CHANGELING HEARTS

THE BOOKMARK
53 TITCHFIELD ST.
KILMARNOCK
01563 573015

Also by Simon Harding

Streamskelter

CHANGELING HEARTS

SIMON HARDING

PAN BOOKS

First published 1995 by Pan Books

an imprint of Macmillan General Books
Cavaye Place London SW10 9PG
and Basingstoke

Associated companies throughout the world
ISBN 0 330 33211 2

Copyright © Throwaway Classics 1995

The right of Simon Harding to be identified as the
author of this work has been asserted by him in accordance
with the Copyright, Designs and Patents Act 1988.

All rights reserved. No reproduction, copy or transmission
of this publication may be made without written permission.
No paragraph of this publication may be reproduced, copied or
transmitted save with written permission or in accordance with
the provisions of the Copyright Act 1956 (as amended). Any
person who does any unauthorized act in relation to
this publication may be liable to criminal prosecution
and civil claims for damages.

1 3 5 7 9 8 6 4 2

A CIP catalogue record for this book is available from
the British Library

Phototypeset by Intype, London
Printed and bound in Great Britain by
Cox & Wyman Ltd, Reading, Berkshire

This book is sold subject to the condition that it shall not,
by way of trade or otherwise, be lent, re-sold, hired out,
or otherwise circulated without the publisher's prior consent
in any form of binding or cover other than that in which
it is published and without a similar condition including this
condition being imposed on the subsequent purchaser.

Changeling hearts beat twice as fast
Twice as long as love will last

                Traditional

PROLOGUES

FLIPSIDE

The intro writes itself, Nicky. Straight to the point.

That's what they crammed into us at college. A straightforward, no-nonsense intro and some good, crisp copy, that's what the lecturer geezer with the wombat wig wanted. I'd do my two-fingered worst and then pour tea over the smudgy pages, give them twenty in a medium oven. By Christ was that copy crisp.

What the hell does crisp mean, anyway? What does crisp mean to you? Ask a dozen people you'll get three dozen daft answers. Tell someone you're a *reporter* and they think you'll believe anything. Hell, maybe we will at that. Taking people's tall stories as gospel, I ask you. I ask you to believe in me, in them, in everything they tell me. Of course, you also get to read between the lines. Between my random reworking of their lines, anyway. Well, as I say, you certainly meet some funny bastards in my line of work. All these years on I still get the funny phone calls. Do I still hear from you know who? Do I pop up to the big place on the moor and check him out? The star of Bleakdale Institute's electro-encephalograph eleven, the supreme sicko himself.

Who am I talking about? David Roberts, of course. You remember him, don't you? The psychokiller who topped his wife after a run in with his fancy woman, his water lily dream demon, whatever she called herself.

Yeah, him. Yeah, right. Like we were such buddies.

SIMON HARDING

He fed me a line and I took it. Same as people are always feeding reporters lines, same as people always go reading between them. Where was I going to check his facts? Who was I going to go to for a quote? The Trafariawhatsit travel bureau?

I steer clear of him, if you want to know. I try and keep his insidious echoes out of my head, make it a rule never to take work home with me.

So you can imagine, maybe, how I reacted when my missus started slipping, started spinning me stories as if she's picking up some kind of infernal/internal vibration from my bad dreams. Stories about strange youths tripping between worlds, bodysnatchers, succubi, changelings. Walking in on my life, my wife, like they own the place and the face.

But whoa, wait a sec! Hold that call to good old Dr Whiteman, the shrink with the shrunken head. This is Clove we're talking about, after all. Just down the road from Glastonbury, with its very own set of caves and chasms and people in pointy hats. The place where straightforward intros and crisp copy run rings around your fingers, set up weird echoes and sidewinding suggestions in your head.

Stand on any doorstep in Clove, down our ordinary two-up two-down street, and yodel at the cliffs as you collect your semi-skimmed. Bloody hell, those ladders and ledges will take your innocent cry apart, stick it back together and send it back with bells on. The Marabar Caves have got nothing on Clove Gorge.

Maybe being born and brought up in Clove's cave breath is getting to her, Molly I mean. My missus. She even forgot who she was the other day. Looked at me in Sainsbury's as if I didn't exist, gazed at the jumbo pork sausages as if they'd fallen from the sky. She's as daft as a brush, sometimes. And other times, she says things that aren't exactly daft, more scary. I'm scared for her, where they'll take her talking crap like this.

Molly reckons these pointy-hatted people on the other side have managed to open a breach between the worlds, torn themselves an emergency exit from their dying lands so they can live a little (and love a little, she said) over here. Down our street. Funny voices, see. Echoes. Corpse-stealing creatures kerb-crawling Cloveside. That's it in a nutshell, if you'll excuse the expression. How about that for crisp copy?

And here come all the echoes, crowding back, crowding me out of my own story.

This is as crisp as it gets. After this you're on your own, pages crumbling under your fingers like cracked icing on stale buns. This is their story, see. I'm just the go-between. Sure, I've dropped in a few letters here and there, a few dodgy documents I managed to turn up during my trawl through the vaults, my tireless wanderings around labyrinthine record offices. I've asked a few experts for their analysis, they've promised to get back to me any day now. I haven't figured whether my extra-curricular research will help you out or muddy the waters, but a fact's a fact, and like me you'll probably want to hang on to them like splinters from the True Cross.

Mostly though, this is their story. These are their lies and legends and fears and fancies. And when I'm finished (or when they've finished with me), maybe someone will tell my story.

I can't wait to find out what happens, in the end.

SLIPSIDE

Imagine my own voice rising and falling, now clear and sweet as the stream down the mountain, now parched and choking, crabby as the dustiest desert pool. Not sure whether I am chanting my birth song or my own epitaph.

Well, there you have it, I suppose.

If what I have to tell you needs must be the story of my death, then I pity the poor stonemason they drag in to chisel my headstone. All these names and titles, where would he start?

Amiarillin, the Lady First and Last, Empress of Trafarionath and Baroness Cloud. Dowager this and Duchess of that. *The ultimate other woman*, my other woman reminds me. Other woman and middle sister, then, that's me.

The ragged runts who tell these tales have never quite made up their minds what to call me either. Now I come to think of it, they had half a dozen names for my dear sister, none of them too flattering.

But she's dead now. Dead for ever, and to be honest with you, I can't imagine *she'll* ever be coming back.

The tale tellers have it I went west, sought out my elder sister's funeral pool the moment I heard she was dead. That I, the miserable exile, danced a jig around my little hut in the wilderness, rode a dozen ponies into the ground racing the clouds to dear Azhiamehet's watery grave. That I lifted my skirts and squatted, paid her out for my years of torment. Not true.

I went north. Out of the wastes of Febalio, crossed Kyle and Egrashia and Doriomothigol, wandered the plains of Kelleth until I spied the long valley and the mountains mirrored. I came upon her wandering tribes, her cast-off creatures, but they could not abide me and fell back before me. Maggots. No, worse than maggots, chrysalides, wrapped tight in their plated jackets, waiting for wings, waiting for something, someone, to happen.

I went north to see my little sister. I hesitate to say living sister, for the patchwork priests who attended her had long since sealed her within her chambers. Aryhannon, their precious virgin priestess, the last uncracked cup in their splintered cupboard. Walled up safe from prying eyes and filthy fingers in the high tower of the Paliastaron. I cannot say whether they had been following Azhiamehet's twisted instructions or whether they had decided to brick her in through some cultish deviation of their own. Living sister? Living death.

Her unwanted acolytes, terrified clowns in ragged gowns, flung themselves out of my way, scuttled screeching for their holes as I found the doorway, the narrow tunnel they fed her through. Poor child, at least our sister had left me an entire waste to roam. I searched the mean streets under the high tower and brought her a chicken and some wine while her scaly servants chanted my doom. It took her a while to be aware of me, who I said I was, crouched like a beggar at her food pipe.

'Ah, you have heard, then?' she said.

I said I had, Azhiamehet dead at last. Swallowed up by magic she could not control.

'And you, sister, I have dreamt your death also,' she whispered.

'Do not be afraid for me,' I said.

'If you are not afraid then you have come for my magic, for my help.'

I said I had. That I would follow Azhiamehet, travel to the land where the stream flows backwards. How she begged and pleaded with me to remember our sister sharing that same dream, her bitter defeat, drowning at last in a bubbling vat of her own bile, the venom of her own making. I insisted she make the spell, begged her to send me where the stream runs backwards.

Hours, we argued to and fro, our mouths pressed to that dribbling tunnel. At length she passed three chicken bones back, gnawed and grey in her thin white hand, covered in tiny runes and arcane symbols even I could barely read.

'Take these bones,' she said. 'Take these names: Maggs and Miller and Klein. I have seen these men in my dreams, and watched them unknowing, building your fate where the stream runs backwards.' I could make no more sense of this but took the bones anyway, all scratched and scored.

'But remember,' she warned me, 'remember what our departed sister forgot. That fate can be a fickle friend, fickle indeed.' That she could talk of fickle fate, sealed by twenty feet of brick and spitty mortar into that toadstool mausoleum, brought the tears to my eyes for the first time in many an age. She told me to pass her a knife, so she might cut a token to make me magic for my journey. I said I would gather tokens of my own, and that, one day, I would return for her. She said her filthy attendants would never permit such a thing. Ah, children, children.

Two years I wandered. Two years the tale tellers made minutes, before I came on Azhiamehet's drowning pool. The little boy lost, Puut Ra, or whatever he called his name, had taken over my dead sister's realms, and stalked them as if he had been born to it.

CHANGELING HEARTS

As if.

The changeling made me smile with his foolish antics, his lousy legions melting away like fat on a grate. He never dared interfere with me, though, and it wasn't long before I had taken powerful tokens of us three sisters, tokens enough for my crossing. For my return. A rebirth with as many complications and twice the pain of giving birth to you two, my children.

From *The Sisters of Shibboleth, a Faithful and Exact Relation of the Lives of Azhiamehet, Amiarillin and Aryhannon*, collected by the Lady First and Last, Baroness Cloud and Dowager Empress of Trafarionath.

MAYDAY

ABSOLUTES' DECREE

This thin boy followed the runes with a grubby finger. Trafarnian love poetry. A faded inscription beneath a fragmented watercolour of a handsome couple, hand in hand, perfectly matched in some kind of shimmering silk gown. He'd found it on one of his expeditions into the dark recesses of what had been their library. Looted now, the books long gone to the latrine pits, the last few fragments curling and misting on the splintered shelving. The fortress had been gutted, desecrated long before he'd come on the scene, but the lonely old chamber still rang with their arrogant grandeur. He could feel it in his bones, standing cold and shivery as the lamp cast sickly splashes over the forgotten hall. No wonder the new owners had been so eager to erase its memories, put everything to sleep. He sighed, glared at the mildewed page, the immaculate runework he had to squint to read, lips moving like a backward child. The male gazing at the female, or was it the female gazing at the male? Both of them had cheekbones sharp enough to shave each other. Trafarnian nobility, sublime superiority. Hadn't done them much good when the goblin legions vomited over the hills and erupted against their high towers. Some daft damsel peering over a balcony. Wherefore, why, where are you? He frowned, concentrated on the memory flitting through the abandoned library of his mind. Flimsy trellis collapsing as if it had been knocked up in his own workshops, spilling a girl in a pointy hat over the hall floor. Or was it simply his brain playing tricks, withering on its stalk like forgotten fruit? It would come back to him, perhaps. One day. The boy reclined in the enormous stone throne, sighed. The snivelling goblin at his feet pulled the rags this way and that as if attempting to find one corner of the robe with some decent stitching.

'I'm not wearing any more skins, Mysheedi. I don't care who you've found to sew the wretched things up, they're not good enough. They itch.'

Itch? Mysheedi Edum, First Counsellor, covered his flaring nostrils and bowed backwards dragging the appalling garment with him. He'd scratch him with something if he wasn't careful. He watched the boy with bright amber eyes as he lifted his end of the robe, tugged it to the cold stone floor and made that nasty clicking noise in his throat. Sitting back, superciliously flicking mousy hair from his pale eyes. The wretched creature retreated a few more steps, tugging the dreadfully stitched hem of the robe with him.

'I can see you're annoyed, no good hiding your hooter here,' the boy snapped, crossing and uncrossing his legs, swinging his foot. His light boots were worn and the sole had begun to peel from the badly stitched upper. The sight of it exasperated him even more. 'And look at the state of these shoes! Where's that damned cobbler you came up with? Gone home again has he, gone four more like it.'

During the past twelve years Mysheedi had grown more than accustomed to his master's tantrums, but just lately his moods had deepened, darkened. As if he was growing more like them every day, hairier, coarser. And if the master was growing more like his goblins then what hope had they? Whither now Mysheedi Edum?

Withering all right. Where was he going? To the dogs, that's where my friend. Gone four they called it, running off wild assed on their knuckles into the wild wood. He shivered. It was a nagging doubt which Mysheedi had been picking over for weeks. They'd conquered all Trafarionath, it had taken them a million years but they'd triumphed in the end. Burnt the last wizened warlocks from their caves in the hills for what, the right to wear their own rags. Tilekin had always said he worried too much.

'We fill our bellies when we want and we've no damned Trafarnians smoking us out of our holes. We can do what we want, where we want. What more is there to worry about?' the old general would chuckle as they shared a pipe in the echoing halls of the great keep under the hill, squinting in the gloom to watch a litter of pups kick a stone clattering along the gloomy passages. Perhaps Tilekin was right, worrying too much about futures which were none of his business.

'Let the boy bother his balls off, we are what we are, we are where we are,' the general would snort philosophically, blowing great rings of smoke at the cloudy canopy of old webs.

Mysheedi eyed his master warily, noted the careless kick of the slipper, the distracted frown as he stared at the hangings. Old banners, smoky threads dimming in the dim lamplight, the guttering candles. Nothing pleased him anymore. Nothing in their slowly rotting world would do. Everything they brought before his horrid human eyes made him twitch and narrow his withering gaze. Is *this* fit for a prince? How dare you bring tat like that before your sovereign lord? Twelve years ago Mysheedi would have been over the floor and on him, cut him and drained him and dyed his cap in his watery blood. But he'd been the Lady's favourite, trotting at her heels on a silver chain accepting sweetmeats from her long white fingers. And when the great queen who'd gathered the lost tribes and ruled them had gone up in smoke, she'd left him to tend their fires. Her final victim, the little manchild she'd snatched from his world, snatched from his crying mother and slipped back under the stream with. A living, breathing totem of a place she'd barely tasted, hardly sipped before the people on the other side had sent her back. Before they'd burnt her out, cut and stitched along ragged red lines like mental tailors. Mysheedi had seen shades sliding and dipping over scenes of slaughter before, seen shape-changing shadows sucking the steam from gravepits, but he'd never seen anything like the great queen, their poor lady, when those otherside people had finished with her. What sort of people were they anyway?

He wondered again what she had ever had in mind for her little prisoner in the first place. Simple revenge? Taking one of theirs with her at the end of her time? And now the boy, her chief beneficiary, all he ever thought about was going back to them. Getting back where he'd come from, back for his skin, back for the shell of himself she'd tossed over the bushes by the bridge, dropped on the grass like lovers pulling off their filmy shirts, skipping into the shallows for a midnight dip. Here, here with his goblins, he was Puut Ra, Prince of Trafarionath. All that they knew, in every direction, all that had been hers, his, and every bit as useless to him. Under every rock and up every tree and behind every blade of grass a cackling gargoyle whispering his memories, calling him home. He'd watched him all right, he'd seen his lips moving, squinting at rocky places as if he could picture himself back there, back with his parents and his people. Sitting on a blanket around a basket of food, his feet crossed just so in front of him as he admired the views, peered at skylarks. Shouted and bawled if any of the bowstring boys forgot themselves and risked a shot at them. It was his, all of this, all of them. All her territory and all her servants, shrivelled and stinking, and he'd leave it like she had, run out on them for ever. Run back down the stream pulling his cracked and dry old lizard skin from the reeds and rushes where he'd left it, trying himself back on for size. What about Mysheedi Edum, what about his trusted counsellor, ever loyal friend? Would there be skins hanging there for him too? New skins, fairer, smoother? Lying in the lush grass where the othersiders had left it? He ran a hand up his hairy arm, glanced at the great green banner tacked behind the throne, the Lady's gown, carefully unravelled from her deformed carcass after the chaos at the bridge, the last battle with the woodlanders and their fire demon allies. They'd choked their own fires, burning their lady like that. Mysheedi had been rambling, lost his master's thread in the smoky threads of his memories.

'I was asking whether you'd ever seen stitching like this?'

It was the best he would get, over here. Mysheedi had thrown his weight around the shabby woodlander's hut, threatened him with all sorts of disasters if he didn't come up with better quality garments for his little prince.

'Haven't you got a son or something?' he'd asked the drooling tailor, cross-legged in his own filth, dull eyes crossed as he attempted to thread a length of gut through a blunt bone needle.

'He ain't the gift.'

Ain't the gift? Mysheedi frowned, picked nervously at a flaring nostril. Puut Ra had finished with the gown and had crossed his foot in his lap to examine his soles. Sometimes he or Tilekin got to wear his castoffs, although the warchief generally preferred iron-shod boots. All the better for stamping on faces, Mysheedi presumed.

'Are you going deaf? Make some more candles out of that stuff between your ears!'

He'd tugged off his shoe and was hopping around the chamber from one foot to the other. Capering about in his filmy underthings, shrouds torn from some old tomb to the north. Their best weavers couldn't come up with anything better than a few yards of sacking, and the master wasn't fond of wearing sacking. Made him itch. Mysheedi had inherited the trousers the boy had arrived in, although he'd quickly snapped the intricate fastening at the front and been forced to hold on to his loincloth to keep them up. He watched the boy pull up his pants and prowl the chamber, lifting his sheepskins from the frame by the guttering fire.

The boy paused by the tattered banners screening the walls, the rocky fortress hewn from the hills countless years before. Puut Ra's best stonemason wouldn't have been allowed a free hand making pots for cats to puke in. The boy frowned at the marvellously embroidered banners, the intricate runes he could barely read. Bardalakalef Lifeguards. Pride of Athretricha? They sounded like football teams to him. He eyed Mysheedi, watching him intently with his bright amber eyes. Sometimes he wondered if the crafty goblin could read his thoughts. Football, there now. Mysheedi wouldn't know, couldn't help. His counsellor had never been and he simply couldn't remember. He could remember remembering, was all. Clutching at the streamers cracking and snapping in his memory. Memories that dissolved, dissolved as if they couldn't take the atmosphere here, as if they died of exposure as soon as he thought them up, left him grasping empty air in the cold chamber. The boy looked up sharply as Tilekin coughed, pulled the curtain from the door and strode into the room. Five foot tall if you could straighten him out for a moment, but grown in on himself, hunched like a withered oak on a bare mountain. Quicker than a snake in a storm, though, milky beads for eyes and a lurid tongue flicking behind his yellow fangs. He bowed stiffly, glared at Mysheedi.

'I 'eard you wanted me,' he growled. 'Something about these pox-scummed bead jigglers of yours.'

Mysheedi sucked in his bad breath as the master twitched, almost crossing his eyes as he tried to summon a suitably authoritative reply.

'Warchief Tilekin,' he began. 'Could it only have been yesterday morning that I sent for you? Doesn't time fly.'

The goblin shrugged, shuffled across to the antique Trafarnian sideboard to help himself to the master's elderberry wine. He took a mouthful of the lethal black concoction, rolled it around his gaping gums and spat it over the wall.

'I can't imagine what you want with them,' he said archly.

Mysheedi snorted. The lying reptile. He could imagine exactly what the master wanted with them. The last warlocks of old Trafarionath, the keepers of the secrets? Ask the dumbest clot in the castle, they would have been able to tell him too. The boy wanted out.

'I've already told you what I think. Knives, dissectin', that's all they understand. The old man's lost his wits, misplaced them maybe. I say, let me have an hour with his nephew. I'll make him sing sweet,' the chieftain suggested with an alarming roll of his tiny eyes, silvery white points under the iron frown of his eagle-beaked helmet.

The counsellor dismissed him with a wave of his inky claw. 'You've had ten years with your damned knives, and haven't got a word out of them,' he flared.

Puut Ra waved his hand as Tilekin fumbled for the

toggle on his chest, tugged a canvas sack open to display a vicious variety of razor-sharp surgical implements. His pride and joy, lovingly washed and polished after every session. His grandsire had taken them from the bloody corpse of a Trafarnian sawbones after the slaughter at Cloud Hangar six score years before. He'd been a bowstring boy then, a lousy archer in one of Morigilim's legions. One of the several hundred the old warlord had hurled at the cliffs to take the castle from the tall men. Mysheedi sighed. All their magic, all their stones and spells, hadn't been enough to stem the tide, stop the sands running between their grasping fingers. Tilekin's grandsire had cut rings from bloody knuckles, kicked gorging crows from their feasts. He'd dropped to his knees to scoop their bright blood in his battered helmet, dyed his cap black in their gaping wounds. So much for their magic. So much for the magic the master craved. The secrets he sought in the cavernous old fortress, from the cracked tablets they'd thrown down into the catacombs under the halls, thrown down with the slashed corpses of the last garrison. Trafarnian magic, bead-jiggling pox-scummed wizard secrets, hadn't stopped the legions then and wouldn't help the boy now. Their prisoners, the ones the master was so obsessed with. The dotard of a warlock and his surly nephew, even that slow-worm Tilekin had recognized they were his only chance of making sense of the ancient runes, of casting the old spells. Tilekin knew well enough when he'd met his match, and he'd met it in Tarkemenis.

'Stubborn?' the old general had complained to Mysheedi, washing the blood from his hands on one of the master's old shirts.

'You'd have imagined I'd been clipping his toenails for him. Never so much as blinked. Ain't natural,' he'd shaken his gnarled head, hadn't slept properly for weeks afterward. His only failure.

'The boy, though, I might be able to pick a few morsels from him before I'm finished,' he'd promised with evident relish. Tell them where they'd hidden their old spell stones, just like the master wanted. Plotting to go back where the impudent boy had come from. The other side where the stream flowed backwards. Mysheedi knew well enough the old general suspected them, their plots and their schemes. He'd been at the battle on the bridge, he'd seen the magic when their lady had tried to cross over, tried to run out on them. The demons they'd summoned down from the skies, out of the water, back in the good old days.

'Wormfood now, the lot of them. Worms. If he leaves Trafarionath it'll be over my dead body,' Tilekin had promised. Mysheedi thought of the skins, lain over the grass, waiting. One for the master and one for him. One for Tilekin too? A great big man skin with red hair and watery blue eyes, like the pictures the master drew for him, drew of his old world on the scraps of paper he was so keen to find around their echoing old hall. As if he could draw comfort from his doodlings. The goblin pinched himself, concentrated on the matter in hand. Tilekin chuckled; Mysheedi, reading his murky thoughts, snorted.

'We daren't risk giving him a free hand with the boy,' Mysheedi said sternly. 'Look what all his knives and torture have done to Tarkemenis. He's quite mad.'

'I'm mad? The warlock's mad,' Tilekin growled, twirling a crooked claw into his scarred forehead.

'I meant—'

'My way's best. Let me alone with the boy for an hour, he'll tell you everything you want to know,' the general interrupted, smiled fiendishly.

'They are Powerlords, sire, warlocks. They don't crack easy. I've known them go for years without as much as taking a piss . . .'

Puut Ra waved his hand. Tilekin grumbled.

'Well, I'm fed up waiting. That's why I called you both here. The warlocks are our only chance to get out of this foul place. All I need is their damned stone.'

Mysheedi glanced at Tilekin, back to the master, smiled weakly.

'The stone was smashed,' Tilekin growled. 'If the wizards had picked up anything other than a few fragments they would have used them on us years past,' he insisted.

Mysheedi brooded as his master paced the chamber. Tilekin was right. If they had found the great Grimoire the goblin hordes would have been stopped in their stinking tracks. Wouldn't they?

'We know they were hiding something when we caught them. Tarkemenis of Peresh wasn't in the habit of carrying a spade around with him.'

Tilekin hawked, spat on the floor and ground his boot over the sticky black mess. 'The boy had the spade, maybe to bury the old man?' he rolled his milky eyes, grinned. 'By the lake, under the trees. His final resting place,' he chuckled unpleasantly.

Puut Ra clicked his thin fingers. 'Teomalik wouldn't bury his own uncle alive! What kind of twaddle is that?' the boy snorted.

'Wandering into *her* territory? Risk getting caught up in the Spawn Queen's nets?' Tilekin carried on regardless. 'Unless he fancied a bit of tickle and slap,' he sniggered, ran his crusty sleeve over his nose.

Puut Ra glared at his commander-in-chief. 'If she exists, if, mind you, she has no territory,' he corrected him. 'A hut in the woods, a few fowls maybe.'

CHANGELING HEARTS

Mysheedi bowed. Perhaps the randy little weasel had forgotten he'd dispatched as many expeditions out after this non-existent queen as her sister, the great Lady herself, had? Who was he trying to fool? Surely denying the sisters' existence was as good as denying his own. Who else had brought him here, if not the Lady Glaistig? Changelings didn't just drop out of the skies, they had to be fetched or summoned or stolen or something. And if Glaistig had existed then so did her sisters, Mysheedi reasoned. Why didn't the stroppy little sod go ahead and pinch himself, see if he could wake himself up back in his clean little bed in his nice little home with his precious mummy and daddy they had heard so much about. Puut Ra had turned his bright eye on him as if he could read the goblin's heresies through his hairy head. Mysheedi covered his nose, coughed.

'I think what Tilekin meant to ask, sire . . . Why would the warlocks have ventured so close to her . . . alleged lair?'

Puut Ra straightened, frowned at the banners and hangings around the walls. The Spawn Queen. The Sister of Sorrow, the daft goblins called her, drooling in their holes. Their legends had it she'd been banished by her elder sister when the Green Lady had been at the height of her horrible powers. That Glaistig, glowing green then white with rage at her own pitiful corruption, had been driven madder still by the sight of her sweet siblings' immaculate beauty, the perfection she had once shared. That she had driven the middle sister out and had the younger one imprisoned in a half-ruined Trafarnian abbey high in the northern mountains years before Puut Ra had ever come on the scene. But she had never forgotten her sister's swarthy beauty. Exiled but never destroyed. Lovers and plots, plotting lovers. Assassins sent to finish her off never seen again, trusted generals who had volunteered to lead a legion after her somehow getting themselves entangled in her nets and webs, troops melting away into the woods, running naked over the marshes. Stories to scare the pups. Drop-dugged grandmothers gabbling by the stream as they paddled and pulled their ragged washing over worn old rocks. And when the Green Lady had been swallowed up in the rearing waters, the great wicker cages of sooty flames, the Spawn Sister had returned at last, gloating over the Green Lady's final fall. Dived for her carcass in the great pool, pulled the very teeth from her twisted and changed hate-racked skull. Picked the wicked white incisors to make herself a necklace, so the daft goblins said. Silent as ice, cold and sharp as a knife in the night. He shivered, blinked at the general, pacing to and fro in the echoing chamber.

'Well, it doesn't matter whether her sisters live or no, they'll never help the likes of you,' the raisin-faced goblin blabbered on. 'If they had any sense they'd be having a word with the wizards.'

'Oh, is that what you think?' Puut Ra sneered.

'Just give me an hour with the boy and I'll get you some answers,' Tilekin insinuated. 'If it's answers you're after,' he added darkly.

'What's that supposed to mean? What else would I be interested in?' his prince demanded coldly.

Tilekin scratched his leather thong, leered knowingly.

Puut Ra eyed him, tugged the sheepskins tighter around his bony frame. 'I don't want to hear about your Spawn Sister, her younger sister or your bloody sister,' he said quietly. 'It's the warlock and the boy I'm after. They had stones, maybe not the whole tablet, but magic stones all the same. They buried them to keep them from us. They buried them in her territory – her vicinity,' he corrected himself, 'to keep you lot from poking your noses in. All we have to do is find where.' He looked from the general to the counsellor, lowered his voice as if the cold cavern had mushroomed with stinking sets of ears. 'I mean to go over, back where I came from. Teomalik's the only one who can help me now.'

Clippity-clop went the ragged pony, picking its way along the mossy streambed with considerably more confidence than its rider. *Clep-clep-cleppity* echoing back down the corrugated granite gorge, jangling Mysheedi's nerves a little more. He bunched his gnarled fists in the beast's knotty mane, dragged it to a halt and tugged its head up as it bent to drink the chill water. Mysheedi hated riding and would have been happier eating the shaggy four-legger than squatting in the middle of its back with his legs splayed uncomfortably around its fat furry belly. The hills had closed in on the ragged column, funnelled them toward their destination. He looked up, studied the dark woods and the gloomy cliffs, ice-cold spirit-sapping spray as the stream bounded from one cataract to another, fell hundreds of feet between towering columns of bare rock. Mysheedi was pondering kicking the beast on, spurring it into the trees once and for all. The master was going or he was going mad. He wouldn't spare a thought for his advisor if it came to the crunch, came to the crossing. Might as well kick the beast on, away from him, away from them all. Over the cliffs and the plains of Kelleth, see what lay on the other side of the mountains. He was just about to kick it on for good when the pony snorted, shook its head. Just ahead the stream had run up tight against the mossy ruins of a bridge. The broken slabs of stone, standing like jagged teeth in a crow-picked skull, had blocked the flow sufficiently to form a large lake into which one of the goblin guard was aiming an arc of steaming urine. His colleagues were sunning themselves on the rocks like iguanas, red tongues lolling in the steamy afternoon heat. The rider shook his head, reflected bitterly how the master had picked the advance party from his best regiment, Igor's Eyeouts. Hah! Most of them had forgotten how to string their bows let alone hit anything. Jakabi now, reputed to be the best captain in the entire army. Mysheedi doubted he could hit a tent from the inside.

'Here they are, then,' the guard called, tucking his tackle behind his loincloth and leaping nimbly from rock to rock to come up alongside the rider. He gazed back downstream wonderingly.

'On your own then, Mysh?'

'That's Mysheedi to you, lizard-vomits. Get your rabble on their feet, Jakabi, his nibs is just around the corner,' the rider warned.

Jakabi raised his crooked eyebrows, smiled maliciously. 'Ventured away from his den, has he? All the way out here, into Sister's pantry?'

Mysheedi clambered down from the ragged beast, held the halter out for the guard, who frowned, took it.

'He doesn't want to hear any talk about her pantry, lair or bloody bower,' Mysheedi grated.

Jakabi grinned.

'I thought he said the warlocks had buried their treasures in her back garden so as to keep the likes of us away?' he enquired.

Mysheedi sighed, tapped his nose. 'You're a nosy skunk. I'm warning you, he's not in the mood.'

Jakabi grabbed his groin and rubbed vigorously. 'After a shag, is he? Haven't you told him what happens when you sleep with the Spawn Queen? One glorious rut and she has it out of you, drowns you in the soggy rags?

Isn't that right now, Mysheedi? We've lost half a dozen this moon already.'

The rider shook his fist under the inquisitive young goblin's nose, turned on his heel as his pinpoint hearing picked up the rest of the column splashing down the gorge. Tilekin out ahead, spear over his shoulder splashing in his great boots as if he was stamping the life from the cold waters. Half a dozen goblins struggling with a rickety litter, the boy lolling in the back as if he'd been at the hoof glue again. A second group of spearboys prodding the shackled prisoners a safe distance behind, heavy chains hanging in the rushing water. Puut Ra didn't take any chances, getting too near the warlocks. Tarkemenis, the elder, grey stubble sprouting from his battered head, his once noble features battered and twisted into a horror caricature, great sooty rings under his crossed eyes. Teomalik, pale and drawn, red hair falling in great matted red coils over his strong shoulders, eyeing the trees as if he was waiting for his old friends to appear. Precious few of them left these days. Tilekin had shaved his mane several times, but it always grew back, stronger, more luxuriant than before.

The exhausted goblins waded to the bank, deposited the master with a jolt. He jumped to his feet, clambered out of the unlikely contraption and stalked angrily down towards them.

'Are we here? Is this the place?'

Tilekin raised his broad-bladed spear, pointed on down the narrowing gorge. 'The Sister's Slit is what we call it.'

Puut Ra eyed him. She was a watermark on his map, a ripple in his pond. 'I go where I please,' he said stonily, flicked his damp fringe from his forehead. What better place to hide the heirlooms of the old houses, these hairy fools afraid to go anywhere near, never daring to rake over her ground, her patch. The Sister's Slit. He stared at the thatch of branches closing in overhead, the broad boughs split from the main trunks, holed and patched by the relentless hammering of hundreds of colourful woodpeckers. Or was it a headache coming on? He clutched his itchy breeches, made himself comfortable, caught Mysheedi's curious look.

'Well?'

'We are . . . here, master,' the goblin repeated, anxiously pulling at his flaring nostrils.

'On a ways,' Tilekin chuckled, nodding on down the stream, which wound between the mossy boulders and on into the deep cleft in the hills.

'Lover's leap, hers to keep,' he muttered.

Puut Ra jabbed a thin finger into the old warrior's notched breastplate. 'Keep your goblin twaddle to yourself,' he ordered. Tilekin pulled his cheek, the tough rinds under his milky eye, as the boy glared, turned back to the column to see what the sudden commotion was about. The old warlock, Tarkemenis, prancing in the water, swinging heavy chains from his bony wrists, slashing at the stream. Downstream, Puut Ra heard his high-pitched screaming.

'You fool! You don't know what you're doing!' Lifting the heavy chain again, one of the spearboys making a half-hearted grab for the flailing end. Teomalik, as astonished as the rest, gazing at the cracked old man as he beat the water, clattered the chain against the mossy rocks tearing great swaths in the deep green beds of algae. Teomalik shouted a warning, wrenched at the chain as Tilekin barked, waved his spear.

'Should have thought of the water before, seems to have loosened his tongue,' he called after Puut Ra. The boy's eyes were glittering with excitement, Mysheedi hurrying after him, lifting his loincloth to rub his aching buttocks.

'Be careful, master, you don't know . . .'

Puut Ra ignored him, leapt from rock to rock back up the stream to the small pool where the old man was shouting. The goblin guards had nervously backed away, craning their necks to eye the trees, the cold cliffs. Schmelker, the grizzled old sergeant, jabbing his dagger into their backs.

'Get back in there and grab hold them chains,' he yelled. 'He's a silly old fool, that's all, what are you afraid of?'

The nervous spearboys ducked under his blade, crouched down into the mulch as Puut Ra trotted up, kept a safe distance.

'Tilekin, get the old fool out of there.' He looked down at Teomalik, holding on to the chain and reaching for his madly capering uncle. Caught his curious glance. So you're the boy? He heard the question rebound in his head and yet the young warlock's lips had barely moved on his grubby face. Puut Ra shivered as the boy dragged the old man into the pebbly shallows. The boy squinted at the mossy rocks the old man had lashed, the smooth surface stripped of its soft green beard, standing like a milestone in the cold flow. What? The boy hurried forward, held his breath as the young warlock followed his glare, wrenched his uncle's chain sparking a fresh torrent of lunatic screeching.

'Tilekin, what are you waiting for? Get him out of there!'

The old man wrenched the chains from the boy, showering the shocked goblins with silver droplets. He spun the chain above his head, thrashed the stream again. This time the silvery spray froze in midair, turned to icicles by an invisible breath.

'Don't, don't you dare,' the wizard called, shakily, into the echoing gorge.

The goblins froze, Tilekin, pausing on the bank, raised his spear a notch, glanced around the ring of trees. A trumpet, no, an animal, a furious honk like a car horn, Puut Ra thought. Car horn? He took a step back, peered over his shoulder. A swan, gliding slowly over the lake.

'Run for it! It's her!'

The goblins bolted for the trees, Puut Ra tugged his dagger from his belt, held it in front of him in his thin white hands. A swan!

'Don't, don't you dare,' the old man moaned, collapsing to his ragged knees in the icy flow, Teomalik standing back clutching his stomach, doubling up as if the doddering fool had caught him one. The boy grabbed his uncle's ragged green tunic, tugged him out of the water, away from the mossy treasures. Puut Ra leapt into the water, waded toward the milestone, the rotten, mossy chest he'd taken for a rock. The dull bands had buckled, the worm-eaten, shell-encrusted wood splintered by the old fool's frenzied assaults. Teomalik deposited his uncle in the dirt, turned back to the triumphant boy. The wind tore through the crevasse, howling and honking through the swaybacked trees, the undergrowth tumbling and writhing from beneath the heavy boughs, snaking swiftly over the mulch. Great tendrils of ivy and bindweed rippled through the leaves, curling and snapping around the old man's weakly kicking legs. Binding him, shackling him with tough green shoots. Wild magic, power to bend trees and summon waters. The magic he needed to catapult himself out of there, to get back to the shell he'd left behind. Bug eyed, laughing, he watched Teomalik, horrified, kneeling to tear the hateful weeds from his uncle's cracking and crumbling limbs.

'The stones!' he moaned between his suddenly blue lips.

'The spells!'

Puut Ra, supremely excited, darted forward. The stones, the spells, so close! The woman reared out of the water in front of him, a halo of droplets, duckweed bracelets sliding slick on her slim brown wrists. The thin boy yelped, tripped on the slippery stones, windmilling arms as he tried to recover his balance before the bank gave out on him. A glimpse of her shiny jelly cloak before he bellyflopped into the water, thrashed and kicked over the bright pebble bed. It's me you want, it's me! the boy thought, despairingly. She ignored him, ducked by his panic-stricken dog-paddle to lock in on the astonished warlock boy, scrambling away from the water on his backside. The woman grabbed him, pinned him by the arms as the roaring water lashed the sky, erupted like a tidal wave down the narrow chasm. Teomalik buckled as she locked her mouth over his astonished cry, sucking the air from his frozen throat. He collapsed over his uncle's writhing body, pinned by her weight, fingers ploughing wet furrows through the sparkling spawn net draped over them. She whipped the necklace from her throat, tugged her head back for a second to noose the jangling teeth around his neck, pulled tight. Teomalik choked, tearing at her iron hands, the burning wire digging into his skin, blue and red spots pulsing and billowing in his double vision. He felt the teeth prickle his chest, digging into his aching ribs as she clamped him tighter, clamped him again. Lungs crushed, throat collapsing, cartilage tearing. Teeth sinking slowly through his taut skin. Her light green eyes bright, sparkling with delirious malice, turning from him slowly, cogs clicking in her neck as she looked over her shoulder at the mad river, waves and spray tossed this way and that, a tornado of shining green water coming for them, spinning weeds and pebbles in dervish frenzy. A feline growl, a last triumphant stare at the shocked boy before the vortex hurled her away, flung her into the breakers. Came on, swallowed him whole, coughing and retching, the loose noose writhing like a silvery snake's tongue, the razor-edged teeth tinkling loose, falling away from him one at a time, falling for ever. He clawed at the vicious burrowing pains in his chest, turned cartwheels over and over in the lurid green tube. Cold, white, green.

THE MEMO

Clove Heights Home no.687
A division of Twilight Homes Investments
In association with North Somerset County
& Budgworth City Councils

Confidential internal memorandum
from Martin Grainger, Manager, to
Doctor J. C. B. Klein, Options for Future Team Consultant,
North Somerset Regional Health Authority

Dear Doctor Klein, just a quick note to keep you abreast of developments at 687. As we discussed last Thursday Mrs Jasper's relatives in Hong Kong have been in touch to confirm arrangements for her move to a more conveniently situated home. She will be flown out at the end of the month. As you know Professor Maggs was proving too difficult for our staff to cope with and was transferred to the Bleakdale Institute last Thursday. A particularly tragic twilight to a glittering career as the region's most distinguished geologist and explorer. I am sure you will join with me in passing on our sincerest regrets to his poor family, who were finding it so difficult to get down to Clove and visit him. I am seeing the Haberfields this week, and hope to convince them of the benefits of moving their father nearer London. As you know Mr Haberfield is a virtual vegetable these days, frequently confused and often disruptive. Some of his remarks and his behaviour toward the female members of staff are not endearing him to the home community. If his family cannot suggest a new home nearer London I am afraid Mr Haberfield might find himself joining his old friend Professor Maggs at Bleakdale. Mrs Ogden is sinking fast, I don't imagine she'll last the month. In the tragic and untimely event of her death we will be left with less than half a dozen residents, all of whom could be accommodated at Ferndale, with the minimum of fuss, if this proves necessary. Hope my continued efforts to reach a satisfactory conclusion meet with your approval. I am by the way very interested in the management possibilities at Ferndale. See you on Friday for your fact-finding tour, yours, etc, Martin.

FRIDAY

GUPPIES HAVE GOT TO GO

I

Couldn't the damned girl see he was in the middle of a good bit? Go on, get out of the way, pour your damned tea somewhere else! The old man leaned over, peered over the woman's nylon-sleeved arm at the chattering screen. Right near the end, to be continued any moment. Watch.

II

The boy looked as if he might have gotten away, but he was on his last legs now. Stumbling along the streambed from one mossy boulder to another. His ragged green gown soaking wet, hanging from him like an old man's skin. He leapt to his feet as if the stream had come alive and electrified him, ran on again because last legs were better than no legs and if *she* trapped him, if she tripped him like she had his uncle . . .

The woman was sitting, laughing on the bank, legs spread brazenly with her gauzy skirts tugged around her middle. She watched the boy pick himself up, stumble on downstream without noticing her. She turned to the old man she'd hung upside-down from the tree, bound neat, his kicking feet shackled by ropes of ivy and wiry willow wands.

The old man jerked helplessly, swung to and fro like a spider's supper, trying to bend his head up and out of the lapping waters, giving up with a despairing grunt. The cold water brought him round again, he came up coughing.

'Here we are then, turkey bollocks. Trussed up like a turkey, Tarkemenis the chief turkey of Trafarionath!' she crowed.

'You may have bested me but you shan't snare the boy there,' the old man snarled, eyes rolling, red face contorted with helpless rage as he nodded on down the tumbling brook.

'Where's he off to, I wonder?' the woman called. 'What does it matter? I have creatures where the stream runs backwards too!'

'I have creatures also, Amiarillin, it's not over yet!' He flopped into the stream again, swallowed another mouthful of freezing water.

'Your creatures don't even know who they are, let alone who we are!' she snorted, giving him another push to set him spinning. 'Here, there's one now! Yes, you, turkey bollocks! You in the chair! That's right! Over the other side. We're coming for you, you know, nowhere to hide! Have you met my little creature, my little darling doer? Here she comes!'

III

Oh no not me please, he shuddered, eyeing her. Aware for a moment, thinking fleetingly: sounds like that *on the mat a pee* word. Onomatopoeia, words that sounded like the things they described. Gurgle, splash, ouch. Hap Haberfield – his occasional visitors could tell it was him because his name was felt-penned above his locker – sucked in his cheeks, held his breath. The nursing auxiliary glared at him a moment longer, held her finger to her lips. He leaned away from her, shifted in his seat releasing another smoke signal from his steaming groin. Her mouth formed a tiny O as she blew away the vapour. She knew, she knew they couldn't help it, but Hap, horrible hateful Hap? She had her favourites the same as everyone else, even though Mr Grainger had warned them quite specifically not to get too attached. Only natural there would be the occasional sourpuss, one nobody liked. Old Hap took the biscuit. Nasty piece of work, no wonder his family didn't want anything more to do with him. She put the empty cup on the trolley, trundled it over the ruckled rug and over to the big bay window, out of his sight, out of his mind. A crabby old man, they all said so, even the old lady next door who didn't have a bad word for anyone. Crabby, maybe crab-appled would be more exact. Looked all right but he was funny inside, sour, sucked in on himself. Crab-appled. Like a crab scuttling sideways, that was how Hap saw things, couldn't see straight to save his life. He wondered what the word was that sounded like scalded skin, like the steam he could see rising from the baggy crotch of his baggily braced trousers. Was he on fire? He couldn't remember. Couldn't concentrate for more than a few moments these days without bringing on another nerve-racking headache. By the time he had uncrossed his eyes he had usually forgotten what he was trying to remember anyway. He thought he knew why, though. He knew damn fine who to blame for his predicaments. Meddling doctors, dedicated to the medicated. Women doctors at that. Women doctors driving him mad! Women had stuck him in here in the first place, he recalled with another sideways snap, a twinge of catheterized anger.

Blow him down, if it wasn't women in here shushing

him and emptying him and telling him what to do all over again. The faces had changed but the apron remained the same. Hap sighed vindictively. A crumpled, crabby old man in crumpled old clothes, his shiny old pincer hands crossed in his steaming lap. His left turnup had snagged on his cushion exposing a shiny leg, somebody else's socks. They'd taken his old pairs away with them, said they weren't any use, all those holes. How had he come to wear them out anyway? It wasn't as if he went very far these days, sitting around the worn mat one of the old fogies opposite had been given by a relative.

Hap looked up from the bedraggled clippy rug, back to the telly. Telly-Visional. Tell-Me-Visual. Thinking sideways had its advantages, brought you round in a circle. Back to the beginning. Back to his special screen that filled him in if he'd forgotten, turned him loose all over again. They were close, Hap and his Telly. Nobody came close any more. He thought the women doctors were worse. The way they would follow his gaze, gazing at nothing, frown, and walk away muttering, scribbling notes on his worn file. He'd seen them, he'd heard them. Wasn't his fault if they couldn't cussing well see what he saw. The Tell-Me came in handy, keeping tabs on them. There, now.

Hap reassured himself the precious set was still there in the corner, a Russian peasant climbing out of his steaming straw to kneel before an icon. On top of the squat set Doctor Clean-Klein's bleeper winked and blinked, strobed him as he steamed in the worn La-Z-Bone, blinking his watering eye in ragged time. Hap groped for the remote, ran his fingers over the worn buttons to remind himself where he was. Might as well have been Death Row, San Quentin. A life/death sentence, delete where applicable. He wondered what he'd done to deserve it. Must have been pretty bad. Worse than those few funny phone calls. They didn't lock you up for enquiring what a girl had on underneath, did they?

He'd been watching too much Telly. Great escapism. Titles cropping up at all the wrong moments, hopelessly muddled with the trailer for the next feature. He could hardly pick beginnings from ends any more. And what was all that shouting? He could have sworn he'd heard somebody shouting. Here he was trying to concentrate, trying to place the slides of his life in the right order, and some awkward old sod down on the ward has to go and make a fuss, pulling the drips from their shiny arms and whipping the bed sheets for giving them sores. Hap blinked at the screen and tried to think. Sometimes it blinked and blipped to itself like a radar set on *Voyage to the Bottom of the Sea*. Dink dink du dink dink. Dink dink du dink dink. If he stared he could put faces to the smudgy contacts. He could see them, see things, moving about, coming closer. Like remembering dreams when you'd only just woken up.

Hap peered into the Tell-Me, pictured a car approaching, three kilometres and closing in on him. Dive dive dive. Abandon ship. What were they after him for? He was in there already, what more could they do? Maybe they weren't after him, they were after those prisoners, the boy and old man he kept seeing. On the run in the water from that bloody woman. Disconnected images skating across the permafrosted screen, pinned up on his concentration's clipboard. Backwards and forwards in a rush he couldn't comprehend. Faces and places and names which wouldn't budge from the tip of his red tongue. He ran it out of his cracked old lips, thirsty.

Hap stopped watching, looked away. He was always thirsty these days, the heat in this damned place and the funny tablets old Will had passed over to him. The funny stones kept him tight, kept him regular but sanded the spit right out of his mouth. Maybe he wasn't supposed to chew them, just keep them safe by. But if he didn't chew he didn't see the pictures, did he? He took a sly look around the quiet waiting room, they must have tranquillized the noisy bugger who'd been shouting, wheeled him away from the rest. The noise would start them off, stampede them into a chorus of restless pleading and moaning. Moaning pleaders. He listened to the bullfrog chorus of uneven breathing, glanced round the rug, the ring of cauldron-watching witches. Weren't dead then. Some life in the old logs yet.

Hap's face collapsed, contorted as he tried to cram the lid on the cauldron of thoughts bubbling and popping inside his head. He pictured a rock pool full of blind blennies stirred by some backward child's stick. Took a stick to his own childhood. They'd take a stick to you as soon as look at you, back then. He remembered, suddenly, grubby pants pulled up under his armpits, paddling at the seaside. His net had fallen off, he'd never catch anything without a net. The little buggers would slip through his fingers, laugh little blenny bubbles at him.

He rubbed his eyes, tried to get his bearings. Still here. The day room. Every fucking day room. He'd been listening in, hadn't he? Minding his own business minding the bickering bra-straps' business along the hall. The auxiliaries never saw him if he sat still, watching, listening. He could see them moving in the other room, he'd been watching them clear and crisp on the great shiny Tell-Me. Scratch the screen, sniff, you could breathe them on in, swim with their secrets. He could do most anything, now he had the stones to power up the screen. Drop in and eavesdrop wherever he wanted. The kitchens, the office, the bedrooms. The other place.

The funny place with the trees and the rocks and the rushing river he didn't like so much. It was like his seaside dream only brighter, nearer. The way the people there seemed to perk up, look about for him as if they wanted to eavesdrop on him, as if they wanted to splash around in his secrets too. Try and latch on to the way the police had tried to trap him when he made the calls to the girl at the chip shop. Just seconds to whisper a few secrets before he'd hang up with a gleeful shudder, picture those coppers cursing the connection. Now he remembered. He'd been sitting there watching for them, waiting for them to bring the tea, waiting for something to happen. Hap tilted his head to listen to their chatter.

IV

'Smarmy bastard. I hope he bloody crashes.' Claire James watched the tall man stride purposefully down the gravel drive toward the smoke-grey Jaguar. 'Lovely motor, mind. Be a shame if he pranged the car.'

'Claire,' Molly chided quietly, splashing milk into a dozen pale blue cups and wiping her hands on her apron. Claire watched the heavy car reverse in a spray of gravel, slide on down the drive toward the gate. Wheels within wheels. Wheels in motion.

'What do you mean, "Claire"? If he has his way we'll be out on our arses by the end of the month. You've maybe got something else lined up in this shithole?'

Molly paused, tucked a strand of dark hair behind her cap, winced at the dull throb in her belly, been bothering her all day. Sickening for something all right, and then they'd be left to Claire. Pyromaniac in a flaming firework factory.

'He's got to make a report, that's all,' she said wearily. 'Walking round like Christ come to cleanse the temple.

This isn't viable, that isn't viable.' She mimicked his smooth public-school accent. Molly picked up the heavy teapot, began pouring the weak brew into the cups. Too much and they'd spill it all over themselves, they'd have to clear up after them. She glanced up at the blonde girl, frowned. Five years younger so maybe she figured it was beneath her, pouring tea for old folks. It was a job, wasn't it? Sure, she'd be happier behind a computer terminal, some fat bastard's knee in an office. You had to take what you could get in Clove. High-flying jobs for willowy brunettes pushing thirty weren't exactly ten a penny. Molly Fish, welcome to your life.

'Are you going to stand there all day moaning or maybe get the trolley? They've got to have their tea before we finish.'

'Might as well pour it all down the drain,' Claire sniffed, easing herself up on the work surface and rifling through her uniform for her cigarettes.

Molly raised her eyebrows. 'You know the rules . . .'

'I know the rules. Jesus.' She took her hand from her pocket, drummed her long fingers on the worktop.

'Are you getting the trolley or not? Come on, Claire, I can't do it all myself.'

Claire eyed the taller woman as she finished pouring the teas, replaced the teapot and reached for the biscuit tin.

'Give us one, then.'

Molly selected a packet of Rich Tea, arranged half on a plate and offered the packet to the other girl.

Claire took one, nibbled it absentmindedly. 'We used to get Hob-Nobs. Chocolate Hob-Nobs.' They'd been taken off the menu during the last round of social service cuts back in the summer. Chocolate Hob-Nobs, three auxiliaries, one SRN and the gardener. The old fogies probably missed the biscuits more than the staff. Claire certainly did. She nodded toward the kitchen door, the main sitting-room just down the passage.

'And what's going to happen to them, eh? Who's going to have them? I wouldn't have them in my house even if they were family. Not in that state.'

Molly glared at her. 'You're really overflowing with the milk of human kindness today aren't you?' she snapped. 'Listen, just because your boyfriend's mucking you about it's no call to go taking it out on them,' she warned, dark eyes flashing.

The blonde girl leaned away from her. Look who's talking. Bloody husband of hers, eyes all over the place, more hands than a vote at the Tory party conference.

'Sorry I spoke I'm sure.'

Molly placed the tea tray on the trolley, pushed it toward her.

'Here, go and give the poor old buggers their drink, then we can all go home, OK?'

Claire slid from the worktop, gripped the trolley by the handle and manoeuvred it clumsily toward the swing door. Sorry I spoke Mrs Bloody Angel-Knickers Fish. No good saying not to worry when the RHA were down just itching to shut the place once and for all. Three years of cutbacks, three years of lousy pay watching these old biddies fall apart. She levered the sitting-room door with her bottom, dragged the heavy trolley into the middle of the room. They'd got rid of most of the old folk already, one way or another. Another world mostly. Mrs Jasper rattling on about her new place in Hong Kong. Hong bloody Kong? They'd given it back to the Chinese, hadn't they?

'Tea's up, everyone,' she called flatly, glancing around the huddle of all too familiar faces. Mrs Trent had slumped forward so far she was practically limbo dancing on the worn carpet. Claire stalked over, tugged her straight and mechanically wiped the old lady's mouth. She whistled tunelessly as she distributed the tea to trembling hands, placed the biscuits on their Formica table flaps. Like a bunch of babies in high chairs. Wipe their mouths and wipe their arses. What a bloody life. And here's Mr Haberfield refusing to take his drink. Claire didn't like Mr Haberfield. She pushed the saucer at his hands, twitching like crabs' claws in his lap.

'Come on now, here's your tea,' she snapped. The old man glared past her arm, glared at the fish tank. Always the same. Stick a few knobs on it and she could tell him it was the testcard. She glanced over her shoulder. That bastard Klein had switched the pump off. Waste of electricity, he'd said.

'There's nothing in there anyway,' he'd told her as he stalked past, bloody smarmy git.

'Come on now, Hap, teatime.' She set the saucer down on his table flap, smiled. He wouldn't take his dafty eyes off the tank, as if there was a mermaid showing him her tits or something. Getting worse by the day, you didn't need to be some poncy trick cyclist to see that. She looked over again, noticed Klein had left his bleeper on the top. Now he'd have to come back for it. She watched the trio of colourless guppies thrash around the murky water. They'd be dead by morning with the pump turned off. Not like your goldfish, these tropicals. They'd had a nice tankful once. Tiger-barbs, angel-fish. They'd all died though. They seemed to be fishing the dead ones out every other day. Fish, fogey, fish, fogey. Pretty soon the tank would be empty the home would be deserted and they'd all be out of work. Molly, Mr Grainger, the lot. Enjoy your tea, you silly old bastards. What, no pump? No bubbles bubbling away all day to get on your nerves?

Claire grinned, looked down the passage. Molly out

CHANGELING HEARTS

in the kitchen clearing away, Mr Grainger up in front reception cooking the books for the next committee meeting. She crossed the room, setting off a curious chain reaction of nodding heads, muttered curses from old Mr Fletcher who liked to talk dirty. Couldn't help it, Molly said. The nurse picked Klein's slim bleeper from the top of the tank, the red button flashing angrily, lifted the lid and dropped it in with the guppies. It fell slowly through the stagnating water, came to rest on the dirty gravel. Bleep bleep, bleep bleep like a little red lighthouse, scaring the fish shitless. Engaged, sucker.

HAPHAZARDS

Goldfish get some pretty bad press, especially from scientific journals. How would you like it if some professor had logged your attention span in microseconds? Round and round your bowl, a constantly new, infinitely interesting though ultimately untouchable horizon. The tormented guppies in the tank by the window, safe and silent behind a layer of lush velvet algae, had more room but tended to stick to the corners. Up and down the narrow angles. Doctors tended to look at Hap in the same way. Up and down. The once over. His attention span wasn't much better than the fish and he had a nasty habit of staring at the old tank, opening and shutting his mouth as if he was agreeing with everything the guppies said. They had all the answers, of course. They could summarize his condition in a flick of the wrist, a ballpointed squiggle. Arrogantly assuming they knew any more what he was thinking than they did the poor old fish, swimming around their tanks.

Somewhere at the back of his mind, though, Hap remembered the tank in all its glory. Flimsy plastic fish, luxuriant weed and a powerful pump that rumbled almost as loudly as the red-hot radiators. That was before the Tell-Me came, of course. Before old Will – his one and only friend – had passed the stones over. As soon as he'd started playing about with the tiny chocolate-coloured chips his fish-tank horizons had fragmented like rays of sunlight through a jar of oily water. And before he knew where he was they'd carried the old tank away and wheeled the TMV in to take its place, same position over by the bay window. Sometimes he wondered if the Tell-Me had actually been wheeled in at all. Maybe it had grown, mutated out of the tank the way young Martin's funny robots turned into aeroplanes or spaceships. Noisy little things, flashing and bleeping.

Bleep bleep bleep. The tone in his head gave out, brought him round with a start. He'd been staring at the Tell-Me, watching the bra-straps in the kitchen, watched the girl wheel the trolley out of the screen. 'I hope he bloody crashes.' Wheels spinning and shrieking so loud it was a wonder the rest of them hadn't heard it. Squealing like feedback from a hearing aid. Squeak squeak squeak as the catty auxiliary backed into the waiting-room with the tea trolley. That's right, that's what he'd been doing, watching that old film. Watching the escape film on the Tell-Me. Hap shuddered, picked at his baggy crotch with his scarlet pincers.

He looked away from the screen for a moment, caught up with himself. The stories of his life unravelling in front of his eyes. Unpicked, teased and tangled. Raw nerves fluttering with misunderstood messages. He wished he could summon the energy to cross the rug, slap the top of the telly, slap some sense into it like his father would have done. That's better. He could see clearly now: some silly prisoners on the run, convicts splashing down the streambed with chains hanging from their bloody wrists and funny dogs running on their back legs baying behind them. The overheating saloon he'd picked up on the screen grumbling up the causeway, the sheriff and his deputies clutching warrants and pump-action shotguns. Closing his eyes, concentrating, he could read the names from the creased papers. William

Maggs, John Miller, James Klein. Scored out with ragged red inks, Hap Haberfield hastily scrawled in the greasy margin.

Hap clutched the remote in his sweaty paw, staring at the flashing screen. Coming for him. Him? What had he done? If he sucked the stones long enough and rubbed the remote as hard as possible he could bring the pictures into sharper focus, the bug-out eyes and lolling tongues. Reaching out for him, splashing and calling out as if they could see him the same as he could them. As if he could hold out his hand and help them up, out of their swamp, into the quiet room. Lend them a hand, they'd hand him the warrant. Voices in his head now, sound bites: Hap Haberfield, that you? Peering, squinting, trying to pick faces and features on the end of their push and shove arms. Young Martin, all grown up now, holding the warrant out for him to sign. I, Hap Haberfield, being unsound in mind and rotten in body hereby agree to my immediate voluntary termination. What?

He swallowed, blinking to read the minute print, getting smaller every second. Inky teardrops splattering the parchment, could I have the bill please. To food, to heat, to medical care and twenty-four-hour supervision. Sorry old chap, you're not exactly worth the upkeep, are you? The car ticking and creaking, the woman in the print blouse holding the door for him. It's for the best. He always told us, if he ever got like it . . . you know.

Hap shivered, watched his life pass before him in a series of flashing, unfocused images. He didn't want to be bothered with visitors. He didn't mind watching their films but he wasn't about to go out on location with them. Get in the car with his stony-faced son and his awkwardly smiling wife, the fat sheriff and his drooling deputies. For your own good. I hope you bloody well crash, he thought bitterly, rubbed the remote for good luck. Don't. That's what they'd been shouting. Don't what? Something must have gone wrong with the remote. He could have sworn they'd been shouting down the ward, not in the film. When he'd dared to peep at the screen again all he had seen was the bickering bra-straps out in the kitchen, coming in for him. Maybe they knew what he'd been watching too. And then she'd, she'd . . . then the screen had blip blop blipped, he'd felt it popping hot in his baggy groin as if he'd gone and grown himself some special receiver, an aerial cum penis to pick up its distress call. Mayday mayday zonk.

Hap waited until the auxiliary had finally moved away, then grabbed the remote, pressed the buttons, ran his thumbs over the worn grooves. He peered and squinted to pick out the prisoners and the dogs but they'd run out on him. Just that mean catty one with the teapot, hovering over them like a flapping vulture, wheeling the trolley from one kill to another. Out on the plain, a ruin of ribs in a lagoon of blood, broken biscuit in a pool of tea on the Formica-topped table beside him. Stuck here in the stuffy stifling greenhouse heat, leopard's breath on his prickly face. Maybe the throbbing radiator in the corner had scalded the Tell-Me's circuits, burned the remote right out, interfered with the signal. Maybe the catty one had done it deliberately, pulling the plug on his life support. The ragged shower of dots and dashes had resolved itself into Saturn rings, unrolling lazily and tumbling abruptly from the bottom of the no picture. No picture? He ran his fingers over the remote again, fixing his co-ordinates, felt like thumbing the cover back and checking the tablets were still there. Maybe they'd run out? Maybe watching the funny film had drained them down to a feeble glow? How long had he watched? Minutes, hours? Difficult to tell over the other side. Running his tongue over the tiny grooves, the funny writing that helped him dream sleep, sometimes. Think. What was it, Friday or Tuesday? One of the two.

He glanced at the woman slumped alongside, leaning away from him and into the comforting wombwalls of her worn La-Z-Bone, hair hanging over her face. What was her name again? T. Began with a T was on the top of his Tina. Tina. Was that it? He pointed at her with the remote. For God's sake, she wasn't on the remote either. He leaned over, tapped the woman's arm. She blew some air down her nose, looked up.

'It stopped. The Tell-Me stopped.'

'I'll call Molly, shall I?' peering at him with her head tilted like a parrot.

'It just stopped.' He closed his mouth, looked back round at the slowly revolving bands of jagged colour. She didn't even try to see it. Tina looked even more puzzled than usual, stared at him.

'What d'you stop it for?'

'Didn't stop it, it stopped,' Hap insisted, jabbing the remote absentmindedly. Come on, come on.

'Never mind, dear, it'll come on again.'

Hap eyed her with ill-concealed contempt as she rummaged down the side of the La-Z-Bone and tugged her hand out tangled in a bird's nest of stringy knots she called knitting. Sit there and knit with the Tell-Me up the spout? What did she think she was doing? He could have backhanded her empty brain right back into the headrest, sitting there grinning like a lizard with the Tell-Me up the spout. He breathed hard, drummed his fat fingers on the remote panel.

'Look. It's gone wrong, all right?'

'All right, dear.'

She didn't give a toss, that was obvious enough. Tina upended her knitting, frowned and picked at the loose ends. Hap glowered at her. She'd been around before the Tell-Me came, hadn't she? He'd seen her without the help of the funny stones. Maybe she'd come afterwards. The doctors had left her to keep an eye on him. Had a good mind to tear the wretched ragged knitting from her wretched ragged knotted hands and tug it all tight over her face, net her up like a gasping tuna, if she thought she was going to spy on him while he wondered what to do about the Tell-Me. Hap looked up and down the room. Didn't do to let them see you moving about. Sitting still patient as a rock you could get them to do everything for you. He thought fleetingly of the girl with the black bra straps leaning in on him, squeezing soap on to the fluffy flannel. Concentrated for a moment and climbed stiffly to his feet, pulling the hot baggy crotch of his itchy trousers away from his prickly pink skin. The others nodded and muttered as he stalked past, thinking he was going to drop his trousers again, wave it in their faces perhaps. They'd be lucky. They'd tell the white coats, the girls with the flannels. He knelt down and spread his palms over the massive screen, tiny pulses of static running this way and that along the chicanes of skin, the loops and swirls of his fingertips.

'Seeing things,' he heard someone mutter loudly to a dozing neighbour. Hap levered himself up, took a look over the Tell-Me-Visual's squat lacquered shoulder. There was a big black lead stuck into the big black socket, and a big white plug stuck into the wall. As far as he could remember that's how it worked. He lifted the auxiliary cable, stared at it, fed it through his hands like a lifeline, dragged himself along the wall into the dusty corner of the room. Up the faded wallpaper and into a mousehole in the plasterboard.

Tina looked up as he crossed to the door, strode into the hall. Going to call them out after him, was she? Soon as his back was turned. Just like the woman in the pub that time he'd choked over his pie, pebble-dashed the bar with bitter marinated carrot. Sold him upriver same as they did in the old days, sold you to a ship. Creaking timbers, gently rocking chairs.

Hap paused in the hall, leaned against the glass-panel door. He rubbed himself a little spyhole and peered down the path. The privet hedge had closed in on him, leaving a narrow tunnel for the man who brought the junk mail. Down over the lawn to his right, a platoon of broken-backed willows. Home guards, fingering and swishing the tumbling stream. Hap narrowed his eyes, wished he'd brought his glasses. Was that someone splashing there in the shallows? Those convicts swishing their chains or an old tree bending arthritically to sip the swirling waters? He squinted, tried to pick shades from shadows. Stood back from the door with a snort, patted the remote, safe in his cardigan pocket. No time for that now. Couldn't be doing with visitors. He looked around the drab hall, the worn carpet stretched like close-cropped pubic hair over the stairs. Reception, a computer terminal like a miniature Tell-Me blipping and blinking to itself. Didn't anything work any more? A squall of static as he strode past, took the stairs huffing and puffing, two at a time. He huffed down a corridor, took another short flight of stairs and paused. A door hanging precariously on splintered hinges where somebody had tried to kick their way through the panels one time. What was his name? Old Will with the funny glasses. They'd taken him away to the multi-screen place. Hap wondered for a moment where the multi-screen place was, and how they watched more than one programme at once. He'd heard Doctor Clean-Klein talk about it with the fat controller one time. Before they'd taken him away ha ha the old man had handed him his big chunky tablets, told him keep them safe they'll keep you regular.

Hadn't told him about the films, the dream pictures he could see on the Tell-Me. Maybe he'd never seen them himself? Hadn't realized their secrets?

Hap scratched his stubby grey hair, let his gaze follow the ragged threads of spiderweb around the hall. You weren't supposed to come this far from the waiting room, this far out of the tank. He sagged against the worn wallpaper, staring at the skull-white plasterboard. He pushed the door open, ruckling the carpet back against the skirting boards. Torn sheets like surrender flags only surrender flags were white, not sickly, lurid green. Tumbled boxes stacked haphazardly and an old budgie cage. What caught his eye though, the thin beam of light speared through the mirror, pulled from its mounting on the chimney stack. A thousand reflections, slices of Hap in the frosted glass. Shivery slivers impacted around the fractured iris. Hap whined, studied the beam. Must be wrong. Must have gone wrong somewhere, a broken connection between the deserted room and the Tell-Me waiting dead downstairs. That's why he'd been called up there in the first place, to fix things. Used to do a lot of fixing before he'd come here. The signal had to go down the wire to the back of the set, didn't it? Wasn't supposed to be shining free like the faulty light in the kitchen. Burnt out.

He paused, looked at the broken mirror. The beam had scorched a hole as big as a fist right through it. The flimsy white plastic surround had warped and melted, scattered molten droplets all over the place. Hap leaned in, wiped a finger over the nearest blob, slick and waxy. He stepped closer, tilted his head to one side, eyed the green beam. If you listened close you could hear it buzzing quietly to itself, all those programmes all his schedules. Going to waste. Beaming themselves to oblivion. He raised his index finger, felt the beam glow warmer.

Tiny flickers arching from the main stem to run up and round his fingernail. Hap giggled, drew it back, jabbed it through the beam again. Maybe he could pick up the signal direct, run the programmes in his mind's eye. Watch the funny films without the Tell-Me in between? Maybe the longer he sucked the stones the easier it would be. Maybe he should swallow them, right now. Turn himself into the Tell-Me. The Tell-Me had turned itself from the tank after all. Hadn't it?

He sniggered. It tickled, the blazing green light spilling and splashing and re-forming itself, wrapping round his finger, twining his hand. He pulled his hand back and tugged the light with it, tugged it like molten glass. Whirled it like a Catherine wheel spilling a lurid comet behind it. He pulled the beam apart and it shredded obligingly, still whirling round on its corrupted axis, spinning and expanding every moment. Hap grinned as he knelt there in the green glow, enjoying the buzzing sensations playing up and down his shambolic nervous system. Pins and needles he could switch on and off just by squeezing the slippery light. The block of stone came out of nowhere and caught him on the cheek. Hap fell back with a grunt, tugging the beam with him, spilling the light all over the floor. The angry coils whipped away from him, sucked back, re-formed themselves into a slowly revolving tunnel of green light flecked with tiny glowing fibres, a plastic tornado turning itself inside out from the fractured mirror. Hap clutched his face, gingerly worked his jaw. He wondered if Tina or one of the girls had crept on up and tried to grab his attention.

'Is anybody there?' was what they always said walking around the haunted castle holding the guttering candle against the grasping spider webs. Thunnk. He spun around on his creaking knees, saw the curtain ring hit the ceiling, fall with a clink into a dish full of old crystals

CHANGELING HEARTS

and things. The green tunnel was spinning so fast he couldn't pick out the individual splashes of colour in the lurid green segments. It pulsed bright hot white, and, a lump of coal rocketed into a roof beam, embedded itself. Hap eyed the revolving beam nervously, wondering if he was some kind of magnet, attracting all this junk out of the Tell-Me tornado, spinning and whistling round his attic. Maybe he'd won something. Booby prizes. Silly rings and bits of stone, audience aahing as the holiday in the sun went down the pan. Uncomfortably aware now, nakedly aware none of this would have happened if he hadn't played about with the stone. The stone made things happen, made the films on the Tell-Me. Old Will hadn't warned him not to fiddle with it. Keep them safe keep you regular, was what he'd said. Licking them, nibbling them, he'd started to see fragments of films, faces and funny places in the Tell-Me/Tank. He should have left well enough alone, slipped them into the toilet when they weren't looking. God, he would have caught it if the catty one had been told to go along and dig all this rubbish out of the pan. Better if he dealt with it himself, got it all cleared up before they found out. What was it they said about curiosity?

After a few moments' deliberation he edged away, spied the curtain ring in the dish. He nudged the cracked china and tipped it into his hand. Curiosity killed the cat, that's what they said. Cold, white. Wasn't a curtain ring. It was a tooth. He stared at it for a full minute, racked his brain to remember the old days. He'd had a tooth out one time, dentist girl holding him down while the man with the glasses leaned in, pulling and tugging at it until he held it out on the end of a pair of forceps, neat and bloody. This was much bigger than his caked old molar though. Twice the size and sharp too, running his thumb along the clean cutting edge. What were those things with the fins called? In the film . . . sharks. That was it, more shark than human. They shed them every week, didn't they, had a constant supply of super-sharp snappers retracted in their jaws ready to cut new ones after every diver and swimmer and fisherman they'd gobbled up. Hap glanced at the green pillar, imagined horrible grey fins slicing through the slippery lurid light. He clutched the beams, felt the wood cold and hard under his hand. Cold and hard? He glanced down. The slab of stone which had clocked him one, who the hell had thrown that?

He peered around again, picked up the slab. Dark, covered with tiny etchings. Some kind of alphabet, like the tiny brand marks on the funny tablets Old William had passed over. There were no As or Bs or anything, just spidery letters more like the funny writing on the back of his Tell-Me. The slab was about the same size as the remote too. He held the stone up to his face, and without thinking ran his index finger over the tiny grooves. Backwards and fast forwards, contrast, vertical hold. Picture. A bundle of towels. Volume, train whooshing by in a tunnel. Hap dropped the stone in alarm, wondering what he could have done, wondering how he could have been expected to know he shouldn't have gone playing about with it. Don't. Telling him not to. Those prisoners running from the dogs waving their arms about, they'd warned him. They'd switched the Tell-Me off so he couldn't play about, couldn't interfere, and he'd gone right along trying to switch it all back on again. The willows out on the lawn, bending and swishing and whooshing at him, warning him off. Shadows rising from the shallows. He could explain. He hadn't meant to fiddle. It hadn't been his fault. Whoosh, rocking lights flickering as the youngster picked up speed, cartwheeled out of the green vortex and into the chimney breast, spin rinsed into the cold brickwork. Slam splat. Dirty towels from a wild washer, a man mangle. A sickeningly slow crunching as the battered stranger collapsed in a heap beneath the broken mirror. Seven years' bad luck, wasn't it? Hap, as usual, couldn't quite remember.

GONE FISHING

'You've been up there, then? Lover's Leap?' Nicky Fish's bright green eyes flickered from his notebook to the girl, just long enough to let her know he could have meant anything and nothing. Something flickered in her eyes too, for the split second he'd looked up. She frowned, smiled a little.

'I know where you're talking about. I've lived here long enough.'

'But you're not from round here though, are you? Originally?'

'My parents were. My uncle runs the pub.'

'The Boar? Roy Jones?'

'That's him. Uncle Roy. I'm staying with him until I find a flat. Not much around here, though, is there?'

'Flats-wise? Not a hope.'

'You live round here, though. I've seen you going past.' She nodded over his shoulder towards the window, the small-town traffic on its way down the gorge. Early in the season, so it was still moving. Older couples maybe taking a quick dekko at the cliffs and the caves before the holiday crowds bussed it down from Budgworth by the battalion to block the pavements queueing for melting ice-creams and tacky souvenirs. It got hot down in Clove gorge, hot up on the cliffs too, when the summer came on. The Miller feller hadn't been too bothered about the traffic or the heat. He'd driven close on two hundred miles to get where he was going. Seemed he'd read up about the place, knew all about the gorge, the gaps. Picked his spot like an archer squinting along his arrow. John Miller from Shepherd's Bush. Quiet sort of guy, the girl had said. Ordered a Cloveburger quarter-pounder, had a diet Coke to go with it. A diet Coke? What the hell was he worried about, counting calories?

'How did you know he was here, anyway?' she asked, looking him over once again. Big guy, multicoloured tie pulled to one side, grubby shirt and gaping collar. He was missing a button too. He smiled, raised his eyebrows.

'Mate of mine on the force. Said he had the receipt in his glove compartment. Had your name on.'

She made a face, looked even cuter. Five-six, auburn hair in a bun under the silly red hat, Clove Burger Pitstop.

'It's quite horrible really, when you think about it. I mean, your name on a piece of paper . . . his last meal. Spooky somehow.'

'Won't be the first they've served up in this place,' Nicky snorted.

The girl frowned. 'You shouldn't make jokes,' she scolded softly.

The reporter shrugged. Wasn't the first top job he'd covered. Christ, those gaps in the hills went all the way down to hell's belly-button. No bloody wonder they hadn't managed to get him out. Miller had taken the precaution of tying the rope round his neck and fastening it securely to his car bumper. He'd thought of everything except the jagged ledges that scarred the cliff faces like badly drawn tattoos on some old lag. Maybe he'd read the tourist stuff, the rosy glasses views. Down there, down in the guts of the hills, things tended to fade to grey fast. Then red, faster. The rocks had razored through his best buy DIY rope, God only knew what they'd done to him. When the police arrived they found the car, pulled the string but hey, no puppet. Fucked up his last great gesture. Maybe he'd been trying to guarantee a suicide verdict, do his wife out of the insurance or something. Most of them just turned up, looked round and jumped. Funny they always looked round. To see if anybody was looking, Nicky supposed. To see if anyone was going to witness their last act of defiance. Seagull shit on a windscreen, what the hell.

'Your badge says Mags.' He nodded toward the lurid plastic caveman nametag.

'Short for Margery. Margery. I ask you.'

'It's nice. I prefer Mags.'

'And you're . . . Nigel?'

'Nicky. Nicky Fish.' He hated it when people didn't catch his name. Christ, wasn't it snappy enough or something?

'And what's your wife's name? The one with the dark hair?'

Shit. 'Molly. Do you know her, then?' Ha ha what do I care? Nicky flipped his notebook over, stuffed it in his well-worn jacket pocket.

'Only to nod to. She goes in the pub with the blonde girl sometimes. And the old bloke with the funny jacket.'

'That's my boss. He's only forty-two.' Christ, what she do, keep tabs on the whole town? She was better informed than he was.

'Had a hard life, has he? Looks as if he's carrying the weight of the world around with him. Anyway . . . look . . . I must do some work. The manageress'll kill me otherwise.' She looked over her shoulder towards the big woman bustling along between the rows of bright orange tables. She wore the same sick-bag costume, bright red skirt and matching blouse, but she got to wear a blue blazer as well. Didn't help her complexion.

'Have you finished there yet, Margery?'

Nicky stepped aside as she slipped out from behind the counter. 'I shan't keep her too long, Mrs Bignell,' he called, nodding to her. She handed the younger girl a tray, motioned toward the tables.

'Six needs cleaning up. I don't know how some of them find their way down here sometimes. Come to see the caves, live in them more like.'

Mags nodded, and took the tray. 'I'll make a start, then.'

Mrs Bignell watched her cross to the tables then gave Nicky a sidelong look.

'How's Molly?'

'Molly's fine, thanks.'

'And Wilf? He keeping all right?'

'His knee's still playing him up a bit. He'll be OK when the weather gets warmer.'

'Warmer?' Mrs Bignell frowned, checked her watch.

'Well, I must make a dash. Thanks for the help.' He nodded to the manageress, waved at Mags and let himself out into the sunshine. Mrs Bignell watched him lumber off along the High Street and then nodded after him.

'You'll be all right with that one as long as you keep him at arm's length.'

'Who's arm?' the girl asked shortly, sponging spilled relish into her cupped hand.

'So what did you get?' Wilf Worthington looked up from his cribbage results, studied his chief reporter over the thin half-moon specs he'd pinched over his thin nose with thin inky fingers. Nicky noted his editor had as usual been hitting the keys of his typewriter so hard you could practically read the copy through the grubby paper. He threw his notebook on to the bonfire on his desk and crumpled into his seat.

'He had a Cloveburger and a diet Coke. The bill was five pounds eighty-six pence.'

'Is that it?'

'He didn't want relish.'

'Oh, well, there we are then. Mystery Londoner throws himself off cliff after eating burger without relish.'

Fish showed his teeth. 'I gave you the photocopy of the bill, we knew all that two hours ago.'

'We didn't know about the relish.' Wilf sighed.

'Anyway, that's not all. I talked to the girl. Margery. Did you know Roy had a niece in town?'

'Of course I knew,' Wilf snorted. 'Left college after some big bust-up with a boyfriend. She's staying in his back room.' Wilf enjoyed getting one over on Nicky and dragged the copy out of the roller with a flourish.

'Well, she said she couldn't sleep all night thinking he'd jumped. Thinking she may have been the last person he spoke to. Said it was like staring in the face of death.'

Wilf looked up slowly from his cribbage tables. 'She said that?'

Nicky nodded.

'She said that, exactly?'

'More or less.'

'More or less?'

'That's the gist of it.'

'Tell . . . me . . . exactly . . . what . . . she . . . said,' the editor suggested slowly.

'She said it was spooky. Spooky he'd carried the bill with her name on it. But it amounts to the same thing. Why must you be so pedantic?' Nicky moaned, flicking through his notebook to find her quotes.

Wilf slid around the side of the overloaded desk and squinted over the big man's shoulder.

'Your shorthand will never stand up in court, Nicky. Look at the state of that. Is it Pitman or something?'

'That's not shorthand, it's my handwriting,' Nicky snapped, switching the notebook to the other side of his desk, sending a pile of Clove parish council agendas crashing to the floor in the process.

'It's a mess, Nicky. I've told you dozens of times you may have to produce those notes in court one day. Look at mine. Proper Pitman's that is. One hundred and twenty words a minute you had to do in my day. Accurate too. None of these new-fangled tape machines when I started.'

'On the *North Somerset Hedger and Ditcher*. Yeah, those slates, what a drag.'

Wilf rapped the desk with his knuckles. 'Twenty paragraphs. I want kosher quotes, none of your Brothers Grimm bullshit. If young Margery said it was spooky you can put that halfway down.'

'Halfway down? The intro surely.'

'The intro writes itself, Nicky. Londoner drives two hundred miles to Clove especially for the views. The vertical views.' He frowned, rubbed his bony chin. 'Why did he do it anyway?' He looked forlorn for a moment.

Nicky caught his eye, shrugged. 'Press Association said he was a typical nine to fiver in some office. Collected rocks and was interested in gravel kind of guy. Wife and kids. Commuted on the Tube. Couldn't take it, I suppose.'

'Two hundred miles, though. Two hundred miles to do that.'

'That's what bothered me.' Nicky paused, looked glum. 'Fancy sitting in the traffic on the ring-road. Stuck behind a tractor coming down Cliff Drive. What he do, beep the horn? Looking for a place to park in the High Street while he had his last meal. Eyeing up the girl in the Pitstop. Taking his change. Getting caught in the one-way system up on the top there. It's like a kamikaze pilot on Valium. One purpose, one thing in mind. Locked in on our nice little hill, it's pretty obsessive, you'd have to admit. What in Christ's name was so bad with his life, made him do that?'

Wilf shook his head. 'What's wrong with you anyway, you've done suicides before?'

'It's just not knowing.'

'Not knowing?'

'Not knowing Roy Jones' bloody niece was working in the Pitstop,' Nicky growled, rolling some copy paper into his battered Smith Corona portable. New technology, Clove. Clove, Hillstones, North Somerset. Tornadoes rocketing over the hills from the air base down the road. Army on manoeuvres through the heather and broken bracken on the top down. Third exit from the Great West Ring Road. Two hundred hairpin bends later a quaint old bridge, leading motorists back in time to the gorge and the quiet, patient caves. Lit up like a fairy grotto at Disneyland, these days. Powerful arc-lighting in the ancient nooks and crannies had awoken ancient seeds. Ferns thriving against the grain of the old rock out of place, out of time.

BLOODY ROMANS

Romans? Romans built straight roads. Everybody knew that. 'Old Ringus Roadus must have had a few too many the day he got stuck into this lot,' Martin Haberfield snapped, flexing his fingers around the steering-wheel as if he was trying to throttle the living daylights out of his rapidly overheating BMW. With the wife and kids on board he was taking no chances, keeping the heavy car in check and watching the bastard in the articulated lorry loom in his mirror. Maybe he knew the road.

'Roman Road. It's marked in red. It's that or a ley line.' His wife Nisha squinted at the badly folded map, then turned it on its side, peered ahead for a sign.

Ley line? Jesus wept, they were trying to get to the old boy's, not bloody Glastonbury. He closed his eyes for a split second, blinked back to the road. It was no good sitting sulking on bends like this. Roman bloody road? He'd counted five hairpins in the last half-mile and he'd never seen – or liked – heights like it. The juggernaut which had turned off the motorway behind them was still there, trying to stuff itself into his rear-view mirror. Breathing down the back of his prickly neck. Maybe he shouldn't have cut him up like that. Martin had never seen gestures like it. He lifted his foot from the throttle as much as he dared.

'Are you sure we took the right fork?'

'We were supposed to take the right fork,' Nisha

pouted, slamming the map into her lap, lip trembling, looking out of the window.

'No. The right fork. Not right as in right–left. Right as in right–wrong.'

'How the hell should I know? You said you remembered the road.'

'It's ages since we came down here. Before we were bloody well married.'

'You said . . .'

'I know what I said. I'm just saying. There's no way on earth the Romans built this. They would have slung up a viaduct. Gone somewhere else. Did they get this far west?'

Martin eased off on the aggression, eased off on the throttle. The juggernaut loomed in the mirror, oily grille sticking obstinately a few feet from his exhaust pipe. He'd have the bastard's number and report him as soon as they arrived in Clove. If they arrived in Clove. Nisha was staring out of the passenger window, forcing herself to look at the horrendous drops which fell away alarmingly to their left. Leaving him out here all alone, all these years. No. Get a grip. He wouldn't have come, he wouldn't have left his old place in the High Street. They'd written, they'd phoned, they'd begged him to move up a little nearer London. Begging that had stopped short of an out and out invitation to come up and join them. Join them in their three-bed semi? She'd told Martin they'd manage, the kids could share a room. It was his bloody father after all. If they went ahead and shut the home the only other place was at Ferndale in Budgworth. Didn't have a warden, they had a commandant. Surely Martin would rethink. Bunk beds. They could get bunk beds when Walter was a little older. Ferndale. We have ways of making you enjoy your twilight years, only don't take too long. Straight down the

M4, they could have visited him once a month. Every other month, say. Martin glanced at his wife, read her look. Another quick glance in the mirror. God, the bastard was close. Too close to give him a quick dab on the brakes. Run into the back of me, pal, and your arse won't touch the ground. Trouble is they had the baby on board as well as their teenaged son, twitching silently to some Godforsaken racket on his Walkman. Sounded like the Bedlam Chainsaw Ensemble.

'Jonathan, can you turn that bloody row down for one second?'

His son's left hand clutched the neck of an imaginary guitar while he spanked out power chords with the right. Dozy bloody sod. The youth looked up, raised his eyebrows and lifted the headphones from his ears allowing a louder burst of feedback into the stuffy saloon.

'I said turn it down,' Martin snapped, switching his eyes back to the road as they came up on yet another hairpin bend.

Jonathan fumbled with the switches of his personal stereo as his mother swivelled round to check on the baby strapped into the carrier.

'If you wake him up you can change his nappy,' Nisha told him petulantly. Jonathan shrugged his shoulders, fixed his headphones and slumped back to watch the scenery. Horrible drops that went straight down to hell, right-angle bends careering madly round the sheer sides of the cliffs. The main road over Hillstones would have given Hannibal sleepless nights. The potholed tarmac didn't stretch for more than a few dozen yards without an all too abrupt switch in direction. It was as if the engineer had been using a compass he'd found in a lucky bag. Not only that but there were sheep and ponies wandering stupidly on the grass verges that seemed to be playing their own bizarre game of chicken, daring themselves to dash out in front of every car moving faster than five miles an hour. It was a hot afternoon and Martin's legs ached. The car smelt bad, he wasn't sure whether to blame his eldest son's penchant for free-form personal freshness or the baby's nappy.

'Are you sure this is the main road?' Martin sounded cross, cross with himself and cross with the map. But there wasn't much point arriving at the home in the middle of a sodding great bust-up. Not now. Not with the old chap lying there rattling his lungs at the poor little nurses. Nursing auxiliaries, he corrected himself. The last trained nurse had been sacked weeks before. He closed his eyes for a second, snapped them back to the road. No daydreaming, not on these bloody bends. Bloody Romans. They'd left the motorway outside Budgworth hours ago. He was sure they should have turned left for Clove, not right at the Full Moon. He didn't see why his father couldn't have taken a place nearer to them. Nearer to them. Christ it was all right Nisha rabbiting about bunk beds and managing but who the hell was going to look after the old boy? Her? Crotchety old bastard, always had been. He'd been OK before Elspeth had died. He'd been all right before the stroke, come to that. Yeah, define all right. He'd run his wife ragged with his white-hot rages, no use trying to work your way round it with some bucolic old ways bullshit. Martin bristled at the memory. The sly, insinuating childhood memories, cutting their way through the shallows of his feelings. Forgive and forget, Nisha said. He remembered the old man bawling his mother out as she pottered around the dining table setting places, disguising her winces behind grave nods and muttered apologies. Didn't like to see her wincing. Too superior or something. Domestic rebellion? Stamp it out. Nisha wondering why he'd never been keen to see his old man.

Never been too bothered about trekking west to look him up. Better to leave him to it, pottering about to the shop, the pub. Three tiny rooms in Clove High Street. Clove with the caves, that's the place. Limestone systems for the sick of living, down there in the guts of the hills. The old chap hadn't even bothered to get up to London to see Walter and he was getting on for eighteen months old already. He checked his mirror. The juggernaut seemed to have closed up as if the driver was trying to freewheel in the BMW's slipstream. He must have taken his HGV test on the Nuremberg Ring. Only a bloody maniac would drive that close on these roads.

'No wonder Dad didn't venture too far. I haven't seen anything like this since the Gambia,' he muttered crossly.

Nisha sighed, patted the map in her lap. 'It's not that he wouldn't, he couldn't. You know he'd have been up like a shot if he could,' she protested, martyr voice set to standby.

Martin sighed heavily. Hadn't moved anywhere for the past seventeen years, as far as he knew. Squatting there in front of the telly for ever. Penance for all those years he'd spent acting the drunken husband, the tyrannical father. Here, have a look at yourself, see what you see. He squinted down at the map.

'Are we there yet? We ought to see that damn bridge any day now.'

'The last sign said three miles. I could have sworn we had to go left.'

'They've probably moved the place,' Martin muttered darkly. 'Perhaps somebody buried it.'

'You always said you liked Clove. We might move down ourselves one day, spend some time.'

Martin shivered at the prospect. 'You know I hate commuting. And how the hell would I manage this every day? It's damn near forty miles to Budgworth, let alone

Peckham.' His advertising agency was based in a small alley off Rye Lane. Just now though, he would have given just about anything to get back, smoke, noise and all. 'Will you get off my fucking tail?'

'Martin!'

'Not you.' Jesus Christ. Bend. Dip. Bloody Romans.

OVER

Some time had passed, certainly, but certainly not seven years. Just his luck, stuck here/there/wherever while tea times and supper times came and went without him. A pang of hunger, upset stomach. Anxious but not particularly panicked. Adrift, from what? The little fish with the tiny attention span, swimming round and round its tank. Each rainbow bend, every algaed corner a new horizon. The poor old fish wouldn't recognize its old bowl from a yard of ale. From a glass pipe a thousand miles long but just big enough for its glistening fins. On and on for ever, nothing, everything new. Mealtimes were Hap's order of battle. The trump card in his confused campaign to keep tabs on what was left of his life. Up tea dress breakfast wash tea Tell-Me lunch tea Tell-Me tea Tell-Me supper undress Horlicks pills bed. His schedules had collapsed, fallen in on themselves like yesterday's newspapers, but those blinking pills were blinkers on a dancing racehorse blinking him in and calming him down. A testing testing testcard for his eyes only. He had to have his Horlicks before he could take his pills before he could go to sleep and dream of prisoners and dogs and splashing in the stream. He had to go to sleep so he'd know when he'd woken up. Hap wondered how long he'd been standing there gaping at the cracked mirror, wondered what was wrong with the slivered reflections. He took one step, another step closer to the smashed mirror. Those spooky old portraits where the eyes stared you down no matter what angle you approached them from. The mirror was spooky but spookily different now. He wasn't showing up. Not so much as a shadow, whichever way he tilted his head. Side to side, trying to catch a flash of reflections, a sudden peacock display of tired grey eyes. First the tank becomes the Tell-Me, now the mirror becomes a window. A pain down his right side. Running away with him again. Chasing the tail of the long lost guppy in front. The window was leaded with hairline cracks, stained with the pale reflections of the view beyond the walls. Hap ran his eye along a shard, squinted out over the quiet meadow, falling steeply into a red-banked stream. He peered around to his right, trying to pick out the shadows shifting in the willow wands, and stumbled over the boy. He groped for the wall, steadied himself. Quite forgotten how . . .

'You fool.' Hap looked up sharply, recoiling into the room, backing into the jumbled castoffs. He eyed the dim green glow of what was left of the vortex nervously, the green tornado that had scoured its way through the glass, left a carpet of shiny grit over the floor. It could cut its way through him if it saw him. If it picked up his hollow heartbeat inside his threadbare cardigan. Fragile beams unpicking themselves from the harder, shiny cartilage, flopped out of the half-melted frame like a lazy, groping arm. Coloured armbands ruckling and rolling down the length of the tube, ringing themselves off the end to wobble in delicate ecstasy for a moment before puffing to nothing. A funny smell like a light bulb left on too long.

Hap glanced down at the huddled body – it hadn't moved from the wall – looked up at the old man's face rippling slowly over the bricks, the rough textures pocking and scarring the taut stretched skin. His eyes, moist and bright, ran like egg whites, swam into focus, swirling in the pitted glass. The features formed up slowly behind the twin points of light as if somebody had rigged up a projector behind his head. Hap couldn't see any dust motes fizzing in the beam, though. He tried to place the face. Old Will, his only friend. Wasn't it? It was his room, that's how he'd known where to come. His creased forehead was steep, his cropped hair smudgy grey. He gazed sadly from the boy and back up to Hap. Looking out of a puddle, the lined features liquid, gazing in at him. Will who'd left the stones only older, crosser. Keep them close, keep you regular, he'd said. Leaning in conspiratorially, thumbing the back from the Tell-Me remote to show him the tiny tiles he'd hidden inside. That's where he'd put them, safe in the remote, safe in his pocket, warm as toast.

'You fool,' the old man repeated, his lips moving like segmented slugs.

'Pardon? Who are you?'

The old man's head fell forward as if he'd staggered under some almighty blow. He coughed a plume of misty breath over the unconscious boy. Fool? Fool? Old Will had never called him a fool. Old Will had stuck up for him. Bright, blinding memory lancing out of the broken window as if the shards had turned in on themselves, pierced his tired eyes. Hap remembered why he was there. Why he wasn't down there in front of the Tell-Me right now, minding his own business minding everybody else's. He pictured the nurse with the black bra straps, looking up from his chair, down the passage. Slowly tipping the hot tea from the pale blue cup over his lap before the Tell-Me had blinked and blipped and gone cold and led him up here. It had been him all the time, shouting, bawling, crying out for her to stop. Hadn't been those convicts in the funny old film, hadn't been some other poor bugger on the ward at all.

'Silly old fool.'

Hap blinked, shook his head.

'You don't know what you've done,' the apparition told him, sadly.

Hap blinked fast, fingers fluttering as he tried to batten down the hatches on the shifting cargoes of his memory. 'Who are you? What have I done?'

'What have you d—' The old man lurched to the left, clawed the air with his thin white hand, crooked fingers raking the empty air, drowning. Caught up in a green tunnel the same as the one which had spat out the boy. The other end of the tunnel, though, the big end. Squirting him out somewhere while the thin ribbed arm hung on grimly to the smashed window.

Hap steadied himself, stared at the window on the never world. He was that guppy. The flimsy piece of plastic fish that couldn't recognize one side of the tank from another, the top from the bottom. Swimming round and round in aimless urgency, the old man's scaly claw reaching for him, rippling the surface, reaching for him like those ragged prisoners reaching out of the stream, reaching out of the screen for him. He edged away again, into the shadows and junk, the tiny green glow all that was left of the tube now, too dim to pick him out. Stabilizing slowly, the waters lapping this way and that in the narrow room. A fool, the old face had called him. Sprouting blond hair, puffing his lips out into a bizarre pout he transformed himself into the girl. A silly old fool, she'd called him, tipping the scalding tea over his baggy crotch, looking up anxiously at the ring of nodding heads. Make sure she hadn't been seen. Spiteful glare.

'I wouldn't have you if you was family.'

Hap watched the bricks balloon in a rubbery rictus, contract against each other, grey mortar oozing like brains between the cracks. Silence. The green beam flickered. Hap waited a moment, crawled forward cautiously and prodded the body crunched into the brickwork. There was a splash of blood halfway up the wall, a horrible smear where he'd rolled to the floor. His T-shirt was way too big, his elbows were sticking out of the green fabric like broken fingers of a ransacked umbrella. Hap reached out carefully, shook the body by the shoulder. The boy rolled away from the brickwork, flopped on his back. His face was already swelling, flushing purple behind the angry cuts and abrasions. His eyelids were flickering this way and that, lashes fluttering. He wasn't dead, then. Your eyelids popped open when you were dead, stood to reason.

Hap leaned closer but couldn't feel any breath from the parted lips. Ragged fabric torn and stained, tugged away from the nasty cut over his breastbone, oozing slow blood. Skin ruckled around the wound, glistening white beneath he guessed must be a rib. Slicky shiny like the shivery green slime light playing up the walls, over the ceiling as if searching for something. Hap manoeuvred himself around, eyed the glowing worm beam, the neon condom hanging limp from the pitted glass. Buzzing, popping away to nothing. You fool. They'd said. He'd show them. The green worm coiled in his head. Hap groped over the floor, lifted the slab from the box where he'd laid it, held it over the fluorescent snakeskin. Who's the fool now? There you are . . . steady, steady. Splat. Hap brought the slab down on the boa-beam, the constrictor condom. Far too hard. Lost his footing, fell. The old-folk F-word. *Fall.*

Children fell over all the time, barked shins, scraped knees. Old people fell over and broke things. Brittle bones, rusted joints. Hap threw himself flat and held his breath, watched the wall slide past his blinking eyes. He couldn't recall the wallpaper, ran a finger over the jagged green bands as he fell, clutching the slab to his chest. The hall was an awful way down. This wallpaper was never right. Never right. No joins. Where were the bloody joins? It occurred to him as the paper peeled from the blinding white walls, rolled itself around his body as if he was ten stone of best Virginia shag. Wrapped him and rolled him like the dusky maidens did with the cigars on that island. Lighting up one end: was that his feet on fire or some kind of light at the end of the tunnel? Slipping away. Tumbling away through the tubes, interference running buzzing bands around his body. Bouncing him off the skies rushing by, receiving him. Whumph. Testing testing testcard. Transmitter down. Poor signal. DO NOT ADJUST YOUR SET. He'd fallen out of the dusty floor of the Tell-Me. Tell Me where I am, somebody. His thigh hurt the most, a wicked tearing pain burrowing into his hips. His hips had never been his strong point. Probably broken, the way he'd fallen. Fallen angel. Hap grimaced. Angel? He'd tumbled past the wallpaper so fast the pattern had blurred and blipped till he could have sworn he was sliding down the sunsplash back at Butlin's with young whatshisname that time. The memory zoomed back in on him, splashed him into the ground with a bone-jarring, spine-rattling thump.

Hap was lying on a bed of leaves, he could feel them curl and crunch under his fingers. Mulch had probably saved his life, falling like that. He lay still, thought it through. There weren't any leaves in the hallway. He must have rolled out of doors, maybe staggered out of the front door and fetched up at the bottom of the overgrown garden. Staggered down into the willows, pulling the fronds and vines from his face. It had been him down there all the time, stamping about in the shallows, hadn't it? You weren't supposed to go out without asking, not that any of them ever did. He didn't know where he was so there was no point in running. Following the stream away from the home, they'd send dogs after him too. They'd catch him and then where would he be?

Shaking his head, fists clenched in frustration. Why didn't they tell them anything? Why didn't they at least tell them where they were? He felt the panic vibrate through his bones, trapped by his tapping fingers. Sour sauces squirted in his gut, left trampled tastes on his tongue, anxiously licking his mouth. Shock. Shock's troops advancing from the wrinkles on his forehead, working their way behind his eyes, over his twitching top lip pushing and prodding cold glistening glitterballs of sweat. This was no place he recognized, this wasn't the home place, let alone his home. They'd be out looking, they would report him. Detention. Lost. The sky he'd fallen through, though, was a shiny bright blue, clear and crisp as a freshly fallen field of snow under the moonlight on the hill. Birds were singing in the trees close by. He hadn't heard a bird sing for a while. The air felt fresh and jagged in his throat.

He sat up, blinked, focused. Screamed. Tried to scream. The yell piled up in his throat, stuck behind his writhing red tongue, gasping for words around his chattering teeth. The scream when it came came straight back, echoed around the dell, bounced back making him jump. Squirmed him into the mulch, clawing at the twiggy roots as he scrambled away from the tottering leg, the furry boot laced with wiry ivy and creeper. A stumpy carving, twitching slightly, the trapped foot tapping some bizarre message as far as the smashed kneecap, shiny white slicked in blood and tattered pieces of skin. Hap backed away on his bottom, ignored the pain in his thigh. The ragged boot bindings were entwined with ivy, hardy vines had thrown shoots around the ankles, locked the foot tight into the mulch. The rough woollen bindings soaked in blood, leaves and bushes splashed and spotted. Hap couldn't even feel the pain. He could feel his toes twitching in his slippers. He opened an eye and peered down. Two tartan pompoms twitching on the end of his legs. He felt down from his knees, felt his shinbones, felt for his ankle before the ache in his back forced him to sit straight.

The leg was standing like a sentry next to the quiet pool, fed by a noisy brook tumbling over the mossy bearded rocks. Lily pads nosed by fat carp and great balloon-throated frogs that ribbited and ribbited in a subdued chorus. The pool filled the floor of the dell, the trees rising abruptly from the water's edge, tall teeth growing straight from the flooded banks, red as an old man's gums. Hap ran his hands over his body, wondered for a moment whether he'd fallen in, the old man leaning over the water to stare in at him, the white hand cleaving the surface, rippling the pool. Calling him a fool and tumbling off into the chimney breast, over and out of the green tunnel into the bricks. His clothes were dry as chalk, brittle as the skin on a roast chicken. He peered around for the rest of the body. The mulch had been trampled, great heavy depressions in the soft leaves where somebody in heavy boots had trodden about next to the water. The trees closed in behind the leg as if jealous of their stumpy rival, annoyed at being plastered with bright gouts of the late owner's blood. Hateful stinktop shrubs coiled and sprang around the great trunks, hungry for some horrible cross-pollination. Hap remembered the body rocketing through the vortex, the lurid rainbow spewing the body against the chimney breast. He looked about him, no sign of a chimney or a wall. Not even a hedge or a rickety fence. Just all this nature, alive and kicking.

Hap couldn't recall whether the body had been minus a leg or not. Surely he would have noticed that. How far had he come, how far had he fallen? He couldn't remember. He leaned over and recovered the tablet from the leaves, brushed the worst of the dirt from the glowing stick letters. Looked up sharply as the trees hissed and backed away, drawing their creaking branches back against their vulnerable trunks. The angry letters dimmed, the pain in his thigh glowed white hot. The ivy snapped and curled around the monstrous boot, which swayed lazily and toppled into the mulch, dribbled tendons and thin sullen blood. Fresh blood, as if he'd only just missed the unlucky owner, blinked and missed the nasty accident. Somebody'll be killed before the council do anything about it. Fencing's what you needed around a pool like this, some nice straight concrete banks, a pretty little cement culvert with a rusty grille, bars to keep the things in the water back. Drown you as soon as look in on you. Long white fingers fluttering the surface, rippling the reflection of the trees, bowing and sighing in the breeze.

Hap gulped, eased himself a little further away. Must have landed on something, stuck himself on something sharp. Put his hip out he wouldn't wonder. Hap tugged up his cardigan, tore at his zip and dragged his heavy cords over his buttocks. His pocket had shredded, he'd lost his change and the lucky-bag curtain-ring tooth he'd put away for safekeeping. He tugged the trousers down, caught a brief glimpse of the horrible white growth on his thigh, thought for a second he'd rolled over on some horrid toadstool spitting spores into his eyes. He tore his shirt-tail back, gasped. The tumour was the size of a chicken's egg, hard rinds criss-crossed like living knitting, knotting. She'd done it to him, what's her name, they all had, stitched him up for this with their scurrying and mopping, scolding and pouring. Ganging up with their cardigans and soggy hankies to send him away just because he'd collapsed in the pub again. Taken him home and he would have recovered, a day in bed he would have been right as rain. Not them. Shaking their heads and wiping crocodile tears from their crocodile jaws, chairs rocking like the creaking timbers of those old-time ships. Elspeth had been talking, telling them to watch out for him, watch out for old Hap. Soon as he puts a foot wrong we'll have him away to the hot place, leave him to stew in his own juice.

Hap's jaw hung open as he thought hard, thought harder. Sitting watching the Tell-Me he'd never had a problem with his leg his heart yes but not his leg NOT HIS LEG. He could feel the earth under his fingers, earth and mulch, not worn wet sheets. He opened his eyes, stared at the tumour again. It wasn't anything to do with him. He prodded it. Agony. Pain shot out of the growth, rocketed into his femur, up under his genitals, crouched there cold and grey and flaccid above the monstrous newcomer. Dwarfed and dominated by this lusty long lost cousin. Hap slid back, stared at the hard blue sky. Oh Jesus! Tears rolled freely down his face, into his open mouth, over his ears into his tousled grey hair. The pain in his thigh faded a little. He scanned his memory, the fragments of a past he couldn't quite remember, the shifting cargo spilled round murky holds. Going to work on the farm until the sun had burned so bright he'd fallen down, face purple and yellow. The pain in his chest that time. They'd taken him away ha ha but it hadn't taken him, not quite. Before the Tell-Me came. Before they left him in the lounge with the Tell-Me on too loud. The rest of them sitting round in big shirts with scrawny necks like turkeys twisting this way and that to watch the nurses come for them. So hot you gulped for every breath even if you didn't want one. Hap sucked a mouthful of cool air, blew it up over his slick face. Sank deeper into the mulch. Come and get me I'm here. Can't you see me any more?

They were always leading the others down the path, out into the garden if it was warm enough. Weren't they going to come for him? He was thinking of calling out when something white moved in the corner of his eye, fogged by a tear. Hap looked round, focused. A swan gliding across the flooded dell, soft white breast easing through the rippling lily pads. Bright white mirrored in the deep emerald water. Here he was, lying dying in a pile of compost with his body growing monstrous mushrooms of its own, and a lovely big swan nodding its smooth head at him. Another and another from behind a clump of trees, a small island in the middle of the lake he hadn't noticed before. Hap lay still as the phalanx of swans crossed the pond, ripples spreading behind them, lapping the muddy bank, spilling him this way and that on his mulchy mattress. The swans had seen him, nosed him. The leader craned his graceful neck and they turned, six of them, headed for him. Hap lay still, fingers twitching in the leaves. Swans couldn't hurt you. Who'd ever heard of a swan hurting you? Spit a bit, but not hurt you. Behind the swans the ripples coagulated around the dark head, cutting through the water, bright eyes studying him. The woman rose slowly, black hair streaming water. The dusky maiden. They'd had a picture of her at home one time. Dusky maiden by a tree on some tropical island, yeah, rolling cigars on her coffee-coloured thigh. Smiling at him with her beautiful clean white teeth. Rolling him on her thigh, puffing him through space to this place by the pool.

Hap squinted as the swans fanned out on either side, made way as she nosed the lily pads aside, green glittery eyes glued on him. Hap saw her rise out from the froggy pond, black hair tumbling over her cloak. It shimmered, moved slickly over her body. A great shifting sheet of spawn. Frog-spawn slimed on a web of spidery silks. Tiny black points shifting and sliding in their slippery bubbles. Primitive tadpoles with feathery fans for lungs, millions of them, a slippery honeycomb of twitching creatures sheened to her cloak. A billion tiny black eyes rolling this way and that, those little steel ball games you had to tilt from side to side to find the holes. Hap lay back in the mulch as the spawn woman strode through the shallows, held out her hand.

'Happy.' Happy? Happy? Don't remember. Don't know. Hap opened his eye, saw the woman leaning over his groin, startling pale green eyes flickering up to meet his astonished stare. He couldn't see her black bra straps. Maybe she wasn't wearing one, leaning over his groin like that with her collarbone standing out on her spicy skin. Slim as an eel but as strong as a horse, the way she'd dragged him through the mulch like a fat plough, rolled him to the door of her blancmange-shaped hut. He'd crawled inside, collapsed on the dusty floor. The woman sat back on her haunches. She'd changed the spawn cloak for something lighter, easier. A plain brown shift hung with tiny stones and pieces of stick. Her long black hair obscured most of her face but her eyes bored through, stared at him like a lion in the long grass. The dozy great gnu lying near by, rubbing its jangly back up and down a dusty rut.

'Happy,' she repeated. 'You said your name is Hap, short for Happy, is that right?'

Work. Cold mornings and bales of hay on the back of a rusty Land Rover. Bullocks lumbering down off the snowy drifts to fall in behind the truck like kids on a parade. 'Get on, Hap! Watch your hoe, mate!' down the vortex of his memory, spinning green bands around the white concertina of cartilage.

'Happy Maggs.' She breathed, rolling the little twig bone thing she'd taken from somewhere under her shift.

Hap frowned. 'Haberfield. Hap Haberfield,' he corrected. She glared at him for a full minute, green eyes gouging his, before nodding back on her heels with a small snort.

'Fickle fate,' she said softly.

'Hap Haberfield,' he repeated, louder. Was the damned woman deaf or something?

'From the home with the stones.'

How did she know about his stones? Old Will's stones, he should say. They weren't anything to do with him. Old Will, she needed to speak to, not him. He had seen her before, seen her face on the films, her place on the Tell-Me.

'You know Maggs? I have seen him in your home place,' she said matter of factly.

'Maggs?' Hap blinked, eyed her as she reached to one side, drew a shallow bowl from a shelf and selected a long thin knife. A pallet of blood and smeared pieces of flesh. What? Hap struggled to scream, the noises rammed solid in his bulging froggy throat, the ballooning air sacs of those great slimy toads around the shallows. She wasn't going to? The blade glimmered in the dim glow from the fire, flickering over the rough wattle roof of her hut. Hap knew he should think, think things through but she'd caught his attention, imprisoned it for three concurrent life sentences hovering over his exposed groin with that long knife. She turned, ran the blade up her thumb.

'Where is Maggs?' she asked dangerously.

'Old Will, you mean? Old Will had the stones, not me,' he whined.

'Who are you?'

Hap's head hit the floor with a thunk. How did he know? He would have been able to tell her, once. He would have been able to tell her where to get off too, using that tone with him. But the stones had muddled his mind, muddled his face and his place until he wasn't sure where he was, who he was or where he'd been. The Tell-Me throwing pictures at him faster than he could see them, strobing images hurt his eyes, made him squeeze them tight shut. The last of his strength, the last of his control had ebbed from his bones, evaporated from the stringy twisted sinews in his arms and down his trembling legs. One time before they'd pricked him on a nail and asked him to count from ten backwards. Watched him fall through the gurney, stood back away from him as he dropped into nothingness.

Opening an eye, he saw the woman snort, lean over quickly and run the blade into the horribly pulsating tumour on his thigh. Hap vibrated with agony, fingers tore chunks from the wooden flooring. She flattened her hand on his white belly, held him for a second, dug the knife deeper. He screamed, shook her hut to the wickerwork foundations, rattled the pots and bottles standing dusty on the rickety shelving around the walls. The woman shuddered, leaned forward, pressing her weight on his chest as she cut deeper into the bulging tumour. Hap was cross-eyed with pain, gasping for breath. So much pain his brain switched off, told him about it in a series of pulses and flickers.

'Keep still, you fool. It's got to be cut out now. You've no business with it, it's no business with you,' she scolded. Hap lay back, rigid with fear, as she lanced deeper and deeper into his flesh. Tough tendrils of skin wrapping round the narrow blade, criss-crossing the bleeding wound like an octopus wrestling its prey from some hungry crab. She moved her hand, took another knife and thrust it into the quivering mass. The tooth rolled out, the tooth he'd picked up and forgotten all about. Put it away safe in his pocket with his old penknife and little bits of change. It rolled, slick and white over his skin trailing wet tendrils of flesh and runnels of blood. She held the flailing skin back with the long knife, tapped the bloody tooth from his leg. It clattered against a pot and came to rest on the dusty floor. She looked down at the man, eyes rolling, mouth opening and shutting like the great carp in the pool. Reached over him as he retched raggedly, picked the tooth from the dusty clutter on the floor.

'Where did you get it? Did *he* give it to you? Maggs?' She prodded the point into his flabby arm but he'd already fainted, dentures hanging horsily in his spitty pink mouth. She sat back, frowned, fished the bone necklace from beneath her shift and ran her bloody finger backwards and forwards over the tiny grooves, read the runes for the umpteenth time: Maggs, Miller and Klein. Fickle fate. Amiarillin shook her head, chuckled softly.

OUT

Mysheedi's hair was standing on end. Puut Ra would have found it comical if he hadn't been so terrified by the ghastly moan that echoed around the dell. He gulped, peered over his shoulder into the gloom, the trees rustling, shimmering about them. What now? What had he been thinking of, venturing out in the wilds with these scrawny wretches? Running off into the woods as soon as she'd shown up, letting the warlocks escape. Puut Ra frowned. They must have stumbled on the spellstones hidden under the rock, the old fool distracting them with his mad antics while Teomalik tried to perform the ritual, the stream bitch hanging from him like a wild cat on a lame hare. Hadn't even looked at him, bobbing in the chop over the squall of pebbles, dashing him senseless against the bank. Swum straight past him as if he'd been a lump of weed, a broken branch. The guards had run off howling while the green tornado had scoured down the stream, rushed the damned prisoners away. 'Not right away, master,' Mysheedi had confided when he'd eventually managed to drag his chief out of the water. He must have slipped, banged his head. Unless the warlock had thrown something, knocked him from the crumbling bank just as she'd put in her surprise appearance.

'Not right away? What are you gabbling about now?' he'd snorted, sitting up and rubbing the livid bruise on his forehead. Mysheedi had rolled his amber eyes, pointed to the stump out in the clearing, the sodden earth silty and slick as the flood waters had slowly subsided. He'd dragged the unconscious boy from the water, up the bank and into the undergrowth, splashed water on his white face to bring him round. Puut Ra squinted in the gathering gloom. 'What is it?'

'It's his leg. The old man's,' Mysheedi told him with a fearful shiver. Warlock magic? Tilekin had been right all the time. Leave well enough alone.

'The rest of him, Teomalik?'

'Gone.'

'And what's become of your brave troopers?'

'Gone.'

'She got them?' he asked awkwardly.

Mysheedi had shrugged, told him about the lurid green tornado flickering and wobbling in the water, swallowing them up.

'Yes, I know all that,' he interrupted. 'Where did she go?'

Mysheedi shook his head.

'Typical. What about Tilekin? I'm surprised at him, running off because of a bit of wind.'

A bit of wind? That ghastly howling, the furious honking over the hill? The wailing had chilled Mysheedi's blood. Sucked and drained the marrow from his chalky bones before he'd seen the something erupt from the stream, fasten itself to the fallen wizardboy, slick and shivering, changing colour as it clutched at him. Another horrible howl rang round the deserted gorge.

'Well?' he hissed. 'Where did it come from?'

Mysheedi wiped his mouth, wiped his hand on his trousers. 'Up ahead, over the water.' The scream was loud enough. Were the boy's ears filled with wax?

'Water? I don't see any water.' It was black and cold

now, under the slowing, shifting trees. The dark canopy had obscured the moon and streamer clouds. Puut Ra narrowed his eyes and peered harder into the woods, drew his knife.

'She's caught someone, that's for sure,' Mysheedi breathed. Another scream echoed out into the night, rebounded from tree to tree. The leaves and boughs quivered in wretched sympathy.

'Well then, she'll be busy and she won't hear us. We have to take a closer look.'

Mysheedi fidgeted in the darkness. The boy had denied her very existence, here he was searching her out when all his senses screamed to run run run and hide in the woods.

'We have to see, see what she's really like, all these stories,' he whined, shook his head and narrowed his eyes. 'We have to see what she can do,' he added quietly.

Mysheedi swallowed, picked at his twitching nose.

'Go on, scout ahead.'

Mysheedi looked doubtful, drew his dagger and slunk off. Puut Ra stepped carefully on his shadow. Over a log, down a bank. Mysheedi hissed as the water closed about his dirty breeches. The boy crouched on the bank, focused slowly on the glittering lake. Smooth as a mirror and silent as a slow-worm in a rainstorm.

'Go on. What are you waiting for?' he whispered down to his frozen counsellor.

Mysheedi, teeth chattering, glowered up at him. Go ahead, you're that keen for her. That keen to ride her to death, beyond. He'd known from the beginning what the master had been after. Stones? Spells? Spawn.

'Didn't you see her? Hear the stories about swimming with the Sister of Sorrow? One night and she adds yours to everybody else's. That's what she'd have done with the boy if the tunnel hadn't come for him.'

'It didn't come for him. It was after me,' Puut Ra argued. 'It had no business with him, he hasn't any power any more.'

Mysheedi raised his eyebrows.

'I know the stories,' his master went on crossly. 'So did Tarkemenis and the boy. They knew what they were doing, leaving the stones here.'

Mysheedi ignored him. 'We'll just make another handful for her to smear over her cloak,' the goblin objected. 'Your life for a night. There's no return visit.'

Puut Ra clicked his tongue, making Mysheedi's pointed ears prickle all over. 'There's a light over there. That's where they are. Come on.'

The boy eased himself down the bank, felt the cold water shackle his thin legs, wrinkle his balls. Mysheedi waded forward, sliding deeper in the night. Puut Ra closed in behind his bobbing head, felt the ledge falling away softly under his slippered feet. Something brushed his shin and he thrashed away, snorting at the oily water. Mysheedi froze, his great eyes wider than an owl's in the gloom.

'A fish or something. Go on.'

'Something moving,' Mysheedi gasped. The boy froze, felt slinky weeds wafting against his skin, the cold penetrating his bones. A rectangle of light fell out of the darkness up ahead, bathed the lake in a silvery glow. Puut Ra saw the swans gliding toward them, heavy wings held erect as they paddled in furious silence. A smoky shadow appeared in the doorway of the hut for a moment. Her. He felt himself bristle in anticipation, expectation. Shiver from his curling toes through his agonizingly erect penis to the very tips of his lank hair. Little boy lost. Stolen child, changeling. Her sister had brought him over – she'd take him back. She'd pity him, send him home. He opened his mouth, tried to call her. Throat muscles pulled taut, he barely managed a strangled croak before Mysheedi slipped his stinking paw over his mouth, flashed him a look. She'd gone. Slipped through the light and disappeared into the gloomy trees.

Mysheedi held his dagger out of the water, tiny ripples as he swung his head from side to side. The swans had swept away to their right, bow waves lapping them as they crouched in the shallows. A sudden yell behind them. Puut Ra peered over his shoulder, lily pads closing in as if they would cut off his escape. Shrieks and cries, furious honking and spitting as the swans reared out of the black water, beat their enormous white wings over some desperate fugitive.

'Get out of it! Feathery bastards!' Tilekin! Whoof whoof wings beating the night air, Tilekin wielding his spear over his head, slashing at the jabbing beaks.

'Get away, you witch spawn, you slime boaters! And you!'

Puut Ra shoved Mysheedi, frozen by the sudden commotion.

'Trust that bloody fool to do his job properly. Hurry or he'll scare her off.' He locked his knife between his teeth, kicked off toward the light. Mysheedi plunged on into the water, splashed after him.

The shrieks echoed back and forth across the dell as the general foundered about in the marshy shallows, lashing about for all he was worth. He'd upended two of the swans already, the broad flat spear cutting deep into their extended necks. The rest had paddled away, left him some room. A curious high-pitched whistling made their ears throb.

Puut Ra swam to the bank, ducked under the tangle of roots protruding from the crumbling earth. He peered over the edge, blinking against the bright light flooding from the doorway. Mysheedi rose from the water beside him, coughing and spluttering. He winced, covered his ears as another whistle cut the air over the lake. The swans ruffled their feathers, bowed away from the lone goblin, cursing and jabbering in the weedy margins, beating their wings like white ghosts. Puut Ra eased himself out of the water, darted over the trampled earth and crouched beside the hut, peered inside. Shelves and pots, roots and ropes hanging from the smoky rafters. A frightened fat man peering up at him from a rush mat, clutching a rag to his stomach. The boy glanced along the bank. Mysheedi slipped out of the shadows and crouched down beside him. Puut Ra pointed inside the hut, then along the neat path beside the lake. He ducked under the flap as the fat man squirmed weakly against the wall, holding his stomach and wimpering with pain. Two legs. Puut Ra glared, bit his lip. Could he have altered himself so much, played tricks with his mind? Tarkemenis, Prince of Peresh, Guardian of Rites of the old empire, Guardian of the Heirlooms. Lying in the dust in a dirty old hut with his right foot kicking and twitching. He was grasping for the knife balanced on the blood-splattered bowl beside the mat. The youth stepped over the floor, pushed the bowl away with his wet slipper.

'Where's the boy? Where's Teomalik?' he asked, uncertain; curious.

'Don't hurt me any more. Don't hurt me, please.'

Puut Ra's green eyes narrowed, a slim snake in the rushlight. Don't be fooled by his appearance, the strangely musical dialect he had to tilt his head to catch. He knew the warlock's powers, whether he was in his right mind or not. Ragged white shirt, baggy trousers bunched under his weakly beating legs. It's a dream picture he's showing you, drawing you closer. He's in it with her. They've plotted all these years to keep prying eyes away from their secret dell. The heirlooms of Trafarionath, the Grimoire, spellstone, Lawlayer. He'd seen its work, the rolling thunder down the gorge, the green tunnel scooping them away, right from under his nose. They'd escaped, left him here to rot with the dogs. This bloated carcass they'd left behind with her, some kind of payment, a skin toll. They go over, he comes back. Is that how it worked? He'd need a skin toll too. He'd need somebody on the other side, the spells to find him, send him. He glanced around the hut, flicked to the tooth lying on the pallet by the dirty wattle wall. He gasped. Shulukayasheen. He'd heard all about them from Tilekin and the others, but never seen one. Pulled from the Great Queen's warped skull, so they said. A charm to slit your throat, drain your life with the faintest whisper, so they whispered. He bent, picked it up carefully and dropped it into the pocket flap on the sodden cloak.

'Master!'

Mysheedi calling from the tent flap. Puut Ra backed away from the groaning man. He peered down the bank, drew back. A silver moth caught in the moonlight, shimmering silver wings wrapped around a dark torso, twisting and writhing toward them. Tiny bolts of bright white light leaping and dancing from the shimmering shape. Mysheedi bolted, leapt into the lake. The splash focused the creature's attention, looming out of the darkness. Puut Ra gazed at her, the Spawn Sister, striding on long dark legs with her arms outstretched, shimmering gown spread over the water like a night heron's doomwatch wings. Mysheedi had dived under the flat black waters, kicking his feet in terror, just like all the rest, no spunk. He giggled. Nerves. She glowered, picked him out cowering by the door. He itched to run and jump into the pool, copy Mysheedi's frantic goblin paddle toward the darkness of the far bank.

'Come out of there, boy,' she rasped, clamping his madly thumping heart. The heart, his life. The soul she'd inherited from her elder sister. Called him to her, whistled him up like a young merlin to prance on her wrist. She folded the shimmering cloak about her, black hair closing over her face.

Puut Ra backed away from the door, frantically looking about him. He staggered over the fat man's legs, fell back dropping his knife. The fat man shrieked, sat up and clutched at his groin as Puut Ra snaked over him, tipping the bowl. The Spawn Sister ducked under the doorway, drew herself up to her full height. Regarded him coldly.

'Your penknife cannot harm me, little swimmer. Don't you know that? Don't you at least know that?'

The fat man drew back against the wall, heavy face contorted in pain as he scrambled out of her way. Puut Ra crouched against her crude shelving, groped for the dagger, felt for the tooth. He locked his thin fingers around it, clutched it to his chest. The woman's cloak shivered as she looked through him, through his heart.

'You've missed the warlock, little swimmer,' she said. 'He didn't even think to drop in and pay his respects. After all this time. I think he must have been a little caught up in things.' She chuckled to herself, enjoying his terror.

Puut Ra glanced at the fat man crouching between them, fat face pasty and white in the sickly rushlight. His mouth compressed to a puckered blue line as he clutched his leg. The boy glanced back at her. She looked indulgently at her terrified patient.

'You think he's such a master of disguise? You certainly have a great deal to learn, young master.' She rolled her eyes, stretched herself. Flung her head back and opened her cloak. The shimmering gown sparkled with a million points of light, a million tiny cells of life flickering and pulsing over her body. Swarming, flushing, changing colour and changing shape. Billowing brightly, so brightly the fat man flung his blood-smeared arm across his face. So brightly Puut Ra couldn't stop his teeth clenching, pulling his gaze away. The kaleidoscope flared, a fabulous sunset, flared and died. The lights went out.

'How dare you assume that tone with me? I am Puut Ra, Prince of all Trafarionath. Down on your knees, insolent creature, and pray to your creator I decide to overlook your fearful insolence. You must know I have a bowstring... goblins behind every tree!' he called, shakily into the gloom. He strained his ears, the fat man blubbering and moaning to his right. A vague shadow stirring the dust to his left, chuckling.

'Do you imagine I am your prisoner?' He tried to laugh, ended up retching on his words, parched and brittle on his frozen tongue.

'Do you think... I'm just another prisoner?'

'Prisoner?' She'd wheeled to her right, must be standing over the fat man, straddling him as he lay whining and muttering. 'Prisoners? I don't take prisoners. Men come here of their own free will. The warlock did, the boy did. Don't you know anything?' Playful, girlish almost.

Puut Ra wasn't familiar with the tone, mistook it for a direct threat. 'I haven't...'

'But you did. So did he. Didn't you?'

'Ouch! Not... yes... yes I suppose so.'

The fat man rolled on his litter, Puut Ra heard the rough mattress grate the dust.

'My, all these visitors in one day. I'm such a lucky girl. It's been so long since my darling sister sent me anyone, these blind encounters are so tiresome, don't you think, little swimmer?'

Panther growl, a furry pad laid softly on Puut Ra's jittery skin. He could imagine her claws retracted, the merest sliver lower and he'd feel them, raking him open, gutting him for later.

'Sometimes I'd blind them before, sometimes afterwards. I never shared my sister's tastes though, decayed carnival hucksters or little boys. Give me men,' she breathed voluptuously.

He closed his eyes, scuttled for the fresh air.

'That's right. Crawl away. Thank you for coming. Do call again, when you're a little older perhaps? When you've put on a bit of weight, especially down there,' she said smugly.

His trembling hands dropped to his aching loins.

'The door's just in front of you.'

He held his breath.

'Changed your mind?'

He froze. He could feel the breeze, tell the door flap was hanging there invisible, just beyond his fingertips. His bolthole. So close he could run his fingers over the cold sheen of her cloak, down the sleek folds gathered around her dark bare feet. She raised her arms, pulling the hem from his stretched hand, lighting him up as he grovelled beneath her.

'Going already? You've only just . . . got here.' She chuckled. 'Now put the token you've stolen back where you found it, and let's have a look at you . . .'

He sensed her step forward, she stopped short. Another outcry from over the water. Honking and hissing and great wings flapping slow air over the silent lake. 'That's right, you feathery frog! Fly away now, you carrion crow! Quill pig!'

Puut Ra felt a breath of air across his face, a tiny smear of moisture as the hem of her jelly cloak blew against his arm. She lifted the flap, he could see the stars glitter sharply over the horizon of her shoulders, the slippery cape shimmering and spangling. She ducked out of the hut, strode to the bank and peered into the gloom after the sudden commotion. Three swans, flying low, beating the water with soft, long wing feathers rippling the surface. Powerful black feet paddling the pool as they picked up speed, hurtled up and over the grasping branches into the night. She watched them blurred white over the treetops, turned and gazed into the lake again. Furious honking, splashing as the last swan craned its neck to jab at the goblin, laughing hysterically as he held on to the thick black feet, twisted this way and that in the powerful bird's slipstream.

'Can't fly? Can't fly! You one-eyed fornicator! Can't fly now, eh?' Tilekin twisted behind the swan, running as fast as his stumpy legs would go, heavy boots splashing and skimming the pool as the overloaded swan made one supreme effort to stretch for the safety of the air. The bird turned its head, redoubled its efforts as the mad passenger pulled and plucked at its tail feathers. Puut Ra darted across the hut, rolled the fat man from the litter and tugged the tablet up, clutched it to his chest in triumph. The fat man peered up at him fearfully. 'Don't hurt . . .' The boy brought the heavy stone down on his head. He flapped his hands, shrieking so shrill he knocked the tablet from the astonished boy's grip.

The boy darted across the hut to retrieve it, the old man crawling feebly behind him like a distressed sheep-dog. He threw out a hand, tapped the boy's ankle. Puut Ra, swivelling on one leg, crashed to the floor, prostrate in the doorway. The furious shouting and shrill whistling built to a crescendo as Hap bellyflopped over the tablet with an agonized, slaughtered bellow. Frantically ran his fingers over the cold stone like he had in the loft. He hadn't meant anything then but he meant it now, all right. Go on, take them away. Suck them into the wall like a bag of washing. The pots and pans jumped and rattled on the shelves around the vibrating hut. Puut Ra stumbled out, saw the woman turn, raise her fingers to him. He closed his eyes as she tore the breath from his throat with a savage twist of her wrist. The boy slid over the floor, gasping in dust, rolled over the bank as the Spawn Sister was knocked aside by the dying swan, blundering through the air with its demented rider clawing and tearing at its tail plumage.

'Pluck you like a turkey buzzard, how'd you like that?' Tilekin yelled as the bird sailed into the hut, crashed into the dust dry timbers. Puut Ra clutched his throat, twisting as he sank through the inky waters, past the floating lily pads and their groping tendrils, past the fat carp mouthing the silt. Tilekin hit the hut with a ferocious crunch, staggered back on his soaked boots and collapsed to the floor, the dead bird crashing on to his chest knocking the wind out of him. The bank collapsed, spilling him and the hot swan into the frothing waters. The Spawn Sister, growling with rage, lunged for him, tearing the tattered campaign cloak tight around his neck. He choked for a second before the lazy stitching burst, set him free. She clawed his face as he slid, laughing, under the black waters.

MISSED

Their time ran out the way sand always seems to speed up, gush down the stranglehold neck of an egg timer. Jonathan had been dozing in the back. He was too hot and the batteries were running down on his Walkman, slurring the music and turning the vocals into whale noises. He'd glanced idly at his little brother, strapped into his babyseat with his slippery chins resting on his bib. Walter, for Christ's sake. What sort of parents called a kid Walter in this day and age? Poor little bugger. Take a nap while you can, little feller.

'Stupid bastard's coming . . . what the hell . . .'

The BMW rocked to the right as his father wrenched the wheel around. Jonathan had been looking the wrong way, he hadn't seen anything. Only the bridge looming up, grey slabs rushing out to engulf them.

'Martin, you're going to . . .' Nisha clutched at her husband's arm as she bounced back from the doorframe. Martin jammed the brake to the floor, wrenched the wheel to the right, overcorrecting. The big tyres squealed on the loose gravel as the back end of the car fishtailed into the parapet. Engine roaring, it careered across the bridge and nosedived into the opposite wall. Behind them, the juggernaut rolled to a halt, agonizingly slowly. Dinosaur body at right angles to the tiny brain. The driver was scrambling out of his seat as if he wanted to climb out of the roof, out of the window, Jonathan caught one momentary glimpse of his big hands flapping in front of his face before he was pitched forward, cracked his head against his mother's seat. He crashed back, flung an arm across the baby's chest as he whipped against his straps.

'Martin!'

The car didn't stop. The bonnet dug into the bridge, flipping the car up on its nose. Jonathan was hurled out of his belt and over the seat in front, crashing into his mother as she cracked her head on the dashboard. His earphones had been torn out but he could still hear a mad cackle over the roaring engine and screeching metal. Spreadeagled upside-down against his parents he grabbed for the mirror as the car tipped over the parapet and hit the water upside-down, crushing the struts, crumpling the roof and trapping the three of them against the windscreen. He could hear his mother screaming and the baby crying. Pain criss-crossed his legs, red knives jabbed at the back of his eyes. He flexed himself, yelped, crushed against the roof. His face was pressed against the fabric cover, horrible velvet against his skin. He'd always hated velvet. He couldn't move his head far enough to see the others, but could feel somebody writhe weakly under his back, an arm brush against his leg.

He flexed again and felt the body beneath slip, giving him an inch more room. He turned his head to the left, groaned in agony. He must have broken his neck. Twisted it at least. He could see Walter bawling in his seat, upside-down pudgy face crammed with blood. He could see his own hand hanging over the back of his father's seat, see a tiny snake of blood slither over his wrist. He flexed it, felt the hurt explode further up, under his elbow. He squirmed again, cricking his neck, but couldn't turn far enough to see the front of the car, his parents mangled underneath him. Walter was bawling, thin strings of spit in his open mouth but otherwise he looked OK.

He heaved again and felt the bones beneath give a little more. He twisted, ignoring the pain flooding up his arm, gripping his knees in jaws of ice. He inched himself over the roof fabric, useless legs flopped over the front seat with his head hanging in the water that had rushed into the cabin. The stream was pouring in through the smashed engine compartment, through the crow's nest of twisted wires and the splintered plastic of the dashboard. Filling dials and gauges, overflowing the ashtrays, spilling out of the cassette holder. Pouring, flooding over the crumpled roof, rising higher. Jonathan heaved against the seat, the crushed bodies. The water was freezing cold against his chest as he crawled, squirmed backwards into the interior. Walter hanging upside-down in his straps, his face redder than a clown, his hair hanging down, hanging in the water that was already flowing up and over the seat. Jonathan pulled himself up by the doorhandles, reached against his little brother's chest, his chubby hands waving like tentacles. He grasped at the catch, folded himself against the seat, water rising higher now, over his legs, over his waist.

He sat up on the broken roof, legs splayed awkwardly under the brown rush, leaned against the seat. The water was pressing cloudy green against the passenger windows, he could still see the sky out of the back, clouds drifting by unconcernedly. He concentrated on the catch, holding the dumpy weight of his brother as he fumbled with the fastening. He could hear him screaming now, flat, monotonous. He'd be out of breath soon, quieten down. The buckle popped open and Walter fell head over heels into his arms, making the joints pop in agony. He rested his brother in his lap to take the pressure off his elbows as the stream flowed darker and darker behind the remaining windows, colder and colder over his legs. He reached for the doorhandle, then remembered the BMW had been fitted with childlocks. They would only open from the outside or with the central locking switch. That was somewhere in the front, under the water, crushed under the broken bodies of his parents. Jonathan stared at his reflection in the glass, the twisted features, the wet hair. He was trembling, cold panic. He stared at his face for forty seconds before he realized it wasn't his. Somebody was in the stream looking in at them. He tugged himself forward, peered out. Knocked on the glass with his good arm.

'Get us out! There's a child lock. Open the doors!' he shouted, hoarse, throat hurting. He could feel the water seep over the collar of his shirt, rush up his back, a green tide swallowing the stepping-stones of his spine. He hitched his brother higher, out of the water, held him against the head rest. Walter was crying, spluttering. As he brought his brother around, Jonathan registered a second face in the glass, peering in at them over the swimmer's shoulder. A filthy hand clamped over his mouth and nose, gimlet eyes sparkling with a revolting hunger. A hunger for them. Jonathan jerked back, stared at his screaming brother, recoiling in terror from the faces flattened on the glass. He clamped his eyes shut, shook his head, looked again. The faces hadn't moved, pressed up close to the car. A flat hand with thin fingers. Jonathan reached up, bringing his arm out of the water. He flattened his hand against the shadow on the glass, palm to palm. The water crept over his chin. He tilted his head back, pushed Walter higher, into the floorwell. Stared at the green eyes that flickered in the green water. The boy on the outside, looking away as if embarrassed at his squalid, rotten death. He pushed his brother as high as he could, pressing his head against the carpet. The window cracked and the stream flowed in for them, flooded the car.

Kicking legs, livid faces with bulging eyes, fingers tearing at the pitiless roof. Bubbles streaming into the ceiling rebounding and rushing along the soaked velveteen to pour out of the broken window. Jonathan kicked out after the fleeing bubbles, reached for the glimmering light. The boy grabbed his wrist, thrust him back inside the compartment. Jonathan kicked, jammed inside the doorframe as the strange swimmer held on. Held on for dear life. Held on for his life.

ABYSS

Nicky swung round the ancient mahogany banister and leapt noisily up the steep staircase. It was pitch dark and he could hear the familiar clunk tap of Bethany's high heels as she made her way down to the front office, clinging to the rail with one hand and balancing a pile of mail with the other. Nicky tripped, dropped his notebook.

'Oh Christ... Beth... thank God you're there. I think I've turned my ankle.'

The big blonde girl teetered three steps above the grovelling hack. 'Get out of the way, you silly bugger. I'll go flying one day.'

Nicky raised his eyebrows. 'I'll take you,' he breathed.

Beth sighed. 'If you don't get out of the way I'll miss the post and this lot'll be late. Come on.'

Nicky climbed to his feet, rubbed the worst of the dust from his creased suit. Bethany Peters was widely considered to be the town's principal attraction after the Blue Boar. The fact that she had a diploma in business management and dated doctors from Budgworth deterred many of Clove's finest but didn't bother Nicky. Sooner or later she'd succumb to his brutal blend of smouldering sexuality and devilish sophistication. Nicky reckoned.

'Wilf's looking for you.'

'I've been busy.'

'Busy sinking pints at the Boar.' She clattered on down the stairs in a halo of Anaïs Anaïs.

'That's lovely scent you've got on.'

She stopped dead. 'I didn't realize there were people around still calling it scent. Amazing how the old customs linger off the beaten track, isn't it?'

'I was only saying I liked your sc— perfume. Essence. Fragrance. That certain something that says you.' He rolled his eyes.

Beth frowned. 'Why don't you buy Molly some, then?'

'She'd think I had a guilty conscience.'

'What if somebody else does?'

Nicky frowned. 'What, buys her some perfume? Why should they do that?'

'Well, you spend all your time racing about like north Somerset's answer to Don Johnson. What's to stop Molly having a fancy man?'

Nicky looked puzzled. 'Molly? Are you trying to tell me something?'

'Yes.'

'Well?'

'Think a little bit more of her, that's all.' She smiled sweetly, went on down the stairs.

'You're just trying to break us up so you can have me all to yourself!' he called down after her.

'Anything?' Wilf glanced up from his pig prices as Nicky crashed behind his desk.

'Usual crap. Malcolm Bell reckons anything he might have to say will be taken down and used against him. Off the record, they reckon the guy had been planning it for some time, marked Clove in on his map.'

His editor shuddered. 'They'll have to get his family down, we can maybe talk to them then.'

Nicky looked unconvinced. 'They've lost bodies down there before. I've been on to HQ in Budgworth, they reckon they've got a team coming over from Snowdon to have a go.' His green eyes narrowed.

'They had the army down there looking for a teenager once,' Wilf went on. 'Ages ago. They said it was too risky, crags, overhangs and all that. To be honest with you I can't see they'll get him out.'

'I'll take a detour round there on the way home. Just in case.'

Wilf looked up. 'Combining business with pleasure, are we?' He peered over the top of his half-moon specs.

Nicky shrugged. 'Nah . . . nothing like that. But if they have got a team going in they'll stand out like a sore thumb on the top there.'

'Lovely view, isn't it?' Nicky asked, letting the Cortina idle for a second before switching off. Mags watched him recline in the worn seat.

'Lovely. But I don't see any sign of this rescue team,' she said suspiciously. He'd called in after work to grab a Cloveburger and happened to mention he was going up the hill to keep tabs on the police operation to recover the body. Must be exciting, being a reporter, she'd said.

'It's like being a soldier,' he'd replied casually. 'Two minutes of action every ten years. Otherwise it's dead boring. Same old faces, same old places.' She was going off duty at six, did she fancy a lift home? To the Boar? It was only two minutes' walk away. Via the hill. Just in case they're having a go. OK. But she'd have to be home by half six or Uncle Roy would worry.

'Don't worry, I'm on a curfew too, remember?' he'd said.

'Oh, yes, your wife.' She'd given him that look again, mocking but maybe a little provocative. They'd driven in silence, sat a while looking out over the hills. The main range marched east to west, petered out in a series of stepping-stone islands. You could just make them out in the haze over the sea. Looking inland, the broad green expanse of the southern moors, criss-crossed with ditches choked with pondweed. Friesians that looked too clean to be true cropping the lush grass as if they were trying to get work on an advertising agency butter account. The main road cut straight across the moor, a black dagger scored by silver streaks. Climbing slowly through the first of the foothills, heavily wooded slopes with picture-postcard cottages thumbed in like tacks. From the lay-by they could see the first of the gaps, hardly more than hairline cracks in the limestone at the top of the hill. They got deeper down toward the edge of the gorge, the biggest gap of all. The main pass snaked through Hillstones carved by an ancient river, not much more than a dribble now. If they craned their necks they could see the stream glistening beside the road that wound down the gorge. The little bridge leading in to Clove. The houses stacked on either side of the steep valley. Biscuit-tin views. The bare grey and bronze rocks reared behind the houses on the new estate, tiny people pruning tiny gardens. Their little bit of the hills, little bit of green.

'I can't understand why you're still here. I mean, you were born here, weren't you?'

'No. Budgworth. I came here when I left college, stuck around. I'd rather be big on the *Clarion* than small anywhere else.'

'Why not be big somewhere else?' she asked.

Nicky shrugged. 'I'm a lazy bastard.'

'I've seen worse.' She absentmindedly smoothed the Pitstop smock over her knee.

Nicky flicked his eyes back to the view. 'No . . . it's OK here, I suppose. You get a lot of stuff because people know you. They come up to me in the shop, in the pub. You'd never get that in Budgworth,' he said.

'I'm not staying.'

'Can't be that bad. You came back didn't you? From college?'

She glanced at him quickly, shrugged. 'I didn't want to be around for a while. I needed some space.'

Nicky fiddled with the car keys. Women started talking space he normally gave them a little.

'He wanted me to settle down with him, move in straight away. God, I'd only been there a few months. I hadn't met anyone, hadn't done anything.'

'He?'

'Bloke in my class. He got in a bit of a state.'

'Bit tough, wasn't it, getting to college and then giving up because of some jerk?'

She stared out of the window. 'He killed himself.'

Nicky thought he'd misheard, knew he hadn't. Christ, what the hell had he said about the Miller feller?

'He was that sort, I suppose. Nothing dramatic, Paracetamols and vodka. If they'd found him in time they could have saved him which was probably what he wanted anyway. They were all out though, all the blokes on his floor. Out on the town. By the time they came back and found him he'd choked on his own vomit.'

'Christ.'

'He was eighteen.'

'Bloody hell. Look . . . I'm sorry . . . about . . . the questions, if I'd known obviously . . .'

'It's OK. It's just that I needed to get away from all of them. You know.'

'And then I come and stick my foot in it. Honest, Mags, I'm really sorry.' She looked up at him. That look. What the hell was she playing at, where was she coming from? Nicky looked away down the gorge. A thin plume of smoke was rising from the bushes alongside the road further down the valley.

'What is it?'

'Something by the bridge. A fire. Dust or something.

'So, so what?'

Nicky showed his teeth. 'It's my town, remember?'

BIG BIRD LIVES

'I'd better get you home.' Nicky leaned forward, turned the key and revved the tired engine into life. Mags stared ahead.

'Oh yes, don't you worry about me,' she breathed.

Fish glanced round at her. 'What's wrong? It looks like a crash, I'll have to go and have a look.'

'Such dedication.'

Nicky looked puzzled. 'Something's hit the bridge, I can't see from here,' he protested. 'It's my job.'

'So you go on as if nothing's happened.'

Nicky leaned back slowly, half-hearted smile slipping a notch. 'What are you on about? Nothing has happened,' he said slowly, deliberately.

'I know.' She sounded . . . disappointed?

'Look, Mags . . .'

'Just drop me at home, please.' She said it without moving her lips, eyes boring into his peeling tax disc.

'Fine.' He crashed into reverse, sent the wheels spinning on the loose gravel of the lay-by. Bumped along the rutted path and turned out on to the main road. Something had gone into the bridge. The plume he'd taken to be smoke was dust, billowing slowly in the afternoon heat haze. What did the girl want, money? He'd driven her a mile or so out of her way, was all. Christ, she wasn't going to make trouble like that, was she? He drove determinedly down the gorge, pulled out on to the main Budgworth Road. Tyre tracks slewed across the highway, slabs missing from the top of the parapet.

'Jesus Christ.'

Half a dozen cars had already pulled over, drivers and passengers scrambling down the bank on either side of the stream. A juggernaut ticking and clicking, black eyes and a bloody nose, the cab twisted violently against the massive grey container. Driver walking back the way he had come, pointing furiously at the cab and the bridge as some motorist tried to pull him out of the road. Nicky slotted the Cortina in behind a small tipper truck and switched off.

'Stay here, then.'

Mags was still staring ahead, drumming her fingers on her knee furiously. Nicky slammed the door, crossed the road and dashed to the parapet. A big grey Jaguar pulled in, doors open. Tall guy fishing for something in the back. The bridge looked drunk, crabbing across the brisk stream. The stonework bulged dangerously, slabs and loose mortar scattered about the roadway. He peered over. A big saloon on its back, half submerged in the fast-flowing water. Half a dozen men pulling at the doors, peering inside, shouting and pointing. They looked like natives trying to pull a giant turtle apart. A big bloke in grubby overalls trotted past with a crowbar and a length of rope over his shoulder.

'Give us a hand, mate. We can't get them out.'

Nicky glanced at his shoes, worn loafers. What the hell? He scrambled down through the undergrowth beside the bridge. The water was about three or four feet deep in the middle, rushing up and around the car, nose down in the flow. The drivers were trying to rock it level to get a better grip on the doors. The big fitter bent down, peered in through the wedge of glass still visible of the rear passenger window. Straightened up and brought the crowbar down on the glass. It fractured but held. He hit it again and the glass shattered, dirty water pouring out. The fitter knocked the jagged edges aside, leaned down and reached in. Fish and the others crowded round as a police car screeched to a halt above them.

'I've got something,' the fitter said out of the side of his mouth, straightening up carefully. Nicky squinted over his shoulder. A head wrapped in bandages. No, a baby. A baby kicking and squawking, clothing soaking wet and hanging from his pink body. A woman with red hair grabbed it from him, waded to the bank. The fitter turned back, ducked his head toward the window. He looked over his shoulder, shook his head.

'I can't reach 'em. They're mashed up in the front.'

'I'm a doctor,' the tall guy called from the smashed parapet.

The fitter glared up at him. 'Well, give us a fucking hand, then,' he shouted.

Nicky elbowed himself alongside the fitter, helped him tug at the crumpled door. 'Is there anybody else in there?' he asked.

The fitter grunted something.

'I reckon the little 'un was driving himself, don't you?' Nicky redoubled his efforts on the door. He ducked down, peered into the dark water, the metal tomb filled with stream. He could see the wrecked seats piled upside-down, dark limbs at impossible angles. He reached inside and groped for the door handle.

'All right, mate. Let's have a look. Good God, what are you doing here?' Police Sergeant Malcolm Bell in plain clothes. No crook would ever have sussed him in that windcheater.

'Come on, Nicky, out of the way, you can interview

them later,' Bell snapped, reaching over and wrenching the door open. Two other police officers moved in as Nicky waded toward the bank. The big fitter was standing by as a middle-aged woman wrapped a car blanket around the young woman holding the baby. Nicky wiped the sweat from his red face, climbed up the bank fumbling for his notebook. The fitter nodded at him.

'He's a lucky bugger.' He pointed at the youngster, crying raggedly and coughing gouts of muddy water over the young woman's T-shirt.

'He's lucky to get out of that. Couldn't get the bloody doors open till the pressure equalized inside and out, see?'

Fish nodded, flipped his notebook open. The fitter grinned.

'You're not from the papers, are you? You jammy bastard!'

Fish had taken a look inside the tomb. He didn't want to hear about jammy just then, wandered up the road splashing in his waterlogged loafers. The baby seemed unhurt despite the peculiar mewling noise he made, alarming Doctor Payne when he'd arrived from the town surgery to relieve the quack from Budgworth. The tall doctor in the grey suit had flapped around the scene of the accident like Big Bird, supervising and shouting without risking his expensive Italian shoes on the muddy bank. The doctor had given Payne a brief rundown on the accident, made his excuses.

'Urgent meeting at Region. You know how it is. Best for you to take over now the blood wagon's arrived. Damned idiot lorry driver ploughed straight into the back of him. Could have been me you know, on the bridge. Missed it all by about twelve seconds.'

Police Sergeant Bell lumbered over clicking his pen up and down as Payne ducked past to examine the baby.

'Won't keep you long, sir,' Bell chimed. The doctor had given him an SS smile, nodded toward Payne.

'He'll fill you in on all the details, officer. I'm due to report to a very important meeting at seven sharp.'

Bell returned a non-commissioned grin, tapped his bulging notebook. 'Won't take a minute to report to me first, sir. I'm told you saw the whole thing.' He guided him toward his patrol car, the lorry driver crouched in the back with a constable, holding his face in his hands and shaking his head. Payne had given the baby a quick examination, stripping the blanket the woman with the red hair had wrapped around his chubby white body.

'How long has it been crying like that?' he asked the woman (Nicky's notes had her as Mrs Ruth Garland, 21, housewife of Cliff Drive, Clove).

'Since we got him out, Doctor. He is going to be all right, isn't he?'

He'd taken off his glasses and examined the crying baby, rolling him from side to side on the tartan car rug.

'Well, he doesn't seem to be marked in any way.' Payne turned the baby on his side, laid him down and tucked him back up in the blanket.

'He must have swallowed some water. We'd best get him in right away.'

Fish had watched the ambulance wailing off toward Budgworth, damn near causing another accident as Wilf and the *Clarion*'s ace photographer and cribbage correspondent Digby Tibble rolled up in the editor's battered Morris 1000 estate: two-tone rust and splintering woodwork. Wilf peered down his nose, slowed to find a parking space among the crazy assortment of slow-down-for-a-better-look ghoul merchants. The recovery van had appeared half an hour later, a couple of big geezers in oily orange overalls swinging chains over their shoulders. They clambered over the wrecked car, tugged doors and fastened tackle. Wilf told Nicky off for forgetting to get the name of the witness and the lorry driver before they'd been driven away.

'That's typical of you, that is. Running around like Clark Kent but forgetting the basics. Who—'

'What where when. Don't worry about it, boss, I can pick it all up from Bell later. They're going to start lifting it now, can't you get in closer, get a picture?'

Tibble was sitting on the verge, wiping a grubby handkerchief over his face.

'I'm sorry, Wilfred, I've never been any good with things like this.'

'That's all right, Digger, you take it steady.'

'Well, can I borrow the camera, then?' Fish insisted, stepping from one squelching loafer to the other in agitation.

Digby handed the Nikon over, snatched it back to remove the lens cap. 'Light's going. It'll never come out,' he called weakly.

Nicky ignored him, crossed to the edge of the bridge to line up the shot. He watched the red car rise slowly from the stream, bonnet hanging open like a fish's mouth, dark water gushing out. The tow truck was pulling away slowly, grinding gears as the heavy chains stretched, pulling the BMW from its watery grave.

Digby Tibble covered his mouth. 'I can't stand blood.'

Wilf clapped him on the shoulder. God knows why he'd bothered to bring the staff photographer down, he'd done nothing but threaten to faint since they'd arrived.

'All right. Leave her there. Come on, please, move back.' Bell waved a constable to keep the crowd back as the fire brigade moved in with crowbars to try and wrestle the front doors open. 'Move back there. Give them some room, please.'

The BMW's engine had been crushed into the driving compartment although the bonnet seemed unscathed, hanging like a broken jaw over the mangled bodywork. The front of the roof had been crushed by the impact, destroying the windscreen and struts. Through the viewfinder Nicky could make out what looked like bags of washing awash with red. Bloody hell. The fire brigade experts peered into the crushed front seats, looked round and shook their heads. The man with the oxyacetylene cylinders switched off the flame and started loading them back on the truck. Bell said something to the blokes in the orange suits and they advanced on the crumpled doors with crowbars. Nicky shot half a roll of film and strolled over to the lanky editor.

'The mum and dad are history. Bucket and sponge job.'

'Nicky. Do you mind?' Tibble spluttered, clutching his mouth.

Wilf rolled his eyes heavenwards. 'Give it a rest, for God's sake. Can they get them out?'

'They're just jemmying the doors. Sergeant Bell's moving the punters back and there's no point in taking pictures of the corpses, you'll never use them.'

'You're damn right there, young man. What are you doing now?' he asked as Nicky handed him the camera.

'I was in on the rescue, too. You'll want a shot of me, won't you?' he asked. Wilf was about to say something, thought better of it and snapped off a couple of shots to keep him quiet.

'Get your foot off the parapet, Nicky, you look like Rommel.'

'I thought it looked heroic.'

Wilf snorted, wound the film on.

'Got any names at all?'

'Victims? No. They aren't local. The little kid sounded weird, screaming like a strangled cat.'

'Give him a break, Nicky, he's just lost his parents in a bloody car crash. What is the matter with you?'

'We're going to be spoilt for choice on the front page now. We'll drop that suicide to the back and splash with this.'

'I draw the layouts, Nicky.'

Fish shrugged. 'You'd better stick your name on it as well, I can't do an eye-witness interview with myself, can I?'

'It wouldn't be the first time,' Wilf sniffed, helping Tibble to his feet.

Nicky looked up the road. The Cortina was empty. Thank God for that. 'I'm off home, then. My feet are bloody soaked.'

'Don't forget your night job.'

'Night job? What bloody night job? You think I'm going to Clove parish council tonight you've got another thing . . .'

'It's not the council. That was last week. Police HQ say that mountain rescue team from Snowdon will be over tonight, have a crack at Sheep Tor Gap. Your mission, should you choose to accept it, is to interview them, get an estimate on how long it'll take and be there if and when they get the bloke up.' Wilf smiled sweetly, climbed into his car.

Nicky strode over, peered in. 'I've got a bloody home life too you know. What am I supposed to say to Molly? I haven't seen her since seven a.m.'

The editor shrugged. 'You can't expect to sit at home watching TV and drinking lager when all of Clove's in a bloody uproar, can you? You get home and see her and pop out later. You'll be home by midnight and you can claim the hours.'

Nicky stood back and watched his boss drive off towards town. Police officers were sweeping away debris from the bridge, placing warning signs and waving the ghouls away. Nicky crossed to the parapet, looked over. The fire brigade men were gingerly easing a woman's body out of the passenger seat, feet first, skirt riding up over her tights. Time to go home.

STILE CONSCIOUS

Mags tucked her coat tighter, stomped off toward Clove as more and more cars and wagons pulled in, spilled people who rushed toward the bridge to get a better look. Sirens wailing on the main road, too many people pointing, pointing her out. Just like the last days at college. There's one mum. Is she dead too? Dead like Jason with a mouth full of puke and an incoherent note they'd found scrunched in his hand. She had it in her bag, folded carefully down with her tissues and a Tampax. Fuck this lot gawping at me. Mags turned down the verge, swung her legs over a gate. That's right, try and look up my skirt, you bastard!

She dropped down to the ground, followed the stony path across the field. A walk would settle her down, and she needed settling all right. Needed time to settle her thoughts and get things straight. It hadn't been her fault and it hadn't been his fault – Nicky's, for driving off like that. Bloody idiot didn't know what he wanted, chatting on and flashing her looks and then Oops look out the wife. Met plenty of his sort. She shouldn't have gone on though, threw a wobbly. She giggled. She'd have to ring, say sorry. She'd walk first, clear her head.

Mags clambered over a second stile and dropped out of sight of the crowds honking and hollering by the bridge. Ambulance wailing mournfully down the valley. She followed the path along the edge of a field of rape seed, bright yellow flowers as far as she could see. Up close they were gritty little weedy things with small flowerpods. Stand back from them they were magnificent. Christ, like people at a rock concert, standing on tiptoe to get a glimpse of somebody on stage. Jason had taken her to Knebworth, flotsam and jetsam of tents and burger trucks swamped in a sea of mud. Deafening music and some funny acid she knew she should have refused. Jason had bought it from a guy in a suit, what did he expect? What *had* he expected? she corrected herself. Not her fault. He was a dipstick, if it hadn't been her it would have been somebody else. His type were doomed to die by the time they were nineteen, the last of the Beat poets although he couldn't write a decent rhyme to save his life. Not that she had. Bollocks.

She looked up. The thin youth was thinking about darting back behind the tree. Just what she needed, an apprentice rapist. She stepped back though, felt the stones under her shoes trying to trip her up, lay her flat for him.

'I'm not in the mood for fun and games,' she called, cursing the catch in her voice. She repeated it, louder. The skinny youth didn't move, she could see his thin arm stuck along the side of the tree just over the way from the path. In the bushes.

'Listen, buster, there's a police car just over that hedge, if I shout they'll be here ... in minutes.'

The boy stepped out from behind the tree. Jason. Don't be bloody stupid. Younger, thinner. Soaking wet. Long dark hair plastered to his skull, framing the pale, drawn face. Holding his Walkman in front of him as if the batteries had packed up on him, as if his battery had packed up too. The headphones were hanging around his ears, tangled in his dank hair. Mags watched him standing there stiffly as if he hadn't made up his mind what he was going to do. Sometimes, they were the worst.

'Are you waiting for someone?'

The youth looked up at that, fiddling with the Walkman. Drops of water running out of the back, spilling over the path. If he'd got it wet it would never work. She looked over her shoulder, realized she'd come further from the road than she'd thought. He was gazing at her now, eyes alert in his pasty face. Run for it in these stack heels? He'd be on her like a cat in ten strides. He wasn't sure what he was going to do. Take control and he's harmless, look helpless and he'd get cocky.

'I saw you walking,' he said. Strange accent. She'd been north for college and south for fun but couldn't place him at all. 'I thought I'd get a bit of air, you know.' He hadn't moved, standing there awkward, gawky. Come on, get a grip of him.

'Walk with me if you like. From Clove, are you?' She ignored her heart, thumping under her sickly Pitstop coverall and plain-cut coat, strode toward him. He took half a step back and fell in beside her. She could hear his jeans grating like cardboard. His trainers squelched horribly, she managed to stop herself giggling.

'You gave me a fright just now. What have you done, fallen in, or something?'

He glanced at her, nodded dumbly.

'Did you say you were from Clove or not? This way. Over the stile.'

'Around and about.' He wiped his mouth. 'We'll take the long way back.' The pretty way. Mags couldn't make out whether he knew where he was going or not. He'd known to take the left fork by the stile, seemed to have an idea where they would end up. The youth had clambered over the gate, glanced up as she tried to manoeuvre herself over without giving him any suggestion of a come on. The boy hadn't blinked, hadn't offered her his hand or anything. She frowned, jumped down. These shoes weren't going to be fit for work in the morning either. They went on, bushes and trees closing in over their heads. Thick mulch over the stony pathway. He could try something now and she'd run for the home, just along the ridge there. Another hundred yards and they'd see the lights. He'd either panic and run off or grab her but she'd be ready.

'What's your name again?'

'Guess.' Mags laughed shortly. 'Well, I'm Margery, but you can call me Mags. Call me Mags.'

'Hello, Mags.'

Fifty yards and the path crossed the long gravel driveway leading to the old folks' home. She'd been for a job there but they'd been laying staff off rather than taking anybody on.

'Guns N' Roses fan, eh?'

'Pardon?'

'Guns N' Roses.' She pointed to his T-shirt, still wringing wet. He'd better change it soon or he'd catch his death. The boy stared down at the colourful logo, gave her a sidelong look. Please yourself. The trees gave out. It was getting dark quickly now. Mags felt the gravel under her shoes and squinted to her right. Dim lights behind the branches. The home.

'Right, I'm off, then.' Brightly. Took him by surprise. She strode off toward the light, waiting for him to rush for her, crunching the gravel at least she'd hear him coming for her. Don't look back, you silly cow, keep walking. She stopped, turned. He was standing in the shadows of the path, looking out for her. She sighed. A fucking puppy she didn't need. Sighed again. Maybe she did after all. Go home, homeboy!

'Are you off then or what?'

Silence.

'You don't want to stand there all night in that T-shirt, you'll get double pneumonia or something.' Steady, not too motherly. He'll be out after you and he'll have you before you've gone ten yards. She strode back toward him.

'Look, whatever your bloody name is, you can't stand there all night, not in those clothes.'

'Take me home, then.'

Mags chuckled. Kid had been reading up. Intrigue 'em, they love it. She closed her eyes for a second.

'Take me there.' He pointed his thin arm toward the dim lights.

'It's an old folks home, not a youth hostel. I thought you said you were from round here anyway? Come on, stop messing about.'

'I want to go home. There's someone I know there.'

'Well, there would . . . Why didn't you . . . Look. I'm going down there, to the home. I can ask to use their phone. OK? Walk with me if you like.'

'All right.'

He strode out of the bushes and followed her, squelching, crunching on the cold bright gravel path.

SATURDAY

ABYSS II

'Coming down with us, are you?' the chirpy guy with the red face to match his cagoule asked cheekily. Fish snorted.

'They don't pay me enough to risk my ass on the end of rope.'

'They don't pay us either,' the Welshman put in, making the straps of his pack comfortable. Only a little bloke. Little bloke with a dirty great pile of gear stowed on his back like a pack pony. The rest of the team had arrived about 10.30 p.m. in a couple of Land Rovers, met up with Sergeant Bell, stomping around in the evening chill in his light blue windcheater. They were going to risk going straight down, just in case the geezer was alive. Bell had shaken his head.

'It's risky enough in the daylight, by night, I wouldn't fancy it.'

The Welshmen didn't seem overly concerned. 'Not as bad as Nant Gwythrin, eh, Reece?'

They had unpacked their gear under spotlights, packed and sorted lengths of rope, checked each other's equipment. Nicky had darted round collecting names, talking to Morris, the team leader.

'It's two hundred metres straight down as far as we can make out. If the sergeant's sure of the spot.'

'I'm sure. We marked it out. But those gaps don't go straight down, there's ledges, all sorts.'

'But no snow, look you. Piece of piss, eh, boys?'

There was a chorus of approval as they switched on the lights on their miner's helmets, prepared to let themselves over the side. Nicky was fifteen feet from the edge, peering over on tiptoes. Bell wandered over.

'You might as well piss off now, son. They're going to be ages.'

Nicky knew full well the time to stick around was when an official suggested you leave.

'I'm fine, Molly did me a flask of soup and I've got stories to write.' He smiled sweetly, made his way over to the battered Cortina and climbed into the warmth. He'd crossed out his intro twice before he fell fast asleep.

Tilekin opened his good eye and saw nothing. He could breathe in but not out, had to let his breath escape in tiny, agonizing gasps. He could feel something bubbling in his nose and there was blood running into the back of his throat. He couldn't feel a thing down his sword side but his shield arm felt as if he was being stabbed by a dozen jagged daggers. He'd tried to move his head but his back felt wrong and his legs wouldn't work. Puut Ra's general lay at the bottom of the abyss, dead to the world but still breathing. He yelled once, felt his throat contract in agony, as if a cow had jumped on his chest. Like he'd jumped on that damned swan, knocked the stuffing right out of it. He sniggered, winced as the broken ribs grated against his bloody lungs. Bloody, broken, battered. Somebody else's agony and he had to stick it, typical. Wasn't his bloody body splattered into an outcrop halfway down the chasm. He'd left that back there somewhere, back in that dratted pool maybe. Felt himself, felt his soul tearing free, popping out of his useless shell of mouldy skin like the cork from a gourd.

Ricocheting off the swirling sky leaving his leafy rags behind him. Hadn't hurt. Much. Did now though. Tilekin twitched, felt fresh darts of pain up and down his spine. Knocked out of his body, knocked cold. Knocked and pummelled and bruised and battered. The next thing he'd been aware of, rushing, pouring pain. Pouring into the heaped leaves, the discarded skin he'd stumbled on in his naked wanderings down the windy gorge, the rocky death trap. Wispy shapes and ragged vapours hanging like grubby smoke over their old camp. Dim faces racked with pain pulled this way and that.

'Get out of it! Get away from me, you bloody sacks!' More of her ladyship's little tricks, he'd supposed, cursing and threatening the grey ghosts. Dirty flimsy snivelling people ghosts, hah, he'd waved them away. He'd gone to thumb his nose at them before he realized he hadn't got one, couldn't feel his face at all. And then he was in the new skin and he could feel it and oh, mother of everything, had it hurt. Soaking up new skin and blood, taking over a trembling network of freaky nerves and jangling impulses, a rickety shell of holes and gashes and leaks and sores and splintered bloody bones. This damned long-pig human at the bottom of the gorge, him. His. Shite. He spat out a ball of bloody mucus, shut his good eye. He thought about the mad ride on the back of the swan, cheered up a little. Then he wondered where in this damned gorge he was.

'That bloody copper wasn't kidding, now, Evan.' Morris hammered in another peg, clipped his harness and took a breather. The team were spread along a narrow ledge at least two hundred and twenty metres down. They'd had to negotiate sudden outcrops and squeeze themselves through a narrow crevasse.

'He never fell through that, Morris,' Reece had said, pointing his torch beam into the slit in the rock.

'Well, he's not along here so he must have done. If the copper marked the right place. God knows what kind of mess he's . . .' Morris stopped, tilted his head.

'Did you hear something?'

'Probably the wind cutting round the rocks. An echo or something.' Morris shook his head, tipped his helmet back.

'I thought I heard a shout.'

'You don't think the poor bugger's alive now?' Reece called from the back.

'Not after this!' Morris ran his torch along the jagged limestone wall, down to the narrowing crack. The strong beam bounced off a smooth rock. He swung the beam back.

'Jesus wept, boys.' Three torch beams converged on the shoe. A decent brogue with the laces tied neatly. The foot was still in it, black sock white bone.

The tiny Oriental girl was half his size but Nicky had grown. She was leaning forward to look out of the window of some manor house, grounds he barely recognized. She was covered in shimmering black silk, filmy underwear he must have tugged up around her waist. She looked round as he reached for her, hands stretching as if he was made of rubber.

'Hey, Nicky.' The gardener was rapping on the window. Must have climbed some kind of ladder.

'Hey, Nicky!' Rapping on the window with his gnarled old knuckles.

'Open the fucking window!'

Nicky jumped, blinked in the front seat of the fossilized Cortina.

'Mimi?'

A pale puffy face smeared against the window, looking in at him. 'What? Open the window, you dozy sod.'

'Sorry, Sarge.'

'You were bloody miles away. Get your socks on, they're bringing him up.'

The face sank back into the deep darkness. A shadow lurched toward the abyss. Nicky blinked, ground his knuckles into his eyes. He'd cornered Mimi for the first time in six months and Bell had woken him up. Bastard. Nicky opened the door and climbed stiffly to his feet. Torch beams playing round the gaps like searchlights in some Bomber Command training film. An ambulance was jolting along the rough stony path from the main road. He squinted at his watch in the dim blue glow. Christ, 3.46 a.m. Nicky looked up, made his way over to the group of figures huddled round the Land Rovers. Bell looked round, raised his eyebrows.

'They're bringing him up now. Thought you might like to know.'

'Cheers, Malcolm. I owe you one.'

'You owe me several bloody hundred, mate.' Bell nodded toward the crevasse, blacker than pitch against the dimly lit grass. Torch beams playing over the worn grey rock, the bright orange ropes the climbers had laid carefully over the edge. One of the team squatted beside the secured ropes, peering down into the gloom. 'They've got him on the stretcher,' he said over his shoulder.

The driver moved forward, helped him clip the ropes to the winch on the back of their Land Rover. Bell stood aside as Nicky fiddled with the camera Digby had left him.

'Easy, boys.'

'Gently now.'

The man by the gap nodded and the driver started the winch. The silver drum shone dully in the flickering blue light, winding the tough rope. The ambulance driver wandered over, lit a cigarette.

'All right, Malcolm?'

'Not much for you tonight, Dave. Bugger's going to look like a bucket of shark bait.'

The stretcher appeared at the lip of the crack, a dark bundle wrapped in a red blanket. The climber eased the steel frame over the edge. Bell played his torch over the head.

'Bloody hell, they could have covered him up.'

'Shut up, I can't hear a thing they're saying,' the climber snapped, tipping his head to one side.

'He's what?' The climber swung the stretcher in, peered at the smashed features, the skeletal grin. The right side of the man's face had been torn away from the skull, exposing the jaw and the ragged cheek muscles. He'd lost his eye and ear and half his scalp. What was left of his face was a mask of blood and dirt. Nicky hung back behind Bell, the camera clutched in his hands.

'Fuck me. What a bloody mess.'

The ambulance crew doubled over, shouldered the climber aside as the first of his colleagues clambered over the edge and stood back.

'Nerves, must have been muscle spasms or something. He couldn't survive that.'

'I bloody heard him,' the leader shouted, swinging a leg over the precipice and pulling himself up. He snatched the miner's helmet off and wiped the sweat from his forehead. 'I heard a moan and we found him underneath an overhang. He's in a dozen pieces but he's still alive.'

His face livid in the eerie twilight. The ambulance man pulled the straps back to loosen the blankets, tugged a bloody arm out and checked the pulse. He looked up slowly.

'Christ Almighty, he's right. I can feel his pulse. Going like a bloody train.'

'What? Are you trying to bullshit me or something?'

Bell sank to his knees, peered over the medic's shoulder.

'Look at the bloody state of him. I've seen people hit by a train in a better condition than that.'

'Check for yourself!' The medic sounded irritated – hysterical as the last of the team pulled themselves up from the pit, beams shining from their helmets.

Bell looked back over the rock-battered body, shook his head.

'Do him a favour, finish him off,' one of the climbers called half-heartedly.

'Reece.'

'Well, he'll be dead by the time they get him to hospital,' the climber snapped, tossing his gear into the back of the truck.

'We've got to get him in,' the ambulance man said, looking round the weird watching faces. 'His pulse is steady. I don't know how he's doing it, but he's breathing. We've got to take him in.'

'Well, what are you waiting for?' Bell shouted, breaking the spell. The team manhandled the stretcher to the ambulance, crooked arm hanging over the steel frame, crushed hand brushing the grass. The doors slammed and the team stood back to watch the ambulance lumber down the path.

'Kinder to let him die here. I wouldn't keep a dog like it,' Reece observed.

'Shut it, man. We found him, we brought him up. Now it's their turn.' Bell swivelled round, stared at Nicky. 'What's the matter with you?'

*

'You look like you've seen a ghost,' Molly said drily, pulling the curtains and flooding the front room with hot bright light. Nicky was lying on the couch, shoes off, a hole in his left sock, arms crossed over his head. He grunted something, turned over on his side.

'What time was it? Four, five?'

'Five,' muffled from the cushions.

'Must have been a long meeting.' She turned, tied her cotton dressing-gown around her waist and ran her hands through her long brown hair. 'I said, it must . . .'

'I heard what you said. I told you before I left. I had to go and check on the rescue team. They got to the guy about half-past three. You want to make something of it check with the hospital.'

'Talk to one of your nurse friends.'

Fish sat up groggily, slumped his shoulders. 'Come on, Moll, give me a break. Ring Wilf.'

Molly stalked into the kitchen, plugged the kettle in noisily. Fish lay back, groaned quietly.

'Ring Wilf. Come on, Molly, do you think I'd be out looking like this?'

'You looked all right last night when you left here.'

'You try sitting in a Cortina for five hours.'

Molly poked her head round the door. 'Do what in a Cortina?' she asked, bitter-sweet.

'Ring—'

'I bloody well rang Wilf, all right?' from the kitchen. Crashing mugs.

'So what's the problem? What he do, drop me in it?' Nicky swung his legs to the floor, rubbed his eyes.

'I rang Wilf after I had the call.'

'What call?'

'The girl for you.'

Nicky paused. What girl? 'What girl?'

'Wouldn't say her name.'

'Well, what did she want?'

'Wouldn't say.'

'What time was this?' He crossed to the kitchen, watched the dark-haired girl wrenching the drawers open looking for a teaspoon.

'Third drawer down. What time was this?'

'About nine.'

'About nine . . . I was chatting to Sergeant Bell. What exactly am I supposed to have done?'

Molly looked up, stared at him. 'You tell me.'

'Oh come on, Molly. Wilf practically ordered me to stay there. Half the town police were there along with a load of bloody Viet Taff. I sat in that bloody car for five hours, on my own. Check it out with whoever you like.' She poured the hot water over a couple of mugs, Fish smelled coffee. 'OK?'

'Well, what did the silly cow want?'

'What silly cow?'

'The silly cow from the burger bar. I recognized her voice. What does she think I am, stupid?'

'The girl from . . . Mags. Margery. Roy Jones' niece. He's looking after her up at the pub.'

'Well, what's she doing ringing here?' She thrust the mug of coffee into his hand, stalked back into the front room. Nicky turned slowly.

'What did she say?'

'I told you. She asked if you were here.'

'Silly cow. I've only met her once. She saw the guy they dragged up this morning. I told you he's still alive, didn't I?'

'I don't give a shit whether he's alive or not. I don't want silly little tarts ringing my home to speak to my bloody husband, OK?'

'Well, she's never phoned before. Not at work or anything.'

Molly was sitting on the couch, foot swinging angrily.
'Ask Wilf.'

'I don't need to ask Wilf. I asked Beth.'

Beth. 'What's Beth got to do with it?'

'She works with you. She sees what you get up to during the day.'

'What's that supposed to mean? What's she been saying?'

'She's been saving your bloody bacon, that's what. You know she's seeing that guy from the *Budgworth News*? He was waiting for her in the burger bar and the little cow chatted him up.'

Nicky thought for a second. 'What, that Arthur? That prat?'

'That prat was waiting for Beth at the burger bar. She practically asked him out on the spot.'

'Beth?'

'No, you stupid bugger. Mags . . . Margery. All over him, apparently.'

'So you figure she must have been all over me as well?'

'I'd trust Arthur, I wouldn't trust you.'

'Well, that's nice, isn't it? Just because she chats up your mate's boyfriend makes her the bloody whore of Babylon.'

'She phoned after you, don't forget.'

'Well, it must have been something about work. I interviewed her, remember?'

'How could she forget?'

'Molly, what exactly are we saying here?' Fish realized the girl hadn't said anything incriminating. Christ, all he'd done was take her for a ride in the bloody car. 'Are you accusing me or what?'

Molly twitched. 'I just don't like getting calls from overgrown school girls, all right?'

'All right. But I've only met her a couple of times.

CHANGELING HEARTS

Whatever she wanted . . .' He waved his hands. 'She can ring me at work. I don't even know where she got the number.'

'Wilf rang as well. Wants you to ring him first thing.'

'Do I take it this matter is now closed?'

She looked up sharply. 'Make sure it is or you'll be bloody sorry, Nicky.'

Bloody hell!

Jerry James poked his head round the reporters' room door, made them all jump.

'Good edition, Wilf. Bloody good coverage. We're printing an extra two thousand.' He nodded and felt his way back up the creaking corridor to his office. The editor folded his still-warm *Clarion*, took his glasses off.

'If we've dragged Geronimo away from his table football we must be on to something. Still, good work, Nicky.' Nicky was admiring the head-and-shoulders picture of the *Clarion*'s chief reporter alongside his eyewitness report on page one.

'I still reckon you should have used the full-length shot. That one of me pointing to the bridge.'

'We know where the bloody bridge is, Nicky. The head-and-shoulders was more than enough.' Beth was scanning the colour piece they'd knocked together that morning while the presses were waiting to run. GAPS PLUNGE MIRACLE: MAN FOUND ALIVE. DOUBLE DRAMA AS DEATH CRASH ROCKS GORGE: BABY PULLED TO SAFETY BY TOWN RESCUE SQUAD.

'Typical, though, isn't it, we get a whole decade's news in one bloody week. It'll be pig prices again next week. Stamp theft at post office,' she observed quietly.

'At least we got the latest, though. That Miller geezer

brought up alive *and* the double fatality. How's the kid?' Nicky asked.

'Home tomorrow, according to the hospital. Cuts and bruising, possible concussion,' Wilf read from his spidery notes.

'What'll happen to him with his parents gone?' Beth wanted to know.

'Care probably.' Wilf took his patched jacket from the peg, shoved his notebook in the worn pocket. 'I'm off to police calls. Are you writing up your court? There's that speeder up for sentence.'

'Wow. Back to earth with a bang.'

Wilf nodded and went out. Beth stood to go.

'Beth. A minute.' Nicky closed the door as Beth narrowed her eyes.

'What do you think you're up to?' she asked suspiciously. 'You touch me and you'll be sucking soup through a straw for a six-month,' she added dangerously.

Nicky held his hands up. 'You spoke to Molly last night. What's it all about?'

The girl with the piled-up blonde hair and piled-up pink chest perched herself on Wilf's desk, regarded him sceptically.

'Panic stations, eh?'

'I haven't done anything. No, really. If this girl's been ringing me up it's nothing to do with me.'

Beth nodded. 'Why do I keep expecting your nose to grow a couple of feet?'

'Seriously, Beth. You know me. I'd have a chat and a laugh but never piss around like that. She said you'd had some trouble with her as well.'

Beth shrugged. 'Nothing I can't handle. She asked what Art was doing, he told her he was meeting me.'

'Thank Christ she did. Molly was ready to rearrange

my urino-genital system. If she hadn't spoken to you I'd have been right in it.'

Beth shook her head, regarded the dishevelled shirt, worn suit. The Las Vegas leer replaced by childlike concern. Bloody great kid. 'Honestly, Nicky. Molly's too good to be mucked about. If I ever find out—'

'Find out what? I've just told you, haven't I? We sat in the car was all.'

Beth sighed. 'Ah, you sat in the car with her. Let me guess. Axeheads Lane, the pylon, the top down?'

'The top down. I was driving her home.'

'Where from, Budgworth?'

'I had to speak to her about the Miller bloke. She was on her way home, we took a little detour. I'm sitting there admiring the bloody view when the geezer in the red BMW had the row with the bridge. I chucked her out and got straight down there, honest, Beth.'

The blonde girl snorted. 'Honest? What did you think you were doing up there with her? For God's sake, Nicky, you treat Molly like a bloody six-year-old retard sometimes. I don't care whether you were discussing the weather, you were up on Lover's Leap with a bloody mixed-up eighteen-year-old. What did you think you were doing?' Beth shook her head in exasperation.

Fish shuffled from foot to foot, rolling his *Clarion* into a club.

'I don't know . . . what do you mean, mixed up? She didn't seem mixed up to me, not much anyway.'

'I was speaking to Claire James. Used to go around with her before she went to college. Apparently she's had some kind of a breakdown. Some boyfriend trouble. The girl's about as stretched out as her knicker elastic. Claire tried to get her a job up at the home but they wouldn't have her.'

Nicky frowned. 'She told me he'd topped himself.'

Beth looked up sharply. 'Proper little heart-to-heart you must have had.'

'It wasn't like that. I was droggling on about the Miller bloke and she comes out with the history repeating itself crap. I didn't know, did I?'

Beth eased herself to her feet, checked her watch. 'I've got to go. Just keep out of trouble for a week, eh?'

'And what's all this about you and Art? I thought you'd dumped him when he moved to the *News*? I heard you were seeing that doctor bloke.'

Beth opened the door, paused. 'He came back, asked nicely. Who else is there in this bloody dump?'

'Apart from me? Nobody at all.'

Fish ducked as she went to slap him, clicked on up the corridor. The phone jangled on the editor's desk.

'Yeah, *Clarion*?'

'Nicky. Wilf. Get your arse down to the press room and tell them to hold everything. They've got names for the RTA fatalities. Nisha and Martin H.A.B.E.R.F.I.E.L.D.'

'Right. I'll try and get it on some late editions.'

'There's more,' Wilf snapped. 'According to the family friend they set off yesterday. All four of them. The elder boy's missing.'

'Well, he could be anywhere, they could have dropped him off on the way down.'

'Get back down there. The cops are going to re-examine the bridge and the truck. They won't say why but they kept the driver in overnight.'

'Christ. You think we may have missed him?'

DON'T CALL US

Nicky Fish glanced up and down the street like an agent in a dodgy spy film, slipped into the cool interior of the Clove Burger Pitstop. A couple of families munched silently in the booths near the window. Nicky strode to the back by the till, slipped into the seat facing the door. Mags appeared at his side to take his order.

'Morning. Sir.'

'Can I have a Cloveburger and a coffee. What the fuck did you ring my missus for?'

'Is that a quarter-pounder or Pitstop special? I was just trying to say sorry for last night. In the car. I was out of order.'

'The special's fine. So say sorry to my face, not to my bloody wife.'

'Is that with relish or without? I didn't know when I'd see you again. I didn't say anything else.'

'When a teenage girl rings a bloke's wife for no reason you don't need to say anything else. You just drop him right in it from a great height.'

'Well, if you're so bloody concerned about this precious wife of yours why did you ask me to come for a ride in the first bloody place?'

'Thank you, Margery, I'll finish this.' Gwen Bignell snatched the order pad from the girl's hand, smiled sweetly at her. Fish rose to his feet but the manageress stepped forward, blocking the aisle. Mags flashed her a look, stalked off toward the till.

'Now then, sir. Let's see. Cloveburger special. Relish?' Gwen leaned closer. 'I've already had Beth Peters in here having a few words with young Margery. I'd prefer it if you could leave your sordid little conspiracies until closing time,' she hissed, straightening up. 'Relish and a side order of buttered mushrooms. Won't be a minute, sir.'

Fish slumped back in his chair with a thoughtful sigh. So Beth had already been in, had she? On her own account or Molly's?

'Here. Excuse me. We know you don't we?' Bald head, piggy eyes and specs half an inch thick, nodding encouragingly. The geezer had slipped over from his seat near the window where he and his family had been pointing him out and making comments into their half-eaten Cloveburgers.

'You were in the paper. The *News*, wasn't it? We're not from round here. Budgworth. Had nothing to do so we came down to see where it all happened.'

Fish smiled grimly. 'The *Clarion*. Yes.'

'Rescued those people from the car. We passed the bridge on our way in. Just fancy.'

Nicky nodded.

'Pity about the poor kids though, wasn't it?'

'The kid's all right, the parents died,' Nicky corrected him shortly.

'Oh yes, that's right. Coming down to see their poor old mother as well. Terrible.'

'Terrible.'

'We saw them dragging that Rover out as well. Lovely car. I used to work for Leyland, you know.'

'It was a BMW, actually.'

'Was it? Bit hard to tell really, all scrunched up like that.' Baldy chortled. 'I'm surprised you can tell the difference. You newspaper people are always getting your facts wrong, aren't you now?' Gwen Bignell strode up the aisle with a tray. Baldy nodded and slipped back to his family, who immediately hunkered down for a case conference. Gwen placed the burger, the coffee and the mushrooms on the table.

'Now you see and leave it alone. I don't want you ruining your marriage on my premises. Is that clear?'

'Yes, Mrs Bignell, quite clear. But—' She turned and stalked off. 'Got any tomato sauce?' he called after her.

Tilekin lay in a strait-jacket called John Miller, balefully watching a nurse checking some clear bag contraption they'd pushed into his arm. He felt hot but no pain. That had gone like it had before, when he'd left his old self behind. This time, though, he was still whole, lumpy. This time he still had a nose, although he was buggered if he could reach it. Wasn't all that special either, all he could smell cloying cleaned clean. The bland body he hadn't bargained for, the last turkey in the shop. The empty skin he'd come across in the gorge. In it before he could blink, blinking before he could think. Blinking this damned human's watering eyes, lying there like a runty pup in his useless long-pig carcass. They'd wrapped it . . . him, in bandages from head to foot, plugged him in to the life support. The nurse leaned over, peered in at his eye like some gaoler checking a prisoner.

'Mr Miller? Can you hear me? Blink if you can hear me.'

Tilekin told his arm to move, ordered his hand to grab the creature around the neck and throttle it before she could do any harm. His arms weren't obeying instructions. He could feel a dull pain below the elbow.

He thought about his shoulder, managed to twitch it. Broken arm. His left foot was itching.

'Mr Miller? Can you see me?'

Tilekin tried his left arm. He could reach across and grab something sharp from the tray near the bed. Nothing. Another dull pain from the shoulder was all. Left foot itching like hell. He couldn't move. They'd wrapped him in chains, they were holding him down. He groaned.

'I'll call the doctor in, Mr Miller. Let him take a look at you.' She straightened up and turned away. The patient gave her the creeps, staring round the room like that. She'd seen them before, failed suicides or bad accident victims. Begging you to finish them off. They'd done a special section on it at college. Self-determination and all that.

'How is he? Any change?' Tim McGregor poked his head round the door of the special care room, raised his eyebrows.

'No change, Doctor. I think he groaned just now.' McGregor checked his chart, frowned.

'His heart's something else. You're sure it's right?'

The nurse nodded slowly.

'Checked it myself. Then I checked it again.'

McGregor replaced the chart and peered in at Tilekin's glaring eye. 'Mr Miller? Can you hear me? You're in hospital in Budgworth. Can you remember anything?' He straightened, stroked his stubble. The spinal injury alone should have killed him instantly. He couldn't have had more than a couple of pints of blood left by the time they'd brought him in. He'd lost half his face, broken his neck, lost his left foot and left eye and they'd been forced to amputate his right arm. Right leg multiple fractures, left leg broken above the knee. Six ribs and a punctured lung, internal bleeding. Ruptured liver. He was breathing with difficulty thanks to the ventilator and yet his heart rate was sound.

'Sorry, Stella, I was miles away.'

'I said, what about the relatives? We've put them off twice already,' the nurse told him. He shook his head.

'There's nothing more we can do for him. If he stabilizes they might as well. I don't think he'll last the night.'

'But his vital signs are all in the black. You'd think he was in for ingrowing toenails or something.'

'That's quite common with injuries like this. Like a guttering candle. You know?'

ARRIVALS

Nicky parked the spluttering Cortina behind the police car, climbed out extracting his notebook from his worn jacket pocket. Bell had detailed one constable to beat the bushes along either bank while he and the second officer had a look at the juggernaut. It had been straightened out and locked overnight. Orange tape wrapped round the door handles. Oh, well, safe as houses then. Bell looked over his shoulder as Fish sauntered along.

'Up early, aren't we? Saturday morning as well.'

'Morning, Malcolm. How's the poor bugger they brought up?'

'Still kicking. Ambulance geezer said he actually tried to sit up while they were taking him in. Some kind of muscle contraction, he called it.'

Fish raised his eyebrows. Bell waited a second.

'Well?'

'What are you up to now?'

'We're going to pinch his fucking Yorkie Bar, what d'you think?'

Nicky peered over Bell at the second constable, busy examining the juggernaut control panel.

'Driver saying his brakes wouldn't work? You want to check the coily pipe things behind the cab,' Fish said helpfully.

Bell smiled horribly. 'On your way now, sir.'

CHANGELING HEARTS

The second constable bent under the dash, lifted a set of keys from a hidden peg.

'Going to open it up, look in the back.'

'You know, Nicky, you ought to be with the Regional Crime Squad, enquiring mind like yours.'

Fish didn't mind the insults. As long as Bell was insulting him he was still around. The sergeant took the keys, clambered down from the cab and walked the length of the container.

'Driver reckons his control panel went wrong,' Bell said. Fish trotted along behind, scribbling it down. Bell paused, glanced at Nicky's notebook. 'This is strictly off the record. One word and I'll run you out of the town, all right?' Nicky nodded. 'Driver reckons his display panel went wrong. He admits he was too close to the Haberfield geezer. Says he cut him up coming off the ring-road.'

'Got his own back more than somewhat. You're going to do him, are you?'

'When we can get him back on the planet, yes. Probably.'

'Local guy, is he?'

'Some bloody Frog. Had to get Rachel our secretary in to understand what he was on about. On his way to Shepton Mallet with a load of cattle additives or something.' Bell fiddled with the heavy padlock, released the door mechanism and swung it open. Fish peered over his shoulder. Big sacks on pallets covered in polythene. The constable clambered up, Bell watching him.

'Jean Claude Dickhead said his controls must have blown. Some funny green light flickering over the back of the cab, he's half mesmerized, tries to duck out of its way. That's what Rachel said anyway. Could have been lost in the translat—'

'Sarge!'

Bell tilted his head. The constable had ducked down between two loaded pallets, looked up, Adam's apple bobbing in his thin neck.

'You'd better have a look at this.'

Bell glanced at Nicky. 'Right. Back. Out of sight. Go on.'

Nicky backed off as Bell clambered up into the trailer. He darted forward and levered himself up to peer down the aisle between the stacked pallets. The young constable had backed against the polythene sheeting tacked over each load, the big sergeant peering at the funny old guy on the floor. Blood splashed all over the bright packaging, running in shiny rivulets down the creases in the polythene, pooled under his baggy clothing. Nicky edged forward, craned his neck to peer around the burly officer. Old chap, funny clothes, looked like cheesecloth. One leg twisted beneath him so far he could hardly . . . oh Christ. No wonder the juggernaut was covered in blood. He coughed.

'Nicky, for fuck's sake! I told you to keep your hooter out of it. Go on, get on out of it!' Bell striding back down the aisle paler than ever, lips twitching.

'Where's the leg?'

'Never mind that. Get back. Go on.' Bell pushed him out, the young constable climbing down beside him. Bell clambered down, bolting the door behind them.

'Well?'

'Nothing for you, Nicky. On your bike.' The sergeant glared at him, stalked off to the police car and swung himself into the passenger seat, barked into his radio. The constable looked at him, swallowing with difficulty.

'It's all go here, isn't it?' Fish asked. The constable smiled weakly.

*

Molly pushed the door open, frowned at the assortment of letters and junk mail on the mat. Claire had obviously called in sick, she usually collected it if Grainger hadn't beaten her to it. Just what she needed, stomach playing her up already. Nerves, period or something. Something... like an aching hole in her belly, as if she hadn't eaten for days. Nicky and his not so cunning stunts, Christ, she should be used to his antics by now, upsetting her like this. The hall was deserted, Grainger's outsize waxed jacket on the hook behind the reception desk. Molly took off her coat, hung it up and poked her head into Grainger's office. Empty. Must be in the lounge. She strode down the hall, looked into the dining-room. Christ, they'd been up early if they'd already finished serving breakfast. Didn't smell as if they'd been cooking. Concerned now. She strode down the passage, peered into the kitchen. Spotless. Peered into the lounge. Bloody hell! Eight old folk, nodding and muttering. 'Morning everybody!' brightly though she didn't feel too bright. Hap was missing from his chair opposite the tank. She bent, looked into the cloudy water. Three dead guppies floating like bits of plastic. Somebody's bleeper resting on the gravel. She frowned, looked around.

'All right, Mr Fletcher? Had breakfast yet?'

'Fucking thing he was doing to him should have fucking seen the fucking thing doing it to that fat bastard fucking hell...'

'Morning, Mrs Trent. All right, are we? Seen Claire? Mr Grainger?'

'No dear.'

Sheepish, worried. Don't worry them, they get funny.

'Not seen anybody?' joky, brightly. Mrs Jasper didn't look well, looked like five o'clock shadow over her chin, sitting uncomfortably in her poorly fitting tartan cardigan. She turned, Mrs Edwards nodding and muttering.

'No. Not seen anything.'

Christ, you'd think she'd interrupted their card school, an orgy or something. Where the hell was Grainger? Claire was always cadging time off. Paul had left her again and she was probably round patching things up. Saturdays were normally a quick shift. Tidy, breakfast, bathtime, lunch, then home. Mr Grainger usually gave them their tea and got them sorted for bed. Molly wiped Mrs Ogden's mouth, straightened her cardigan. Soaking with dribble she must have been wearing it . . . she looked up and down the room. They'd all put on the clothes they'd had on . . . wait a minute. Molly straightened, looked at her palm. A smear of blood.

'Mrs Ogden? Are you all right?' Leaning over, easing her forward, gently tugging the old lady's buttons with trembling fingers. 'Have you cut yourself, love? Are you all right?' The cardigan was soaked. She'd never dribbled . . . somebody had been wiping her off. Left her in a bloody soaking cardigan, what the hell was Grainger trying to do, kill the lot of 'em?

'All right, Mrs Ogden?' Perhaps she'd been coughing it up? Fresh and red. The slack mouth dribbled pale spit. Molly straightened, calmed herself. Where was Grainger?

'I'm off to find Mr Grainger, I'll be straight back, OK?' She strode out of the room down the passage toward the hall. The thin youth slid out of the kitchen, threw his arm out and leaned against the wall, blocking her way. Molly stopped short, swallowed.

'Who the hell are you? Where's Mr Grainger?' Thin kid. Familiar. She racked her brains thinking where she'd seen him.

'He's had a bit of a turn. Left me in charge while he popped up to town.' Mr Haberfield's bedside cabinet, framed family photo third on the left behind the woman holding the baby. Jim, James, Jonathan. Molly relaxed, frowned at him.

'He shouldn't have done that. They've not had their breakfast or anything.'

'Oh, they weren't hungry.'

She glanced at him. Where was Hap? 'Is your grandfather all right?'

He looked perplexed, then smiled. 'He's fine too. No need to worry.'

Molly paused. 'Well, I'll make some tea and you can take it on in to him.'

'Very well.'

Brightly, helpful. Something wrong. Very wrong. Hap wasn't even in there and he wasn't in the habit of taking morning constitutionals.

'Didn't he say anything else? It's not like him to go off like that. How long has he been gone?'

'Not long.'

'Taken his car, has he?' Grainger's Volvo had packed up on Tuesday.

'Yeah.'

Molly ducked under his arm, caught his musty odour. Looked as if he'd been dragged through a hedge backwards. He let her go, watched her tug open cupboard doors in the kitchen.

'We've got to give them their breakfast,' she said stonily, hanging on to a door, not looking at him.

'That's fine. What's your name?'

'Molly. Molly Fish.'

'Angel Fish.'

She wobbled. Nicky used to call her that. Used to whisper it after they'd made love, warm and plastered to each other at her mum's house next door to the post office. Just down the road. Just down the road. She got a grip, tugged the pale white cups and saucers from the cupboard. Keep going. Keep going. As long as he didn't hurt the old folk. She couldn't bear the thought . . . stop it. He's not hurt them yet. Apart from Hap. What had Mr Fletcher been babbling about? You should have seen him do it to the fat bastard. Fat bastard meant Grainger, not Hap. She pulled the biscuits down from the shelf, tipped them out automatically. The boy stole up to her, a waft of rank underarm odour as he reached one of the biscuits, nibbled it.

'I'm starving. These are nice. What are they?'

'Rich Tea.' Jesus. A psycho. Hap never said anything about . . . Hap never said anything, period. Sat all day in front of the fish tank, hands clawed over the armrest, bent up on themselves like nasty plastic claws. The front door bell rang, shrill and loud. She spilled milk over the worn Formica work top, looked up. He slid down the hall out of sight. Make a break now. Lever the kitchen window up, smash it with something. He was opening the door. She waited. Voices from the hall. Somebody knew him. Grainger back from town, bellyaching after one too many curries. A dark girl walked into the kitchen, gave her a curious once-over. The girl from the Pitstop.

IN THE MOOD

Hap went to open his eyes, reminded himself where he was just in time. Didn't do being too nosy, they'd be on him with their sponges, pulling and straightening him up in his chair, tugging his cords, the flex he'd tugged from the back of the Tell-Me and set himself adrift. He tuned in to the hushed hut, the tiny patter as she pottered with her pots and pans. Way off the dial, lost in the jagged bands of colour that had dotted and dashed themselves from the screen. Dotted and dashed him over here. He groped in the soft dust but the tablet was nowhere within reach. Maybe, if you pressed the funny writing in the right place, it would flick him back where he'd come from, back in time for tea and no harm done. Hello, Hap. But the bra-straps wouldn't leave him now, now they'd started on him. Pouring and pinching, any chance they got. Everything was easier second time around. He thought about Elspeth. Hadn't thought of her for ages. The way she'd never take a hint, never let it lie. He bristled, remembered their neat little house in Clove High Street. He'd hit her once, right across the front room, soon after young Martin was born. Hit her into the middle of next week. But had she taken any notice? Had she borne it in mind? No, she'd gone right on nagging and chattering, on and on a second time, a third time and a fourth time as he sat in front of the fire, quiet like. Rolling the newspaper around the poker, still grey from the warm ash. Easier the second time. So much easier the third, didn't think about it at all the fourth.

'Feeling better?' The dusky maiden. She slid into sight as he opened an eye, lay still on his litter running his crooked fingers through the dirt. She was mixing something in a mortar, bending her pretty nose to sniff the mixture. She was wearing the plain brown shift again, hair caught up in a clasp behind her head. She had a small dark mouth, sharp nose and prominent cheekbones. Like the girl that used to work in the Chinese takeaway in Clove. He thought of the farm, the big heavy Land Rover they used to drive. Mikey Harris. That was his name. Used to work on the farm as well. They'd take the Land Rover and drive to Budgworth, drinking a safe distance from Elspeth and her nagging.

'You can have some of this. I made it up for Hurry but it'll work just as well on you,' she said casually.

Hap inched himself up, looked round the hut. It looked neater in daylight, fresh air streaming in through the flap. He could see a pair of swans standing near the doorway, angel-winged guardians. Hap watched her kneel beside his pallet, lift the dressing from his leg. His leg. He'd forgotten all about it. Didn't seem to hurt much now anyway. He peered down the length of his white body, watched her lift the wad of gauze from the wound. Hap blinked, tried to focus. A nasty little hole at the top of his thigh, the blue and purple skin folded in a series of puckers around the bloody muscle. She'd cut the tumour-tooth from his flesh and healed him all up. Kept on, where'd he gotten it? Asked him about the boy. The thin nasty boy?

'Not that little pipsqueaker. Puut Ra. Hah! The other one. Teomalik. We're practically related.'

Hap had shaken his head, decided against mentioning

the boy, cartwheeling into the wall with a wet-towel splash. He wondered for a second whether the boy was still there, up in old Will's room with the grit and the junk. Hap watched her smear some of the paste in a leaf, press it to his leg. She looked round, startling green eyes paler than gemstones. The way the bra-straps would look up, cleaning round your balls and stuff. Pity and disgust as they leaned over so he could squint down their crisp cool uniforms. Trying not to think about maybe getting like it themselves some day. He could read their minds, read them the same as he watched them, flickery and filmy on the Tell-Me. Read her mind as she leaned over.

'I wouldn't have you if you was family.'

Now she'd done it once she'd want to do it again, and again only worse. Hap knew all about that. She frowned at him, as if she could see thoughts too, see things inside his head, in other people's heads.

'He hurt Hurry. Cut the main muscle in the back of his wing.'

She was talking about the swan again.

'He killed Swift and Skyspeed and Diver.' The woman straightened, looked at him coldly, piece of meat in a freezer. 'That's why I wasn't in the mood.'

The mood for what? She glared, rose to her feet in one fluid movement, slammed the bowl down on one of the overloaded shelves.

'I don't want you taking an infection, dying on me.'

'Thanks.'

She gave him another cold look, eyes like limes left overnight in a snowdrift, frostier than the brook, brittle and bent through the never ending winters.

'You've no call to be thanking me,' she snapped.

He shrugged, decided to keep quiet. He watched her standing in the doorway, looking out. She bent to pat the swans, arching their elegant necks as she ran her slim brown hands over their smooth plumage.

'He's gone, though, the boy? Puut Ra? The boy who was here last night?'

She bowed her head. 'They're nothing to me, dirty scuttlers. Beetles on a dungheap. My sister's tastes . . . aren't mine.' She tossed her head back, ran her hands through her thick dark tresses as if she were sorting tobacco to roll on her thigh. She glared as if she was expecting him to argue the point. Hap elbowed himself up, looked about him. The tablet was lying next to his litter. The boy had wanted it, but she didn't. Ignored it, stepped over it, walked around. The tablet had whisked the boy away the way the remote whisked the programmes from the Tell-Me-Visual, whisked you away across the world. Like flying. Flying to exotic places in the sun, white beaches and warm blue seas and dusky maidens just like

'You haven't mentioned your name?' she'd chuckled.

'I'm H—'

'I know who you are. Don't bother me now.'

'Must have impaled myself when I . . . when I fell,' he said lamely.

'It impaled you,' she snapped. 'Although I can't for a moment understand why.' She frowned. 'I'll be back for you later.' She rose, straightened her shift and strode out of sight. The swans waddled forward, nestled down in the dusty doorway and started preening themselves.

Nicky Fish watched the ambulance men manoeuvre the stretcher from the back of the container wagon, red blankets strapped down tight over the body. Bell was hopping from foot to foot, trying to make sure the reporter couldn't get a good look.

'Come on, Malcolm, give us a break,' Nicky said wearily.

'Come on, Nicky, give us a break,' Bell mimicked. 'I told you. Anything else, anything else you're going to have to get from Public Relations in Budgworth.' He lowered his voice. 'And remember what I said about the French bloke. Anything appears in the papers and I'll have to have a close look at your Cortina. Do I make myself clear?' Nicky nodded, watched the medics load the corpse and climb aboard the ambulance. The pair of them watched it disappear up the Budgworth road, past the looted lorry. Regional Crime Squad officers had been swarming over it all morning. Arrived by the Granada-load down from HQ, plastic gloves and those dinky little seal-top bags.

'D'you reckon he did it, then? The driver?'

Bell frowned. 'He was babbling about this green light, didn't mention a passenger. Or a stowaway, in case you're wondering. He may have been on something mind. Crack, heroin. You never know the crap these foreigners bring in.'

'You can't drive a truck zonked on that stuff though, can you?'

'He didn't, he hit Haberfield, remember?'

'You said he'd followed the Haberfields since the ring-road. That's thirty miles of hairpins and God knows what. Wouldn't fancy driving that sober, let alone . . .'

'All right, Sherlock Fish. Let me have a report on Monday morning, I'm sure my boss'll love to hear your opinion.' Bell tugged the collar of his windcheater up as far as he could, strode over to the bridge. Nicky followed, rubbing his hands together. A dozen constables, an equal number of Scouts and Air Cadets helping to search for the boy. Maybe he was at a friend's house somewhere. Maybe he'd gone on holiday? If they found another body that would be... what, four in one weekend. Nicky did some slow mental arithmetic, grinned. Expenses and overtime and he'd be able to afford that new video he'd had his eye on. Another Granada pulled up, disgorged a couple of suits, designer stubble and mobile phones.

'Hello. The Macs have arrived.' Bell clicked his tongue, trotted up to the newcomers, saluting and nodding, nodding and pointing. The heavy mob.

Puut Ra watched the girls wheel the trolley down the passage to the old ones slumped in their worn leather thrones. The lounge reminded him of the ruined hall at Cloud Hangar. Carved stone seats all around the walls. The council chamber had been burnt to the ground decades before, heaps of knotty black ashes, all that remained of their great oak table. The table where they'd drawn their maps and planned their campaigns. The table where they'd drawn the dispositions for the last battle under the walls. Mysheedi had told him all about it. His grandsire had been there, Tilekin's too. Shouting and bawling with the rest of them, millions of them. Endless legions surging out of the marshes, down the hills, along the shore. Gone now. Blown away. So many shadows sitting in their stone chairs watching the tide pouring over their ditches and castles. Great white gouts of seagull shit crusted over their broken crowns. The girls were snapping at one another as they served the old ones their drinks. He'd taken a pale blue cup from the tray, swigged the murky brown contents and burned his mouth. He ran his tongue over the tiny scorched ridges, enjoying the taste. Had to have their tea, she'd said, the pretty dark girl. Taller than Mags. They didn't seem to be getting on, whispering and hissing at each other as they passed around the room. The funny old muttering man spied him in the doorway, raised a blotchy hand, veins standing out starkly like tree bark.

'Fucking watch out here he fucking comes again fucking little bastard did you see the fucking . . .'

Puut Ra held his breath, ready to run this time, run for the window. Take a running jump the way he'd hopped skipped and jumped out of Trafarionath. Molly shushed the old man, eased him back in his chair and wiped his foul mouth. Puut Ra eyed the girls nervously. The old man glared at him, shaking his head and nodding to himself. They didn't seem to want to listen to anything he said, to any of his foul-mouthed accusations. He should have cut and run, gotten out of that ruined old place as soon as he'd arrived, as soon as he'd gotten his bearings. Off over the fields, into the woods. He'd catch small birds, strangle things to eat. He'd hide himself away in the deep wood until he'd gotten used to his new skin, his new powers, new place. The boy closed his eyes, swallowed. Run run run! He would have to run like a hare, slip away from his pursuers like an eel in a basket, not try and stand up to them, fight for his place like Tilekin in the shallows back over. He should have known, should have used his brain if he wanted to stay here. Fighting, killing? What did he know about it? Goblin stories. Tilekin's tales of battle and blood in the shield wall, Mysheedi the courtly assassin, master of poisons and the stab in the back. The short sharp stab in the back he'd tried out on the fat man.

He winced, cursed his stupidity. They would never, ever let him free now. Let him get on with what was left of his life. They'd hound him to the ends of the earth, to the ends of everything. For one second of blind, childish panic. For one second's curiosity, what his magic tooth could do. The big man – Grainger he supposed –

had seemed all right at first, almost as if he knew him. Come on in son, where've you been? Taken him by surprise trying to get his bearings. Have you seen your grandad? Mags had looked awkward, said she'd found him walking up the drive. Fallen in the water apparently. Asked him if he was all right as she called a taxi to take her home. Grainger, preoccupied and not overly pleased to see them on the doorstep, had changed his mind, insisted the boy went upstairs, got into some clean clothes. His son had left a wardrobe full of them when he'd gone to France. Help yourself and we'll find your grandad for you. Mags had given him a nervous wave, gone for her taxi.

Puut Ra had followed Grainger's bulging backside up the stairs. Dizzy spell on the landing, tottering there with his hands held out, balancing himself in the strange body as if he'd been walking a tightrope carrying a glass filled to the brim. As if he couldn't afford to spill a drop of himself from his precious new pot. Feeling his feelings rushing along unfamiliar passages, expanding to fill one chamber after another like a cave diver in a new system, ducking and diving off the edge of his chart. He'd swayed back and forth for a moment, got his new limbs under control. Good as new, better. Followed the fat man into a room smothered with colourful banners the same as his T-shirt, pulled jeans and sweatshirts from a drawer, flung them on to the bed.

'Can I stay here, then?' he'd asked him, not thinking things through at all. 'Is it all right if I stay here?' He should have known. He should have known he'd get funny. The fat man had looked sheepish, rubbed his small mouth. How come he'd gotten so fat with such a small mouth? He must have had to scoff his way through millions of mouthfuls to get as fat as that. He'd almost giggled, giggled despite the fat man's pasty, serious face.

'Trouble is, Jonathan, I'm afraid we've had a bit of an accident. It's the cuts you see, aren't allowed the staff we should have. Should have more cover. When your parents arrive I'll explain everything, of course, but in the mean time we might just be able to sort things out for ourselves, between ourselves.' He'd nodded. Stay alert and listen, this isn't your place and they'll be after you if they find out. He'd had to think hard, remind himself. Jonathan. That's me, we're talking about the new me. No time to think. '... so we hadn't really expected, that is, he never had before, you know, got about too well on his own. None of them do, as I'm sure you already know. That's why we didn't really expect him to ... get up and go like he did.'

'Who?'

'Your grandad,' Grainger had insisted quietly, maybe losing his temper a little. Was the little shit taking the piss or something? OK, so the old fool had done a bunk, was it his fault? He hadn't lifted as much as a buttock in all the years he'd been in, then he suddenly ups and leaves. It was ridiculous. And if they didn't find him ...

'Your parents dropped you off? They'll be here what, half an hour?'

'They stopped on the way.' The car upside-down in the stream, swimming around the shiny red metal with Mysheedi looking in on the boy with the big eyes. Me. My eyes now. Where had Mysheedi got to? Where had they taken the little red-faced one? Had Mysheedi got in too? Taken himself a new shape out of the flooded car? He blinked, watched the fat man stomp off toward the stairs. Changed quickly and came after him. Feeding the old folk their late drink, looking over his shoulder, sweaty.

'Listen, I'll just finish here and we'll pop out, around the grounds. He can't have gone far. You came up with your friend, you didn't see anything?' He'd turned, sighed so heavy he'd made his chins wobble.

'Look, I'm sorry, OK? I'm really so bloody sorry but if they won't give me the staff it's hardly my fault, is it?'

'Hardly your fucking fault you fat bastard you fat git you fat—'

'All right Mr Fletcher. Give it a rest for a second.'

'Jonathan, just give me a moment. Let me finish with this lot and we'll go and look for your grandad.' Exasperated, losing patience. The old folk muttering and dribbling and nodding, the jury out on his frightful incompetence. Shit. Klein had promised. Get it done without a fuss and there would be a new posting. One of the big homes in Budgworth, videos, jacuzzis. Lots of staff. Klein had promised. Losing one though, what the hell was that wicked bastard going to make of that?

'That's not Jonathan.' Mrs Trent, tiny Mrs Trent slipping down her chair looking up at the gangly boy. Was all he needed.

'Here we are now, Doris. Up we come. Of course it's Jonathan. You've seen old Hap's pictures, many a time.'

'He looks different,' she'd protested.

'He's older, that's all. It's a while since you've seen him.' Bending to lift her straight. The look on his face as he'd peered over his shoulder, sweaty and red. Judging him, passing sentence. Impostor, fugitive, changeling. Jonathan shook his head, watched the girls moving around the nodding ring of old folk. He glanced down, his new shoe caught up under a fold of the ruckled old rug. He pulled his foot back, swallowed, felt the tooth sharp and slippery in the outsize pocket of his borrowed jeans.

Molly glanced at him, leaning in the doorway frowning to himself, back to Mags, fidgeting nervously. What the hell was going on anyway?

'I told you. Mr Grainger said he had a bad head. He'd be popping in to Budgworth in the morning, asked me if I'd cover for him before everybody else arrived. He said he didn't want to have to bother anybody else. I couldn't get away from work though. Mrs Bignell's got it in for me, I tell you.'

Molly looked hard at the younger girl, dark eyes wide.

'I was hoping . . . I was hoping he'd change his mind. About the job. I don't want to work in the Pitstop all my life.' Garish uniform ruckled up round her knees.

Molly shook her head. 'There's something wrong with him. Didn't even know his own grandfather. When I asked about the car he said he'd taken it but it's been in the garage since Tuesday.'

Mags sighed. 'He probably wasn't even listening. He's like that. You know.'

'Well, how long have you known him, then? I'm surprised you've had time to get round to him.' Her brown eyes flared, mouth set.

'What's that supposed to mean?'

'You know well enough, young lady.'

'Listen, don't come the holier-than-thou with me. If your husband—'

'If my husband what?'

Mags tossed her head, hair swinging free under the clasp. She had to clamp it down to get the Pitstop cap on. 'Sort your own life out before you come accusing me, lady,' she snarled.

Molly eyed her, straightened up and cracked a cup and saucer down on the trolley.

'Where are your parents, anyway? Normally send you off on your own, do they?' Molly demanded, glaring at the youth.

'Probably delayed somewhere. Trouble with the ... er ... car.'

Uncertain. Something was wrong here but she couldn't put her finger on it. Mags, apologetic, touching her shoulder. Thin nylon housecoat.

'Look. I'll help with them. There's nothing to worry about.'

'Where's Hap, then? You seem to have forgotten we're one down already. Some help you are.'

'Well, let's get them settled here and we'll look. OK? He can't have gone far.'

Can't have gone far. That was true enough. Hap hadn't moved since the day they'd brought him in here, not of his own accord anyway. Molly breathed hard, wiped her hand on a tissue.

'Right, then. Take the tea things back to the kitchen. They've got to have their dinner. I'll ring Claire and get her up here.' She waited a second while they exchanged looks. 'Well, go on, then. I'm going to start looking.'

The youth shrugged. 'I'll take the garden. He's my grandad after all.'

FAULT LINES

'You can start by telling me who you are. What's going on. Come on.' Mags had flung her coat over her shoulders, followed him out into the garden. He wandered on another yard or two, paused, looked lost.

'Come on. I covered for you but she's not stupid. She knew who I was and I never even mentioned my name. Where's Grainger? Where's the old man? Where had you been, getting soaked like that?'

He looked round sharply, she thought for a second he was going to hit her. He shrugged, hastily rearranged his features around a careless smile and stepped after her. She realized she'd taken a step backwards without meaning to.

'I'm Jonathan.' He stuck out his chin. 'Mr Grainger said my grandad disappeared yesterday afternoon. While I was out walking.'

'You walked with him, you took him somewhere? Just before you bumped into me?' she suggested. He's only gone and lost his bloody gramfer.

Jonathan shook his head. 'I haven't seen him for ages. I've forgotten what he looks like.'

Sounded as if he was on the verge of tears, looking out over the garden, the hills rearing away behind them. He shouldn't have to feel guilty about that. Happen to anyone, losing your gramfer, forgetting what he ever looked like. Forgetting what your boyfriend looked like.

Shouldn't have to feel guilty when it WASN'T YOUR FAULT. She'd had other things to think about, she'd had her own fucking life to get on with, stick worrying about him and his silly songs. Jonathan was the same, he had his own life too. She understood, she could relate to that. Christ, she was beginning to sound like the doctor woman at college. Let it go, Mags, it wasn't your fault. She sighed, nodded down the garden.

'I'll have a look by the shed there. You take a walk down to the fence, look along. If we can't find him we're going to have to call the police.'

He'd turned, stridden across the grass toward the shed.

'I said I'd look . . . oh never mind.'

'Thank Christ. Where the hell have you been?' Molly hissed into the receiver as Claire answered, groggily.

'Molly? What's the matter? Look, I had a bit of a late night . . .'

'Surprise surprise. Guess who's holding the fort? Look, did you speak to Grainger? Did he say he had a headache or something?'

'He looked pretty fagged out after that meeting with Dr Klein, but he didn't—'

'When did you last see Hap? He's gone missing.' Mumbling. Come on girl, think about it.

'Grainger's missing?'

'Grainger's missing and Hap's missing. I'm here with that little tart Mags and some dopey sod who says he's Hap's grandson.'

Another silence.

'Hap's grandson . . . You haven't heard, then? You haven't seen the news?'

'I've been up here bloody looking after eight old

folk while you've been lying in bed screwing your lousy boyfriend,' Molly screamed, a fingernail away from hysterical. 'When have I had time to watch the news?'

'Molly . . . for God's sake. The crash on the bridge. It was the Haberfields. The mum and dad.'

Molly thought quickly. Nicky had been on about it all night. Couple killed on the bridge, the little baby rescued. No mention of—

'They were all on their way to the home. The elder boy's been reported missing. They think he might have been in the car as well. If he's up there he's in . . . he must be in some kind of a shock.'

Oh God. Molly winced, closed her eyes.

'Molly? You there? He must have been thrown clear, wandered around. Had he hurt his head?'

'I don't know, I'm not a bloody brain surgeon.'

'OK, Molly. Slow down. Take it steady. Where is he now?'

'Out with Fancy Knickers in the garden. You know. Margery. She's playing Florence Nightingale for him. Well, he's wearing trousers even if they are too big for him.'

'Molly. Think for a moment. He's had a crash, possibly got some head injury. Confused. You hang on, I'll ring the police. OK?'

'Yeah, yeah. OK. Ring them. Hap's missing, God knows where Grainger's got to. I'll go on searching the house. Give my love to Paul.' She hung up.

Claire James sat back on the rumpled bed next to her rumpled boyfriend. Cheeky bitch. She rang the police station. Uh oh, answerphone.

'Inquest Monday. Identity only,' Wilf called across the office. Nicky looked up from his battered portable, nodded.

'They must be doing three at a time. Might as well take your sleeping bag with you.' He rolled his eyes winningly. Not a pretty sight. 'Course, you could always let me go. You get all the juicy jobs,' the tousled reporter accused. Wilf glared down his half-moon specs.

'With that shorthand? I wouldn't trust you at a' – he thought for a moment – 'at a place where it was vital to have a good shorthand note,' he added crisply. Nicky's lip hovered under his left eyeball, settled back over his teeth as he poked his tongue out, finished the following week's soccer fixtures with a flourish.

'Coming down the Boar for a quick one?'

His editor clambered to his feet, pulled on his ancient sports coat. 'Go on, then. Your round.'

The two of them held the wall, negotiated the horrifying passage to the suicidal back stairs. They were halfway down when the telephone trilled. 'Sod 'em. It's half-past one already,' Wilf declared, feeling for the loose banister rail.

'Anything?' Molly asked as the two of them appeared at the kitchen door. She'd taken a quick look around the house while they had searched the garden. Telly on in Grainger's office, drawers pulled about as if he'd left in a hurry.

Mags shook her head. 'We looked as far as the lane. He must be in here somewhere.'

Molly nodded. Come on, think about it. She'd telephoned Claire, she'd telephoned social services but got no answer as it was a Saturday. Clove police were engaged and by the time she'd got an emergency call through she had spotted the pair of them making their way back. Right.

'Look. Jonathan, you have a sit in with them, you look knackered. You give me a hand looking upstairs.'

Mags bristled, looked as if she was going to argue. Exchanged a look with the youth, who shrugged, loped on down the passage toward the lounge. Molly waited a second, guided the younger girl down to the hall.

'He's been in a crash. His parents were killed last night coming over the bridge. He must have been wandering ever since.'

Mags stared at her, shook her head.

'It's true. I rang the girl who should have been here first thing, it's been on the news. Now he might have had a head injury so we'd do best to keep him calm until the ambulance arrives.'

'Ambulance?'

'The truck thing with bells on?' Molly asked snidely. 'He might have hurt his head,' she spelled out slowly.

Mags bit her lip. 'I saw him walking, soaking wet. Didn't think.'

Her brown eyes were welling with tears. Come on, for God's sake.

'I didn't . . .'

'Never mind now. He's all right there for a moment. I rang 999 but they were stacking the calls. We'll try again in a while. Let's have a look for Hap while we're waiting. OK?'

'Yes. Sorry. All right.'

She followed the girl up the staircase, paused on the landing.

'You check the rooms, I'll go up to the store. Find him and shout, don't try to move him, OK?'

Molly watched the girl stride off down the landing, Pitstop overall tight over her shapely bottom. Sort you out later, Nicky bloody Fish. She fished her keys from her housecoat pocket, tried Grainger's sitting-room. The cushions on the sofa were pulled about, scooped out by the shape of somebody's head. Magazines strewn over the floor and the telly on. She crossed the room, switched it off, walked into the small alcove kitchenette. Pretty small place for the supplies the manager had stacked in here. Big fridge-freezer standing open, frozen food thawing on the floor. Cereal boxes ripped open, discarded wrappers everywhere. Somebody had enjoyed a real pigout in here. Molly shut the fridge door, walked back into the main room and on down the corridor. Grainger's bedroom. Big double neatly made, immense clothes folded neatly over the chair. Make somebody a lovely wifey. Huh. She closed the door quietly, went on down the passage, up the small flight of stairs to the next floor. Mr Maggs' room, the door panel dented where he'd gone funny that time. Had to ship him over to the big place on the Downs, getting too disruptive for the rest of them. She turned the key, realized she'd locked it. The door must have been left unlocked. Claire! She left the keys in the lock, pushed the dented door open.

His room was as he had left it, a shambles. Hadn't had time to clear it up and they weren't exactly short of space in this rambling old dump. Be all right with a couple of million to spend on it, but Molly had worked there three winters, she knew only too well it was a right bugger to keep warm. That broken window wasn't helping either. She'd have to report it. She looked down, wondered why old Mr Maggs would have had a sleeping-bag. With somebody in it? She doubled forward, knelt beside the body, tried to remember her first aid. Don't move them, they might have a neck injury. But it wasn't Hap and it was far too small to be Grainger. Younger, much younger. He'd hit his head pretty badly judging by the blood smeared down the wall. Or maybe somebody had hit him. Maybe Grainger had caught him prowling, there had been a struggle, the manager had staggered off to raise the alarm?

Slow down. Get a grip. Molly took a deep breath, bent down over the boy. He was wearing a T-shirt five times too big for him, a nice leather belt loose round his waist. His dirty reddish hair was clogged with blood and needed a good wash anyway by the look of things. Hippie. New Age Traveller, whatever they were called. Had a lot of problems last year with the convoys stopping off on the way to Glastonbury, asking if they could have a pail of water or camp out the back. Grainger out there on the drive telling them he'd have the law on them. Where the hell was Grainger?

The hippie stirred, groaned something. At least he wasn't dead. She eased him away from the wall, stretched his arms out by his sides. Hands were covered in grime. Hippie. How the hell had he got in here? Maybe the Haberfields or whatever their names were had given him a lift, he'd staggered in with the other dozy sod. Maybe he'd broken in, fallen or something. She twitched, nervously watched the youth rolling his head from side to side. He opened his eyes. Blue grey, like a seagull's wing. He looked at her, blinked.

'Where's my uncle?'

Weird accent. Wherever the hell he'd come from. He focused on her, scrambled away on his lean buttocks. Came up against the abandoned bed. On something all right.

'You're all right now. In an old folks' home. Don't worry.'

Don't worry? He looked at her suspiciously, fingered the nasty cut on his chest, sat up quickly with a wince. He looked anxiously around the floor. Pink spiders, Molly supposed. He held a dirty hand to his dirty head.

'Don't worry? Oh, all right, I won't,' he snorted. 'Where's my uncle? Has he left you here with me?'

Molly took a pillowcase from a shelf, held it to his head. The youth took it, nodded. Dabbed it to the cut on his forehead and looked at the bloody smear.

'You're not the Spawn Woman, are you?'

She wondered if she'd misheard.

'Sperm woman? Are you trying to be funny, because if—'

'Where am I?' Picking at his chest, angry now, trying to get to his feet. Molly backed off. He stared at her.

'Where am I?' he repeated.

'Clove Heights Old People's Home. Clove,' she said shakily. Some kind of lunatic. Mags down the corridor. She could shout, get her down to help.

'Clove? Cloven Vale?'

Fucking Eden Vale, how the hell should she know?

'We're still in the valley. By the stream?'

She paused. Clove Brook. There was a reservoir two miles up the road. She told him.

'So we know ... where we are,' he added lamely.

Big lad. Six foot at least. Great big tie-and-dye job over his trousers. Yeah, those red shoes too. He glared at her, reached out his grubby paw and felt her housecoat.

'Silk?'

Hippie smartass. 'The best,' she said with a cold smile.

He turned, walked to the broken window, sniffed. Definitely on something. He ran his fingers around the warped window frame, stood on tiptoes to look out. Molly backed for the door.

'You haven't seen my uncle? Old man, beard, clothes like these?'

'Don't think so. Look, if you don't mind me asking, you shouldn't really be in here.'

'That's not asking, that's telling.' Still looking out over the garden, the hills swarming up behind.

'All right, then, I'm telling. You shouldn't be here. If you want to look for your uncle you should have knocked.'

He chuckled, turned to look at her. He was quite good looking too if you scraped off some of the dirt. Another bloody cramp. Just what she needed. She held the shelving until it passed.

'You're right about that. I shouldn't be here,' he recited as if talking to himself. The door clicked closed. Molly whipped around, grabbed the door handle.

'Mags! Open the door! Don't be so bloody stupid!' she yelled, frightened now. The youth strode across the room, she thought he was in on it, thought he was going to hit her only he raised his fist and slammed it on the panel. Molly kicked, rattled the doorknob. Christ, the bastards must be in it together. Locked in with one of them, out of his mind on something, he couldn't tell her from whatever daft fantasy he was imagining. She kicked the door in frightened frustration.

'Let us out of here! Mags, for Christ's sake.'

BREAKDOWNS

'Money? What, this?' Jonathan tugged the wad of notes from his pocket, waved it under her nose. Mags told him to put it back, looked up and down the main road as if they were in the middle of some parade.

'For Christ's sake . . . where did you get that?' As if she didn't know. As if she didn't know? She didn't know nothing. She didn't know anything about him and here she was aiding and abetting whatever it was he was up to.

'The desk. A little tin box. I thought it would help. The way it had been hidden away, had to be worth something.' She sighed, strode on down the verge, coat pulled tightly about her Pitstop uniform. They would have to hurry, the ambulance would be on its way, maybe the police too. Christ, he'd already admitted taking the bastard's cash. She glanced at him, loping along with a bemused smile playing about his mouth. Bugger's enjoying himself, she thought. They should have stayed where they were, waited for the ambulance. Cleared things up straight away. That cow Molly had been right all the time. Look for the old man, wait for the ambulance. He could be shutting it out, the trauma of the crash. He could be mental or something. And here she was walking along a deserted lane with him for the second time in twenty-four hours. Must be cracking up. Breakdown, that's what it was. B word. B for bummer. Dragging it around with her since college, since Jason. A bulging laundry bag of bad memories and body odours. Forget it. Doctor Jervis, patting her shoulder. Not your fault, let it go Mags. Think about something else. She'd finished searching the rooms, been on her way after Molly when Jonathan had slid up the stairs like a ghost, grabbed her arm and made her jump. Held his finger over his lips and pulled her down to the landing.

'We've got to go. We've got to go now.' Insisting, insistent. 'They're looking for me because there's been a crash. It was on the . . . the box thing that talks downstairs, just now. The Telling box.'

Mags nodded, sorting through his chatter. Molly had left the TV on for the old folk while they searched. Mr Fletcher moaning it was the wrong channel. Switch it over that was wrong as well. He'd been in a crash and his head wasn't working properly. She tried to pull away, he gripped her arm.

'My mother and father are dead but my little brother's still alive. In their hospital.' He said it as if it was some kind of alien concept.

Mags nodded. 'So we'll wait for the ambulance and they'll take you to him,' she said tearfully. Christ, she couldn't handle this. He wasn't crying, and it was his parents. Was she crying for his parents or for herself? He shook her.

'It'll take too long. Too many questions. My little brother . . . won't know where he is, won't know anything. We have to find him now. Right now.' His green eyes bored into her brown ones, gripped them, held her tight.

'They'll be talking, talking when we should be with him. We must go now. Leave her. Shut her in, we'll have more time without her bothering us.'

Maybe he'd taken a dislike to the older woman too.

Couldn't be all bad. Outcasts together. Fugitives from what? Reality? He'd motioned up the stairs. All right. All right, we'll go. She'd steadied herself, wiped her nose on her sleeve and crept on up the stairs. She'd heard Molly talking away to herself. She knew how she felt. Glanced at Jonathan, his eyes were damn near popping out of his head. She'd raised her finger to her lips, he'd swallowed, nodded. Molly would be all right, though. They'd ring 999 and get them to sort it out while they went to find Jonathan's brother. When they'd got that straight they could relax, work things out properly. Repeating it over and over inside her head, a mad mantra.

She'd slipped along the corridor and eased the door shut, locked it as Molly finished talking to the sheets and started banging the door. Girl packed a punch too. Wouldn't have liked to be on the end of that. Mags had rushed off, blocking her ears against the furious shouting. She'd be all right. She'd apologize later, when everything was straightened out. Molly would understand, eventually. The kid needed to see his brother, didn't want a lot of grown ups talking at his face telling him what to do. They'd taken coats, had one last look in on the old folk. Nodding and muttering to themselves, TV on way too loud. Down the path like robbers, out on to the main road back to the village. Odd car trundling past but lifts wouldn't be a good idea, not yet. Jonathan had practically jumped over the fence every time one drove by. Was he in some kind of state? Was *she* in some kind of state?

'There's something wrong with me,' he declared, just like that.

Not now, please God not now.

He raised his eyebrows, sighed. 'I don't even miss them,' he said, throwing her again. What had she expected? Some kind of confession? What's he got to confess about? She closed her eyes, held her breath.

'Who?' she asked at last.

'My parents. I don't feel I miss them, if you know what I mean.'

Mags gritted her teeth. 'Don't think about it now. It's the shock.' Shock you could never quite shake off. Shock you had to live with, on and on about his family, his problem. Her problem.

'Let's get some clobber and we'll catch the bus.'

'Get some clobbers to catch the bus?'

'To get to Budgworth. It's thirty miles away, if you're thinking we'd walk.'

He looked bemused, strode on beside her.

'City? With a defence like that? They'd do better to buy me,' Nicky said, finishing his argument with Roy, who shook his head, took his glass. Wilf wasn't keen on football, not that you could really call Budgworth City a football team. He had spread a copy of the city *Herald* over the bar and was following the latest on the Haberfield deaths with a grubby index finger. 'They've drawn a blank on the elder boy. Bit of a loner, it says.'

'I wouldn't believe everything you read in that,' Nicky warned him, slipping from his barstool for a trip to the gents. He wandered back two minutes later, spotted Mags heading for the door with a bag over her arm. Roy hadn't moved from the bar, Wilf slumped over it with his nose in the paper. He dashed on out, caught her as she headed across the small market square.

'What do you want? Get out of it.'

'Look. I'm sorry about this morning. It's just—'

'Your time of the month, piss off out of it,' she snapped, tugging the bag over her shoulder and striding off across the square. Cheeky little cow. Only trying to apologize and all. Nicky elbowed his way back to the bar, crashed on to his stool and swigged from the fresh pint Roy had pulled him.

'I told you, Nicky. She's got problems enough without you pissing her about,' the big man warned, eyebrows twitching.

'I just . . . wanted to tell her something, that's all.'

'Do us all a favour. Leave her alone. Mary promised her mother.'

'Off in such a bloody hurry. Where's she going anyway?'

'Friend's in Budgworth. Staying the night. She's a big girl now,' Roy said easily. Nicky raised his eyebrows, went back to his pint.

'Did you get them, the clobbers?'

Silly sod.

'What do you think this is, sweets for the journey?'

He looked hurt. Shit. She touched his arm, walked him toward the bus stop. Best if they kept out of sight as much as possible, get to the hospital and get things sorted.

'Did you enjoy the burger?' She'd left him for fifteen minutes in the Clove Pitstop, asked Gwen if she could have a staff discount for him. Gwen had frowned but nodded him into a seat in the corner.

'It was lovely. Really tasty. What was it again?'

'A Cloveburger quarter-pounder with relish.'

'It was delicious.'

She'd glanced at him, wondering if he had been taking the piss.

'And the cheeps. They were out of this world.'

'All right. Don't go on.'

CHANGELING HEARTS

Walking along swinging his arms studying the shop windows as if he'd never been inside Woolworths in his life.

'Hang on. Look at those.' He pointed out a pair of Lycra leggings in the windows of Dorothy's. 'They're smart. Do you have a discount here too?'

Mags chuckled. 'We haven't got time to window shop. I thought you wanted to see your brother?'

He tilted his head, looked that cute way he did. 'Let's get them first,' he asked. Presents at a time like this.

'Come on then, hurry. The bus is here at three.' She followed him into the shop. He went straight to the display, began peeling the leggings from the model.

'Excuse me, can I help you?' Miss Dorothy Frobisher, sister of the Air Vice-Marshal, looking a little peeved. Christ, it was a customer, wasn't it?

'We'd like the leggings, please.' Little hussy. Seen her walking around before. New boyfriend?

'I have them in ten, twelve and fourteen,' she said sweetly.

Mags gave her a flicker of a smile. 'I'm a twelve actually.'

Jonathan accepted the leggings, held them up against his legs. 'These'll never do,' he moaned.

Mags took them from him, gave him a look. 'They stretch, you idiot,' she hissed. Miss Frobisher pursed her lips. 'They'll do nicely.'

'I'll wear them now.'

Mags froze. Miss Frobisher froze, thawed, boiled.

'Listen here, young man you come into my shop—'

'He was only joking. He's got a great sense of humour. How much are they please?' Mags interrupted, fishing for her purse.

'Nine ninety-nine. Please.'

Mags handed her a ten-pound note, tucked the leggings under her arm and pulled him out of the shop.

'Do that again and I'll leave you to it, making a fool of me,' she snarled. He glared at her, snatched the leggings from under her arm.

'They're my bloody leggings, you get your own,' he snarled back, thrusting his jaw at her. Mags looked into the shop window, Miss Frobisher peering out like a goldfish, opening and shutting her mouth. Mags stomped away, Jonathan striding behind her. The single-decker bus pulled in at the stop. Mags stood staring at it.

'Bloody hell.'

'Is that it, that the bus?' Jonathan called, catching up with her and touching her arm. She tugged away. It won't wait. 'Are we going then?' Bastard. 'Is this the bus? Mags?'

The driver took her money, gave her the tickets and her change. He wondered why she was crying. Lovers' tiff, he reckoned, pulled away.

'Darling, I'm home!' Nicky hung his jacket over the stairs, threw himself down on the sofa and rifled under the cushion for the remote. Half-time scores.

'Moll? All right?' He called out toward the kitchen. He levered himself up, strode to the door. Spotless, Mollyless. Bottom of the stairs.

'MOLLY?' He checked the coat rack where he was supposed to hang his jacket. Her coat was missing. Must have had to do an extra shift. That Claire girl again probably, always messing them about. He picked up the telephone, dialled the home. Waited. Somebody usually got around to answering it in the end. Come on. He let it ring. And ring.

'What the fucking hell do you want you noisy fucking

bastard ringing all the time ring bloody ring bloody ring.'

Fish thought he'd got the wrong number. Thought again.

'Is that . . . Mr Fletcher?'

'Bernie fucking Fletcher mate what the fuck do you want?'

The foul-mouthed old boy Molly was always complaining about. Swearing and pinching their bums. Saying what he'd do to them. 'I wouldn't mind if you had half his spunk,' Molly had told him one night. What? What was he doing answering the phones, putting off malicious callers or something?

'Is Molly there?' he called over the deluge of four-letter words.

'Upstairs with the rest of the bastards. You should have seen what that bastard did to him as well. He tore his fucking guts out I tell you.' Mr Fletcher went on describing events at the home, a stream of filth with facts floating in it. Nicky wasn't listening. He was in the Cortina, fumbling for his keys.

He ran the heavy Ford into a wall and leapt out with the engine running. Doubled up the stairs to the front door. It wasn't locked.

'Molly? Molly?' He dashed down the hall, peered into the kitchen. An old man in a threadbare gown pulling cupboard doors open.

'Who the fuck are you?'

'Where's Molly? Where's Mr Grainger?' The old man returned to the cupboards, taking out the tins for a good rummage. Fish lumbered down the passage, the old folk nodding like those daft dogs in the back of car windows.

'Where's Molly? Anybody seen Molly?'

'Went upstairs with the boy and the girl. Looking for Mr Haberfield,' a tiny old lady said from the floor. She'd slipped down from the smooth vinyl throne, propped herself up on the carpet. Nicky paused, lifted her awkwardly to her seat.

'Bless you. I called and called but nobody came. Mr Fletcher's gone wandering as well,' she said shakily.

'All right, my dear. I'll find them. Hang on here and keep an eye on them, will you?'

She nodded, tugged a handkerchief from her sleeve. Nicky dashed out of the lounge, on up the stairs. They could hear him 'Hallo' and 'Molly' all over the house.

'Nicky! Nicky, in here!' Muffled, from up the stairs. Nicky took them two at a time, rattled the door knob.

'Molly? What the hell's been going on?' He unlocked the door, pushed it open. Sweaty warm air, tangy, salty, coppery sort of smell. Sort of smell? His wife in dishevelled housecoat, a grinning youth in a T-shirt. Smack.

'What d'you want to go and hit him for? Can't you see he's already got a lump on his head? You could have killed him!'

Molly, bending over the unconscious youth, dabbing his bleeding mouth with the pillowcase. She opened her mouth, gasped something, held her abdomen just below her nylon rustling breasts.

'What's wrong?'

'Nothing's bloody wrong,' she snapped, eyed Nicky standing by the shelves, frowning at her.

'What was I supposed to think? What the hell's going on anyway? It's a bloody madhouse downstairs.'

Molly glanced up at him. 'Grainger's off on his travels, Hap's missing . . .'

'And that funny feller with the mouth's in the kitchen making mudpies,' Nicky added helpfully.

'Go and ring the police. Don't worry if they stack the call, just get somebody up here. Better check the ambulance as well.'

Nicky glared at her. 'Give him the kiss of life, why don't you?'

Molly sighed. 'If you're going to start . . .'

'Well, who is he anyway? The plumber?'

'His name's . . . Theo something. He's had a whack on the head, Nicky, you can't expect him to give you an interview straight off. Now stop pissing me about and listen. That little Mags tart has gone off with the kid from the car crash.'

'The little baby? He's in—'

'The elder boy. Jonathan. I caught him wandering about this morning, thought he was some kind of a thief. Course what with one thing and another I—'

'Jonathan Haberfield? The kid they've been looking for?'

Molly nodded. 'He must have wandered up the valley, dazed or something. Christ knows where they think they were going.'

'I'll ring Wilf.'

'Ring Wilf afterwards. 999, remember?'

'Right. I'm on it.'

VICTORY VS

Hap watched the woman hang her cloak and fiddle with the crudely stitched shoulder of her gown. Been gone ages. The light fading, turning the guardian swans' blinding whites to hazy greys. He was hungry. They usually came round with the trolley. Hadn't they missed him yet? Why weren't they looking for him? He'd sat up, crawled about the hard-packed earth floor. Nosing pots and tasting potions on the tip of his finger. Taking bunches of dried roots down from the rafters creating his own little dust storms. A scatter of crystals and shiny worn stones in a bowl on a shelf. Old William had been keen on crystals and rocks. Peered at them with a little spyglass screwed into his eye. Old William, gone now. The multi-screen where you could watch ten channels a day, all at the same time. His stomach rumbled alarmingly. He'd gnawed the breadstuff he'd found on the table, sipped the brackish lake water from a leather pouch. Perhaps she would cook them something. Wasn't in the mood. Mood for what? He ran his finger through the bowl of stones, picked the flatter ones, tried to read the tiny writing. Letters too small to make out even if he'd known their funny alphabets. Victory Vs. That's what they looked like, these miniature tablets. He wondered for a moment if they matched the set packed carefully into the remote, or the funny slab thing the boy had tried to steal from under his nose. Maybe he could find some glue, stick them all back together like those floor tiles in the old days. He put one on his tongue, ran it around the inside of his mouth. Pepper pebble. Salt stone. He'd managed to break one of his stones once, chewing it so hard, sucking it small and grinding it down with his dentures, chewing the chalky fragments. Thought perhaps he had better not eat her stones. She might have counted them, needed the exact number for some recipe or other. Her swans eyed him as if he'd gone mad, eating all the funny woman's stones like so many boiled sweets, rattling round the plates. Wasn't in the mood. She turned, glared at him.

'Been out, then.'

'Don't talk.'

You fool. Pouring the tea over his lap just because the Tell-Me had gone wrong. What gave her the right to treat people like that? What gave this woman the right to use that tone with him? He looked round for her knife. She tugged the door flap down, plunging the hut into virtual darkness. He could hear her rustling, moving across the floor. She knelt beside his litter, breathing hot over him.

'What's wrong? You can't see in this light. It's not come back, has it?'

He'd thought the wound had healed remarkably. You had to squint to see the scar on his shiny white skin. He'd meant to thank her but she didn't seem all that big on conversation.

'Not yet. It will. It's time.'

'Time for what?'

She gave an irritated snort, ran her finger up his thigh, over the crinkled wound. In the mood. 'What do you think? I need my strength for what is coming. I need your strength.'

'My strength? What . . .'

She clamped her hand over his mouth. 'You're a man, aren't you? You've got one of these,' she tugged at his trousers, made him jump. 'And that's close enough,' she whispered. Pushed him back, gently but forcefully, same as she'd gently cut him open, eased the knife under his skin as if she'd been peeling potatoes. Cool hand splayed over his white belly, hot breath over his cringing genitals. My God, she wasn't going to . . . she was! Hap reclined, eyes popping into the darkness as she moved over him, threw a tawny leg over his twitching trunk. He stifled an astonished giggle, closed his eyes and enjoyed her hands sliding slick down his belly. He swallowed, looked down. A tiny chink of light fell across her arched back. She looked like a cat, crouching over an old fish in an alley. She pulled the dark hair away from her face, looked over her shoulder.

'What's wrong? Don't stop!' he pleaded, clutching at her slim arm. She tugged it free, glided to the door. Stark naked in the torchlight. Stark naked in with him. In the mood. Torchlight? The Spawn Woman eased the flap apart, peered out. Hissing swans waddled to and fro, craning and dipping their heads. The light, casting orange splashes over the silent lake.

'What is it?'

She glided to the cloak, eased it over her bare shoulders.

'They're back,' she snapped, and slipped outside.

Jakabi. Youngest captain in the entire army. Tilekin's nephew, he reminded the stragglers, hopping from one stinking boot to the other in the gloom under the trees. Tilekin the great, Tilekin the magnificent. Stormchaser, swanrider. He'd thought the old general had lost his wits, gotten himself lost when the wind howled down the Sister's Slit, when the lake wobbled and the trees sang and the swans flew in great white phalanxes over their cowering heads. Jakabi had scattered with the rest of them, holed up behind logs clutching his spear in trembling claws. Dusk, and they'd emerged like frightened field mice, scaring themselves silly as they bumped into each other under the quiet branches. Schmelker and his blockhead sons claiming they'd stood their ground, fought it out with the stream demons, hacked and jabbed at the green tornado which had spun down the gorge, sucked the warlocks away. The lads had been twitchy. Make for home or wait in the hills for the master and Mysheedi and boss Tilekin. By nightfall a couple had slunk off into the whispering, creaking trees. Get a grip on them or they'll all be gone by morning. Right. That was the night they'd heard the screams over the hill. Shrieks to fill the woods, send shivers up their hairy spines.

'What be that?'

'Echoes, innit. Echoes of our boys she's caught for her supper.' They nodded and jabbered and rolled their eyes, twitching for the trees, the rocks, a stone to crawl under. Standing around their watchfires chewing dried meat, eyeing the trees, the leafy whispering closing in on them. Jakabi had doubled the watch, toured the lines all night. Keep them on their toes all right, that screaming. Stop any more wandering off alone under the branches. Somebody had caught it hot, a straggler? Puut Ra? One night with her and a handful over her cloak. Toppled in the lake with the cold bones of all her legion lovers. They'd muttered, eyed the hills and the trees, sniffed the breeze.

'We go on and take a look.' Pale watchfires burnt down now, greying embers and gnawed bones. They followed him, muttering, scouts ahead. They'd whistled for him that afternoon, he'd run up on his belly and flopped into the mulch behind a great oak. Pointing down, down into the dell and the great green lake, fed by the whispering stream winding down the crevasse where the warlocks had disappeared. His nose twitched as he dissected the swarming odours. Pungent water and slippery weeds. Cold wet smells of frogs and tadpoles. Spawn sheen.

'It's her. The Spawn Witch,' one of the scouts breathed, hardly controlling the mad tic above his eye.

Get a grip on him or he'd be gone, start a stampede he couldn't hope to hold.

'See the swans, each end of the lake and around the island,' a younger scout called from the branches above.

'She'll have us, have it out of us and use our skins for arsewipes,' the frightened cadet muttered.

Jakabi gripped his ragged cheek between his finger and thumb, tweaked him. 'I'll do it myself if you say another word. We'll work our way around, keep our eyes open. You stay here and you wait,' he hissed into his pointed ear. The scout nodded, eyes flashing right and left. Running silently over the mouldy mulch and popping toadstools. Her enchanted woods. Jakabi had called a halt as the sun went down, been about to crawl forwards on his belly when the trees erupted with shouts and yells, furious honking and splashing. They'd frozen themselves in cover, blended with boulders or scampered up into the sentinel trees. The shouting and crowing went on, agonizing minute after agonizing minute. Another of the stragglers surprised, the wood bending its many heads to trip the lost boys with vines and grasping ivy. Jakabi cursed, slid over the mulch like a slowworm, found a vantage point on a rocky shelf on the eastern fringes of the lake. Splashing and honking, one of his goblins caught in the shallows by a phalanx of angry swans. After their eggs or a stray cygnet, no doubt. Jakabi whistled up his party, who arrived somewhat reluctantly and dropped down on to the rocky ledge beside him.

'Who is it? Schmelker? That bastard Ombuda?'

'Can't see . . . looks more like . . . Boss Tilekin,' one of the scouts whispered, squinting into the gloom.

Down below, across the lake, the lone goblin seemed to be locked in a mad dance with the swans rearing around him. Jabbing and slashing at them with his spear. Tilekin, all right. What was the old fool doing there?

'We ought to help him,' the scout suggested half-heartedly.

'Get between him and his loot?' Jakabi whispered. 'If the swans don't get him she will, she will now.' They watched as the swans retreated.

'He'll catch it now. Look, he's grabbed one of them. What's he trying to do, stuff it?'

The party chuckled and laughed into their hands, peering over their fingers at the bizarre ballet.

'If it was frozen he could skate across,' one of the scouts called.

'It'll be frozen once he gets his hard ass in it,' another called.

'Shut it, the lot of you,' Jakabi hissed. 'Who knows what she's got down there, what she can do.' He watched with the rest, watched with growing astonishment as the old general wrestled the big swan around. Plunging and rearing, beating the water with its great white wings. Pulling him over and under the water, coughing and spluttering and screaming his head off. The bird flapped forward, Jakabi swore it had been airborne before colliding into the trees. He shook his bullet head wonderingly. He looked around the rest of his command, open mouthed, drooling. The lights flashed, dimmed, flared. Now what. The witch's revenge. The lake seemed to rise up at them, rise into the trees. Water coagulating, ballooning into vast wet shapes, spilling and sliding, flowing and flopping. A hundred great watery bags suspended above the lake silt, the flapping fish and braying frogs. A slow-burning flash, a pop, and the water fell back into the empty bowl of the dell.

Jakabi stood open mouthed as the water seethed and rolled, lapping and splashing the surrounding trees. The lights flared and died. It was at least an hour before any of them had recovered their wits or voices, and then they could only mutter to their nearest neighbour, peer around the trees to see what she'd sent up for them. Jakabi flexed his fists, pinched his balls to wake himself up. Come on, they'll bolt. Any second they'll run off, gone four for ever. Cawing and crawling and bounding on their knuckles. He'd called them around, sent runners off to the others. Crawling back from the rocky ledge he'd scrambled down a red bank and squatted in the middle of sixty reluctant heroes, eyeing the escape routes through the closing trees.

'We saw Tilekin ride the swan to nothingness,' Jakabi said when he had finally secured their wandering attention. 'We saw our boss fly into the trees on the back of a bird. We saw the lake throw up its arms to take him.' He gazed around the anxious faces, sweaty, smeared with dirt. Tired and hungry and scared. Listening.

'You know as well as I do, no goblin has ever, ever had the magic on him.' Nodding heads. 'You know we followed the lady, you know we followed the old masters before her. The dark men who came and drove the Trafarnians west till there was no more west for them to go. But, brothers,' – he gazed about the staring faces – 'we have never followed our own. The boy came to us and we followed him because if he was a boy he must be magic. He must have the magic old Tarkemenis forgot he had, the magic they tried to hide from us. But last night we saw our boss ride the swan with the magic on him so strong . . .' His voice caught, he choked it back. 'We saw one of our own with the magic on him. And if it was on him, it's on us. In us, now. We can ride the swans too.' Jakabi paused, wiped the dribble from his chin. 'We'll not linger in the woods, waiting for boys to come for us, lead us out like cattle. We'll go in after Tilekin, we'll go in after her.' He pointed a trembling finger toward the dell. Silence. The goblins looked at each other, examined their claws.

'Well? Are there any here who'll ride the swans with me?'

One of the big archers at the back got to his feet, leaned on his bow. A sword boy and his brother climbed to their feet nearer the front. Before he could identify individuals the entire band had sprung to its feet, waving weapons, calling. Quietly at first. Then shouting, roaring, shrieking to the sky. Jakabi and his war band were coming.

Hap had crawled to the door as the flap came down wetly against his face. A nasty sharp arrowhead protruding through the fabric. Could give somebody a nasty cut that. Thunk plink thunk plink. All over the roof of the grubby hut. He eased the flap aside, saw the fires light the trees around the dell. Light them and fire them to the sky. Black branches on blood-red flames. She strode along the bank, turning slowly to watch the fires flicker and flare around the rocky rim of the dell. The swans were rearing and splashing, waddling along the bank craning their necks at the tangling undergrowth. Arrows were falling steadily from all directions, thudding into the woodwork or snapping harmlessly on the hard-packed earth. She strode through the arrows as if they were midges over a summer pond.

'Come on out,' she cried. 'I'm not afraid of you vermin! I'm ready for you!' Echoing around the dell, the chattering trees. The swans paddled away over the lake, a white arrowhead attracting a fresh deluge of missiles. They flapped, dived, honked and reared as the goblins swarmed over each other out of the darkness. They were clinging to logs, paddling with their broad stinking feet as they steadied themselves to fire their bows. At the front of each log a warrior clutching a shield, spear ready to throw. The swans were scattered, white feathers fluttering as the slashed shrieking birds sank into the lake in clouds of bloody bubbles. Jakabi, thighs gripping a roughly hewn log, hurled his spear at the tall figure on the island, pacing to and fro in the storm.

'Here we are! Bring on the swanriders! Up!' he shrieked, yelled to the rest paddling furiously behind. She whirled around, cloak blossoming with light. Faced him as the log ran into the silty shallows and the goblin leapt out into the lily pads tugging his dagger from his belt. She held out her hand, flexed her long dark fingers. Jakabi staggered, dropped his dagger into the lake. He clutched his hand, growling with pain and fury. He glared up at her, yelled over his shoulder. The dozen warriors who'd dropped down with him quailed, ducked and splashed in the deep mud.

'Fire! Cut her down!' Jakabi bellowed. She flexed her fingers and his mouth clamped shut on his tongue, dark blood splattering his face. He fell forward, foundering in the shallows. One of the scouts reached the bank, ducked down and hurled his javelin. It sailed through the witch's slick cloak and pierced her arm. She staggered back, glared at him. No time to challenge and shriek with half the goblins of Trafarionath emptying over the water, choking the shallows. The javelin thrower's head exploded in a flash of grey and red splinters, his limp body twitching and jumping on invisible strings. Jakabi was clawing at his mouth, spitting words past his clamped fangs.

'Ire! Ire! Cu n dn!' The goblins arriving over the lake dashed forward into the first wave, still splashing and clambering over each other, spilling the archers from the logs. Chaos. Jakabi screamed to himself in frustration, his arm and skull locked up in agony. More arrows. More spears. One of the warriors pushed forward and worked his way behind her, slashed the taut tendons behind her knees with his wickedly notched scimitar. Her legs buckled as she swung round, gutted him with a fiery finger. She crawled, bleeding, toward the hut as Hap ducked under the flap, the tablet tucked under his arm. The goblins came on, over the bank like ferocious beetles, horn-plated breastplates clamped to their chests, scrawled symbols. Long tongues lolling and eyes blazing. She flailed about, used up her spells in a rush of green and blue darts of flame. Hap glanced at her as he doubled past, caught the look of furious defiance in her blazing eyes.

'The stone! It's time!' she cried over her torn shoulder. 'Damn their magic!'

'Damn yours!' Hap watched the pale shape rise from the turbulent waters, thought for a second she'd summoned up some old man from the deep. The goblins shrank back, suddenly silent, their crude canoes tipping this way and that on the wavelets. She raised her arm slowly, as if she was unsure whether to glare at the apparition or shield her face. Hap ducked down, recognized the watery shape from old Will's room, the watery shape looming up over their crowded pond. He hadn't touched it, the stone. Not this time. Maybe the old man had his own stones, had his own streams now. Free to roam and pop up where he liked. The Spawn Queen certainly seemed to think so, at bay on the arrow-tufted bank. She leaned back on her haunches as the old man raised his hands, balled his fists.

'I know what you're planning, Amiarillin,' he called over the cowering goblins' backs. 'And I know what you've done.'

'You can't stop me now, you miserable old swindler. I don't need you to stoke my fires!'

'But you know what happened to your sister. You know . . .'

'I know what happened, Tarkemenis of Peresh.'

The goblins looked from the shimmering apparition to the crippled woman in astonishment, hounds beaten to the kill. She glared at them, clicked her fingers as if releasing them from their spell. Before the old man could say any more they shrieked through him, charged through his shadow as if they were capering in a fountain. An eruption of shouts and screams rushed in on her, a raging tornado from the depths of the lake, tearing at her cloak, lashing her flat on the slippery bank. Hap fell sideways against the hut, rolled behind the cracking snapping wickerwork. She elbowed herself up, black hair pulled back from her clenched features, the boiling green eyes popping in some furious contest of wills with the fading, flaring vision. Strove against him. The old-man shape exploded into glittering droplets, fell down over the frantic goblins splashing in the shallows. Hap leapt to his feet, ducked out of the doorway as she was knocked backwards by reeking boots, speared and slashed as the goblins swarmed through the squall, hurried up and over the bank with redoubled fury as if inspired by the warlock shapeshifter, the shade which had gone before them like a tatty campaign colour. She clung to the bloody spear points, wild eyed, saw Hap scuttling off into the undergrowth, arrows snapping at his heels. The big spear boy ducked under her grasping hands, held her down with his boot and ran his broad blade into her throat. She collapsed as the goblin held the dripping scimitar to his mouth, ran his dark tongue over the slippery blade. Hap stumbled over the decapitated scout, tumbled into the lake. A dozen others swarming, wading for him, knives ready. They leapt for him, unstoppable, stabbing and throttling. Dragged him to the bank and rolled him out, stepped back muttering. An immense carp, opening and closing its mouth. Fins and scales slashed by their sharp blades.

SUNDAY

TOR ORDERS

Detective Sergeant Colin McNair watched his governor turn his small gold cigarette lighter over and under his hairy fingers. You would have imagined they would have cottoned on. You would have expected the punters to recognize the frustration they were causing. Shorting out all his patience circuits. Blowing his reasonable-persuasion fuse. Detective Chief Inspector Matt Macall blew a column of blue smoke toward the faded ceiling tiles.

'Come on, Theo.' Measured, precise. But not for long. 'We know you know the old geezer in the truck. The same party, you two would have scratched each other's eyes out.' The suspect was sitting straight in his chair, stiffly formal in his hippie robes. Funny combination. Standard-issue convoy smugglers slouched over the desk as if they had Silly-Putty spines. Not quite right. He'd refused a smoke, watched with interest as the officers had lit up. Acting dumb but looking alert. Another annoying combination. Bound to get up any investigating officer's nose, that. A right smartass. McNair had mentioned it to his boss before they'd gone into the interview room at Budgworth CID.

'He's been knocked about enough already,' Macall had chuckled.

'So who'll notice a little more?'

'Remind me to mention your initiative the next time your promotion comes up,' he'd snapped. Bad mood all morning, Sunday overtime and all. Macall flipped the files open. Glossy five by sevens of the funny guy in the robes in the back of the juggernaut, the fat guy under the tarpaulin in the shed behind the old people's home. They'd dug him out while searching for the old guy. Haberfield. Still missing. McNair's money was on the stream. Bloody bodies they'd fished out of that. Place was a regular slaughterhouse. The bodies had been found less than a mile away from each other the previous day. This Theo Malik character had been found unconscious at the home, woken up started asking witnesses if they'd seen his uncle. The other two suspects, the boy and girl, had scarpered before they'd arrived to find that reporter feller shouting and bawling into the phone.

'Of course I called them first. I told you, they locked Molly in a bedroom! Yes, that Molly.'

Hadn't been too happy about finding his missus with the hippie either. Don't blame him. Good-looking bloke, long red hair, bright eyes, chiselled cheekbones and all that palaver. McNair figured he would have clocked him one too, worried about it later.

'Got him bang to rights. Some kind of drugs scam went wrong,' McNair had theorized. 'The four of them are on their way down to Glastonbury loaded with smack. Two mainstreamers and the couple of kids as runners. The fat guy bumps into them by accident, they bump him off and fall out over it. Textbook case.'

Macall wasn't so sure. The Theo character was either colossally stupid or a complete iceberg. He'd barely twitched when they'd shown him the pictures of the old guy. Barely. His eyes had given him away. The tiny, almost imperceptible intake of breath. He hadn't moved a muscle when they'd shown him the picture of Grainger. Either he'd managed to get a grip on his facial expressions or he didn't known the fat guy from Adam.

CHANGELING HEARTS

Way he handled the pictures, ran his finger over the prints then looked as if he was expecting it to come away wet or something. Still warm. Their bodies had been. Macall sighed to himself. And then the truck. Double locked, keys under the dash in a little hidey-hole the driver had been forced to explain three times before the translator had gotten what he was on about. He'd not exactly hidden it under the mat.

'I guess the last time you saw the old guy he had two legs. Am I right?'

Another involuntary twitch.

'So where is it?'

'Where's what?'

'The old guy's leg,' slowly.

'Could be anywhere,' Theo Malik said simply.

'Okey-doke.' Macall pulled the plastic bag across the table, weighed the lump of coal in his hand.

'This mean anything to you?'

'Bit of stone.'

Macall pushed the bag toward him, stubbed his cigarette into the overflowing ashtray, kid's eyes on him all the time.

'We pulled it out of a beam in the room where you were found. Maybe you were practising your pitching technique?'

'My what technique? Pitching?'

'As in baseball. You know.'

Theo clammed up again, shrugged.

Macall weaved the lighter through his fingers, faster now. 'OK then. So you don't know anything about the murders. Maybe these guys cut themselves shaving or something. You're in the clear. So what about the home. How did you get to be lying in that bedroom?'

'I was looking for my uncle.'

'Your uncle . . . what, him?' Macall held up the photo.

The youth paused, nodded. 'That's him.'

'Right. OK. So what's your uncle's name?'

'He's not my real uncle. I just call him uncle.'

'And his name is?'

'I call him Tark. Tarky.'

'Tark? What kind of a name is that? Uncle Tark!' Macall snorted.

'Short for Tarkus, sir. Album by Emerson Lake and Palmer. D'you remember it? Early seventies pomp rockers.' McNair interrupted helpfully. 'Probably called himself after it. You know what they're like.'

These people. Travellers. New Age Wanderers. Crystal Maizeheads. Kind of prats who marched round cornfields stamping out their star signs. Macall looked up doubtfully.

'So, Uncle Tarky, the last time you saw him was when?'

Theo closed his eyes. 'The day before yesterday.'

'Friday. Where?'

'Near the lake.'

'The lake. The Axehead Reservoir?'

'I preferred it as a lake.'

Macall narrowed his eyes. 'The reservoir was opened in 1958. You maybe remember it as it was? Previous-life experience? Something like that?'

'Something very much like that.'

'Listen, son. You don't seem stupid to me. You seem to understand the question, so what I would like to know is WHAT THE FUCK YOU THINK YOU'RE PLAYING AT?' Macall bawled, jumping halfway out of his seat. The table vibrated. McNair stood back, swallowed. Theo gazed back unconcernedly. Guy had balls, he'd give him that.

'Look, I've told you I know him.' Pointing to the

truck picture. 'But I don't know him.' Pointing to the tarpaulin. 'And I don't think I can help you any further.'

Macall strode through the closely packed desks in the incident room, paused by the fax machine to run his chubby finger over a pile of grubby copies. 'Still nothing?' he snapped.

The pretty blonde WPC raised her eyebrows.

'We've been all over. Margate to Manchester. Interpol hasn't got anything either.'

'Well, check again. They got down there somehow. This Tark geezer, that's got to be some kind of handle, a callsign. Check it out. What's Dover got to say?'

'Logged and inspected. Cattle-feed additives. Puts lead in bulls' pencils.'

'So they must be hitchers. He picked them up coming down the M4. Somewhere before the bridge Theo gets out and walks, leaving his uncle to bleed to death in the back.' Macall lit another cigarette. McNair was thumbing through a computer printout listing missing persons.

'And no mention of chummy in the car. Where does he fit in? How come he had his parents in tow if he was in on a drugs job?'

'Perfect cover,' Macall suggested.

'And the girl . . . she's based herself in the town what, a couple of months?'

'Yeah, his friend. She's just moved back from college, we're checking it out. Funny the truck should be following them just before the crash, though. I tell you, it's all there in front of us, it's just making the connections.'

'The girl's got no previous. According to the uncle she said she was going to visit a friend. Bus driver remembers her crying, the boy laughing, acting like a big kid. Dropped them off . . .'

'Here, where they haven't been seen since. Why here?'

'His little brother, we thought. Maybe he had a pang of conscience. The boy was released from hospital yesterday, being looked after by an aunt in . . . let's see . . . Rookton. We've got a car outside keeping an eye on things. Long shot, though.'

'Long shots are all we've got at the moment, Sergeant. Where's the . . . shit. Did you pick up the stone thing?'

'I thought you had it.'

'I did. I . . . I must have put it down when I . . . must have left it on the desk. Better run and fetch it Col, we don't want him destroying the evidence.'

He'd endured a quarter of an hour of *Songs of Praise* with the sound off. Sure, the hymns were coming through loud and clear but Molly hadn't said a word since he'd returned from the pub at lunchtime. He toyed with the remote, aimed it at her head as she stared at the screen.

'What are you doing?' she asked flatly.

'Changing your channel. Seeing if I can tune in a smile or something. Oh sure, that's a smile.' Sort of sour grimace you saw strippers slap on their kissers. 'Come on, Moll. What's the matter? I said I was sorry for lunch. You know how Wilf goes on and it's not as if we haven't got things to talk about, all that's happened.'

'All that's happened? I'll tell you what's happened,' she snapped, perking up a little. 'I've been scared shitless, locked in a room by a couple of maniacs, my boss has been brutally murdered and I've lost my fucking job. What's Wilf think about that?'

Nicky paled, fiddled with the remote. Wished it could transfer him out of there.

'The police arrive and I tell them. I found the guy in the bedroom, out cold. The money's missing from the cash box but they don't find any of it on him. This Jonathan's done a bunk with that Mags and yet they still insist on carting Theo off to Budgworth.'

Theo, is it? 'They had to cover all the angles, Moll,' Nicky wheedled. 'The bloke's wearing . . .'

'He's a hippie. A traveller. He told me himself. As far as the cops are concerned that means psychotic serial killer, of course.'

'Well, it looked a bit suspicious. Turning up like that with all the other shit going on. You trying to tell me he wasn't involved? In any way?' Nicky picked up the ball, kicked it in her face. Silly cow had had a face like a fiddle all weekend, giving him the sulks as if it had been his fault. PMT, he supposed, hadn't been near enough to find out and if you asked . . . if you asked! 'What sort of shithead man-question is that? Of course I'm not on!'

Good Christ, he'd been the one breaking his ass getting to the home. He'd been dead worried about her, got to help as soon as he could. Waited with her as the cops arrived, searched the grounds. A shoulder to cry on when they'd dragged the logs from Grainger, stood back shaking their heads.

'Maybe you're still miffed I interrupted your little tête-à-tête with him,' he snarled, getting to his feet and walking to the kitchen. Molly sat stony faced, swinging her foot. Light blue touch paper and retire. Do not return to a firework if it fails to go off. Nicky watched her from the kitchen.

'Of course, you know he's guilty. He's a hippie, he wears funny robes instead of button-down shirts. Must be a menace to society.'

'Thinking of joining up with the next convoy, are we?' Fish asked archly.

'They're all villains, obviously. Might as well throw the bloody book at them.'

Fish poked his head out of the kitchen. 'Damn right. It's about time we got a grip on the lot of them, running around in their clapped-out trucks from one bloody Giro to another.' He drew a breath, held the lager can to his overheating forehead.

'Look. I know it's been a shock, it's been a shock for me too, remember. Just because they've moved the old folk out, it doesn't mean . . .'

'It does mean just that. And they haven't moved *all* the old folk out. Hap's still missing. I was in charge.'

'Grainger was in charge.'

'Grainger was bloody dead. What the hell they have to go and kill him for? What did he know?'

'You can't blame yourself about Hap. Who knows what he was thinking? Maybe they'll keep you on anyway,' he blundered on.

'Klein was down on Friday talking about the closure. All this has done is bring everything forward six months. Face it, Nicky, I'm out of a job.'

'You and three million others. We'll manage.'

'Huh!'

'What's that supposed to mean? I've got a hundred quid overtime this week already, everything that's happened.'

'So as long as we get two deaths, a murder, a suicide and a couple of missing persons every seven days we'll do all right, will we?' she yelled out, muscles in her throat contracting.

'Oh fuck off.' Nicky ripped the tab on the can, spilled the cold bubbles into his mouth.

Molly got up, fetched her coat from the stand. 'I'm going out.'

'Don't hurry back, give me time to defrost the atmosphere.'

She slammed the door.

'Molly.' Fish wandered to the door, peered through the glass panel. Molly was climbing into the Cortina, fumbling for her keys. He should have never allowed her to learn. Give 'em their own transport, they wanted the bloody world.

Jonathan wandered down the ward peering down the crumpled sheets at the sleeping children. Some were wired up to drips, others were propped up on three pillows, tubes taped to their cheeks. One parent who hadn't dragged himself away had fallen asleep in the chair, head tilted back against the wall, still holding his daughter's white hand, the little plastic nametag dull in the twilight. The next bed a boy boxed in some kind of metal contraption, lying out still and cold with a blanket over the metal frame. He paused, looked down the bed at his pasty face. He'd swap too, wouldn't he, given the chance? If they told him he had to stay like it for ever, he'd have gone over. He'd have changed places. Wouldn't have hung around, wasting away on his funny frame. He'd have taken what he could, got out while he could still walk properly. The boy stirred, opened an eye. Stuffy air sucked from the over-heated ward, chill darkness. Treading water in the stream, the red box upside-down, the terrified face looking out at him, flat hands white on the glass.

'Jason? Where's Mum?' the boy croaked. Jonathan fidgeted, went to walk away.

'Can I help you? You've missed visiting time.'

He jumped, looked round at the red-headed nurse in

the stiff purple uniform, two light blue lines round her white cap. Jonathan shook his head.

'I asked on the desk. They said you had my little brother in here. Walter Haberfield is his name.'

The nurse thought a moment, smiled.

'Sorry. I thought you were somebody else. You've missed him. He went home with your aunt. Susan? Steph. Aunt Steph. You must be . . .'

'Jonathan.'

'Ah. They were looking for you, weren't they?'

'They found me.'

'Ah. So it seems. Look, you wait here and I'll get somebody to have a look at you if you like. Did somebody bring you here?'

Peculiar look. Short smile.

'They're waiting in the front.'

'Let me just . . .' Her hair was darker at the roots and didn't match her eyebrows. Big brown eyes, a mole on the side of her nose. Trace of what was it? Lipstick. Lipstick. He reached out, pressed his index finger on her lower lip. She jerked back quickly, looked at him quizzically.

'What's your game, eh?'

'I've got to go now.' Nervous. She frowned, watched him saunter back down the ward the way he had come. Blinked, picked up the receiver on her desk.

'Mellie? Look, there's a kid, there's a kid in the ward.'

The girl on the switchboard whistled.

'Go on. A kid on the ward. You all right, Stell? Still with us?'

'Yes. Mellie. Look, he's on his way down.'

'Who? Dr Kildare?'

'The boy.'

'What boy? Look, Stella. Get a grip, it's only seven thirty.'

*

Tilekin elbowed himself up so he could see up and down the ward, flicking his good eye over the half-dozen or so beds. The people in white had taken away the pipes and tubes and strapped him into some kind of linen breastplate so he couldn't move his head. The old fool in the bed opposite was peering over at him, nodding.

'How are you today then, Skip?' He was as old as anything, his slack skin hung from his face like the folds on a lizard's belly. He would laugh and wave at the people in white as if he didn't know they'd brought him here to die. Why didn't they just knock him over the head and have done with it? Groaning and sighing in his sleep like that, or was it him? He tried hard to remember. They'd taken him from the rumble wagon and stretchered him to the smaller death place, fitted him up with the padded collar before he could get his claws round any of their scrawny pink necks. Just wait. They'd kept him waiting, tested his limbs one by one.

'Can you feel this? And this?' Tilekin had glared at them, throttled his throat trying to find the words but found none. He'd managed to hook his good hand under the covers and lift them sufficiently to peer underneath. One horrible white foot with long white toes splayed to the right, a heavy bandage wrapped over the stump a little below his left knee. Now he'd have to learn to walk all over again, learn to walk before he could do anything any more. He slumped back on the pillow, felt the bones in his neck grate, gasped.

'All right there, matey? D'you want me to call the nurse?' The old fellow opposite, peering over again. Get his dagger and he'd cut some bloody squints the other side of his wrinkled bumface, the bastarding scum sucker of a pig-featured fart fucker.

'Hello, you're a popular bloke all of a sudden. Visitors.'

Tilekin glanced sideways down the ward. A big man in a white coat, gaggle of smaller males and females following him around like goslings. Like cygnets. Tilekin remembered his death ride on the back of that sad-sack swan, sniggered. What a way to go. His boys would have sung him a few verses for that. He'd slipped along, above the rushing water as if he'd turned into the bird. Flying down the water with his feet flapping, windmilling arms caught up in the whirlpool which had whisked and sucked him out of Trafarionath and blew him down into the earth. Darkness closing about his head, rocks pressing in on him, scratching, bumping him. Pummelling and hurling him from one jagged outcrop to another. What a way to go. Only he hadn't gone, had he? Not all the way. He'd flown out of his shell and down the chamber, the ghost alley jammed with pale pigging human shades, blown them away on his foul breath, spiderwebs with dewy eyes. Suicides.

'You fucking jumped, you lousy scabs, what are you looking so fucking humped about, eh?' he'd challenged them as they fled, shrinking back up and down the rocky chasms like haze over a pond. And then the dead fish he'd found in the shallows, this broken-spined sack of shit he'd inherited. Tilekin lay still, held his breath as the live ones closed in on him.

'Is this him?'

'They said bed five.'

'Mr Miller?'

He could feel the human's tired breath on his eyelid, about the only part of his face the people in white hadn't smothered with bandages. Tilekin was no stranger to torture – he'd extracted information from the hardest woodlanders, confessions from thieves and deserters and barking drooling four leggers – but he'd never stooped to methods like this. Tiny knives no bigger than a sharpened quill, beams of light shone into the eyes. He'd never tried that. They cleaned you to death, wiped and poked, smeared and prodded. They lit the place up so bright they burned his eyes. They encased his bones and strapped his neck and bottled his dark blood, ran his amber urine into a funny smooth sack. Maybe they had something in mind for that as well, way the females carted it away like it was the finest Febalio wine. He hurt all over, sometimes it was like fists thumping his skull inside his head. He hurt and they watched and waited and hovered over his bed like vultures. Tilekin hadn't figured what they wanted, unless they knew he'd come over. Perhaps they wanted to know about the other side, about Trafarionath and the Spawn Witch and the bridge by the cliff. He couldn't tell them even if he'd understood all their babble.

'Mother!' He hadn't called for her since he'd been a pup, one of six the stinking old crone had borne to his blind sire. He called for her now. He clenched his chest and coughed her name, spat the word across the clean white of the prison.

'What did he say? Courier?'

'I . . . didn't catch it. Sorry.'

Tilekin opened his eye. The enormous smooth pink face pressed down over him, red mouth moving wetly, watery eyes widening. He worked his jaw, trying to dislocate it far enough to bite the stinking creature's head off. The muscles were smashed beyond hope, all he could manage was a deathly grimace. He glared furiously instead.

'John? It's Doctor Klein. How are you feeling today, any better?'

'Get your stinking carcass out of my sight, you pus bladder,' Tilekin moaned, clamping his eyes tight and clenching his remaining fist. Speaking slowly, shaping the words from the rasping bile stuffed full of broken glass that seemed to have clogged his throat. The man leaned closer, smiled weakly.

'Sorry, I didn't catch that.' He mumbled something in the white-people talk.

'I think he's delirious,' he said over his shoulder. 'Didn't sound like English to me,' he mused. 'Did you catch it?' The man looked enquiringly around the crowd around the bed.

'Babbling in tongues. Chapter three,' the doctor joked, leaned closer.

'We're going to get you up to X-ray, have another look at your internal injuries. All right?' He stood back as the shifty porters moved in. Pain came at Tilekin in multicoloured legions, pouring over hills of his bones armed to the teeth with stinging sharp spears. The lights swirled overhead, arms reaching this way and that. Down the ward past the vulture-necked old prisoner, down the passage to a metal box which opened a massive mouth to swallow him and the people in white whole. What hell was this? A great square pot to boil the flesh from his bones? Tilekin gritted his fangs, sat up to stare at the thin human lounging in the corner. Holding his thin human hand to his thin human face to flick his hair out of his eyes. To flick his hair and flick his head on his skinny shoulders. Realization, then recognition came seeping along the clogged culverts of his mind. He turned the memory over in the tinkling sparkling waters. Smiled crookedly.

'Master?'

'What he say? Isn't this the one gave Dave that fright the other night?'

'Puut Ra? You rode the vulture too!' Tilekin gasped.

The porter shook his head. 'What's he on about? Poor old bugger. I don't know why they're bothering to keep him ticking over. X-ray, pathology more like. No offence.'

'He seems to know you anyway, mate.'

The thin youth cowered back against the cold steel wombwalls of the lift, smiled weakly. 'I've never seen it before in my life,' he said shakily.

Tilekin lurched forward, the porters trying to hold him back without hurting him. Tubes popped, bandages flowered with bright blood. Streaming from his mouth, his smashed eyeball.

'Fucking hell. Get him back, Stan.'

'Keep him off!' The boy, scrambling away from him, ripping the ashtray from the steel panelling in panic.

'You rode the swan too! Puut Ra, we brought you home, just like you wanted! Puut Ra, here too!' he cackled, grasping for him with his big human hand.

'Putrid? It'll bloody fall off, much more of this! Del, get a grip of his leg before he has us all over.'

'Careful of his chest. Jesus, ring the bell!' The porter turned to the youth, pointed to the flickering buttons on the control panel.

'Hit the emergency button, he's pulled all his tubes out!'

The youth squeezed away from the stretcher, the struggling porters and their grisly passenger, groping for him with bloody hand. The lift groaned to a halt, doors slid open. Shocked nurses and patients milling round the reception. Jonathan dashed out spinning one of the porters to the floor. Stan made a grab for the handles as the trolley crashed into the lift door, tipping the bloody bandaged bundle to the floor. Screaming. Tilekin lay still for a second, bright lights bouncing off the shiny metal walls. Screaming and coughing raggedly as he tried to prop himself up on his blood-splattered stumps. He turned his head to one side, saw the lift doors heave shut, closing massive jaws of steel around his battered head. He'd seen them coming, looming out of the fiery flaring mists on the edges of his vision. Tilekin had always had a hard head. The boys had joked about it, told tall tales around the campfires. Better than any helmet, a good thick skull, and old Tilekin's thicker than most! He'd had his share of wounds and scars. The battle by the bridge with Pizog's lot. He'd wondered where the light had gone that time the arrow had hit him above the eye. Groping for the broken shaft to work the bloody barb free. Ha! Kill me with your arrows? That swan, flapping and honking as it tried to gain height. I'm riding you, you feathery pig! I'm stuck . . .

But it wasn't Tilekin's skull the lift doors clamped. John Miller. That was the man. Fracture lines zooming over and around his skull, the doctors barely believing their own eyes as they stood holding his smudgy X-rays up to the light. He's alive? Alive inside this? Not any more. Stan tugged the doors open with his bloody hands, crying and blubbering as he forced the steel shutters apart. Meshed with blood and splintered bone. Tilekin kicked John Miller's last foot one last time and lay still. What they couldn't figure, when they'd gotten the crowd back and fished his body away from the splattered walls, what they couldn't figure was the smile. Bastard's knocked to pieces, lost half his limbs and a third of his internal organs. Half his face hanging off the other side hanging on some outcrop somewhere, crow food. Smiling up at the bright lights bouncing around the jammed lift. What a way to go.

MOVEMENTS

'Heard you had some trouble with a prisoner,' Dan Gillings chuckled, rolling up his sleeve as he passed the slim file over his desk to Macall. Sergeant McNair stood a little behind his boss, frantically signalling with his hands. Gillings ignored him, carried on regardless.

'Did he bend the bars or did you forget to lock the door?'

McNair frowned. 'He must have been carrying something, we must have overlooked it.'

'And he scarpered? From Budgworth CID. Tut tut.'

Macall eyed him. 'We had him, we lost him, we'll find him. You want to waste any more of my time?'

Gillings had been principal police pathologist for long enough to know exactly how far to go with the arrogant DCI and long enough to know exactly when to stop, get down to facts. He shook his head.

'Well, his funny uncle was carrying something as well.' He tossed the plastic zipper bag to McNair, who held it up against the light, squinted in at the dirty bracelet.

'Carrying them in his bowel. Not the first place you'd have looked.'

McNair put the bag on the table, wiped his fingers.

'We washed 'em just for you,' Gillings said mirthlessly.

Macall peered at them. 'Lozenges? What is it, cannabis?'

'Way off. Some kind of charm bracelet. Charming place to keep it, there you are.'

'What's the writing? Egyptian?'

'Jilly up at the Uni's taking a look for us. Nobody in this department has seen anything like it. Twelve tablets, each about one centimetre by two. Leather thong through the lot. Quite uncomfortable. Reminds me of a story about the nurse who knotted—'

Macall looked up. 'I heard it already. Why'd he have it up his arse?'

Gillings raised his eyebrows. 'Clashed with his robes, who knows?'

Macall blinked slowly. 'And what about the leg?' he asked, patience wearing thinner every moment.

'Nasty that. No sign of any blade. The skin and tissues are torn rather than cut. I'd say somebody pulled it off.'

'That's what you say here?' Macall tapped the slim report.

'The wound's as ragged as you could get. Bled to death in a little over twelve minutes. Time of death, difficult, but say Friday night. Something like that.'

'Drugs, chemicals, conditions?'

'He wasn't a big man. Looked like he hadn't had a good meal in a while. Stomach contents some kind of bread, meat. No sign of any kind of drug. Not a trace.'

'Hippie. Some kind of recluse, back to nature guy.'

'Nature? Red in tooth and claw. He's welcome to it.'

McNair growled. Gillings looked at the officers expectantly. Macall sighed.

'What else?' he asked flatly.

Gillings grinned, took a second file from his drawer. 'I thought you'd never ask. Grainger. The manager.'

'So?'

'You wanted a cause of death. You'll have to keep looking.'

'Spit it out, for God's sake.'

'That's what he was doing. Spitting things out. His liver for instance.'

Macall studied the file cover-notes. 'One entry wound? For all this?'

'I've never seen anything remotely like it. The cutting edge must have been moving. Somebody must have shoved it around . . . with incredible force.' Gillings, for once, short of wisecracks.

'Drill?'

'If you could fix one to some kind of flexible rod, perhaps. The cutting edge is actually . . .' He shook his head.

'What?'

'Nearest thing I've seen, a tooth. Something large as well. Big cat, maybe a shark.'

McNair chuckled. 'Are you kidding us or what?'

'I'm not kidding, Sergeant. Three-sided cutting edge. Like a Bowie knife, but there's evidence of minute serrations as well. Consistent with a shark tooth.'

'He was bitten to death?' McNair snorted.

'No. Just the one tooth. All the marks are the same, and there was only one puncture wound,' the pathologist repeated.

Macall shook his head, weaving his lighter through his fingers. 'What're you saying, we're looking for a fucking gap-toothed Great White with a chainsaw on the end of an ice-pick?'

'Told you you'd have to keep looking,' Gillings said.

Molly leaned over the passenger door and flicked the lock. Teomalik looked down the busy street, climbed in.

'How did you do it? How did you get out? You haven't hurt anybody else?' she asked anxiously.

He shook his head, pulled the stone from his robe, passed it from one hand to the other as if it was still warm.

'I used to play with it when I was young, didn't do anything. Streaming must have invigorated it, I don't know.' He raised his bushy eyebrows, tucked the stone somewhere in his baggy shirt. Have to get him some new threads for a start, going round like that.

'Streaming?'

'Like I told you at the home,' quiet, curt. 'Or did you think I'd made the whole thing up?'

Way she was hurting she knew damn well she hadn't dreamt anything. He glanced away, nervously, guiltily. Streaming. Hang on, don't tell me. Slipstreaming. Going between. Between the worlds, between the sheets. Yes, he'd explained it all, those three hours stuck in the jumbled bedroom. She'd been rolling her eyes, just beginning to believe him when Nicky had come shouting up the stairs three at a time, punched him on the nose for his troubles. Nicky. Sitting at home getting plastered, she supposed. Thing that bothered her, if she hadn't believed it, what was she doing here with him now? She pulled out into the traffic, peered into the mirror.

'What did you do, hypnotize me?' Teomalik grinned weakly. Goddamn Cheshire cat they send over. What was he anyway, a courier, a carrier? The worrying warrior. She glared at him, cut the small talk: 'And what about that thing? That thing you stuck in me?'

Teomalik bit his lip, awkward. 'I told you, I didn't realize . . . hadn't realized I was carrying it. She must have stuck me . . . stuck me before I came over.'

'Why? What is it, what'll it do?'

'I don't really know.'

'Jesus,' she sighed, eyed him squatting alongside her in the juddering Cortina. Shook her head slowly. Much more of this shit it was going to fall right off, roll into his lap. Again. Umm. If only he'd not started on her with his big eyes and boyish grin and bruised bloody vulnerability. If only she'd not started, she reminded herself tartly, started picking at the leather thongs holding his top together. It was no use going over it again; maybe like he said, it would work itself out.

Bit of charm bracelet, was all. Bit of enamel stuck inside me, what the hell. Funny, she knew she should be worrying, rushing to the nearest hospital to have it cut out, have him locked up while she was at it. The charm must have been smeared in Mogadon to keep her as calm and collected and believing as this. A little voice in her head soothing her down, telling her it would be all right, everything would be all right.

'It came from her necklace. I . . . I don't really know. Maybe it'll work itself out, like it did with me,' he repeated.

'All I've got to do is think of something to tell Nicky,' she said. ' "I didn't know you'd had your appendix out," ' Molly mimicked horribly. 'Do I have to tell you everything I do on my afternoons off?'

Teomalik smiled nervously, swallowed. They drove in silence for a while. Listening to him you would have imagined they'd been playing pass the parcel up in that damned room. A sexually transmitted tooth-totem, an interuterine icon. Seductive sedatives, what next?

'OK, then. What did you do, how did you get me up here?' Apart from the obvious, er, excuse me, but would you mind seeing your way clear to getting this fucking tingling thing out of me, right now, buster. She'd thought she'd been imagining it, some kind of funny sensation in her stomach like Nicky thrusting his tongue into her belly button. All those nerve circuits, an erogenous Underground, lines and lights splitting off into the distance, fuzzy faces. Connecting her up inside. Maybe the tooth-necklace thing had cut some of the wires, loosened her connections. She wasn't making any sense, she knew that. After the tingling, the half-expectant orgasm that had rushed up and bucked her, and with it, cloaked and daggered, the hurt. Hurt like a knife. By the time she'd scissored herself away from him, a single bright runnel of blood trickling from the tiny cut to her dark pubis. She felt her face flush, swallowed and concentrated on the road. Say something, say anything.

'You were the first, actually.' Hah, he wasn't kidding about that. 'A suggestion word. I whispered it to you as they were leading me away. I pictured you, sitting at home, suggested the word and you did it.'

'Came up and rescued you. What was the word? Abracadabra?'

He giggled. 'Honey. I thought of you, I thought, honey.'

She glanced at him, glanced back to the road. He could picture her sitting at home and tear her away from it with a word. One word? Fucking pushover she was, leaving his mark in her like the fuzzy numbers the farmers sprayed on the sheep at Clove market.

'But I can think OK. Didn't feel much like a zombie,' she insisted. 'I had some arsehole driving up my exhaust halfway up here. I stopped, got some drink.' She nodded to the plastic bag at his feet. He reached down, selected a carton of orange juice. Thought about it for a minute, rattled it experimentally then ripped the top off, took a good swig.

'What did you expect, cross eyes, moaning?'

'I've seen people go under before. Staring, sleepwalking, whatever you want to call it. I knew you'd called me but I . . . I knew I didn't have to . . .' She sighed.

'But you did. That's why it works see, suggestion.'

'Honey.'

'That's it. Honey, come and get me.'

'And here I am,' she said archly.

Teomalik took another drink, watched the crowds moving on the cramped pavements, the bright stores splashing them with gaudy colours.

'So what happens now. D'you go back . . . back to the other place?' Never mind that shit, what about the tooth? The tooth-tab belly ring-pull shooting ideas into her head, switching on the illuminations up and down the seafronts of her mind.

'Saying it won't harm you, you know. Go on.'

'Trafarionath.' She spelt it slowly.

He wagged his finger. 'Right first time.'

'*Land of the Three Rivers.*'

He glanced around sharply. 'I never told you that. Who told you that?'

She frowned, shook her head. 'You must have done. What's wrong?'

'I . . . nothing.' He sat back in the seat, went on slowly. 'Old Trafarionath, where it all started. When my uncle's ancestors ran the power through the land, lit the corners of every cave to chase the bloody goblins out.'

'Goblins. Oh yes. And not just goblins,' she said, matter of factly.

Teomalik studied her for a moment. 'Are you all right? Are you . . .'

'Of course I'm not all right. You've left your bloody calling card in me, remember?' she snapped back, drumming her long fingers on the wheel.

He bit his lip. 'It's just . . . that was a funny sort of thing to say.'

'So sorry.' She smiled ironically.

He waited for a moment, continued. 'With the power running in the land, in skanes, we called them, we ruled all the world. The warlock order used the power to charge their spells, energize weapons our enemies hadn't even dreamed of. Then they... we... tried to... we over-reached ourselves. No more power. The skanes dimmed, left the warlock order and our armies high and dry, thousands of miles from our homes. They threw us out, all the conquered nations. Rose up, threw us back to our original borders. Then they invaded Trafarionath itself. Morigilim the Lame in a litter made from the bones of our barons. We held them off, outnumbered hundreds to one. The last battle, by the sea, the end of it.' He sighed. ' "The Hallowed Halls of all our heroes, we dig determined here beneath",' he recited. 'That was one of Uncle's epigrams. He wasn't always... like he ended up. He was quite a wit in his day.' Teomalik shook his head, went on. 'They kicked us out of everywhere, but it's still Trafarionath. To us and to them.'

Molly stared at him, traffic snarled around a city-centre roundabout.

'And they were keeping you prisoner? Before you escaped?'

He smirked, pulled at his nose. 'We didn't exactly escape. I'm not sure what happened. This is the last place I wanted to end up anyway.'

She caught his eye, held it for a second.

'I mean... I meant to say...'

She shrugged, studied the road. 'The stones brought you here. This Puut Ra found them?'

He shook his head, little boy lost. 'He never touched the tablet. He must have heard something, had some idea where we'd hidden the heirlooms, that's why he'd dragged us along.' Teomalik gazed at his hands. 'I didn't recognize the place at all. I would have tried something, you know, distracted them. We walked right into it, into the stream, the place we'd hidden the Grimoire.'

'Grim what?'

'Grimoire. Book of spells. The tablet I told you about. Uncle must have thought . . . I don't know. He wasn't right, here.' He tapped his thick red braids. 'They'd hurt him so much, you know, tortured him. He started prancing about, I still didn't get it. He kicked the chest open, right in front of them. By the time I'd registered what was happening it was too late. The spell had been made, she'd . . . here I am.'

Molly frowned. 'But if you didn't make the spell . . .'

'Somebody here. Over here, I mean. They helped make the spell and summon us. They must have had stones like ours, locked in on them, bridged the breach between our world and yours.'

Molly drove on, frowning. If she was going to believe any of it she would have to believe all of it. The breach between the worlds. The breach he would have to seal to save them. Christ, he hadn't exactly cut the mustard yet, this fucking Saviour of theirs. Mission Improbable.

'How could anybody here have had your stones?' she asked.

'No idea. But it must have had something to do with the old place, the home.'

'Why?'

'Because that's where I ended up. The stones made the spell, locked on to the tablet in the stream and brought me over as well.'

'And your uncle? He wasn't at the home?' She nodded at him, waited. 'What happened to him? Your uncle?'

He turned away, steamed the window as he breathed. 'He's dead. The wagon people showed me pictures of him.'

Molly breathed hard, forced herself to concentrate.

'It was her fault, she wouldn't let him go. She set a

spell to keep him there and he was . . . torn. Torn in half. They showed me pictures.'

Pictures? 'She? I thought you said Puut Ra was . . .'

'Puut Ra wasn't the only power in Trafarionath,' he growled, slumped back in the worn vinyl seat. 'I'll tell you sometime.'

'You'd better tell me now, all of it, or you can get out and walk. Honey or no.'

'You . . .'

'I didn't have to come. I could hear you in my head, I could hear voices, but I knew there was a part of me left that could have said no. D'you know what I mean?' Changing the subject, giving him a break. She could see the tears welling in his eyes, the way he pulled at the door lever as if he was going to bale out any moment. He nodded, looked glumly at the honking cars, waving arms. The pedestrians threading their way through the streets. Frowned at the blaring horns, a wailing car alarm.

'I could have used a stronger suggestion. I have spells for every occasion,' he said. Smile hopelessly artificial.

'You began to tell me. Tell me now.'

He took another drink, wiped his mouth.

'My uncle, Tarkemenis, was a powerlord as well as a poet. Quite a good one in his day. He belonged to the ancient order which had ruled Trafarionath, he could trace his family back to the great rebellion, when they tried to take a ship and get away.'

Molly narrowed her eyes. 'When was all this?'

'Thousands of years ago.'

'In Trafarionath.'

He nodded, went on. 'The warlocks found the broken tablet in a wrecked ship, tried to use it to build their own. As soon as the fleet realized what we were trying to do . . . they destroyed them. The stones, the tablet, the warlocks that were left picked them from the wreckage, hid them away for years. They worked on the largest fragment, built what was left of their magic into it, but it was too late. The goblins took the last of our castles, over-ran our defences. We had to run, hide in the hills as they swallowed everything in sight. They knew about the stones, wanted them for their own magic, the bloody dabblers.'

Molly glanced at him, staring at the windscreen, the lights blooming and fading over his set features.

'Their chieftain, Morigilim. He'd captured any number of our women, you know. Forced them into his harem although they would rather kill themselves than submit,' he sniffed. 'It wasn't long before he had his reward. Three lovely daughters by Miativoon of Tielemek.' He paused, slowly shook his head. 'My uncle . . . when he was younger, I suppose you'd say he fell in love with one of them. The eldest, the cruellest. Azhiamehet. Totally against his nature, but he'd always been fond of pretty faces and . . . it's a long story. It took hundreds of years, from the moment he saw her to the moment he agreed.'

'Agreed to what?'

'Make the spell for her. Send her to your world.'

'What . . .'

'Yes, the breach has been broken before,' he told her. 'But every time . . . I don't know, it weakens something, dilutes the little bit of power we've got left.'

'How?'

'We haven't time for the whole thing,' he snapped, exasperated. 'The spell failed. It was never supposed to be. The spell did something . . . upset the balance if you like. Ruptured our hold on things.'

'You ruined your environment, you should see what

we're doing to ours.' Molly nodded toward the crowded streets, the snarled traffic.

'The environment was all right. We were the problem. Trafarionath.' He shrugged. 'You should see it sometime. Maybe when everything's died away. The creatures. The goblins.'

'Maybe it wouldn't be the same without them?'

He raised his eyebrows as if she'd suggested some particularly outrageous heresy.

'Well . . . anyway. The spell failed. If she was mad before she went you should have seen her when she came back. We ran, we hid. We hid the spells and the lawstones.'

'So you couldn't do any more magic? You couldn't get away?'

'We couldn't let the stones fall into her hands. She had power of her own you see. Slipstreaming, it changed her too,' he said flatly. 'She was more powerful than ever but she couldn't stop the rot. Tarkemenis said we should destroy the heirlooms while we still could. We didn't have much time or many places to hide. We did our best to get rid of them. We gave some of the simpler stones to her sister, buried the rest in her territory.'

'Her sister?'

'Yes. She'd left her sisters behind, see, the youngest one in a convent in the far north, the other one . . . the other one she didn't get on with. She'd already banished her.' He sighed, ran his hands through his thick red hair.

'It was her necklace you . . . we . . . we sat on.'

Sat on? That's one way of putting it.

'*Amiarillin*. It was her necklace, but it wasn't . . .' Molly paused, raised her eyebrows.

Teomalik edged away from her, lips twitching.

'What?'

'I never mentioned her name. I might have mentioned the three rivers but I didn't mention her name!'

Molly felt her stomach churn, felt the bony splinter shift under her skin.

'I must have picked it up... from you. Another suggestion?'

Suggestion? She was on first-name terms with their bloody Spawn Queen but couldn't have told him her own mother's maiden name to save her life! Fucking hell had he done to her? She felt a surge of panic over the sandbanks of her sanity. The curious calm she'd felt driving to him, joining him, beginning to buckle under the flood, peel the fuzzy layers of insulation from her imagination. Unpicking her reason. He turned, stared ahead.

'We knew she'd abuse it, we knew she wasn't right for it, wasn't ready for it. Maybe we were stupid, naïve, but we thought if we set her up she'd keep the others away, the goblins, the rest of them. Keep them away from the last hiding place. The place we'd put the stones and the tablets, the most important items.' Teomalik sighed.

'Anyway, her sister came back for a while, then her boy came. We were captured near by but we wouldn't tell them where we'd hidden all the spell stones.' He gazed out of the window. She could see the tears run down his face in the reflection on the glass. She turned back to the road, quiet. He wiped his face mechanically, blinked.

'They tortured him for hours, days, weeks. On and on. They never gave him a moment's rest until... he shut them all out for good. You know?' Molly nodded.

'He put the shutters up. They couldn't touch him. They could have set fire to his eyes and he wouldn't have blinked. Then they came after me. Where had we hidden the looms? What were the spells? First her and then him, the boy. Puut Ra. Younger than me, smaller too. He wouldn't come down to the dungeons with us because he was scared we would hypnotize him. He had his goblins do all his dirty work, knew they were too stupid to brainwash. Ignorant apes. But they didn't get anything out of me either. Not a thing.'

'She . . . Amiarillin, was the one who made the spell, that trapped your uncle?'

'Somebody must have been handling the looms, handling some of the stones. They made the vortex, opened the breach. We didn't want to be slipstreamed. Uncle . . . he didn't know anything, he didn't know where he was or what he was doing. I got sucked up into it, he did too only she must have . . . the Spawn Sister must have set a spell on him. A confinement spell.' Teomalik swallowed. 'She'd never forgiven him, for sending her sister.'

Molly eased the Cortina into the outside lane, put her foot down for the ring-road. Spawn sister? Hell they call her Spawn sister for? *Amiarillin. Three little girls running through the woods, the spearmen smiling down on them, patting their tresses.* Molly blinked. Spawn sister. She frowned. 'That's why, when he arrived . . . he was dead. In the big wagon.'

'He was dead,' he repeated. 'He'd lost his leg. He'd bled . . . all over the . . . those pictures they showed me.'

'Your uncle?' He nodded. God. She was imagining things. She was imagining she was here with this mad stranger when in actual fact she was at home on the sofa, head resting in Nicky's lap while he fed her garlic crisps. Kissing her a mouthful of wine like he'd always used to. They'd driven for a curry, she'd swallowed a chicken bone. She'd be fine when she woke up. 'So who was it? And how'd they get the stones in the first place?'

Teomalik shrugged. 'That's what we'll have to find out.'

'How? What do you do now?' she asked finally.

'We go back to the home. That's where everything ended up, started out. Whoever it was, maybe they won't be far.'

'And this Puut Ra . . . you think he's here too? Think that he and this Jonathan are connected? Connected to the home as well?'

He nodded.

'What makes you so sure?'

'A feeling, I guess.' He could talk about feelings. Fuzzy signals from her belly button, radiating out over her body, glowing, seeping veins. This fragment thing, this part of her, it could be, do anything. Foot down for the hospital, get them to whip it out for her. Teomalik watched her, lips moving nervously as if she was reciting something to herself, keeping things close. Keeping close to things. The heirlooms. Lost now, scattered. Swallowed up by the vortex, spat into this madhouse world of horns and shrieks and noise and sirens. The Lawlay stone, the bloody teeth. His uncle would have wept to see him, miserable slinking boy, haven't you learnt anything? He'd recovered the stone from the wagon people easily enough. A suggestion word, a flick of his hand and he'd had it. Burned the lock from the door and fled down the passage, down the deserted staircase at the back of their castle. The Lawlay, though. Where was it, who had it? And the tooth? Not the one he'd carried over, passed to the poor girl, he could keep an eye on that, whatever happened. The other one, the one that had been used on the fat man, butchered and bloody. The wagon people angry and scared, thinking knives and drills and shoving the pictures back across the desk at him.

Who had the tooth? Who'd killed the fat man, knew the secrets of the Spawn Queen's necklace? She did, Molly. Thinking things out of the rarefied air, sucking things out of Trafarionath, knowing things she should never have known. Not her though, he'd been with her, he'd watched for her. Somebody had used the other tooth on the old man, tried it out to see what it could do. To see for himself. It could only be Puut Ra. Teomalik sat up with a start. He'd been playing with them from the beginning, arranged the march to the stream, arranged their escape. The boy, the stones, together. Molly couldn't see it, kept asking where's the harm? The harm? Cold dread surged through his bones, seeped through his skin, sucked in through the windows. The way the boy would bring his ragged legions through the breach, set them loose like rabid wolves in a nursery. The icy blast from the instrument panel froze his features. Straight to the treasures, and he'd taken them! Teomalik pressed his hands over his mouth.

'What's the matter? You look awful.' Molly, glancing anxiously at him as she drove into the night. Eternal night come down on me! He'd led the boy to the heirlooms, let him take them from under his nose! The boy and his pack of goblin hounds, cackling and howling as they led him a dance into the hills, into the dale, down to the stream. And now he was here too, leaving trails of his own. She'd been talking, irritated he'd not been paying attention.

'I'm sorry?'

'I said,' Molly breathed, 'what's all this we business?'

'Oh, it's you.'

'Sorry I'm breathing, I'm sure.'

'Nicky. What is it? Are you at home? Molly out, I suppose.'

'Well, as a matter of fact . . .'

'I thought so. I've told you, Nicky, I don't want you involving me in some sordid fantasy. I'm not going to take a drive up to the reservoir with you . . .'

'Beth, can you shut the fuck up for a moment? Thank you. Look. Molly's gone off. Taken the car. I wondered if you'd seen her, been in touch?' Silence.

'No.'

'What, no, or no, no?'

'No no. What's she done, packed her bag?'

'This isn't funny, Beth. There's a maniac out there chopping people up in old folks' homes. Who knows what he'd do in the privacy of his own car? Get a little imaginative I suppose.'

'All right. What do you want me to do, help you look?'

'I thought . . . if we found her, maybe you could talk her down? We've been at each other's throats all weekend, don't ask me why. It was as if she was preoccupied . . . it was as if she wasn't there at all. You know?'

'I know. OK. She's taken the car, I better pick you up.'

'Cheers, Beth.' What, no jokes?

NEW BOY

Mags was giving Dianne a hand with the washing up. Takeaway pizza and garlic bread, a few cans of lager to wash it down with. Dianne nodded at the boy lounging in the cluttered front room, feet up on the table watching the video with his headphones on.

'Not exactly a new man is he?'

Mags chuckled. 'I don't know what the hell he is, what he's about. He's just . . . cute. Nice to be with. Not like some of the bastards I've known.'

Dianne looked up at her from the dishes. She'd meant that all right. Dianne had met her at college. Her kids had grown up and her husband had left her, left her enough to scrape by while she did a BA in English. Mags reminded her of Janey, her daughter. Same hair, same morbid fascination with no hopers. She could talk.

'I don't understand how he can listen to that rubbish and watch the box at the same time,' Dianne observed.

'He's a sponge. Devours anything he gets his hands on.'

'Including you.'

Mags smiled. 'Sometimes he's like an overgrown kid. Other times he's like . . . you know. Masterful.'

Dianne raised her eyebrows. 'Bit young to have learned tricks like that, isn't he? Had much practice?'

'Nothing I noticed. I had to . . . slow him down a little.' She wasn't kidding. Holding him back, pushing his skinny chest back as she struggled to get her breath and bearings. 'For God's sake, Jonathan . . . take it easy. Nice and easy. Look. Like this. OK. No . . . no you stay still a second. Stay still. Now when I do this . . . you do that. Not that hard. No. Stop again.' He'd spluttered and flustered and hammered home till he was done and flopped over dead to the world. Well, there's a change. Ten minutes later he'd been ready again, his green eyes popping over her body, his hands running over her skin as if she was a map showing buried treasure. Buried treasure. My little treasure.

'He's a bit young too, isn't he?' gently.

'He's almost seventeen.'

'God Almighty. Almost seventeen. Isn't it against the law at that age?'

'Do me a favour, Di. He's only a few years younger than me. My Toy Boy. Never had a Toy Boy before. Plenty of Toy Men.'

'How long were you planning on staying, anyway? Not that I'm trying to get rid of you, mind. It's nice to have a bit of company. The girls in my class said I ought to go out along with them, but you know how it is. I didn't want to be mother hen all night.'

'You ought to go. College has knocked years off you anyway.'

'You know, that's just the sort of remark will get you some toffee ice-cream for dessert.'

'Jonathan, want some ice-cream?' Mags bawled. He rolled over, smiled, waved his hand.

'Yeah, give him some too.'

'What next?' Beth wanted to know. Nicky shrugged, dug himself a little deeper into the comfortable bucket seat of her souped-up Fiesta.

'What about the reservoir? You never know.'

Beth glanced over at him, slumped as if he was wearing a gorilla suit three sizes too big for him. 'If you think I'm falling for that . . .'

'Oh come on, Beth, give me a break,' he croaked.

Beth shook her head. 'She could be anywhere. We've tried the Downs, we've tried the town. I don't see what else we can do.' She pulled into the Blue Boar car park, switched off the engine and looked at him, staring morosely at the brick wall of the pub.

'Come on. I'll buy you one.'

'Thanks, Beth, but if I'm out when she calls . . .'

'She'll miss you. Come on, I can't stand the thought of you moping around like this. I must be round the twist but there it is. Come on. It might never happen.'

'What might never happen? Going off, you mean?'

'She's a big girl, Nicky. If she's gone, she's gone. You could hardly lay claim to being the best bloody husband in the world, could you now? No, don't start objecting. Come in and have a drink. I'm going to anyway.'

He climbed out of the low-slung seat, straightened up. 'Just deserts, eh?' he called over the sunroof.

She bent, locked the doors. 'Come and have a drink. Forget it.'

He followed her up the steps, half-heartedly eyeing her peachy rear in a pair of worn Levi's, closed in behind her as they entered the sudden light and noise of the pub.

'I thought you wanted to see your little brother,' Mags said quietly, lying back on the rumpled single bed wishing her boobs would stop hurting. She felt as if she'd been breast-feeding a couple of orang-utans. He'd thrown himself on her as if she wasn't there. Hardly said a word. Fucking her hard staring at the old posters on the walls. Dianne had let them have Janey's room, as long as they wanted. How long did she want this? Why did she want this? Some kind of self-mutilation, lack of self-esteem? She'd keep a shrink busy for months, working her brain out. Instead of fucking her brains out. She'd lost her temper eventually, bucked him off and rolled him over. Leapt over him and scissored down on his thin thrashing thighs. He'd focused then all right. Given him something to think about in the real world. Let's have it my way for a change, buster. She'd enjoyed it, she'd come and she hadn't the previous however many times. Was it eleven or twelve? Whatever, it was a miracle she hadn't turned her insides out all over him.

'What are you laughing at?' he asked her, glancing up from the weighty Sunday paper he'd folded over the pillow. Lying crushed against the wall for fear of falling out.

'Nothing. I said I thought . . .'

'I heard what you said. I told you. There were some weird people hanging around at the hospital. Really weird.'

They must have upset him out there, colour he'd been when he'd run out like a shoplifter, bug eyed empty handed. He hadn't said a word for an hour, she'd touched his arm and he'd jumped a mile. Best leave him to it, brood his way out of whatever he was feeling. They'd taken his brother away, an aunt or something. Jonathan had claimed they'd never seen eye to eye, he'd leave it a while. She was about to argue but she'd caught his glance, same look he'd given her outside the clothes shop when he'd snatched the leggings from her hands. Mine all mine. All my thoughts, all me, locked away here. Maybe she should aim to be more like him, straighten herself out a little. She shrugged. Leave the analysis for another day. It would keep. She rolled over with difficulty, tugged the paper to one side.

HIPPIE SUSPECT SOUGHT IN HOME DEATH RIDDLE

Funny how newspapers always used words nobody else would dream of. He'd had his nose stuck in the bloody thing since Di had thrown it on the coffee table that morning.

'Theo Malik. Sounds more like a Pakistani.'

'Pakistani? That's Teomalik. That's who they're after. They think he must have killed that man at the home.'

Mags frowned. He'd babbled on about the home and what he'd been doing there, damn near driven her out of her mind listening to his daft stories. What was he trying to do, upset her or something?

'What's the matter?'

'You. Going on.'

'What do you mean, going on? Don't you believe me, don't you believe me yet?'

'I do believe you. But it's so . . . far fetched isn't it? I mean. The crash. I saw it happen.'

'So did I. I had a bloody grandstand view of it,' he snarled.

She rolled on her side, hanging over the edge of the single bed staring at their tangled clothing. He made himself comfortable and she rolled out in a heap, landed awkwardly on his discarded clothing.

'Ouch. Shit. What the hell did you have in your pocket?' Mags reached behind her, fingered a cut halfway down her back. She raised her finger, smeared in blood. He looked down at her. Giggled.

'You bastard, you did that deliberately.' She picked up his jeans, rattled a few bits of change and a balled tissue from his pockets. He leaned back, drank her body, got drunk and stupid on it. Eyes glued to her small breasts, her neat little triangle.

'There's room, if you get on top again,' he said smoothly. Too bloody smoothly. Where did he learn all this lounge-lizard stuff anyway, back home in what was he calling it, Trivia something? Liar. Little bloody liar. She snaked up the covers and slowly pulled them away from him. His boy's body, slimmer than a snake, warm from the sheets. She smiled, threw her leg over his thighs and drew herself down. Frowned.

'Ow.' Rubbed the cut on her back. 'Must have been the zipper. Bloody hurt me,' she complained.

'Aah. Let me make it better,' he leered. Grinning now, the little bastard. The little bloody bastard.

'My turn this time.'

'I'm not complaining,' he smiled. A watery, preoccupied smile. The Trivia place could wait, just this once.

MONDAY

GRIDS

'Skein? What's that, something to do with swans, isn't it?'

'Geese, actually.' Jilly dipped her big blue eyes behind those horribly large but fashionable black spectacles. Power dressing in red tights? McNair had met her briefly at some conference. Remembered her barely concealed excitement as she led them through the complexities of something so exciting he'd entirely forgotten what it was. Pick his moment, maybe he'd ask her for a refresher. Not now though. Macall blowing smoke down his nose like a bull brought to its bloody knees by bloody red-handled swords. The chief super had been on: the chief constable had been on his back already. Bent his ear down at the club house the evening before. Any progress on the mess down in Clove? No progress, plenty more mess. Macall weaved the lighter through his fingers, realized she was watching him intently, bristled up all over.

'Geese. So they're, what, some kind of pygmy bird-watcher's homing device?'

Jilly raised her eyebrows over the big black glasses, cracked a smile. Jilly. For Christ's sake why hadn't she caught the mood, called herself Jill. Better still Doctor Freeman, whatever the hell initials she had stuffed in after her name. What he needs, more aggravation. Red tights to a bull.

'S.K.A.N.E. It crops up once or twice on each stone. The computer's still getting to grips with the text but it's already deciphered part. Terribly exciting really.' She pronounced really as *rilly*, got on Macall's fraying nerves some more.

'Skane. What's that? Nordic or something?' The Vikings had got as far as Glastonbury, according to some local legends. Local legends he didn't want to hear. Glastonbury, on the other hand, something to go on. Something to tell the super. Funny stones, substances, weird inscriptions, it all fitted.

'It all fitted up, you mean,' McNair had snorted as they'd arrived at the University building in Budgworth that morning. He'd got a real look with that one, kept it buttoned ever since.

'I don't think it's Nordic, no. It's more like an early Minoan script, Linear A, possibly a stronger Phoenician influence. I've sketched some of the principal symbols for you.'

Macall looked from the sketches to her, studied the sketches again. 'What can I say?' he growled.

'You see Skane keeps cropping up. That funny squiggle there next to the upside-down V.'

'I see it, but I don't see what you're driving at,' Macall smiled sweetly. McNair winced, sipped his coffee. Better than the rot-gut brew they dished out at the station. He glanced around the walls, ranks of books, files of decaying spines. Titles he couldn't even read in one go.

'I think this fellow of yours was a scholar, certainly. A linguist, probably. You see, when I first studied the stone, I thought I was looking at one script. But in actual fact, if you look closely you can see there are two sets of marks, one on top of the other as if somebody has copied – or adapted – the original symbols. The writing is also very precisely arranged within these small grids, twelve of them around the central square, look.' She tapped the sketches, the squiggles next to the upside-down Vs.

'Yeah, so?'

'I thought I'd concentrate on the runes in the central panel. The decipher program has come up with something but you won't like it,' she warned. Macall waved his hand anyway. 'I think it says something like "noises fondly on a mountain".'

McNair closed his eyes. Macall bowed his head, ran his hand over his chin.

'I know it doesn't make any sense,' Jilly went on quickly, irritated. 'I don't see how it fits with the arrangement of the blocks . . . if it wasn't for the inscription, and if, if, you wanted my opinion, I'd say it was some kind of early astrological chart, possibly some kind of navigational aid.'

McNair nodded. 'Well, that would fit what we know about him. On his way to join the convoys, tripper kind of guy, some kind of funny stall, joss sticks and stuff,' he went on blithely as Macall clambered to his feet and marched around the bookshelves.

Jilly brightened, tossed her neat pageboy haircut. Rattling away about star signs, planetary influences, astrophysics, the university's world-renowned space-research department.

'A neolithic horoscope, is that what you're suggesting?'

'Neolithic? I've no idea. But old, certainly very old,' she agreed eagerly. 'We'll have a preliminary carbon dating for you later today.'

'Could it be valuable, an . . .' McNair began, Macall interrupting rudely from the other side of the room: 'And our one-legged friend was carrying the whole thing scratched on to a dozen stones which he'd had stuffed up his bum?'

Jilly's smile slipped a notch. McNair coughed.

'Are you taking the piss, Detective Chief Inspector Macall?' she demanded coldly.

Macall waved his hand. 'I'm investigating a murder. Two murders and a disappearance. Two murders two disappearances,' he corrected himself. 'What I don't need is to be baffled with sideshow science.' He met her stare, turned it.

'Now can you tell me in words of one syllable or less whether the information on these stones has anything to do with the body we found in the lorry?'

'You're the great detective, you tell us,' she snapped, riffling the papers into the large leather bucket she'd pressed into service as a handbag. McNair was mumbling platitudes to nobody in particular, Macall was already halfway down the corridor. McNair gave her a smile, a shrug, a sigh. She eyed him as he backed out, hurried after his boss. Weaving his way through a crowd of eager young things he couldn't tell were students or lecturers. He caught up with the detective, hurried alongside as they took the refectory steps three at a time into the sunlight outside the main university building.

'Marvellous. Stone Age star signs, just what Evans is dying to hear about.'

'You could have ... I mean, I think ...' Macall ignored him, ducked down and climbed into the unmarked police car they'd left parked in the principal's bay.

'Goddamn cranks.'

'Who?'

'All of them. Skanes. This hasn't got anything to do with bloody Star Wars research or theoretical physics.' He lit another cigarette as McNair clunk-clicked.

'We're barking up the wrong trees. I know it.'

'You didn't tell her about the stone. The way he got out.' McNair risked a sideways glance at his boss, drumming his fingers on the hot dashboard.

'He must have had something else. Something we missed. Christ, coal's coal, isn't it? Or maybe it's some carbon-based ray gun or something.'

'Maybe she'd have been able to shed some light on it,' McNair said flatly. He knew he was right. He knew his boss knew he was right. Give him a second but don't give in. Macall shrugged.

'When we've finished, go back and apologize. Ask her for a short summary of her findings and her views on our one-legged friend's interests, origins. If he's so fucking clever he must have made an impression on somebody sometime, even if it was only long enough to get himself thrown out of something. Check out the science journals, the off-beat ones, you know. These guys are definitely left field, definitely out there somewhere.'

McNair nodded, pulled out into the traffic. 'Right ho. Now what about that letter? What was his name, Grainger, had it in his safe.'

'The letter to Klein at the RHA. Yeah. Right little creep getting the place set up for closure like that. Can't see it ties in though.' Macall blew smoke, watched the traffic. 'Close the place down he needed the people out of there. Old man Haberfield's one of the few they haven't managed to shift. Funny that his folks buy it on the way down. And Grainger gets done in himself around the time they were due to arrive. Christ, it's all there for us,' he moaned. 'Maybe Theo and his uncle were brought in to arrange an accident, something like that.'

McNair shook his head. 'Sounds about as likely as Jilly's bloody astrological chart.'

Macall sighed. 'We're missing something. It all revolves around Clove. The home, the bridge. The whole lot. Get down there we'll pick something up. Something we've missed.'

Sure, Monday morning, but that was no excuse to feel... what exactly? Anxious. As if she hadn't come on. Christ, when the hell was she due on? Twelve... thirteen times and counting and she couldn't remember taking her pill on Saturday. No. It was more than that. Worse. She'd stretched and showered. Felt the cut on her back tighten. Rubbed it gingerly. A little better. Smell of toast and coffee in the kitchen. Jonathan looking sheepish as he moped about the living-room, watching the TV with the headphones off now. Di spreading butter, eyeing him nervously. False smile. Mags had taken a piece of toast, towelled her hair.

'Anything wrong?'

'No.'

'Di?'

'No. Honest. Nothing's wrong. Why should there be?'

Mags imagined big red hands pointing accusing fingers at her head. Di was getting along fine with Hardy and Lawrence, but lying she'd never master. Had he said something? Thrown a tantrum like the time in the shop? Said something to give them away? 'We'll take a trip in town. See about bus timetables.'

Di swallowed. 'You're moving on, then?'

'We can't go on imposing on you. Really appreciate it.'

Tugging her things together watching him mince about the bedroom in those ridiculous leggings. Thin matchstick legs encased in shiny black fabric stuffed into outsize trainers. On second thoughts he'd probably blend in all the better out on the street.

'What's wrong with Di, did you say something?'

He looked lost, more lost than ever. Frowned, shrugged his thin shoulders in the outsize top he'd bought along with the jeans on Saturday. 'There was a picture of me on the telly.'

'What?'

'They must have got it from . . . home. Picture of me and my mother and father.' Stiff, formal. No Mum and Dad or anything. The parents he'd seen mangled in the car. The car she'd seen ducked under the water. It had done something, shut something off inside his head. Christ, she needed controls like that. Shut things off now and again.

'Did she?' He nodded. 'Say anything?'

'She started to say it looked like me, then she started on the toast like it was growing mushrooms or something.'

'Fuck. We'll have to get a move on now.' She'd fished her spare underwear from her bag, watched him mope by the window, hanging on to the pink curtain.

'What's wrong? They're bound to want to . . . you know, take you in. We have to go on until everything's blown over. Until things have settled down.' She settled herself. 'When they find that Theo bloke we'll drop in to the police station, straighten things out.'

'He's looking for me too.'

'Who?'

'Teomalik.' That stuff again. Every time they had a problem, Teomalik. Triviawhatsitcalled.

'We'll get a bus, go to London. Look up some of your friends, eh?'

He shook his head. 'They'll want to speak to me about the fat man. That was . . .' He waved his hand wearily, felt again for the tooth, the tooth he'd carefully wrapped in his pocket the day before. The missing tooth. Eyed her nervously. If she'd fallen on it ... if she'd ... he closed his eyes, remembered the stream, the home. The fat man. The way the Shulukayasheen had trembled as if it was living a life of its own, vibrating under his fingertips. He held the curtain, the plastic rings tugging white around the flimsy metal runner. Grainger, the fat man, bending down over one of the old ones. Great bag of corruption, all fat and blubbery like that, he could hardly stop himself, hardly control his hand, groping in his pocket for the tooth. The Shulukayasheen hot to the touch, like the goblin stories said, glowing white.

'Of course it's him, Doris. Hap's grandson,' Grainger had explained, straightening to wipe a fat hand over his sweaty forehead as she peered nervously over his shoulder.

'Where did Hap go?' she'd asked again, nodding all the while.

Grainger jumping up like that, jumping from the worn carpet as if he'd been stung by a hornet. Little bastard had stuck him with something! He'd groped around his bulging belly, looked from his stained sweaty shirt to the boy, standing back shivering as if he was afraid of something, afraid of what he'd done.

'What did you do that for, you stupid little bastard? I told you I'm sorry we've ... ah ... ah Jesus!' The fat man had danced about, grasped at his back as if he could dig the Shulukayasheen back out, rake his own flesh open after it. Red face now. Red face shouting. He'd backed against the muttering old man who'd flailed at him with his blotchy hands.

'Get away from me you little bastard you fucking horrible little ...' going on and on while the fat man straightened, eyes popping, fell to his knees tearing his shirt open to spill his big white belly over the worn carpet. Rolling and crawling, huddled into a big fat ball. Bawling and pawing his big white doughboy belly. Stranded whale on the shoreline, the terrible tooth razoring through his organs, grating on his ribs. Clattering against knotty cartilage and ricocheting through beds of slippery fat. He'd crawled over, clutched at Mrs Ogden's frail stick legs, great gout of blood splattering her clothes. He'd stridden over to him, pulled him back by the ears, laid him out on the carpet while the tooth finished with him. Out of control, what he'd started. What he'd let loose.

The big man coughed more blood, loads of it, splattered over the threadbare threads. He coughed and choked and spat the tooth out. Shiny and bloody. He'd picked it up, wiped it carefully on the fat man's shirt as they all looked on, slack mouthed. Wondering maybe if he'd stick the tooth on them too. He'd tugged a handful of tissues from the trolley, wrapped the tooth and replaced it in his pocket. The fat man had kicked, groaned, died. Taken him hours to drag the carcass out of the lounge, down the passage to the back door. Down the path and under the trees in the big garden dotted with broken-down plastic chairs. What they do, leave the old ones to sit on them, break their spindly legs? He'd left him under the logs in an outhouse, rushed back to find water and rags to clean the old folk off, brush the blood from their clothes and hair. On his knees past midnight scrubbing the carpet. Old ones nodding and muttering amongst themselves. He'd left them to it, searched the home.

The boy's room stuffed with clothes and any amount of other stuff he hadn't been able to identify. Searched the bedrooms, narrow beds and cabinets loaded with pictures. He paused in room six, snatched a picture up and stared at it. The boy in the car, not him. Him now. I'm the boy in the car and they'll catch me if they can. The fat man had called him Jonathan. Jonathan was the missing man's grandson. He'd finished his tour, wandered back in on them on tottery legs, slumped in Hap's chair. They were dozing and snoring all round him but he didn't mind it. Dozing and snoring till morning when he'd woken up and stared at them staring at him. They'd looked away then, all except the muttering one with the foul mouth.

'What?'

Mags sighed. Staring out of the window, he hadn't been listening.

'They'll catch the other fellow. That Theo. He must have done it. It's in all the papers.'

'So am I. And I'm on the TV too. Di recognized me. They'll all recognize me. The people at the hospital, the girl, the men with the trolley, Ti... the others.' He trailed off, shrugged his thin body in the outsize clothes. Nappies he'd pulled around himself. Her little kid. Was that it, she needed somebody to mother? She closed her eyes, shut the thought away with all the others. Too many others. Pressing, hurting.

'Well we'd better get a shift on, then. Come on, don't stand there gawping.'

It was two o'clock already, hot sticky and smoggy in Budgworth. Wilf had decided he'd had enough of the social services committee and rolled out of County Hall, dusting the worst of the biscuit crumbs from his heavy tweed trousers. With Nicky moping around the office he hadn't minded pencilling himself in for the monthly meeting. Wilf had warned his reporter a million times not to exaggerate, two million times to remember he was a happily married man. Shouldn't go around chatting every woman up as if he was running an understaffed massage parlour. The way he talked to Beth at the office. If Molly had taped ten seconds of it she'd have stapled his scrotum to the desktop. He shook his head, made his way across three lanes of stalled traffic on the way to the city-centre bus station. Paused to buy a copy of the city *Herald* from some retard alien on a news-stand. Papyrus? Gerraya Papyrus! Some kind of bloody Egyptian, sounded like. Nicky's anxiety about his absent wife must have rubbed off. Everything else did. He was edgy, irritable.

'Sorry, love!' The girl, striding along bent almost sideways under the weight of a large holdall, had lost her balance and staggered to her knees.

'It's Mags ... Margery isn't it?' The second youth pulled him back, twisting his arm in the patched tweed jacket.

'Ow! Careful!' Wilf twisted after his arm, too close for comfort to the angry youth who'd been following her. Fierce eyeballs itching for trouble.

'Jonathan! Leave it!' Mags called, climbing to her feet and rushing between them.

Wilf glared at the youth, recognized the face from the fuzzy close-ups they'd received from the police PR department in Budgworth.

'Wait a tick. You're the Haberfield lad, aren't you? Jonathan? Let go of my bloody arm!'

Mags pushed the boy back, held his arms. 'It's OK. It was an accident.'

'Course it was. Just bumped in to you by mistake. Where are you going, back to Clove? Police are looking for you, you know. What were you thinking of locking young Molly in that room like that?' Wilf bristled up, holding on to her coat as she tried to propel the youth through the gawping crowd and on into the bus station.

'Nothing . . . It's all a big mistake. We're on our way back now,' Mags insisted over her shoulder. The gangly editor tagged along.

'On your way back. I'm going back too, I'll come with you.' She glanced at him as he twisted his head on his thin neck looking around furiously for a policeman. The bus station was a big grey smoky building with a funny smell. Coughing buses disgorging ashtray-faced people. The warmth given off by the close-packed humanity attracted pigeons, tramps, vagrants and pickpockets. Usually a copper about if you looked hard enough.

'Run!' Mags pushed the boy into an old lady who fell over obligingly. Curious onlookers rushed to help as the youth lumbered off, Mags running behind him swinging the bag over her shoulder.

'Oy! Stop them!' Wilf stepped over the fallen pensioner, skittered after them.

'Come back! Margery! Where the hell you think you're going?'

GALL STONES

He'd felt the first twinge twenty miles back. A steady knotting in the pit of his stomach. A slow churning in his bowel. Molly had wound the window down for him, jabbed the air-conditioning slider to the floor. White faced, thinking so hard, thinking his thick eyebrows right off his square face. He hadn't felt queasy before, in the home. He'd banged his head, been locked in a cupboard for three hours but hadn't remembered feeling like this. Molly glanced around again.

'You look terrible. Was it the kebab?' They'd stopped off an hour earlier at a roadside café, ordered the chef's special. Teomalik wiped his mouth, ran his hand down his strong chin and around his throat.

'Maybe it's the necklace . . . maybe I got stuck on more than one?'

'What are you asking me for, I'm the expert all of a sudden?' She sighed, smiled.

'Thirsty?'

'Tight. I don't feel right.' Don't feel right. What was right, when right was at home? What the hell was she doing here driving an escaped prisoner over the narrow causeways of the north Somerset levels when she should be at home getting Nicky's tea? She always got his tea. Back from her duties at the home to her duties at her home. From her elderly charges to Nicky. Not today. *Not any more*, the little voice whispered, somewhere in the corners of her head. She should have rung at least. She owed him that. She owed him a damn sight more than this. Running off to drive this crazy boy to his destiny. A bloody psychiatrist would be a better bet. Maybe he could kill two birds with one stone and ... ow! She felt the pain lance behind her eyes, shivered, holding her breath. The pain flared, faded. She breathed out quietly, blinked carefully as if she'd upset more apple carts of agony. He hadn't noticed her attack, groaning beside her with his own problems.

'You'll have to stop the wagon.' Curly head backwards and forwards as his shoulders heaved. Molly glanced in the mirror. Green fields, Friesians and some sheep in the far distance. Pulled up as Teomalik wrestled with the door, leaned out and was copiously sick over the road. Mostly over the road.

'Bloody kebab.'

They'd been hungry. Driving down from Budgworth the previous night, the sudden, crippling weariness which had overcome the pair of them. Or had it been him again up to his tricks, suggesting she was tired, suggesting they pull in for some rest? Parking the car out on the Downs, away from the main road. Sexy seclusion. They'd taken the scenic route out of the city, climbed into the hills and headed for Wells before swinging back across the levels to approach Clove from the south-east. Teomalik talking, talking quietly all the way, all the time. Soothing her. More suggestions. If you're cold, climb over the back with me. There's more room. Suggestion. Piling Nicky's old fishing jumper into the parcel shelf, easing herself between the worn seats to cuddle up beside him. Suggestion. You'll never sleep like that with your neck stretched out. Running his finger down the taut skin to the top of her T-shirt. Falling away to his lap. Suggestion. Was he suggesting things or merely reminding? What had he said, works better when the subject's willing? Hadn't tried it before. Not on a human anyway. First time. Suggestion. What a fight she'd put up. Holding his hand.

'I don't want... with the tooth thing. I mean... what if there's more?' she'd asked. What am I saying? Listen, pal, you've stuffed me once already, remember? Sitting back away from her, the bulge under his oversize shirt subsiding abruptly. Then she'd felt sorry for him, cuddled him in all over again. Thought, weirdly, that she'd put them in him. The teeth. *Put them in to get over.* Over where? To get here, with him? She'd frowned. Couldn't even think straight now. She'd done nothing of the sort. Must be tired, thinking silly thoughts, seeing silly visions.

'I feel awful,' he announced, wiping his hand over his mouth. Join the club. He sagged into the worn seat, licking his blue lips.

'Do you think it's some kind of reaction... to being here?'

Earth tummy. Reality attack. Humanity's revenge. He shook his head slowly, running his fingers over his temples.

'It's the stones. We're near now. I can feel them. I can feel burning. They're burning them.'

'Who?'

'Whoever. The wagon people still have Uncle's. The boy has... a set, or something. Something at the home. One of those old people you told me about.'

One of the old people? Molly frowned.

'Well, it must have been. One of them must have had the stones to create the vortex. Like I said, it was nothing to do with us. We were summoned, just like I summoned you.' Irritated, distracted. Not really talking to her, just keeping her quiet while he tried to think.

'Well, do I go on or what?'

He nodded. 'We must take a look at the home. There has to be something. Something you've missed.'

I've missed? Molly pulled away too fast, stalled, pulled away again. Something I've missed. Oh yes, of course. I had time to search them for funny bracelets and secret stones when I was giving them their tea or a bloody blanket bath.

'I'm sorry. It's me. Forgive me.' Short smile. They hadn't had any stones or bracelets or books of magic spells. None of the last lot anyway. Old Mr Maggs had his itty-bitty collection of old rocks and things but they'd had to take him away to Bleakdale. Nice old gentleman, always tried to hold the door for you even when he had the arthritis so bad his hands were doubled up under his arms, growing back into him. He'd gotten funny when his family had stopped coming. Holiday, they'd told him, only it was a holiday that lasted for ever. A holiday from him. He'd stood it what, three every other Sundays in a row before he'd flipped. Clawed at Claire, pushed Molly into the trolley. Caught Mr Grainger a fourpenny one across the mouth with his nasty *Tyrannosaurus* claws. Molly had walked behind as they wrestled him up the stairs, making sure Grainger didn't think about getting his own back when nobody was looking. Up into his room, cool down in there you miserable old git, no wonder your family aren't fussed with you. Molly bit her lip. Remembering him walking backwards into his bunk as Grainger jammed the door shut on him. The sudden rattle on the door as he hurled his . . .

'Stones. What sort of stones, exactly?' she asked slowly, eyes fixed on the narrow road arrowing across the wetlands.

Teomalik, arm thrown over his face, groaning. 'I'll

show you sometime. Sooner than you think, the way I feel.'

She looked puzzled. Hadn't noticed anything around his neck when he'd taken his big thick fragrant top off. Only the healing hole in his chest. Yeeees.

'The other old man at the home. Mr Maggs. He had stones. I've just thought about it. Loads of them, all shapes and sizes. Stalagtites and that.'

Teomalik eyed her. 'What sort of stones?' he asked.

'He'd been a geologist. Quite famous around here. I think his family had been paying for him to stay at one of the posh homes up in Rookton. Must have fallen behind with the payments, had to transfer him back to local authority care. He was always nattering on about them. His stones, his travels. He'd explored all under Hillstones, found all those different chambers.'

Teomalik chuckled mirthlessly. 'Explored under Hillstones. Carried all these rocks around with him.'

She bristled. 'He had a collection in his room. All sorts of small bits and pieces. But he was transferred away to Bleakdale months ago. Got too confused being at Clove.'

'I'm not surprised.'

'We couldn't handle them when they got too disruptive.'

'Lock them away someplace else, eh?'

'What's that supposed to mean? Look. I'm sorry, all right? Much more of this and you can get out and crawl.' Cheeky bastard. Get smart with me Mr Stranger on the fucking Planet. *Wizardboy meddler*. That little voice again, that voice in her head.

'He had stones in his room, at the home?'

She frowned. 'Where I found you,' she said.

Teomalik clutched his stomach, gave her a ghastly

smile. 'Funny you should remember,' he snapped. Brakes. Bump.

'Listen, mate. You may be a dab hand—'

He waved his hands to calm her down. 'Sorry sorry. Look. Describe these stones.'

Imploring her. Little boy lost look. As if he was slowly losing his grip. Losing *his* grip? He belched, flushed.

'Different stones. Coloured. Crystals and little chips of old tablets. You know.'

He knew, all right. 'And he went to Bleakdale?'

'Yes. Months ago. So he couldn't have summoned you, could he, couldn't have interfered with your astronomic arrangements.'

'But he could have left them for somebody else.'

'I never saw anybody with any stones,' she grated. 'We didn't tend to use his room much, left it pretty much as it was.'

'Rocks and all.' Teomalik turned his not-right eyes on her. Not the right colour for that bloody red hair. He was summoning patience from somewhere, pissing her right off. 'The man who was missing. Not the dead one, the other one.'

'Hap. Mr Haberfield. Everyone called him Hap. Don't know why really, just did.' She paused, shook her head a notch. 'He never had any stones. He never as much as moved out of his chair.'

'But he went missing anyway.'

'So somebody took him.'

'Puut Ra. The boy and the girl. They were there.'

She frowned. 'They just went,' she said wearily. 'Hap was nothing to do with them. Coincidence.'

He was staring at her again.

'He never had any stones. Just the remote. He'd play with the bloody thing all day. Didn't work, sort of a placebo, you know placebos?' He nodded. 'We let him keep it, kept him quiet, you know.'

Teomalik nodded. 'How big is a remote?' Molly held out her hand. 'That's it.'

'What?'

'Maybe he had them in the remote. They wouldn't take up much space.'

Molly groaned. Get out of there, get back to Nicky while you could still explain things, talk him down. She calmed herself.

'If he's got the stones . . . I can't go any nearer.'

'What?'

'I can't go nearer the stones. Think about it. We buried the heirlooms of the great warlock houses in the stream, in Trafarionath, in our time.'

'Yeah, so?'

'So whoever it is must have got hold of some of our stones in a different time zone. Your time. They used the stones to connect the vortex to the originals, back in our time, summoned us all over.' He explained it patiently, devoted teacher with a wayward pupil. 'Now I'm here in your time too, with some of the originals . . .'

'They can't be in the same place twice?' Molly theorized. All made perfect sense now. Get out, leave him to it. 'But you left the stones in the chest . . .'

'Not all of them. We'd recovered some of the smaller fragments before they caught us.'

'They never searched you?'

'They didn't find them.' He frowned darkly.

'And what happens if they are in the same place twice?'

'Who knows? We were terrified they would fall into the wrong hands back home. Over here? Anything could happen.' He retched, wiped his sweaty face.

'Anything?'

'Bad things. Things coming over from my world to

yours.' He shook his curls, glum. Bad things coming from his world to hers. 'It was never meant to be,' he went on, ignoring her squirm. 'Against all the laws of our existence and yours. Whoever has the tablet . . . the main fragment I told you about, they have to be stopped. They have no idea of its power.' He shivered. 'Look. Keep going for now. If it gets too much for me you'll have to check it out yourself.'

'Wonderful.' She pulled away again, flashing hedgerows and curious Friesians. The occasional farmer, dressed in scarecrow castoffs beside ancient Land Rovers. Closer now. Hillstones rearing over the wetlands, slopes and shoulders bathing in the afternoon sunlight. Battlemented brows keeping the quaking bogs from running up over the granite faces, running up through the cracks and gaps. Old Professor Maggs groping in some pothole, running his hands through some silted fissure to find the stray stones, the Trafarnian warlock hoard. Tipped and washed from the rotting chest down the stream, under the hills who knows where, who knows when. Hurling the precious stones at his door when his family abandoned him in the home, left him with his crystals, his fragmented fossils. Tiny chips in the paintwork, the curious gravel they'd trodden into the worn carpet as they'd hastily packed his things, packed him off to Bleakdale. Tiny chips in her life, tiny chips from her mind falling through space like vast anvils, pinning her to him and his derailed destiny. Tiny chips he'd carried over with him, squirmed them into her belly before he rolled over on the ruckled old sheets they'd pulled from the shelves in Mr Maggs' room. Bloody marvellous. Molly sighed, twisted a hank of her dark hair through her fingers as the long straights over the moor gave way to the chicane lanes twisting up through the foothills. Sunday drivers on warp speed, stoned. Stoned all right. Bumpy ruts, dandelions growing in the crumbling tarmac. The Cortina coughed and shuddered as Molly swung the heavy car along the lane through the trees, rolled it to a ticking halt at the end of the drive.

'Here we are. Want me to go on?'

'They're not here. Keep going.' Hand over mouth, eyes watering. Not tonight, Josephine. But last night . . . Molly gripped the wheel, reversed the Cortina down the drive, crunching gravel as she went. Crunched the thoughts springing into her head. Arm over the seat peering down the dim lane toward the brooding house. Empty now, just the way Klein and those money-grabbing bastards at the RHA wanted it. Maybe the whole thing had been set up, some scam to throw everybody out. They rolled to a halt, stared at the gaping windows and formidable door.

'We don't have to break in or something, do we? We're in enough trouble already.'

He didn't pay any attention, brushed past her. She watched him stagger up the steps and press his face to the window, cool the raging vices clamped behind his eyes. Molly peered around the side of the house, made her way down the wall and past the full-length dining-room window. Empty tables, chairs stacked against the wall. Vandals hadn't turned up yet, then. Probably too many police around. Around the corner no doubt. Wouldn't they be interested in hearing her story? Wouldn't Nicky? She heard Teomalik stumbling along behind her, holding on to the smooth stonework to prevent himself collapsing in a heap. He nodded her on. The garden, neat, empty. Questionable plastic furniture so many traps for the unwary.

'What's over there? That shed?'

'Outhouse. Tools and lawnmowers, stuff like that.'

'He was there.'

He was there all right. That's where they'd found Grainger's body. She'd seen them milling around the woodpile when they had escorted her out. Out to the police car . . . when was it . . . Saturday. Two days ago? Seemed a lifetime.

'That's where they found the manager. Mr Grainger. Under the wood.' He brushed past her, made his way across the grass. 'You won't find . . .' What the hell. She scampered after him. The scatty logs had been pulled away from the wall, the neatly stacked rails a shambles. He picked his way over the wood, one hand on his stomach.

'What is it? I told you, this is where they found the body.'

Don't bloody listen, then. Molly peered around at the house, half expecting to see police snipers levelling rifles over the old walls. Remain where you are do not move. Teomalik pulled the stacked logs away, stood aside as they bumped and crashed to the hard-packed earth beside the shed. He bent down, blowing hard as he pulled the peeling logs away, the logs nearer the back of the rickety shed. He puffed, stood back a little. Dirty grey logs sprouting mould and mushrooms, blotchy white leg, cornplasters. He'd found Hap. She darted over, peered down at the body, smothered face-down into the woody, peeling corruption. Woodlice and slugs making inefficient getaways from the scene. Molly sucked in her cheeks, stood away. Teomalik watched her, leaned in closer to lift the matted grey hair. 'It's him?'

Molly closed her eyes, felt the tears accelerate away from her eyes.

'Is it him, then? Haberfield?'

She strode forward, a robot in a morgue. Is this your child? Is this your father? Only the loose laundry bag of bones and flesh wasn't laid out neat on the slab, cold and deodorized. It was swarming with bugs, popping with fetid colours. Purples, yellows. Off-colour death hues. Bruising around the upper back, the neck. Stubby grey hair they all had. (All had?) Teomalik lifted the head, tilted it toward her. What was that, rope? Fucking hell. Knitting. Molly closed her eyes.

'Well?'

'It's Mrs Jasper.'

'Who's she?'

'One of the old folk. Tina Jasper. One of the people we looked after.' Weren't looking after her now, letting her lie in a heap of dirty logs in the dirt and the bugs like that. Weren't looking after her when . . . when? She'd spoken to her what, Saturday morning? Looked so dumpy and grey in her tartan cardigan. The five o'clock shadow she'd noticed on her chin. Teomalik watched her stride away over the grass, collapse into a rickety plastic chair. The youth wandered over, tried not to make it too obvious as he wiped his hands.

'I can feel they've been here, feel them in the soil. But they've gone now.'

Molly held her mouth, wiped her eyes. Mrs Jasper. Fiercely independent. Nine children. Survived the Blitz after losing her husband at Dunkirk. Mortified to find she couldn't go on looking after herself. Had to be taken in like an old donkey. Always trying to help where she could, push the trolley for you even though her legs weren't any good. She'd said, she'd told Molly often enough, she hadn't wanted to go on. Being like it. It had killed her but not like he had. Not like the bastard who had done that to her. With her own knitting. Shit. The fucking shit taking away her last little bit of dignity and rolling logs over her legs as if she was a withered old twig too. Only fit for the fire. She looked up, made him jump back slightly. *Scuttling away from the hut with the stone under his arm.* She closed her eyes, opened them. What hut? The outhouse?

'They took eight old folk to Ferndale,' she said stonily. Teomalik shrugged.

'Hap was missing, Mrs Jasper . . . never went.'

He glared at her.

'He must have done it. He must have done it and dressed up . . .'

'As her?'

Molly shook her head. Difficult old sod, always staring at the fish tank, peering round them as they attended to their needs. To their knees. Could he? Could he have killed her? What for? Whatever the hell for? Dumpy and stubbly in the tartan cardigan she always wore. The tartan cardigan he'd worn away from here. Lightning crackle of pain behind her eyes again. Barbed wires grating through her optic nerves. Two birds with one stone. Two birds inside her head. Vivid like the dreams that spilled out of sleep into misty mornings. Visions: *Hap scuttling off in the baggy jumper. Scuttling away from the hut. Calling him back. Throw me the stone. Scuttling off into the trees.* She swayed in the sway-backed chair, toppled over into the grass. He knelt beside her, steadied her, concerned. Her fists were clenched, fingers raking the long grass, eyelids flickering. Breathing in in short ragged gasps but not breathing out.

'Molly? What's wrong?' Shaking her gently as she twitched in his goose-flesh arms. She came round after a minute, opened an eye and glared at him.

'What have I done?'

'You fainted,' he said weakly. 'The shock.'

'I killed her.'

'What? Who? Molly? You didn't kill her, it wasn't your fault,' he cried. She closed her eyes, a single tear running down her cheek and over his wrist.

'I threw her off the cliff.'

'You fainted. You were dreaming, that's all,' he reassured her, swallowing nervously.

'I saw her on the cliff, I could see her swaying and I pushed her.'

'The old lady's been strangled. It's the shock... you're in—'

'Not her,' she barked, voice free-falling throatily. 'The girl. I saw her, I pushed her. She fell.' She lay still for a few moments while he breathed quietly over her cold face. She pushed him away, clambered to her feet.

'We're going to catch whoever did this.' He nodded, lost. 'We're going to catch him and you're going to lend me that stone. The coal that does the tricks.'

'We catch him, it's yours.'

'Molly? What's wrong? I've had Nicky on to me twice already,' Claire squawked.

'Never mind. Listen. I've been up to the home. I found Mrs Jasper. She's dead. No, listen. You were there when they carted them off to Ferndale. Was Hap with them?' Agonized silence. Sobbing.

'Molly, what's wrong with you? Mrs Jasper's not dead.'

'I saw her for myself, Claire, she's dead, all right?'

Crying now. 'But we moved them all out to the coach late Saturday night. After they'd taken you and that funny bloke away. Are you sure you're OK? I watched them put them on the coach. All eight of them.'

'Look, Claire. Think carefully. Did you actually get a good look at Mrs Jasper? Did you actually speak to her, did anybody? It's really important.'

'Of course I spoke to them. I spoke to them all.'

'Claire. Please. Think exactly what you said.'

'I said... you know what it's like. Of course I was speaking to them. I spoke to all of them.'

'Did you look in her face?'

'Not that I can remember but I must have done. Look, Molly. What are you saying? They're all up at Ferndale now. Only takes a call.'

'I want you to call the police. Get them to look in the woodpile.'

'They looked in the woodpile, Molly, they found Grainger.' She was losing her temper now, shouting back down the line.

'They found him and stopped the search. Mrs Jasper was lying nearer the back. Right by the shed.'

'Molly.' Pleading, crying.

'Ring the police. Get them up here now. Who's on duty at Ferndale, any ideas?'

'The matron's called Mrs Buck. Don't know her first name. Look, Molly. I'm sure Mrs Jasper was there on Saturday. We helped her into the coach. All eight of them. Quite simple.'

'It was Hap.'

'What?'

'Hap dressed up as Mrs Jasper.' Silence. 'Look, Claire, just do me a favour and ring the fucking police, all right?'

FALLING FOR HER

Ancient Budgworth. Dark alleys, cobbled courtyards. Lanes wound around towering inns, knees bent and sagging over their expanding beer bellies, popping their worm-eaten beams, stretching their shredding belts. Office blocks kicked city sand and hi-tech flotsam at their lowly neighbours, shouldered their way on up to the sun. Glittering banks of chrome, mirrored glass. Steel girders and concrete slabs. Dwarfing them as they ran like bugs along concrete chicanes, the mouldy grooves in dead bark.

'Go left. No, left.' Mags pushed the youth into the shadow of a medieval gateway, tenth-century stonework splashed with Day-Glo graffiti. Writing on the wall. Writing's on the wall for you! He leaned against the wall, wide eyed, catching his breath. Mags pulled in alongside him, whirled into his arms as an elderly couple hurried past giving them suspiciously fearful glances. Mug me lovey.

'We lost 'em.' He shook his head, resigned. Standing there straight enough for something without a backbone. Straight enough for a fillet of dogfish washed up on an oily beach. 'For now. They've seen me, they've all seen me,' he said shakily. She gripped his arm, gave him a friendly shake.

'We'll make our way on to St Lucretia's market. They'll never pick us out of that,' Mags insisted. Damn that interfering old fool, bumping into them at the bus station, shouting and flapping after them, the dozy old heron. Police appearing out of unmarked cars as if they'd had the whole place staked out. They couldn't have known they were on their way to the station unless... Di had told them. She wouldn't have, would she? Warn her what she was getting herself into, but report them? What the hell had he done anyway? That Theo was the bloke they needed to speak to, not Jonathan. Not my Jonathan. Running after him, leaping barriers and ducking overcoated arms, out of the cavernous station and down past the Old Hart. A mad dash across the stalled traffic and over the barrier dividing the central reservation. Past the queue for the pictures and on down the maze of back alleys into the older part of town. Beggars and prostitutes, grubby bookshops with lurid signs. She dragged him past the titillating displays, dragged him deeper into the underbelly of the inner city. Sirens wailing down the grooved streets. After them.

'Come on. Keep going. They'll never catch us in the market.'

'I'm not going back.' Staring at a faded set of pictures clipped from some magazine, topless girls tacked to a grubby billboard.

'No, it's this way. Keep going and then go left.'

He shook his head, slack jawed.

'No, Mags, I'm not going back. I'm not going back to Trafarionath.'

The Sikh shopkeeper squinted at him, moustache bristling as the youth stared at his turban.

She hurried him on past the curry house next door. 'Don't start on that now, for Christ's sake,' she snarled, grabbing him under the armpit and manoeuvring him along the street. Funny looks on all sides. Bright yellow neon glowing against the dull concrete. CAR PARK. She pushed him down the narrow alley to the stairs, rancid smells streaked along the dingy walls. Stale beer and a squeal of brakes behind them. Mags peered over her shoulder, spotted two uniformed officers clambering out of a hideously colourful police car. Somebody had been busy with the Day-Glo canister on that too. She was crying now, crying in his ear.

'Keep going, come on, you stupid bastard, they'll catch you. They'll catch us both!'

Taking the steps two at a time. First floor, another police car slewing to a halt by the stairwell. She wrenched the youth on and up the next flight. Switchback sirens wailing, echoing down the steps. Car doors slamming. Shouts. Up again. And again. Mags could hear the officers shouting and panting, running a little more, shouting and panting. Two storeys below. Dragging him easily as if he'd turned to vapour, a scarf blowing in the breeze on a winter beach. She felt as if she'd filled her veins with energy, muscles pulsing with vitality. She'd get him out, get him away. She'd save him and if she couldn't save him she'd stand up for him, stand up in court, tell them they had it all wrong. She pushed a reeking door back and throttled him out into the sunlight. The roof. One or two cars parked at odd points over the worn Tarmac, the walls scratched and scored by a dozen shades of car wing, rusty bumpers. She jammed the door shut, backed away, looking this way and that over the deserted rooftop. He hadn't moved. Leaning against the peeling yellow door, the grubby glass a dark mouth ready to chew him up for his cheek.

'We'll double back down the fire escape,' she called, pointing it out. Another jabbing pain in her back where she'd fallen on his bloody jeans, cut herself on his zipper. She staggered, reached for the throbbing wound, felt something grate over her kidney, yelped in agony. He stared at her, open mouthed. 'It's nothing. Winded, that's all.' Mags pushed him back against the door as the first police officer barged his way out on to the roof. They fell over each other in a mad tangle of blue serge and black Lycra.

'Less it, mate,' the PC called, scrambling to get a grip on the youth. Mags darted forward, snatched at his outstretched hand and snapped the fingers over. The officer gave a shrill cry, pulled his hand back. Toppled into his colleague, red faced as he squeezed himself through the blocked door. Jonathan scrambled away on all fours after Mags, backing against the wall. Framed between massive pillars, hair blowing over her face against the city-skyline backdrop. Difficult to read her intention, impossible to fathom her. If he'd had days to stand and stare, stare at her as if she'd been sprayed against the grim scenery, he wouldn't have been able to work out what she felt, what she felt about anything. He would never know. Realization a terrible, malignant lump behind his ribs, catching his breath.

She stood at bay, tearing her hair back from her face with one hand, the other clenched behind her. 'Jesus wept!' she called crookedly, doubling up. The city closed in behind her as if he was gazing at her through the bottom of a glass, holding out its hands, holding its hands to catch her if she fell. Blowing up a sudden storm of shiny, steely grit, stinging her eyes. Jonathan hauled himself to his feet, reached for her as the second policeman dashed forward, rugby tackled him to the rough Tarmac.

'No! Mags! The tooth!' he yelled, struggling like a maniac as the heavier policeman manhandled him to the ground.

'Mags, it's the tooth! You fell on the tooth!' he spluttered, struggling against the burly officer. Mags twisted from side to side, felt the bloody blade cutting through her stomach, slicing through muscle, tearing through her packed abdomen. The blade he'd used on the Grainger man. There, thought it. Acknowledged what she'd known from the beginning. The strange boy's secret. He'd killed Grainger. Panic stricken, cracked. He'd cracked the old man like a soft-boiled egg and let his double yolks spill over the worn carpet. What had he done to deserve that, being cut up and rolled under the logs, the papers said. She should have confronted him, made him face up to it. She'd known and she'd done nothing but run, run nowhere with him. Some help to him. Some help to any of them. And now they'd caught him, caught them both. The struggling officer rolled past her boots, entwined with the shouting youth who grasped her jeans and raked his fingers through the sharp gravel. The first officer, shaken and pale, holding his hand under his armpit. Glaring at her open mouthed, astonished she'd done it. Recognize her again, pick her out of the line up or nod his head when the quiet attendant pulled the sheet from her pale face.

'Mags!'

'Come away from the edge, love,' the officer called shakily, realizing now.

'MAGS!'

Jonathan wriggled out of the policeman's constrictor grip, a conger in the bottom of a boat, sliding and sliming over the harsh Tarmac, uniformed arms flailing after him as he launched himself to his feet, dashed over the rooftop. She'd straightened before he'd taken a step, lips sucked into her clenched mouth as the blade accelerated under her ribs. She grasped her throat, mouth pulled in all directions, comical. Horribly comical. Nodding and retching and swallowing, nodding and contracting the cartilage of her throat against the remorseless fragment, the killing thing he'd used on Grainger. She should have stopped him, she should have shopped him. Jonathan staring at her Adam's apple bobbing under the taut skin of her neck, contorted in agony. Mags straightened in a series of convulsive shudders, raising her trembling arms as if she was balancing herself on a surf board. Jonathan collided with her, clamping his good hand on to her shoulder as she staggered, wracked. A thin dribble of blood running out of her tightly compressed lips. Death's head grin releasing a dozen tentacles of bright blood over her chin, splashing her coat.

'Mags! Mags? The tooth! I'm sorry! Mags!' Screaming at her, incoherent. Eyes wide, wider, clamping her mouth shut against the rush of blood. She staggered, coughed and splashed him, arms clamped over her chest, hands spread over her stomach as the second policeman dashed forward. She could see his mouth pulled in all directions as he bellowed at her, but couldn't hear him. Only the little voice in her head.

'*Two birds with one stone. Fly away, little one.*' Turning, twisting her head to see who'd spoken, who'd drifted over to gently whisper in her bleeding ear. They struggled to and fro in front of her, arms everywhere. A thin hand, a woman's hand thrust into her vision, thrust between her eyes, clamping her contorted face. For a moment she'd imagined Molly, pictured her face twisted with hate. Why did she detest her so much? What had she ever done to her apart from sit in a car with her lecherous husband? They hadn't done anything. What gave her the right to give herself airs, queen-bitch it over her like that? She felt the wall, cold and hard behind her, sticking her up as the woman shape in her vision closed in. Closed in for the kill.

'*Two birds, one stone,*' the whispering voice repeated. A hollow laugh of triumph, a supercilious hand waving her away, pushing her over the precipice with deadly supernatural force.

'Mags! I'm coming with you!'

No time now. No time to say anything more than he'd said already. What had he said, what had he told her? He'd told her his life and this was it. It would have to do, same as things had always had to do. If he could only have told her, told her it was worth it, his three days away. The officer dived for the boy's feet, the outsized trainers already kicked and scuffed, splattered with red dots. Jonathan flung his arm behind her back, propelled them both against the wall, tipped them over. The officer grabbed the youth's flapping hood, wrenched it around as the gravel crunched under his DMs. He flung his weight backwards, held the youth for a second.

'Mike! Hang on!' The officer spread his legs, braced himself against the wall and grabbed the hood in both hands. Enormous, unbelievable weight. The weight of the world, straining, pulling him over too. Back bending with the effort. The girl had sailed on down eight floors, hit the concrete with a shockingly repulsive slap. Mike dragged the kicking youth up a few inches, muscles in his forearms popping with agony.

'I can't help! I can't fucking help!'

'Grab him, for Christ's sake,' he growled through gritted teeth. Looking down, the boy twisting this way and that in his outsize jacket. Twisting round to scratch a handhold in the brickwork. Looking up once. No fear, no anger. Dead eyes. Cat's eyes in the road under the remorseless wheels of the juggernaut. The youth leaned forward, he thought for a mad second he was going to kiss his hand. Bit him. Sank his teeth into the straining tendons.

'Don't be . . . ahh you bastard don't be . . .' Wrenched his hand back, the hood with it, flapping around the semicircular wound. 'Stupid bastard!' yelling at him as he fell head over heels over head to the floor. The officers stared down at the red lake around the spilled laundry, the broken doll-limbs snapped at awkward angles.

'Fucking maniacs. Fucking maniacs.'

'Fucking maniac!' McNair wrenched the Granada to the left, missed the bridge parapet by seven inches. Luckily the tyres were in order, got a grip on the gravel as the heavy car slewed to a halt. The Cortina barrelled past, sickly mauve sprouting rust. Macall thumped into the windscreen, wrenched his head around despite grating pain to watch the Cortina seesaw from one side of the road to the other. The driver stabilized, shot around the corner in a puff of dust.

'All right, guv?'

The blue minivan screamed past the Granada, launched itself from the end of the bridge and bellyflopped into the road in a shower of sparks. Clove road. Hewn from the Hillstones motherlodes. Maybe the mini would have survived those spongy streets of San Francisco but it wasn't made for Hillstones' calloused limestone. The axle crumpled, the driveshaft snapped, king pins gave up the ghost in a tiny explosion of rust and rivets. The minivan pancaked into the verge, nose first, reared up on its smashed suspension for a moment and then came down with a hideous, spine-jarring clang.

'What the bloody hell . . .' McNair levered the Granada door open, took a few steps forward as the minivan disgorged the dazed driver. A shaky leg in badly creased trousers followed by a badly creased reporter on shaky legs. Nicky strode away from the smashed mini as if it was going to blow, looked round sheepishly at the astonished officers.

'Sorry about that. You OK?'
'You are fucking nicked, mate!'

'Don't give me all the aggrochat. That was my bloody wife in that car.'

'So you said,' McNair growled, watching the police constable dabbing Macall's forehead. His boss winced, glared round at the twitching reporter. McNair sighed.

'You could have killed somebody. I don't care if it was the Queen of bloody Sheba you were after.'

Macall waved the officer with the first-aid kit away, strode over. He gave Nicky a knowing leer.

'And who was that with her, eh? I made it curly red-headed male in early twenties, what about you, Sergeant?'

'Didn't see, sir. Too busy avoiding the bridge.' McNair, stiff and formal as Macall let off some steam.

'Theo Malik.' Macall rolled the name around his mouth before spitting it in the reporter's face. 'So what's going on, eh? We knew there was something up with this place but we hadn't figured Clark Kent was involved. Had we, Sergeant?'

'No, sir. Hadn't thought that at all, sir.'

'If you're suggesting I've had something to do with all this you'd better come right out and say so,' Nicky protested feebly, seeing double, feeling queasy. Rotten and queasy.

He'd taken the firm's delivery van to pop up to the high downs. Wind-blown wild country where only the most determined and masochistic fell-walker ever ventured. When Molly wanted to get away from things, and things generally meant him, she'd drive on up over the rutted lanes, park out on the top under the low-slung rain clouds, under the cold black sheet of night sky. Look at the view and calm herself down. He'd generally creep out to the kitchen and slime a cup of coffee together for her as a peace offering. This was going to take more than a cup of coffee though. He'd left the office early, knowing Molly would either be there or she'd be gone. AWOL. For good, for keeps. He knew her enough to know she didn't do this sort of thing lightly.

The Downs had been deserted apart from half a dozen daft sheep who tried to headbutt the mini from the lonely track. As if they were short on space up there in the nothingness. Nicky had blared the horn, driven on despite the thunk-clunk as one of the muttonheads got too near the battered bumper. He'd watched it in the mirror, tottering on down the track. Cursing the stupid creature as he bumped over a cattle grid and turned back on to the main Clove road, just in time to see his beloved Cortina roar past with his beloved wife behind the wheel, face like death. He'd caught a glimpse of curly red hair behind her hunched shoulder too. Stared after his car as Molly shot on down the road towards town.

'Well, you've been involved all along the line as far as I can make out. You were there when the Haberfields crashed, there to find your missus locked in a bedroom with curlytops. Grainger's outside with his guts hanging out while you're sorting out a domestic tiff? Have a word with yourself.'

'I told you before, I only turned up later, when it was all over. The crash as well.' Nicky glared at him. 'You know that as well as I do, so stop wasting my time. Are we going after them or what?'

'What d'you mean, are *we* going after them? You're going down to the station where we'll do you for reckless driving. That's just for starters. *We* will get after your missing missus, mate.'

'You ought to set up a roadblock—'

McNair gripped the big man's shoulders, led him away.

'Give him a minute or he'll say something he'll regret,' he murmured.

'Give him a minute? He's just accused me of God knows what! We've been through the whole thing soup to nuts a dozen times. Why won't he believe me?'

McNair raised his eyebrows, tilted his head to one side. No, he was serious.

'Come on down to the station. We're on to them already. Won't get far now.'

'Well, what the fuck are they up to, where are they going anyway?'

'We were hoping you might be able to tell us.'

Teomalik bent down, peered back in through the window at her. 'You're sure you're all right? You look worse than I do.'

'I'll pick you up here. Just watch out for me,' she told him shortly.

'I'm sorry. I can't go any further. I'll . . . I don't know what.'

Well, he looked like shit, that was true enough. If he was faking he was a damn good actor. If he was suggesting it somehow, suggesting all this whirling about her head, he was a damn good magician. *Party trickster*. Only it wouldn't work unless she was willing. She was willing this all to happen. Like she'd willed Mags over the cliff. Stop it. Get real. Mags had pissed off with her toyboy, was all. She hadn't fallen from any damned cliff. Had she. Had she? Seeing things, was all she needed right now. She concentrated hard, scoured her mind for more answers. The little voice had gone, the funny shadows had shrunk back into the gloomy corners.

'Molly? Are you really going to . . .'

'Get out of sight but keep an eye out. Don't let Nicky see you, for God's sake.' She glanced up into the mirror. No sign yet of her furious husband. She hadn't noticed him until it was too late, driving along the main road heading for Budgworth, the other home. Hap. If it was Hap. If he was the bastarding bastard who'd done that to Mrs Jasper. Bastard. Sitting in her chair with her old tartan cardigan tugged round his body. A cuckoo with a bad back and three days' beard. Shuddering to think of it, blinking as a blue wreck barrelled out of nowhere, damn near drove into the back of the Cortina.

'Oh, Christ. It's Nicky.'

Teomalik had peered round, squinting at the furious red-faced driver, opening and shutting his mouth bellowing silent obscenities.

'Doesn't look too pleased,' Teomalik had observed. 'Do you want me to use the stone? Knock a wheel off?'

What was he asking her for? Knock a wheel off, kill him? Christ, he looked as if he'd kill the two of them happily enough. She'd given him a withering glance, put her foot down. The wrecked Cortina did sixty tops. The van, on its last legs, about fifty-nine. Nicky had glued himself to the Cortina exhaust, waving his arms and changing lanes as they switchbacked down the hill into the town, skidded past the pub and took the fork for Budgworth. The bridge, looming up ahead. The mini a few lengths behind. A pale Ford nosing over the ramp.

'Jesus!' They couldn't miss. The other driver must have been on his toes, swerving out of their way to avoid them. Gravel flying about like shrapnel, brakes screeching. A terrified face pressed to the glass and they were gone. Teomalik heaving, buckled into his seat. Thank God he had nothing left to spew, just bad breath and little ropes of spit.

They took the bend way too fast, Nicky's worn tyres slipping over the worn Tarmac, fishtailed and corrected, sped on toward the city. She eased back, kept one eye on the mirror as they took bend after bend, climbing over the Hillstones peaks, descending the tortuous trail towards the sprawling city. He slipped further and further down into the worn seat, looking up mournfully at her.

'Thank you, for helping, you know,' he gasped, half dead by now. She pulled in.

'It's the stones, I can feel them in my guts.' He wasn't kidding. She hadn't seen these precious stones of his. Where the hell did he have them stashed?

'You'll have to go alone, it's the only way. I've told you what to do.' He'd told her all right. Do this do that. Get the stones from him, whatever happens. Whatever happens? He was only here for the bloody beer, she had to live, go on living here. The curious surge she'd felt, a rush of emotion she'd not been able to catalogue. She shook her head, avoided his gaze.

'You must. You know him. You'll pick him out. Get him away from the stones, get them to me. Leave him. It's up to the wagon people to sort it out. If he's got the stones they'll never catch him, only his skin. His shell. He'll be able to move between, here and there. Anywhere.' He blew a gust of rancid breath.

'But you've got the stones, you know, you can feel them. I can't.'

'You'll know. The remote. It's got to be the remote.'

'So I go in, grab it and run for it. The bastard strangled Mrs Jasper and all I'm after is the stones. What the hell did he need to do that for, anyway? He was never like it before.'

Teomalik fiddled with his lip. 'I . . . well.' He shrugged.

'What?'

'I was thinking about that. About slipstreaming, how it changes you.'

'Changes you into a granny-killer?'

'I haven't killed anybody.'

Molly glanced at him. Yet. Was it his suggestion or had she read it off his mind, picking up on his thoughts too? Maybe slipstreaming had changed her as well. Madam Molly, Queen Molly, Our Molly. Amiarillin. How had she known her name?

'What I mean, slipstreaming, maybe it alters your personality, maybe it brings out parts of your character that weren't there before.'

Molly nodded. 'Changed the nice old man into a cunning, murderous bastard. So how's it changed you?'

Teomalik grimaced, shifted uncomfortably in the broken seat. 'You tell me.'

'I didn't know you before. You'll have to be honest with me, with yourself.' Christ, now she sounded like Marge Proops. Come to me with all your supernatural problems.

'Before? I had my uncle. Tarkemenis. When he was about you didn't need to ... you know ... take too many decisions. He was a warlock, an elder. He was a Powerlord, first rank. You didn't need to think when you were with him, just go along,' he said glumly. 'He looked after me, when he was able.'

'Marvellous. I'm your substitute uncle, I get to make all your decisions for you.' She thumped the steering-wheel hub. 'It's up to me to make your mind up for you. No wonder your suggestions weren't that strong.' Now he looked hurt, sick and hurt. Go ahead, kick him when he was down.

'What about the boy? This Rabbit whatever his name is.'

'I've no idea. He's used to dealing with his creatures, not humans. He may find it more difficult persuading you people to go around doing his dirty work.'

Molly thought of Mags again, following him around like a sheepdog on heat. Toppling over the cliff. The hell was she thinking about a cliff for? She sighed. Grainger, slaughtered and dragged into the woodshed. Mrs Jasper. Mrs Jasper. Christ, she'd been in charge!

'The wagon people will punish him, if they can catch him,' Teomalik repeated wearily.

'The bastard. What did he have to do that for anyway? She was no threat to him,' Molly cried.

Teomalik shrugged, spent. 'Get the stones, then we'll find out, find out everything.'

She leaned over, thought about kissing him. Held a finger to his caked lips instead.

'Just wait, keep an eye out. OK?'

'Hokay,' he said, stood back. Molly put the Cortina in gear, pulled away. Watched him stagger up the verge and clamber over a stile. Green T-shirt too big for him, big heavy boots. Up to me, then. Didn't know whether to laugh or cry. Tried both.

LOGGING IN

The blinking bright strip-lighting running in triple rows along the length of the incident room flared, faded. Generator up the spout probably. Macall looked along the room, two dozen officers looking as busy as possible. Nobody wanted another bawling-out from the DCI. McNair playfully punched a socket, returned his finger to the enormous wad of missing persons the police central computer had obligingly spewed out for them. 'Must be overloading the bloody thing, all this lot,' he joked mirthlessly. Macall ignored him, blew smoke toward the buzzing lighting. A result at last. Bloody messy one but a result all the same. The dopey kid and his wacky girlfriend, trapped in a city car park after being spotted at the bus terminal. Eighth floor, no way out, the pair of them had taken up hang gliding.

'Some kind of lovers' tryst,' McNair had theorized. 'They'd been involved in the whole scam since the beginning. He'd been involved with Theo·Malik and the old hippie, running God knows what down to the convoys. Somehow the whole thing falls apart, Grainger gets stabbed and they do a runner. Realize we've got them bang to rights so they jump.'

Macall had nodded, totally unconvinced. Turning the tooth they'd picked from what was left of the girl's pelvis over and over in his hand. He'd already managed to prise a couple of nicks in its plastic zip-top bag. Sharp as anything. Shark, McNair had thought. Shark with a chainsaw. Thinking about the Prof again now. Jilly Freeman. He'd have to send McNair over, smooth things over with her following his outburst that morning. They'd missed something, something small which would tie the whole thing together, tie it up nice and neat. Christ, they needed a break, bodies piling up down in the morgue like a bad day in Dodge City. Chief Super popping his pacemaker in frustration. Get me a result, get me something to take to the boss. Three days we've got five bodies. Six if you count the geezer they fished out of the gorge. Had a bit of an argument with the lifts at Budgworth Royal Infirmary. Last known sighting of young Master Haberfield before he takes a nosedive from the car park. What the hell had the Haberfield kid done to stir the poor bastard up so much? There couldn't be a connection, could there? Miller hadn't had more than a few speeding tickets. Nine-to-fiver in some office in London. According to the doctors he should have been dead on arrival. Those porters stuck in the lift with him, they'd be off work for weeks. Come out looking as if they'd gone down seven floors too. Seven million floors, straight to the basement. A couple of PCs down there waiting to interview them, get the story straight.

Macall looked up wearily as the lights faded to a submarine dim glow, spluttered back up again. 'Any chance of getting Maintenance up to shove 50p in the slot?' he called. A few polite laughs. Keeping the boss quiet for the afternoon. The telephone trilled, McNair lifted the receiver.

'You what?' As if on cue the computer terminal behind the pretty blonde WPC erupted into life, a wave of blue paper rolling and folding from the printer. Made the WPC jump so much she spilled her coffee over the table. Macall leapt to his feet.

'It's doing what? What's it call you?' McNair barked. Macall danced backwards, piping hot coffee staining his trousers. 'Well, fetch a cloth, give us a tissue or something,' he ordered, pinching his trousers in a little wigwam away from his skin. The WPC was poring over the computer readout, pulling the sheets through her hands. Macall yelped, unzipped and tugged his trousers down over his boxers. Whistles and catcalls along the office. The WPC looked up quizzically.

'Well? What's wrong with the Flintstones?'

She didn't get it, shook her head. 'It's gone into machine code or something. Look.' She passed the crumpled sheet over to the detective, who pursed his lips, snatched the paper from her. Wasn't much on high technology but he was fluent in Gobbledegook.

'What's all this rubbish?'

'It's the trawl program I was running on the old chap, Tark. Seems to have struck a chord somewhere.'

'Get the bloody thing to spit it out in English and we'll be laughing,' he snapped.

McNair put the receiver down, raised his eyebrows.

'Flintstones?'

'Never mind. What's your problem?'

'Computer's gone mad up at Uni. Jilly's— er, Doctor Freeman's department. Seems our lozenges have crashed their system.'

'Do what?'

'The lozenges, those little stone things we pulled out of his . . .' Macall waved his hand.

'The stones have done what?'

'Locked me out. I can't access anything. It didn't accept my password.' Albie Keen's high-pitched voice had climbed a few octaves since he'd buzzed up from Backup. Jilly flicked her hair behind her ears, closed her eyes.

'You're the expert. I told you my terminal was playing up.'

'It's not just yours. The whole network's down.'

Barbie down? The whole shooting match?

'What about Ken? He's supposed to cut in if there's a problem on the mainframe, isn't he?' Jilly losing her temper now. She had a wad of data waiting to file before she went home and none of that was making any sense either. Preliminary carbon dating on one of the stone tablets they'd been analysing for those bloody rude coppers. No way. Somebody in the lab must have made a mistake. Do it again? They'd done it three times already. The stones were between 1.2 and 1.3 million years old. Made them what, mid-Pleistocene at least. Glaciers retreating, development of early forms of modern man. Chemical composition way off the spectrum, closest the lab could come up with was some sort of incredibly concentrated lysergic diethylamide. LSD. Neanderthal man on acid? Make some sense of that before you report back to Detective Inspector Snidey Bastard. Make some sense of all that before you get home, grab a bath, get changed and get down to the Waterside cinema by eight to meet Allan. He was over from the Sorbonne for a week on an exchange and she'd got to him first. Bollocks.

'Ken's down too,' Albie squeaked.

She pictured him in his cubbyhole office looking out over the mainframes, blips and bleeps running zigzag colours over his glasses. Worried technicians poking and prodding their glossily packaged icons. 'What is it, some kind of virus?' With so many whizzkid wankers about the university they were fishing oh so clever little packages out of the system every week. Shredder programs, melts, double-whammies. If they put half the effort into serious research they'd have cured cancer by now. Jilly wound her fingers around the receiver, squeezed. Albie's voice rose another three octaves.

'If it's a virus it's eaten up all our protect programs,' he wailed, slammed down the phone.

Jilly buzzed Liz, her assistant. 'Get through to French. Get a message to Allan I might be late.'

'Late? Are you off your trolley?'

'Just tell him, OK? The mainframe's gone down. Looks like one of the students we cut last term has left a little going away present.'

'Well, if you're sure,' brightening, 'no problem.'

No problem all right, she'd probably nip over the quad, maybe give him the bad news herself. Conniving bitch. Probably her who threw the wobbly in the system to keep her occupied while she moved in on M. le Hunk. She stormed down the hall and ran into a gaggle of lecturers shouting at the tops of their voices across the corridor, ducked underneath and shouldered her way to Backup. Punched the door code and walked in. Albie had wheeled his chair away from his terminal, turned the mouse over to check it was rolling properly. He looked up, gulped.

'What do you mean, locked you out?' she snarled.

He froze, pointed to the screen, light blue triangles, parallelograms, all meshed together like a child's Spirograph. She watched a new line snake from the central hub, straighten to form a new axis. Another and another, blooming brittle branches. Albie jumped out of his seat as she pulled up her chair, dragged the keyboard toward her.

—Log on Cruella.
—Log on Cruella.

'Come on, you bastard. It's not letting me in at all. What's the override?'

'Sindy. I tried all that, it froze me out, then spat out twenty feet of Cantfail.'

'Cantfail?'

'The basic interpreter. Machine code, you know.'

'Twenty feet of Cantfail,' Jilly snorted, tapped — Sindy. Another eruption of light from the screen, the forest of fibre optics resolving, reshaping themselves. Triangles to squares. Twelve neat boxes stacked around the central glowing hub. Christ, it reminded her of the . . .

'What? Who's been fucking around? Come off it, Albie, it must be one of your anoraks doing all this.'

Albie held up his hands. 'I swear on my Amstrad it's not any of ours. It's far too deep in the system. It's rewritten all our basic functions, jumbled the command words. I've tried rerouteing the basic functions around Cantfail, everything.'

— Sindy. Sindy. Sindy. The block of squares cascaded to the right of the screen, bloomed, re-formed around the central hub. Lines stronger, glowing, the faintest trace of the strange script beginning to form orderly ranks in each glowing grid.

'You'll fuck it all up if you piss it off,' Albie moaned. 'That's what they do, these hackers, take you on and let you annoy them so they've got an excuse to nuke the entire databank.' He was hopping from foot to foot, flushing red under his specs. Jilly ignored him, concentrated on the lurid green letters popping up on the screen.

'Some bloody sci-fi freak. One of your bloody anoraks, Albie.'

'What, asteroids? Do me a favour. Look, I'll get on another terminal, see if I can patch in some kind of retroprotector while you keep it busy.' Albie scuttled out of the office, colliding with puzzled deputations from half a dozen departments. Old Professor Nelson from Astrodynamics moaning his dishes were running helter-skelter idiot jigs of their own. 'What's going on? The Government's not paying my grant to tune in to the Albanian Top Twenty,' he shrieked as Albie ducked by. Jilly slammed the door, pulled herself up to the overheating terminal. The box was revolving slowly, the bright edges running into the dark margins as it rotated as if, as if it was meant to be viewed on a circular screen. A circular screen? Jilly leaned back, drummed her fingers against her compressed lips, lost in thought for a moment. Jerked the keyboard back toward her.

—S.K.N.

—S.K.A.N.E. The box stopped in mid-orbit, rotated slowly back the way it had come. The squiggles next to the upside-down Vs glowed, stood out from the rest of the incomprehensible runic text. 'Noises fondly on a mountain,' the little stones said. The little stones that had just gotten themselves a big brother, a big brother in their system. Jesus. It recognized something maybe. The funny squiggle, the upside-down Vs on the stones. The stones the lab reckoned were over a million years old. Jilly bit her lip. They'd loaded the computer with text from the bracelet found on the elderly hippie murder victim. Standard binary decipher program they used for any odd bits of data they came across. It was supposed to be giving them a rough translation not the fucking Spanish Inquisition. Jilly chewed a fingernail as Albie came back in, shouldered the door on the noisy gaggle in the main computer room.

'Any luck?'

'Total lockout. Still talking to you?'

'It's something astrological, twelve signs, look, twelve signs and this central shape here. "Noises fondly on a mountain" the computer came up with. It was supposed to be working on the rest of it.' She tapped a red nail against the buzzing screen. Albie frowned. Jilly played her fingers over the keys.

'What is it, then? Some kind of limbo, something outside the planetary configuration? The thirteenth sign?' Albie shook his dark head.

'Whatever it is, it's switched everything off.'

'Where the bloody hell did they get those stones?'

Jilly sat back in the gull-wing chair, swung it this way and that. The door burst open and the principal bustled in, somewhat agitated, Jilly would have guessed. He pushed the astrodynamicist back out of the stuffy control room, practically chopping his arm off in the process. Pulled his wiry grey hair from his eyes and caught his breath.

'Worked it through yet? Was it that bastard American we threw out? The one who made all the letters on my screen fall down that way?' The principal made snowflakes with his fingers.

Jilly raised her eyebrows. 'We're working on it, sir.'

'Er . . . Jilly? The screen.'

Jilly turned. The thirteenth segment, the central hub, had sprouted tiny black veins, little octopus arms flailing and running over the neighbouring segments, running along the lines of letters. Turning them on their sides so the upside-down Vs became sharp backward Cs. The principal squinted at it, looked from Jilly to Albie.

'*Space Invaders*, is it?' he barked.

FERNDALE

Molly had turned off the main Budgworth road at the next junction, taken a winding farm track back up over the Downs to approach the suburb of Rookton the high way, hard way. Verges lined with gutted old armchairs, black bags of garden refuse. Hedges and trees hung with cables, robins nesting in smashed TVs. The council had closed down the old refuse tip further along the road and not many people bothered taking their crap home with them having made the long drive out. Molly bumped over a roll of lino, came down to first as the slope fell away abruptly toward Budgworth. Six hundred thousand people in a vast bowl formed where the Hillstones range dived down to throw up older Oldstones. She checked her watch. Coming up to five now, but the long detour would have been worth it to avoid the cops. The mauve Cortina tended to stand out in a crowd. Hoping nobody had been hurt when that Ford had slewed off the bridge. Blinking back a tear as the hedges gave way to brick walls and slatted fencing, bigger homes higher up the green slopes, smaller semi-ds giving way to row upon row of tidy terraces. Reps' cars every other drive. Lots of kids on the open-plan gardens. Kids. She had enough of her own. Some kind of mother complex coming out here.

Some kind of complex all right, something to do with the itchy thing in her belly. Thinking about it as if she was floating ten feet above the car, not driving it God knew where. Driving around with a tooth in her gut. She spotted the sign for Ferndale, drove another two hundred yards and parked behind a garage forecourt. Shouldn't be too visible here. She took her bag, rummaged for her council pass. Glared at it as if she hardly recognized herself. Bloody awful picture, frizzy hair everywhere. She'd had it cut the very next day as well, neater plaits she could tuck up under her cap with the minimum of fuss. Well, if they catch you doing this you won't need to worry about a pass. You ain't getting in anywhere, sister. Sister? Possibly won't get out for a while. She closed her eyes, composed herself, walked briskly back the way she had driven, on down the Tarmac drive toward the big house.

Purpose built, energy efficient, warden controlled. Jewel in the crown of North Somerset County and Budgworth City Social Services department. Little round windows gave the home a nautical appearance. A tanker, container ship with a hundred refugees clutching one-way tickets. Run aground on sandbanks outside the city. Molly made her way between neatly kept flowerbeds, walked into the reception. A young black girl in a housecoat like hers punching a keyboard, snorting in frustration.

'Hello. Playing up, is it?'

'Tell me about it. I've only been here six weeks and they've got me on records already. Think I must have got it confused. Sorry, can I help you?'

Molly smiled, flashed her badge. 'I'm Molly Fish. I work at Clove Heights. They transferred some of our people up here on Saturday and I thought I'd pop in and see how they are getting on. Got quite attached to some of them, you know. Been there so long I was wondering if they'd settle all right.'

The black girl nodded. 'Go on through. They had some trouble with one of them . . . Mr . . .'

'Fletcher?'

'Swore a lot. Called me a . . . well, you have to make allowances, I know.' She looked hurt. 'But Mr Derek said if we had any more trouble he'd transfer him out to Bleakdale. Didn't want anybody rocking the boat.'

Molly nodded, pointed up the hall.

'They're all in the main lounge. Can't miss it.'

They had a super-duper wall-size Tell-Me-Visual with stereo sound and everything. Made the tea for them all as well, Hap wouldn't wonder. Wouldn't have to worry about the bra-straps getting funny, tipping saucers over him. Only Hap wasn't wondering, wasn't watching. Wasn't watching the Tell-Me, at any rate. Had to keep an eye out, had to keep on your toes in case that damned slime woman came back after him. Her or those bloody pale horny things swarming over the lake as if they'd turned it to scum and ashes under their filthy feet. Trampling the reflection, the old man's face, cracks in an old plate swimming with watery soup. His bony hands grasping and searching up over the bank at them, maybe he'd gripped her heels, holding her on the crumbling bank as the stink things swarmed out of the shallows for her, tongues hanging out and their knives held ready. Had no choice, had to run. He shuddered.

'Cold, dear? Do you want to go nearer the fire?' A nurse. Beatty, she'd said her name was. On him as soon as he moved. 'Want another blanket for your knees?'

'I'm fine, thank you,' Hap said politely. Remember polite, remember new life.

'OK, then, Mrs Jasper. Shout if you need anything.'

Beatty strode on out of the room, past the nodding

heads. Fletcher. Look at the old buzzard eyeing him like that. In the coach, glaring at him, pulling the driver's arm.

'He's not one of ours!'

He's not one of ours. All right, Father, give us a break.

'He's not Mrs Jasper!'

'If you say so. Who is it, then?'

'I wish you'd tell him to be quiet, driver, none of us are feeling up to his nonsense now,' Hap had told the driver primly, tugging Mrs Jasper's tartan cardigan around his shoulders. The rest of them had nodded nervously or just plain nodded. Hell, they knew they were going to be locked in with him, whoever he was. Ten, twenty years some of them had been up at Clove Heights. Out in an afternoon, packed up and boarding the coach for Ferndale that evening. Still in shock, most of them.

'Give 'em a break, old son.'

'I'm not your fucking son, mate!' Fletcher had snapped. That's it, keep going, keep droning on swearing every other word. You're my ticket out of here, you foul-mouthed old git. As long as we've got you along making all this fuss they're going to let me walk right on into my new life. Long as I keep alert, keep my eyes open, remember who I am. Just because I'm not paranoid doesn't mean to say they're not talking about me. Talking about me when they'd arrived at the big place with the lights and little windows. Fletcher throwing his arms about as they helped him up the steps behind.

'I'm not going anywhere with that bastard, he's as bad as the little cunt that cut Grainger! Ask him what he's done with Tina why don't you . . . Stop pulling me about, you bastard!'

Helping him to his room along the end corridor on

the ground floor. The restraint suite, where he couldn't disturb the rest of the guests. Guests. Hap reached into Mrs Jasper's handbag, untangled the letter from the knitting. Let's try and remember. Dave and Maggie. Nephew. Moved to Hong Kong 1967. Hadn't seen dear old Aunt Tina for years. Wouldn't recognize her now. Spiky iron-grey hair, bit heavier than last time. Maybe talk to a beautician about these whiskers. That was what it was all about really, having somebody there who'd take the trouble to pluck 'em for you, spider-leg nostrils, caterpillar ears. Couldn't play it too dumb, though, too hopeless. Had to be able to get about under his own steam. They'd be giving him baths otherwise. Monday and he hadn't had a bath yet. Understaffed, they said. Poor old Beatty run off her feet. Run off her feet the way those creatures had run over the lake, skipped and paddled the filthy water as they scrambled up the bank like beetles, overcome the Spawn Witch as she kicked helplessly in the old man's sinewy grip. So much for your magic lady. Just like all the rest, wanting a piece of him, tearing strips from him. If he'd been twenty years younger she wouldn't have treated him like that, pushing him back, cursing his useless body as she held him down with one hand.

They were all the same, wanting a piece of you. He saw that clearly now. Funny how he'd never managed to bring things into focus before, seen things the way they were. The way they'd taken him off to the home just because he'd collapsed in the corner shop that time. Couple of weeks and he'd have been as right as rain, back home in the High Street along from the Boar. Easy walk and a restful pint by the roaring grate, could have gone on for years, his own boss. Instead, they sold him to the Tell-Me, lashed him to it so he could hardly think straight, think how they'd wasted his time, taken his life.

He didn't need their wall-size super-duper Tell-Me now. He'd manage without it. He could run his funny old films in his own head now. Hap tapped the bag in his lap as if reassuring himself the stones were still there. Get out of here, get out to Kowloon and bye-bye Dave and Maggie. He had money. He'd retrieved a hundred from his sock drawer, another wad from Mrs Jasper's handbag along with the slip from her post office account. They'd emptied it for her as she was going away.

He closed his eyes. No. I won't think about that. I won't think about that, not now, not ever. It's mine, it's mine now and it's my life, just starting up again that's all. Throw that knitting away too, first chance he got. She was finished, he wasn't. Starting up while there was still a chance. Nature's way. Bloody tooth and claw. Survival of the fittest and all that. Hap arranged the uncomfortable heavy skirt, tugged at the thick surgical stockings itching so bad he could have cheerfully scratched his legs right off, managed in a wheelchair. He'd manage till Friday. Friday they were coming for him. Coming to take him away. Ha ha!

'Mrs Jasper? Hello, it's Molly. Molly from the home.'

'Oh and Nicky,' Bell called from the steps of Clove police station, 'don't go too far in the mini tonight, all right?'

Bastard. Funny bastard. Nicky showed his teeth, stomped off along the High Street. Too late to go in to the office, he'd catch up tomorrow. Wilf would have plenty of copy from the county social services committee. See if Molly still had a job. See if Nicky still had a Molly. Nice to have things straight like that. They could have their pick of the gorge death-crash stories as well. Write a bloody book. He paused in the market square, checked his watch. Five past four. Might as well. He pushed into the Boar, early drinkers standing near the fire, bent over their pints. He eased himself up on his barstool, nodded to Roy.

'Evening, Roy.'

'Evening, Evel.'

'Evel?'

'Knieval. First twenty-year-old minivan in space. Good one, Nicky.'

This town. Didn't need a fucking newspaper, everybody living here tuned in twenty-four hours a day to the bush telegraph. Nicky sighed.

'We saw it on our way back from town. Write off, I said.' He pushed a foaming lager across the polished mahogany. Nicky gulped at the froth.

'It wasn't my fault. I spotted Molly.'

'In your car with that Theo character, yeah, I heard.'

Jesus Christ!

'Heading for Budgworth, almost killed those coppers. What are they going to do you for?'

'Reckless, without due care, something like that. In the circumstances they'll probably let me off with a caution.'

'Pigs might fly.'

'They damn near did,' Nicky muttered.

Mary ducked under the red curtain into the bar. White faced.

'What's wrong? Mary?'

'I've had the police on.'

'He's walking home, don't worry about that,' Roy said, wiping the bar down with a cloth.

'No. Roy. It's Mags. She's . . .'

Roy twitched, looking around the astonished drinkers, back to his wife, crying gently. Never seen Mary cry before. Big woman with big arms and cartoon postcard cheeks. Roy touched her thick forearm, awkward.

'She's dead. She jumped off a building with that kid from the crash.'

Silence. Police Sergeant Bell hurried in, snatched his hat from his balding blond head.

'Roy, Mary. They've only just got through to us . . .'

Roy waved his hand slowly, Mary crying into his chest in front of the drinkers, twitching, not knowing where to look so looking in their pints, the future.

'We've just heard. There's some flap on up at HQ. I would have . . . you know, told you myself.'

'Don't worry, Martin. We'd better have a drink,' Roy said stonily.

'Where are you off to in such a rush?' Bell asked, holding his arm across Nicky's chest.

'Give me a break, Sarge. Molly's with that Theo bloke. If he's got the same thing in mind . . .'

'Leave it to us,' Bell advised, raising his eyebrows.

'We left Mags to you,' Nicky said coldly, brushed him aside and walked out into the suddenly chill evening air.

'See this?' she whispered, close to his twitching face. Five o'clock shadow, how the hell did he think he was going to get away with this shit? How many people was he going to fool, a gorilla passing itself off as a donkey? Christ, he'd managed all right so far, she reminded herself, got past her once already. My responsibility. She eased the plastic tube from her bag, watched his grey eyes flicker from it, back to her. 'It's called Mace.' Not supposed to have it but Nicky had got it from a bloke in Budgworth when he'd done a feature on self-defence courses for women. 'I spray it in your face and you'll cough your fucking lungs up if your heart lasts that long. Do you understand?' she hissed into his hairy ear.

He nodded slowly, iron-grey hair combed and teased in half a dozen directions. Looked like Sid Vicious. Sid Vicious. Hap Vicious. Vicious old bastard, finger millimetres from giving him a faceful anyway.

'We're going to the bathroom, you and I.'

Grey eyes flickered to her face, back around the nodding heads.

'You can walk, presumably. You had enough strength to hide Mrs Jasper's body in the woodpile,' she hissed.

'It was an accident. I didn't mean . . .'

'Shut your mouth, you miserable old bastard. You took her last little bit of dignity with you and that was . . . that was, never mind now. Get up, go to the bathroom, I'll help you. Try anything and I'll tear your skirt off, let them see who they've got here.'

Hap glanced at her, white faced, no pretending. Eyes colder than the Spawn Woman's, for a moment he thought she was the Spawn Woman. Bent over his groin with that knife. Keep going, do what she says. Wait. He rose slowly, tucking his bag under one arm as Molly eased a hand under his armpit, slipping the canister into her pocket.

'All right, dear?' Beatty, bright, efficient, overworked.

Molly smiled broadly. 'Molly Fish. From Clove Heights. Thought I'd just come and see how our lot were settling in, didn't I, Mrs Jasper?'

'Huh? Yes. See how we were getting on,' Hap repeated flatly.

'Glad of the help, to be honest. You're OK, are you? You look a bit pale yourself.' Concerned look.

'Period. Just what I needed.'

'Know what you mean. All right then, love, you go with your friend.' She strode off across the room holding a large urine bag away from her. Molly gave him a shove, propelled him toward the hall. Fletcher held up his hand.

'It's not Mrs Jasper,' he whispered, eyes darting around the room. 'There's nothing wrong with my eyes,' he said, rolling them. Molly nodded.

'Everything under control. And Bernie.'

'What?'

'You said that without swearing.'

'Did I?'

She left him puzzling, helped Hap on down the hall, the toilets she'd spotted on her way in. The black girl looked up from the terminal.

'I think I've buggered it. You aren't any good with them, are you?'

'Not my department, sorry.' *This is my department. Molly Von Stern, She-Wolf of the SS. Confessions extracted while you wait. See how I look after my charges. I'm in charge now, queen bee around here.* In through the oversized door, big enough for wheelchairs or frames. Bright shiny light bouncing all ways over the white tiling, the pink tiling of her brain.

'Don't even think it, Hap. Faceful of Mace and your heart won't take it, I promise.' She let him go, wiped her hand on the towelflow. He stood away against the wall, looking around, furtive. Pathetic in the cheap print blouse, tartan cardigan, the thick skirt and wrinkled stockings. A drag act from hell. *Cornered you now, you old bastard, eh? Watch him though, who knows what he's got left.* *Scuttling from the hut, the stone under his arm. The stone which would have kept them off, kept them away.* Away? Kept who away? She blinked, concentrated hard.

'I want the stones. The remote and the tablet.'

'Remote?'

'You heard.'

'It's in my bag.'

'Throw it down. Not the stones, the bag. Carefully.'

He clutched it to his chest, Molly pulled the canister from her pocket, took a step forward.

'Don't fucking try it, Hap, or so help me—'

He threw the bag in her face before she'd finished her sentence. Molly pressed the nozzle, squirted a wall as she staggered back. Hap ducked his head, lower than she'd have imagined, bulldozed into her stomach knocking the wind out of her and the Mace canister from her hand. Cold, slippery panic trembling in her arms and legs. She slipped backwards on the shiny tiles, Hap collapsing on top of her. Tearing pain in her stomach where she must have pulled a muscle. He yelped, wriggled on top of her. She caught him behind the ear with a punch, knocked him sideways, brought her knee up into his stomach. He retched, rolled over grasping for the bag. Molly kicked him off, crawled fast for the Mace. He clutched her shoe, pulled her leg back. Rolled over, horribly athletic now, tore the knitting needle from the bag and brought it around in a vicious arc. Point buried inches into her thigh. She screeched, fingers scrabbling for the rolling canister. Hit a wall, stopped. Hap knelt up, pulled the knitting from the bag as Molly slithered over the floor. No lock on the door. Shit. Be quick. He pulled the yarn between his fists, knelt behind her and threw it around her neck. Just like Mrs Jasper walking in on him back in the home.

Saturday afternoon, the whole place still in an uproar, police moving in, old folk moving out. Launched from the chaos by the hut into the chaos in the home. Walking in on him as he sat on the floor in a puddle, dead carp flapped over the rug. Trying to think where he was, where he'd been, who he was. Who he'd been. Boiling, writhing. Blinking against the jagged light flowing in from the hall. Who was she talking to? Who did she think she was? Gazing at him as if she couldn't register. Couldn't register but he could. Tina Jasper, out of here they'd never catch him ever again. Those pale goblins, that dusky maiden, sliding out of the mist to slice bits from his body. Impaled like a block of fly-blown meat in a kebab shop. They'd be looking for him, they'd never find him dressed like her. That's right, work the knitting around her neck and tug it tight, didn't take long, didn't even hurt. Hap took a second, thought about hurt, the ache in his belly. Molly grasped the canister, worked the nozzle over her shoulder and sprayed. The door opened, Fletcher standing crooked, looking from Hap, rolling and choking over the floor, to Molly crouched by the wall tearing the knitting from her neck, needle bent awkwardly into her leg.

'His bag, get the bag.' She pointed it out to him as the black girl burst in, wide eyed.

'What happened? What's that smell?'

'He tried to spray me with Harpic,' Molly said, coughing. Mr Fletcher strode across the room, picked the bag from Hap's grasping fingers.

'I think he got a faceful.'

'Mr Fletcher?'

'She. I think she got a faceful.' Climbing to her feet clutching her leg as the black girl reached for the big red panic button.

'Don't worry. You'll only upset the lot of them. She used to play about like that back at Clove. Let's get her back to the lounge,' Molly said shakily.

'But your leg . . . she could have cut an artery . . . Jesus!'

Molly eased the needle from her thigh, dropped it, faint. White. Fletcher stood awkwardly, tucking the bag under his arm. The black girl knelt as Hap rolled from side to side, features stained a bright puce, tongue thick and furry between his lips. The dusky maiden. He could make her out in the stinging goblin mist. She'd come back for him. They wouldn't be far behind, the rest of them.

TOGETHERNESS

'Sprayed you with Harpic?' Beatty looked from Molly to Mr Fletcher, eyebrows twitching private codes, back to Molly.

'She used to do it all the time back in Clove. Used to be a cleaner, see?' Fletcher told her, fanatical gleam in his eye she didn't like to challenge. Wasn't exactly the model guest himself, now, was he? Shouting and bawling obscenities since they'd brought them in. Calmed down a little now, perhaps this Molly woman had some kind of steadying influence. Standing there quiet, gingerly running her fingers over the livid bruising on her neck. Civilians and they would have been pressing charges. Nurses? Part of the job, wasn't it?

'How's the leg? I'm sure we should get one of the doctors to have a look at it for you.'

Molly waved her hand, drained. Beatty shrugged, rigorously assisted Mrs Jasper to the room along the corridor, wiped the worst of the stuff from her face and ensured she was breathing properly before paging Doctor McGregor at the hospital. He was on his way.

'We'd best leave the restraints on, until she's calmed down a bit,' Beatty said. Needed something all right. Bullet between the eyes would do the trick.

'She used to throw a wobbly if she didn't think the place looked clean enough,' Molly added unconvincingly, looking about the lounge.

'Not clean enough?' Beatty bristled. Kept the place like a new pin, staff cuts or no. Nobody could go around saying her guests weren't properly looked after, she wouldn't have it.

'Well, if you're sure about the leg,' she said, breezing back down the hall. 'I'm just sorry you've had such a miserable trip.'

Molly nodded, cracked a smile. The stones, the tablet. Teomalik waiting out in the fields. Miserable trip pretty fair description. Beatty strode into the lounge to prop up one of her charges. Fletcher nodded his stubbly grey head toward the hall. Molly followed him out, limping as the cold pain spread up her thigh. The old man ducked into the telephone alcove, handed her the bag. She tilted her head, studied him. Cheeks sucked dry over the bony jaw, unevenly shaved black and white bristles.

'In there, are they?'

Hell did he mean by that? She rummaged quickly, retrieved the remote from the broken strands of Mrs Jasper's knitting. Slates in a fishing net.

'You knew?'

He nodded, bristles rippling like seaweed on his rocky chin.

'You didn't say anything?' Molly looked down at the smooth tablet, tiny runes in regular shapes, engrained with centuries of waxy grime. Tucked the tablet in her pocket, patted it safe.

'Off then, are we?' Beatty back already, ruthlessly efficient in her crisp white uniform. An overworked angel. God she was jumpy, holding the remote to her chest like a gun, sticking the old fellow up.

'From our TV lounge. Mrs Jasper must have taken it by mistake. We're stuck on Channel 4,' Molly improvised.

Beatty frowned, clicked her tongue. 'How dreadful.

Time you were going now, I expect.' Wanting her out now, not sure why.

'I was just saying goodbye, to Mr Fletcher,' nodding for emphasis.

'Right you are. Back to your place, that's enough excitement for one day.' She eased a powerful, professional hand under Fletcher's armpit, manoeuvred him toward the lounge. He glared over her shoulder once, nodded. My last friend. Who'd have thought it? Whatever he was thinking, whatever he'd seen. She could have screamed out loud right there and then. She'd never know. They weren't going to let her come trawling through the old folk again, upsetting them, making them remember. All those years stuck down in Clove, never saying a thing unless it began with *F* and ended in *off*. Molly straightened her coat, limped on down the hall past the black girl. One of the gardeners was leaning over her shoulder, ingratiating smile as he punched keys.

'My kids would know what was wrong with it, whizzers they are,' he was telling her. The black girl looked up.

'OK, are they? Are you sure your leg's going to be all right?'

'It's all settled now. Everything under control,' she lied. 'Apart from this bloody thing.' Out into the open air, street lights spluttering into life along the busy road, traffic building up now. She tugged the coat about her, closed her mind to the fireworks going off all colours inside her head. Pain registering now, dull first but sudden thrusts in her leg muscle as she hurried along the cracked pavement. She reached the garage, stopped dead. Two police constables prodding the Cortina as if it was going to bite. She bowed her head, hobbled on down the road toward the lights of the city, twinkling down the hill.

*

'Whoa, there she is!' Nicky pointed to the huddled figure hurrying along the passenger-side pavement. Molly. Beth checked her mirror, pulled in.

'What are you doing? Get after her!'

Beth shook her head. 'Lift up here's fair enough, but this is your problem, Nicky.' She watched him fidgeting in his seat, watching his wife limp toward the city centre. What was she doing, disguising herself as Quasimodo? Nicky's green eyes glittered maliciously. Been up all night, had she? Worn herself out, couldn't keep her legs together. He nodded slowly.

'Right. Look, cheers, Beth. Even if she . . . you know.'

She leaned over, giving him a start and a waft of her scent. Perfume. She flicked the door catch.

'Oh yes . . . right. Let's get it over with, then.'

The afternoon had been a complete daze, kaleidoscope of faces and places. He'd walked back from the pub thinking about Mags and the boy, trying to work out the connections. Him and Theo. Mags and Molly. He must have pushed her. Maybe she pushed him? Somebody had carved old Grainger up after all. Locked Molly in with Theo while they made their escape. He slumped behind his typewriter, studied Wilf's bleak message. Roy doesn't know yet. He does now. It could wait, they had all week until the next edition. Maybe it ought to go out with black borders, the Somme casualties they were getting. Black borders for Molly maybe, for their marriage. Black borders for that bastard Theo if he got his hands on him.

The telephone had rung, he'd answered first time.

'Nicky? It's Claire. Look, has Molly been in touch yet?'

'No, not a word.'

'She rang me before dinner. I don't think she's very well. No, calm down. I didn't say that. Look, she told me to ring the police but I don't think she's making any sense. I've been trying to get in touch with you all afternoon.' She sounded on the verge of tears. He soothed her, fingers clutching the note from Wilf.

'What she say?'

'She said we'd got it wrong. They'd taken Hap up to Ferndale, not Mrs Jasper. I told her she was out of her . . . I told her she was upset but she wouldn't listen.'

'They'd done what?'

'That Hap had killed Mrs Jasper and disguised himself and they'd taken him to the home instead.'

She wasn't making any fucking sense either!

'You what?'

'Molly says Hap killed Mrs Jasper so he could take her place, get away. Took her clothes and dressed up to make them think he was her. She said she was going on up there after him.'

'This afternoon?'

'This was about midday. I don't think she knows what she's on about, Nicky.'

'I'm sure she doesn't. Look, she definitely said Ferndale? I saw her on the Budgworth road, damn near ran me into the bridge.'

'I've been trying to ring you,' she wailed.

'OK, OK. Look, thanks, Claire. I'll get up there, take a look.'

'What about the police? She told me to ring the police.'

'I think you'd better hang on. Let's sort it out before we get her into any more trouble.'

'That's what I thought. That's why I rang you.'

'OK. As soon as anything happens I'll give you a bell.' He'd dashed along the narrow corridor, poked his head into Beth's office. She was just climbing into her coat.

Ten minutes later they'd been over the bridge, slowing down as they passed the wrecked minivan.

'Jerry doesn't even know yet. He'll skin you when he finds out.'

'Bollocks to that. It's Molly I'm worried about. You heard about Mags and the boy, jumping from that car park. You never know what they'll get up to, what they're involved in.'

'Not Molly. I'm sure she's . . .'

'She went off with him. He didn't force her to go,' he insisted.

Beth frowned. 'Wilf said he'd been on their tail. Spotted them in the bus station. You can't believe it. I mean, what made them do it? Do you think it was him, murdered old Grainger at the home?'

Grainger, Mags, Jonathan. Where the hell was it going to end? He climbed out of the car, paused, hurried after the tiny windswept figure of his wife.

She jumped a mile, he had to cling on to the slick cold leather coat to keep her inside her skin.

'Oh, for Christ's sake, what did you do that for?'

'Do what? Chase halfway across the county to catch up with you? Where the hell have you been, you damn near got me killed!' He was that close to belting her one, fists clenched.

'I had things to do. Not what you think,' she sighed.

Sorry I spoke. Sorry I'm breathing. Where the hell had she been? 'Where's Theo?'

'Theo? Oh . . . I left him . . . back in Clove. I had to see them, you know, the old folk from the home. They're all there.'

'Mass murderers included? Look, Molly. Hang on a minute. What the fuck is going on? Tell me. Level with me. Claire's been on with some crap about Hap. You find him or what?'

She was breaking away as if he was a pesky kerb crawler trying to pick her up. Making him feel like this!

'Hap killed Mrs Jasper, took her place when they shipped them up here.'

Nicky let go her arm. 'And Molly Fish, private eye, is on the trail with her headcase sidekick. Wonderful. I mean, don't bother telling your husband any of this.'

She glared at him, through him, as if he was some kerb crawling creep trying to pick her up.

'*You mean to say I sleep with you?*' she said, voice dropping to a threatening, hungry growl.

'What the fuck is that—'

'I told Claire to phone the police. They ought to be there by now.'

'What did you say? Before?'

'The home. Mrs Jasper's in the woodshed.'

Nicky tensed, eyed her. 'Grainger was in the woodshed, what's the matter with you?'

'She was nearer the back. They must have found him and given up. She was covered in logs and stuff. He'd strangled her with her knitting, taken her clothes, God knows what else.'

Nicky opened and closed his mouth. 'When did all this happen?'

'In the confusion, some time on Saturday. Hap must have done it before they took them all away. You know what it was like, you were there.'

Indignant. Indignant with him!

'And nobody can tell girls from boys any more? Nobody noticed? Come on!'

'They weren't looking that closely. Eight old folk they were told, eight old folk they got.'

'Bollocks. You're not even bothering to give me a

convincing excuse. You've fucked off with this Theo bloke and that's all there is to it. You haven't even got the guts to tell me to my face. That's what hurts, Molly.'

She wiped her eyes, staggered. He was in two minds whether to push her on over and walk off or help her up. Sighed, held her arm and stared back over her shoulder to Beth's car, headlights blinding. Traffic slowing to see what was going on.

'It's not what you think. I'm not going anywhere,' she said fruitily.

'Well, don't sound so fucking disappointed.' He held her stiffly, raggy doll with smeary eyes, running make-up. Christ. Beth was going to have to see her like this.

'Where's the car?'

'The police were looking over it back there,' she nodded up the road.

'I bet they are. Well, we'll go on over, get it over with. I'm looking at a reckless driving for a start. They know it was you with Theo so don't get any ideas about denying it. Perverting the course of justice, aiding and abetting an escaped prisoner, blah blah blah.'

'We've got to get it sorted out first,' she said flatly. No room for argument or contradiction. Nicky shook his head, she eyed him coldly. Strangers.

'And whose name's on the log book? It wasn't me chasing around . . .'

'I don't care about that. I've got to get back to Clove, get something to Te— Theo. It's not what you think, it's just not what you think.'

Crying now. Nicky looking at the cars, the staring faces behind the frosted windscreens. Ooh look at them.

'Right. We'll talk about it in the car.'

She nodded dumbly, allowed him to frogmarch her toward Beth's Fiesta. 'What's wrong with your leg?'

'Hap stabbed me with a knitting needle.'
Well, she would say that, wouldn't she?

Molly eased the tablet and worn remote from her pocket, laid them carefully on her lap. Beth and Nicky stared as if she'd just secreted them from her right nostril. Artefacto ectoplasm.

'That's it?'

'He told me not to play with them. They're dangerous.'

Nicky snorted. Beth gave her a short smile, cuddled her in. Nicky had clambered into the back of the Fiesta, Molly in the passenger seat sobbing into the blonde girl's shoulder.

'A bloody remote controller? Abandon ship,' Nicky snarled.

Molly looked up, turned the plastic box over and thumbed the battery compartment open.

'There.'

'Where?' She held the remote up in the feeble glow from the courtesy light. Brownish clay tablets a few centimetres square packed in a mad mosaic. Nicky squinted over, prodded them with a grubby forefinger. Molly snatched the remote back, eased the cover on. Thank God there was something there, some proof, some sense. Nicky wasn't the only one needed convincing. Maybe Teomalik had been spinning her line after line, tangling her in his deceits.

'He said don't touch, we can't begin to understand them.'

'What is he, a fucking puppet-master as well? Got his hand up your skirt, has he?' He let the remark hang.

Beth turned both barrels on him. 'Isn't it obvious? Hasn't she convinced you yet? She's told us everything.'

No, she hadn't. She'd edited half an hour of sweaty scrambling from the bedroom scene. The tooth and the tangled sheets. Arms stretched along the shelves hands gripping the uprights. Housecoat he'd so admired unbuttoned, tugged up around her waist. Teomalik so ragged and hungry, thrusting up and at her raging with sexual energy. Suggestion? She hadn't needed much. Any. Kept going back to it as if it meant more than . . . whatever it had meant at the time. Heat of the moment. Heat all right. Wham thwack cracking her head on a shelf. She stared through her reflection out of the window at the traffic, lighter now towards Clove. A small lay-by off the main road, steamy windows. Smiled.

'Convinced me about what? So some wanker's stuffed a few Victory Vs into a remote. Big deal. That's proof of some supernatural invasion plan, is it? Bodysnatchers in the brook? I'm surprised you couldn't come up with something more convincing.'

'Your attitude isn't helping,' Beth simmered.

'My attitude's not the problem,' he snarled back. 'She's the problem.' He turned his watery green eyes on her, supremely frustrated. 'What's got into you?' he cried.

'What's got into me? To me? It doesn't matter. Look, our world, their world. They share the same space, see? Like a tent with two layers, the outer one's waterproof but if the wind blows it against the inner sheet, the rain runs right through. That's how he did it, he came in with the rain.'

'Slipstreaming.'

'Like a sort of magical osmosis.'

'Why don't you come right out and say it, you fancy the bastard.'

Molly sank her head back on her chest, sighed. 'There's only one way to find out, to convince you. Get to the home and find the body.'

'If the fairies haven't moved it first,' he crowed.

Molly shook her head, eyes running over her sunken cheeks.

'We saw the body. We've got to get the stones to Teomalik. They're not supposed to be here, it's dangerous for all of us.'

'Well, how are we supposed to find him? It's pitch dark outside. Maybe you were planning to run over the Downs, do a Heathcliff?'

'He's got stones. He'll find us. All we have to do is drive. I left him near the Axeheads turn-off.'

Nicky snorted again, the girls ignored him.

'Right, well, keep an eye out, we're not far now.'

SHADES

Teomalik took almost an hour, weaving his way up across the field toward the stark granite cracks. Lifting his heavy feet, thinking about every step, forcing himself towards the summit, the fall. Pushing against the wind which had picked up from nowhere, seemed to be whistling out of the massive fissure. Stay put, Molly had said. By the road but out of sight. The stones sliding and churning in his suddenly sour gut. He stopped, belched loudly, retched some pale strings of spit into the grass. He looked up slowly, squinted into the shimmering heat haze on the top down, the thin, windswept trees bowing this way and that. Teomalik felt his skin prickle as if it didn't belong to him, as if it would peel and pull itself away from him, leave him cold and naked on the hill under the rushing clouds. He shivered, walked in circles to try and get warm. Staring all about now, sure there was something behind him. Open air, jaunty breeze. The sun flaring like a wilting rose, sinking slowly on the tree-lined horizon. He fell down into the lush springy grass, stared at the clouds. He covered his eyes, peered up. If he looked hard enough he could pick out his uncle's features in the billowing shapes. He leapt to his feet, thought where to run. His feet felt heavier than ever, clogging him in the grassy mush. Holding him down as the shapes wheeled and dipped, white shapes closing in on him as the sun went down, cold smears of misty breath rising from the grass, features taking shape from the vapours. The tallest figure holding a cold white hand for him.

'Teomalik, my boy.' The breeze shaped words, tipped them into his flaming ears. He wheeled round, saw the pale shadow of his uncle detach itself from the shadowy host, skim over the grass toward him. The stones, playing tricks. He ground his knuckles into his eyes.

'Turning away.' An ironic sneer.

Teomalik blinked, saw the shimmering boy appear beside his uncle. Tarkemenis held his arm out but the boy shape flowed through it, concentrated in front of his face.

'Satisfied now? Now you've killed us all?' Puut Ra. The boy King. Jonathan. The girl materialized beside him, looking from one to the other, horribly mutilated, face reassembled by a blind chimp from a creased photograph. Dream pictures. Mist and breeze. More shapes rising from the crack, flexing and blowing in the wind. Faces, features, torn, distorted. Hands clawing the grass, dragging smoky arms out of the fissure. Ragged clothes, rotten misty skin unfolding to hang flapping from snapped bones like broken-backed men-of-war. Hopelessly smashed skeletons hanging around pale white hearts, beating grimly behind shattered ribcages. A graveyard fleet, blowing slowly, becalmed.

'Why didn't you let him go? Why did you have to chase him to this?' the girl, peering hideously at him, asked from the side of her smashed mouth, her jawbone working under a gauzy layer of flesh. 'You slimy shit! So fucking high and mighty deciding your destiny and interfering in his! And have you told your little girlfriend about the tooth, about what happens when she gets a grip on it, eh?' she garbled through her smashed mouth. 'I saw her push me, the bitch. I felt her hands on my face, her fingers on the tooth! How are you going to feel, watching the tooth go to work on your lovely prim and proper Molly, eh? The Spawn Queen's puppet, the Spawn Queen's zombie! Watch it the next time she gets on top, Teomalik, you'll never know when she'll take over!' Mags crowed horribly, eyes blazing.

'Away! Back to the pit, you shades!' Tarkemenis, pushing them back as they closed in on the cowering boy. Outnumbered by hundreds to one, unable to hold them back as they whirled closer. Pale clothing, torn suits and billowing dresses, a neat uniform of spiderwebs on a man without a face, milky brains pulsing in his opened skull. Lovers in period costume, a Roman auxiliary far from his farm in southern Gaul, his breastplates rimed with rust, clutching a bent javelin in his skeletal fist. A little boy clutching a kite.

'Uncle,' Teomalik warned, voice rising as the wind picked up, blew the shapes this way and that, ghostly washing. 'Uncle . . . make them go away,' he called over the hissing voices, the ragged breathing. More and more shadows rising from the crack. A broken-limbed man with a shock of misty silvery hair, a half-eaten hamburger alive with maggots held in front of him like an offering.

'Uncle . . . make them go away,' Teomalik pleaded, turning from the glaring youth to the furious girl.

'I didn't know about the teeth!'

'Liar!' she bawled back.

Puut Ra's face contorted with manic rage. 'They were meant for me all the time! I was supposed to take them over, bring her back as my queen, for ever!'

'Idiot! She meant them for Teomalik, she knew what she was doing!' Tarkemenis called over his cowering nephew.

'Oh, and of course you'd know all about the Spawn Queen's plots, wouldn't you?' Puut Ra commented snidely. 'You sent her sister over, you broke the spell for all of us. She came over and she took me,' he said shakily. 'She took me from *my* home to your damned Trafarionath. She killed me back there, left me with you wizard skins. And you have the gall to tell me what I can and cannot do, is that it?' the boy snorted as the lost legions climbed from the chasm, formed wispy ranks around the capering vapours, the fallen youth in his dew-soaked clothes.

'There has been wrong on all sides,' Tarkemenis allowed gravely.

'Wrong? Wrong? Well, that's something. This is wrong, it's all wrong, and your precious nephew had better get it sorted, unless he means to leave us here for eternity, this damned pit for ever!' Puut Ra screamed, misty eyes popping from his cracked skull.

'Uncle, use your powers, make them go away!' Teomalik wailed.

'I cannot. They are all here with me. You must release us.'

'Release you? How can I release you?'

'Break the spell, give us the stones! All of them. Let us go back!' the youth jabbed a misty finger into his jacket, watched it smoke to nothing. Teomalik glared into his white eyes, stared the boy out until he succumbed, sank to his knees.

'It was me she wanted, it was me she picked,' Puut Ra told him, nodding. He pointed a misty finger at the broken-doll girl. 'She picked me too.'

'They are trapped here with me, my boy. They torture me with their sleepless dreams.' The old man raised his bony hands, shrugged his frail shoulders. 'They give me no peace,' he wailed.

'No peace,' the grey host chanted.

'No peace,' Puut Ra snapped. 'Who wants peace?

Peace to stew in our own juice back there?' He pointed behind him, the yawning chasm.

'I will give you the stones,' Teomalik mumbled. 'I will show you back.'

Puut Ra capered on the grass, the girl reaching a broken-wristed hand for him.

'I don't want to go back, you shan't make me, not now!' He drew himself up to his full height, rose from the ground, hovered above him, pulling his arms this way and that.

'You haven't the power, with or without your precious stones,' he sneered.

Tarkemenis waved at him as if he was an enormous hornet, buzzing about them.

'Mind your mouth, you imp! I could deliver you steaming to the deepest holes of Shibboleth, the highest towers on the black mountain!'

The youth opened his mouth in an appalling grin, skin tearing, stretching over his smashed skull. He exploded into a thousand wispy fragments, fell like blossom over their heads, whirled and spun himself up again.

'Dotard. You couldn't spell it, leave alone spell me there! Where could be worse than this? This damned limbo?'

The old wizard ducked round as he flitted from shadow to shadow. 'There are worse places than the land we fled,' he said.

Puut Ra snorted, eyes popping from his head in exasperated, hateful fury.

'Fled? Fled. You seem to be forgetting, I never wanted to go over in the first place. I was snatched, snatched from my family! You made the spell to send her over, send her over to get me. Now you threaten to spell me the other way?' He shook his wispy head slowly. 'I should have pulled you to bits when I had the chance!' He coughed a storm, a gust of frozen air and steaming vomit over the cowering old man, shivered in the air above them.

'I'll bring all the stones,' Teomalik promised. 'I'll release you all!'

'Where? Back there? The other side of the gorge? I'll try and stop the tears of gratitude running down my cheeks!' he snorted.

'I'll bring the stones,' Teomalik repeated. 'I'll lead you back.' They drew away with a gasp of triumph. Tarkemenis bending to touch his shoulder. Teomalik focused on the gently rushing cloud, and toppled over into the grass.

FINDINGS KEEPERS

Macall worked his legs in the trousers he'd borrowed from the store to try and give himself a little more room. They'd only had a pair of cords with a thirty-two-inch waist, much too tight, clashing terribly with his double-breasted jacket. McNair spotted his boss fidgeting, remembered Fred and Wilma. Didn't feel too much like making a joke of it though. The lean DCI eyed him suspiciously.

'Anything wrong, Sergeant?'

'Nothing, sir.' Where would you start, all this lot? They stood back into the telephone alcove as four constables escorted the old geezer down the hall. He pulled his arm away, gap-toothed grin. Their Great White?

'What are you going to do, eh?' he shouted. 'What you going to do that's worse than this?'

Macall waved them on, the constables frogmarching him on down the hall and out to the waiting car. The pretty blonde WPC followed behind, nodded. 'Should have sent Joe in. It's a bloke all right.'

Jesus Christ. That's all they needed on the case report. Read like something out of the *Cloud-cuckoo-land True Crime Collection* already. Latest suspect, a foul-mouthed old nutter. Latest victim a transvestite octogenarian, for Christ's sake.

'Read him his rights, have you, Lou?'

The WPC nodded, followed the other officers down

to the car. Black girl on the reception whispering to the matron woman, Beatrice Buck. Hadn't been too happy to see them arrive, in two minds whether to make them call again tomorrow. Arguing with her in the hall, until he'd flashed his badge.

'That's it, love. DCI Macall, Budgworth CID. We're looking for a young couple, could be dangerous. We found their car a little way up the road.'

'This is an old people's home, officer. We don't get too many teenage tearaways in here,' Beatty had snapped back, overtime, overtired, overwrought.

Macall had smiled, shaken his head. 'We have reason to believe there may be a connection to the case in Clove. The old folk you transferred up here on Saturday.'

Beatty had looked up sharply. 'Clove?'

'That's right. Anything wrong?'

'Not wrong, no. We had one of their staffers up here about an hour ago. Had a bit of a dust-up with one of the old folk.'

Macall had nodded, cool as a cucumber in his too-tight trousers. 'Really? Give her name, did she?'

'Molly something. That right, Deb?'

The black girl scratching her head over the computer terminal had nodded.

'Molly Fisk, something like that.'

'Fish. Molly Fish.'

'That's right.'

'Bit of a dust-up, you say?'

'Nothing unusual. Some of the old folk . . . can be trying at times.' Say that again.

'One of the patients up from Clove?'

'A Mrs Jasper. Took their remote, apparently. Must have become a little confused when she took her to the toilet.'

'A little confused? How exactly?'

'She stabbed her with a knitting needle, tried to strangle her,' Deb called out helpfully.

Macall exchanged a glance with McNair as the uniformed officers fidgeted behind them. They'd spotted the Cortina, called in to HQ and got the detectives down to take a look. Garage forecourt Ferndale Road. Two doors down from Ferndale House old people's home. Ferndale where the old folk from Clove had been sent after they'd found the body of the manager. Had to be worth a look, Macall had played a hunch. Come up trumps.

'And you didn't think this ought to have been reported to the police?' McNair chipped in.

Beatty shrugged. 'As I said, it's an occupational hazard. If I told you every time one of them slapped me you'd have somebody down twenty-four hours a day,' she explained, wanting to get on. Christ, had that Molly woman gone and made some sort of complaint?

'Complaint? No, ma'am. We're investigating a murder. Two murders. Down in Clove. We believe this woman has some knowledge of the events down there, may be accompanying a suspect.'

Beatty swallowed, looked at Deb.

'Now you said the woman was alone? And she was assaulted . . . involved in a fracas with one of the patients. Mrs Jasper, was it?'

'Mrs Jasper. Came away with their remote, couldn't change the channel.'

'But the home's closed anyway, what would they need a remote for?' McNair observed.

'Molly . . . the girl took the remote?'

'Stuck on Channel 4, she said.'

'We'd better have a word with this . . . Mrs Jasper.'

Beatty frowning. Didn't like people putting their noses into her business, her old folk.

'We've had to restrain her, you understand?'

'We understand.' Macall had nodded quickly.

'No. I mean, it upsets some people when they see old folk . . . you know, under restraint. It's not pleasant but it has to be done to ensure the safety of my staff. She'll be as gentle as a lamb in there now, you'll think we're monsters.'

McNair smiled, patted her arm familiarly. 'We understand, honestly. If you could just show the way.'

Down the passage, Beatty fiddling with the lock.

'That's odd. I could have sworn I'd locked it.' She pushed the door open. The old man sitting on the edge of the bed, gazing down at the headless old woman, the crisp white pillow pummelled over her face.

'Jesus Christ! Colin!' Macall dashing forward knocking Beatty aside, dragging the old man off the bed as McNair tugged the pillow from the woman's purple face. Swollen tongue stuck obscenely between the protruding dentures.

'Mrs Jasper!' Beatty shouted.

Fletcher smiling, shaking his head.

'That's not Mrs Jasper. Take a fucking look, why don't you?' He nodded at the slumped body. 'Have a look up her skirt, see what you find,' he advised.

Macall stood back from the bed, shook his head.

'She's dead.'

Beatty pushed him aside, checked the pulse.

'It's Hap. Hap Haberfield. He killed Mrs Jasper, took her clothes,' Fletcher told them.

'Mrs Jasper?'

'She tried to spray Molly with Harpic,' Beatty wailed, straightening up from the bed.

'That's not Mrs Jasper,' Fletcher called again, higher.

'Get him out of here, for Christ's sake,' Macall had ordered.

Beatty had shaken her head, dashed out of the room. The DCI had called in the new WPC, told her what he wanted.

'What is it, some kind of joke? Stuck something up there have you?' Nervous, jittery. Getting one over on the girlies. Bloody prats.

'It's no joke, love. We reckon it's a bloke.' A bloke all right. All done up in her gear too. Every last fucking bit of it. He shook his head, sighed.

'Where to now, then, sir? Charge him?'

Macall shook his head. 'He can wait. We'd better find this Molly character. Maybe she put the old bloke up to it?'

Beatty had given them a full statement, told them she had seen Fletcher talking to the girl.

'That remote's got to be the key. My money's on it being packed with heroin. Diamonds, something like that. Small but high value. Her and carrot-tops must be acting as couriers. Maybe they've tried to burn a deal, things have got out of hand. First this Tark geezer gets chopped, then Grainger down at the home. Maybe this cross-dressing bastard was their contact, maybe it was Fletcher all the time.'

McNair snorted, started the car. 'And the other two? The hang-gliders?'

'Part of the same gang. Catch this Molly, she'll give us some answers. Must be a bloody plausible bitch.'

'Well, she can't have gone far. Their Cortina's still there. Any more hunches?'

'Back to Clove. The whole thing, whatever the fuck it is, revolves around Clove.'

*

'So it's locked out the entire staff and realigned our radio telescope to beam one-million-year-old messages into space?'

Principal Jeffries turned from Jilly to Professor Nelson. Anxiously pacing his study, pausing at his terminal. Fat fingers poised over the dead keys. Jilly looked awkward, disguising her excitement under professional concern.

'The implications are quite staggering.'

'I've been on to our research unit on Top Down. None of the discs are answering. They seem to be locked in on something, all right.'

'You realize this is out of our hands? If what you seem to be suggesting is true . . . it's a matter for the authorities.' Jeffries sighed, ran his fingers over his creased temples.

'Who the hell do we ring, James Burke?'

'I think we ought to attempt to establish precisely what has happened before we go making fools of ourselves. If it is an elaborate virus program . . .' Jilly trailed off, examined her nails.

Professor Nelson slumped back in the worn leather chair, folded his hands behind his head.

'It's no virus. Some student with a grudge? Come off it. Accessing our database from Backup? Disengaging all our protective programs? It took me weeks to set up those discs. If somebody's managed that we'd better sign them up damn quick before somebody else does.'

Jeffries bit his thumb. 'And these stones . . . is there some way the computer could have been nobbled to spit out those figures? One point three million years old puts it smack bang in the middle of the Glacial Pleistocene period.' The principal tugged at his unkempt grey thatch. 'Is it possible it could be some kind of hoax, somebody's been tinkering with it to give a false reading, increase the value, prove some point?'

'I think rather it's the stones that have done the nobbling, if you see what I mean. We started running a translation program this morning. Standard binary-based decipher operation. By lunchtime it'd crashed the system, locked us all out of the mainframe. Just about every screen we've heard about seems to be running this bloody box thing, the funny letters.' The horoscope with the extra star sign.

The principal frowned, noting her eyes, glittering behind her outsize spectacles. 'By four it'd located and accessed Professor Nelson's equipment, realigned all its boxes. Some point one way, some the other.'

'If we could locate the central point, the reference it's giving us, we could maybe discover exactly what the program's doing . . .' Jilly trailed off.

'Fascinating.' Nelson shook his head in admiration. 'If we could get to the bottom of it.'

'I'm still not sure. I think we're out of our depth, there must be procedures for this type of thing,' Jeffries worried. 'If it has managed to take over and access our systems there's no reason why it can't communicate with others. Hack into a bank, the military.'

'Power stations,' Nelson mused.

Jilly shook her head. 'Well, I don't think there's much point in calling in the police for a start. If the ignorant swines I had the misfortune of meeting this morning are anything to go by they're probably yet to be convinced the Earth is round.'

'Well, what do you suggest?' Jeffries wailed.

'Let Albie and me go on studying it. The grids have responded to certain letter combinations, prompted some sort of reaction. Maybe we can trip it up, spot a gap. Albie's been working on a containment program, might be able to get in, get things under control.' She stood, looked from the principal to the professor. 'Of course, you realize what we're saying? It's either a gifted hacker or an unknown intelligence?'

Jeffries closed his eyes. He'd worked his way up through the philosophy department. Hated having things presented in such unforgiving shades of black and white. Go for the grey areas, talk all night. Hackers or aliens, for God's sake.

TUESDAY

CHILD'S PLAY

Are we there yet? Nicky wondered, opening his eyes slowly and yawning about as far as his mouth would go. Stretched his arms in the baggy jacket he'd put on. Borrowed from his dad. What? He jerked himself up, hedge scratching at the car windows. The girl with the pigtails swivelled around to stare at him.

'Where's Nicky? Who's that?'

The chubby blonde girl was shaking her head.

'I can't reach the pedals. What the fuck's going on?'

'Beth? Molly?'

The pixie-faced dark girl made a face. 'You swore. You're not supposed to use the F word.'

'You are when you're driving. My dad does. I heard him.'

'Beth? Beth, is that you?'

'Bethany, if you don't mind. B. E. T. H.—'

'I know how to spell it.' Nicky leaned forward, sticking his curly head between the two girls. Beth was wearing a blue frock with white lace trimmings, Molly her best denim overalls, big bib stained with raspberry jam.

'Where's your mum and dad? They haven't left us out here?'

Beth thought hard. 'They didn't bring us. We brought ourselves.' She giggled, covered her mouth.

Nicky closed his eyes. He'd fallen asleep, any moment little Mimi would come along, curl her finger and lead him along the passage of the big house. The home. The home! He ran his hands over his body, buried beneath the outsize clothing. Clutched himself instinctively. Oh my God. What the hell's that, a couple of acorns and a bare twig.

Molly peeped at him. 'I'm telling. Nicky's playing with his thingy.'

Beth peered over her shoulder, giggled. The shadow stumbled out of the bushes, collapsed against the car with a thump that rocked the huge Fiesta's suspension. They jumped, hid themselves down under the seats. Molly peeped over the doorframe.

'What was it?'

'Was it a cow?'

'Was it a bat?'

'A bat?' Beth snorted. 'That wasn't a bat!'

'Can you see anything? Molly?'

'There's a man on the grass. He's gone to sleep.'

'He's dead.' Beth leaned over, took a look over her pigtailed shoulder. Nicky crouched in the back, rose slowly like a lion cub in the long grass. A big man lying on the floor in funny outsize clothes.

'Who is it?'

'It's Theo. It's whatshisname. The one with the stones.'

Beth frowned, thought about it. 'We were looking for him. We were driving the car,' she whispered. They looked at each other.

'The stones, can't be in two places at once,' Molly croaked, looking round from the misted window. Her pigtails had wrinkled, shrivelled up like dead vines on her brittle shoulders. Skin dried and wrinkled in papery folds around her mouth. Tongue suddenly red against her pale face. Nicky stared, giggle transformed, mutated into a chesty gargle. His hands, veins standing out starkly pulsing slowly, ropes on a sinking ship's deck.

'The stones,' Molly repeated, 'they're interfering with time. Changing our age.'

'Change the bloody record, why don't you?' Nicky moaned.

'Well, something's going wrong,' Beth snapped. 'How else would you explain this, LSD in our cornflakes?' She twisted away from his arrogant sneer, stared out of the dark window. Huddled into the driver's seat for a moment trying to make herself comfortable. She studied her reflection, looked up slowly. Puffed cheeks, worn red splotches like old apples. More tricks. 'You stay here with him, we'll take the stones,' she suggested.

'We mustn't leave him, he'll catch his death,' Molly cackled, fumbling with the lock. She pushed the door open, sticking against the grassy verge. Beth clambered out of the driver's door, held the seat back for Nicky to ease his bamboo legs out. He levered himself up with a puff, caught his breath.

'Why do they make 'em so low down?' he moaned, rubbing his back. He followed the blowsy blonde woman around the front of the car, peered over her as Molly bent her knees, pulled the vivid red hair back from the youngster's face.

'Teomalik,' she whispered.

Nicky bristled, tried to remember why he felt annoyed, left out. Left behind.

'He's breathing, anyway,' Molly said, heaving his head into her lap. They watched as the whites of his eyes rolled down, focused slowly.

'Molly. You made it,' he breathed, chest heaving with the effort. Molly rested her liver-spotted claw on his strong hand, squeezed. Nicky eased himself straight, looked out over the hedge, the dark fields stretching away toward the peaks. Used to walk them, in the old days, way back when. When he and Molly had a thing going, courting. Nicky swivelled back to the geriatric tableau, swiped at her.

'Get your hands off him. What do you think you're doing, woman? You're married to me, remember?' He felt like crying, felt like kicking out with his shiny new shoes, kicking out and running off, off to hide behind the hedge and gobble his sweets and everybody else's share too. Molly lost her balance, collapsed into the verge. Beth struck out.

'Leave her alone, you. You're just jealous,' she accused.

Nicky stood frowning over them, the two girls and the funny man with the flickering grin.

'The stones. You've brought the stones, aggh by the spawn . . . you've got to . . . don't look at the shades! Don't look in the mist!'

Oh ahh! Hark at him, silly old tosser, groaning like an old tramp in the gutter. Cars zooming by on the main road, heading for home. It was ever so late. Nicky checked the outsize wristwatch, God, a quarter to one! He'd missed all the telly and everything. His mum would be worried sick.

'We have to get him in the car.'

'Can't bear it!' The funny bloke was dribbling all over his chin, spluttering the words out in a ragged hail of spit. Uggh.

'What do we do?' Molly wailed.

'We get rid . . . of the stones. It's the stones,' Teomalik warbled, clutching his stomach. 'Give them the stones now.'

Nicky looked unconvinced.

'Where do we do that?'

'Molly!' Grasping at her arm. He was about to die. He was going to die in her arms. Her eighty-year-old arms. Her eight-year-old arms. Eight eighteen eighty, her useless arms. Coughing and rattling, one puff and he'd be gone, puffed out over the hills like dandelion seeds.

'The gaps. The gaps aren't far. Over the field and up the hill. We'll throw our stones down there,' she decided, laying his head to rest and clambering to her feet. She took the remote from her pocket, thumbed the dull stones into her palm. His eyes were glassy as he lay staring at them, trying to nod and smile but only managing to puke some pink fluid. Molly jabbed them at Nicky.

'Do it.' What? Talk to me like that, woman!

Beth pulled at his cardigan. 'Do as she says. Come on.'

Molly laid the stones in her pudgy palm. Beth closed her clicking fingers around them, nodded at Nicky.

'Throw them away, you say, and what then, eh? They could be valuable, these stones of yours,' he argued.

'They're killing him. They're choking out his life. Get rid of them, away from us for ever.' She looked imploringly at Beth, the blonde woman nodded her puffy head seriously.

'I'll go with him. Sheep Tor Gap.'

Sheep Tor Gap. Lover's Leap. The wailing walls. Nicky muttered under his breath, stamped off along the verge after Beth, dragging her high heels behind her. She kicked them off, smiled playfully.

'Come on. The grass is all dewy. Feels funny.'

Nicky bent down, eased the giant loafers from his holed socks, tugged them off and balled them into his shoes. As if easing off his shoes had untied the laces on his mind, undone his imaginations. He took one look at the pigtailed girl leaning over the funny man, sprinted off after Beth. Over the hedge, across the field.

'Watch out for cowpats!' he called to her.

'Don't go too close! We'll all fall down,' she warned.

Nicky ran in smaller circles, toppled over and kicked his legs in the still night air.

'What's wrong?'

'Buzz buzz, dying fly,' he told her.

She held out her hand, helped him up. Felt her spine grind agonizingly.

'Oh my word, I've done me back in,' she gasped.

Nicky clambered to his feet. She held out the stones.

'You do it. It's not far. Do it and we'll be all right, Molly said.' He took the cold stones, weighed them in his palm. Dull brown tablets. He nibbled a corner, spat in disgust.

'Throw them down the gaps, right down,' Beth called, doubled over in pain. Nicky ran around her, leap-frogged her. Beth collapsed into the wet grass, crying. Nicky stumbled, recovered. Ran on. Where were the gaps? Hello, hello gaps? Slowed, thinking about it. What if they just opened out underneath him, opened out to swallow him whole? He dived down on to his stomach, inched forward through the lush grass. Stars up above, glittering bright for him to see his way. Twisted between the grey statues somebody had left around the field. Funny faces he didn't recognize. Statues of great men and lovely women somebody had attacked with an axe, hacked stony limbs from their bodies, buried hatchets in their backs. Nicky frowned, ducked his head and crawled on through the cold hissing grass, damn near fell right down though, the crack opening abruptly like a giant opening his mouth to swallow a fly, a massive fissure in the old stone. Nicky drew himself up, stood back. He could see the road away away. Car headlights illuminating the quiet hedges, dozy daythings in their brambly holes. Moonlight glimmering faintly on the frozen army, granite victims he didn't know. Oh well. He swung the stones out into the cold night. They shivered, basking in the starlight as if they'd been caught on fine silver wires, suspended from the heavens. In a blink they were gone. He tilted his head, listened as they tinkled and tapped, tinkled and tapped down the rocky crevasse. Quiet. Dark. Nicky blew a cloud of dragon vapour, looked over his shoulder. Those statues, a trick of the light? Grey auroras in the frosty night air. Across the empty field, the quiet hedge, the Fiesta parked on the verge. Women drivers, Jesus. Planning to leave it like that, was she? He stomped on down the hill, Beth standing there gawping. Silly cow.

'Did you leave it like that? It's a wonder you haven't had somebody up the back of you,' he called. She wrapped her arms tight around her, gave him a dirty grin.

'Don't you go giving me ideas, Nicky,' she called tartly.

He smiled, nodded.

'Did you see where they went? All those people?' she called, suddenly curious.

'All what people?'

'That queue up the top there?'

'Up where?'

Beth raised her arm, waved it idly. 'Oh . . . I don't know.' She frowned, waited for him. He shrugged, walked back down the hill with her, following the bizarre trails they'd cut through the drenched grass. Funny shapes the stones had made, standing there like that.

'It's over,' he called, clambering over the fence and wiping his hands on the back of his jeans. Teomalik sitting on the bonnet of the Fiesta, Molly, hand on his shoulder. She saw him, dropped it to her side. Guilty as hell. Teomalik looked up, nodded drunkenly.

'Gone?'

'Gone,' Nicky grated, watched as Beth came alongside, wringing her hands for warmth.

'What now?'

Nicky watched Teomalik lift the tablet. 'Get rid of that too?'

The red-headed youth shrugged. 'It was the stones. The old man . . . Hap . . . only had a set of stones. The tablet was ours. Couldn't have been found.'

Nicky shook his head, took a sideways look at Beth. No point in expecting Molly to argue, the way she was looking up at him, taking it all for granted.

'The tablet was never found? What's that, then?'

'This is the tablet we lost.'

We?

'Hap had their stones here, they buried them, over there,' Molly said weakly.

'Trafarionath,' Teomalik snapped, level grey gaze on Nicky.

Trafarionath. Molly mumbling, crying all about it in the car earlier. She'd spilled the beans, he'd spilled the stones. What the fuck had that red-headed bastard Teomalik spilled, eh? He eyed him murderously.

'They couldn't be in the same place at the same time. The nearer we got to Teomalik, the more the stones clashed. Time fluctuated, made us think we were grannies, little kids.'

The fucking expert speaks, Nicky thought, slowburn. Looked up at Teomalik, busy fingering the tablet, crossing his eyes reading the tiny writing.

'Did you touch this?' Looking up sharply, accusingly.

'Listen, mate, I don't know what the—'

Molly waved her hand wearily. 'We never touched it. I told them you'd said not to,' she said flatly.

Them? Them? 'Listen, fuck you, all right? You lead us on a mad chase halfway over Hillstones and you're talking to us like a couple of idiot children,' Nicky snarled. Beth pursed her lips. Molly shrugged.

'Well, somebody's been touching it. It's working.'

'What's working?' Beth enquired.

'The tablet. It's active. The circuit's glowing.' He held the tablet up in the feeble light. They squinted, caught the faint green glimmer etched around the dark tablet. A series of tiny margins around the distinct blocks of characters. Teomalik jabbed the corner, ran his fingers over the smooth grooves along the top edge. Turned slowly, held his arm out, levelled the tablet over the fields. Out of the darkness, a glimmer of lurid green light, flickering from one invisible horizon to another.

'They're working. They've opened the breach,' he breathed.

'Who has? What's that line? Somebody signalling?' Beth peered over the road, over the hedge. Hard to tell how far away. Steady green beam. Teomalik shook his head, held the tablet back to his face.

'Whoever has the other stones, they're using them. Opening circuits. They're activating skanes, the old power grids they left behind.' He glared at the circle of tired faces, closed his eyes. 'It's what they're for. It's what the warlocks wanted, don't you see? They wanted to make the stones work for them,' he insisted.

'We've just thrown the bloody things over the cliff,' Nicky grated menacingly, fists clenched. Beth touched his arm.

'Not those. My uncle's. The wagon people must have his set.'

'We haven't got to do it all over again, for Crissakes?'

Nicky moaned, green beams wrapping filaments of fire around his eyes.

'They've opened a breach by activating the skane, look,' Teomalik repeated, fingers poised over the tablet. 'I told you . . . I told her what these were for, they're drawing power from somewhere,' motioning the stone at Molly.

Nicky bristled. 'Well, how about letting us lesser mortals in on the secret too, eh?'

'We hid these tablets, back in our land, Trafarionath. The old man made the spell and brought us over. Against our will.'

'With the stones old Mr Maggs had found here, under Hillstones,' Molly added.

'How come you're the expert all of a sudden?' Nicky snarled. 'Taking it all for granted. Funny lands and freaky creatures. I had to listen to that prat Roberts that time, remember? Get to the bottom of all his fucking stories. Maybe you've forgotten what happened to him, I haven't.'

She waved her hand dismissively, pulled his pin.

'I'm not going to let you end up like him, staring at the walls at some damned funny farm.'

'I don't need you telling me what to do,' she said levelly.

He cursed, pushed her aside. She staggered, fell into the hedge. Teomalik pushed him away, helped her to her feet.

'Right. Feeling better now?' he snorted, dusting her down.

She held a finger under Nicky's nose. *Don't ever, ever, touch me again. Is that clear?* she grated. Something in her voice, her different voice, cut him short, made Nicky take a step back, look nervously at Beth.

'What's wrong with her?' Staring back at his stranger/wife.

'What's the matter with you? What's the matter with you all?' She glared at him. Nicky stomped away cursing.

'Well, what do we do now?' Beth asked.

'We start with a few phone calls. We can't leave her there another night,' Molly said.

'Who?'

'Mrs Jasper. In the woodshed.'

Christ, they'd forgotten all about her. Forgotten all about . . . Nicky looked round, sheepish. 'There's something else. The boy . . . Jonathan. He's dead. Mags as well.'

Molly wheeled round on him, raised her finger, paused. 'Dead?'

'They jumped from a car park in Budgworth. That's why I came after you, why we came up to find you,' Nicky growled. 'In case you're interested.'

Beth wiped her face.

'It's true. Wilf was there. He'd spotted them in the bus station and called a copper.'

Molly glanced at Teomalik, intent on the tablet. 'The girl on the cliff,' she said quietly.

'Cliff? I said car park.'

'I thought I saw . . . I thought I saw her fall,' Molly explained, rubbing her forehead.

'You're such a happy fucking medium I'll buy you a crystal ball when we sort this out,' Nicky sneered. 'Seeing as you're going to need a new job anyway.' He paused, thumbed in some armour-piercing rounds. 'Pity about Mags, though, getting involved like that.' He raised his eyebrows, looked spitefully at her. 'I mean, she was only a kid. Bit mixed up, didn't really know what she wanted,' he said darkly. Molly looked at Beth, about to say something. 'We'd better get home, ring the cops. This is all out of our league,' Nicky cut in, exasperated. 'We're in enough trouble as it is, we've got to live here remember,' he told his wife. She looked blank.

'We can't afford to let this happen,' Teomalik said, holding up the tablet. 'We have to stop them before they do something . . . they will regret.'

'So we leave this old lady lying under the logs, do we?'

'We'll go now. I'll get her out, dress her at least. I owe her that,' Molly said, cold, hard. 'We'll think of something up at the home, ring the police afterwards.'

Teomalik climbed into the Fiesta, Beth folded the seat and got behind the wheel. Nicky stared at his wife, this dark ghost, this wife-shadow. My Darling Doppelgänger.

'Well, you know best,' he said, lifted the seat and let her climb in the back beside the frowning youth in the Robin Hood outfit. Beth switched the headlights on, pulled away into the night.

LUCKY MAGIC

Jakabi, up to his wrinkly balls in the freezing lapping lake water, gritted his fangs and clamped his bladder. The urge to lift his wet loincloth and urinate was pressing on the back of his mind as well as everywhere else as he flicked his beady amber eyes along the bank, the hushed ranks of his war band waiting expectantly. For something to happen. For him to make something happen. Bastard Tilekin riding that swan out, they were already slinging rough verses together about it, lauding him to the hushed heavens around the quiet lake. They'd looted the hut, piled their treasure, picked stones and gravel from the dusty floors as if it was gold dust. Knocked the flimsy supports away and set fire to it. She'd been sweet all right. Jakabi, working his frozen jaw with difficulty as he chewed the last pink meat from her hands, had shouted it over the gloriously mad camp, raised the bone and shaken it above his head. They'd grunted and slavered and roared in approval. They'd dragged the great Spawn Witch over the red earth and rolled her in her dried-out cloak, smaller, lesser now, her beautiful face scored and spoilt, her eyes starred like frozen ponds smashed by children's sticks. They had gathered handfuls of wet mud from the shallows and smeared her, caked her, cocooned the body in her own red claw-scored oven and rolled it into the embers of the gutted hut. Armfuls of branches and dry leaves, they'd sat up all night waiting, opened her at dawn with the first blood mist staining the clouds over the hills. 'Jakabi the great, queen-eater!' he'd called, mouth full of succulent meats. They would have followed him to the stars just then. Now, they weren't so sure. Now they wanted more, more magic. Goblin magic, no witches or boys or fugitive wizards to worry about worshipping. They were in it for themselves now, they made their own destiny, Jakabi's war band. The slow muttering spread from the rearmost archers to the brawny spear boys standing along the water's edge.

'Well?'

Schmelker. One of the old crew, a veteran of half a dozen campaigns. Maybe wondering if it should be Big Chief Schmelker now. Jakabi shivered, stood straighter in the lapping waters.

'Throw your stones into the water! The Green Lady, the Thin Boy, the Trafarnian bog trotters, all used the stones,' he shouted. Echo bouncing back at him from the sheer walls of the dell. Water Water Water. The front rankers exchanged looks, unsure now.

'Tilekin had no stone,' Schmelker called, the fangless old croner. He'd had one of his sons chew his meat for him, guzzled the mash with the rest. He was rolling the shaft of his broad bladed spear in his ropy claw.

'Tilekin rode the white bird to the place where the stream runs backwards,' he called along the spear boys.

'Where is Jakabi's magic now?'

'I led the attack on the great queen, I am Jakabi queen-eater! I have given you fresh meat, I have given you the Spawn Witch herself!' Jakabi bellowed. 'How dare you challenge me to prove myself?' The young chief knew he was a match for the old one. Slack muscles, poor eyesight, tired old legs. But his sons there, they'd be obliged to stand up to him if he slaughtered the sire. Jakabi felt all his elation, all his hold on them draining out of his skin into the fragrant green water.

Schmelker jumped in, steadied himself.

'You and I, impostor!' he cried.

Jakabi tugged his dagger from his belt. He'd left his spear up on the bank, cursed his stupidity. Schmelker hurled the heavy javelin. Ten years before Jakabi would have been skewered like a pig, but Schmelker's arm was loose in the joints and the heavy spear was dipping before Jakabi darted forward, deflected the blade with his armoured gauntlet. Barks and shouts, fierce clashes. Someone shoved Schmelker's eldest son into the lake. Someone stabbed the other goblin under his short breastplate, held him there howling. In a moment the war band had turned on itself, spear boys thrusting at the lighter archers, scouts tangling among their stinking leg rags, throttling each other. Jakabi watched the massive brawl spill into the shallows, shook his head and swam off toward the shore. An arrow or two plopped harmlessly into the water as he paddled over the lake, the water turning sluggish and syrupy under his feet, against his hands. Must be tired. The water bucked, splashed him. Jakabi stopped swimming, trod water in the middle of the lake. He swirled around, the fighters standing still, staring at their feet. He looked at them, watched them as they slid beneath him, as the great slopping bag of water rose from the lake, a mass of trembling, gelatinous bubbles. He flapped and kicked in the ooze, felt his body compressed by the throbbing, livid water. Squeezing his head, sucking the breath from his lungs. Up, up, up toward the hurtling blue skies, the gently floating clouds.

*

Sergeant Bell removed his hat, placed it on the counter of the tiny police station. Two cells, a couple of offices and a reception. Six extra constables and Macall's team from city HQ lounging about as best they could. McNair, the sarky bastard with the twitchy moustache, looked up from his desk.

'Not a sausage. I told you there wouldn't be.'

Bell grunted. 'May have been a little mixed up but she was no druggie. I've known her, known her people, I told you.'

McNair nodded wearily. 'We know all that, Sarge. We had to check it out, though. Way she went off with him like that. He wasn't forcing her, was he?'

Bell shrugged. 'There's ways of forcing somebody without bending their arms,' he said.

Macall watched him, typical village plod but not as dumb as he looked, not by a long chalk.

'What about the home? Anything there?'

'We went through the rooms like you said, around the grounds. We'd been over the place with a fine-tooth comb already,' he said.

'Well, we found Haberfield disguised as Mrs Jasper, so she's got to be somewhere,' Macall told him, arranging his trousers more comfortably around his crotch. Still no time to get back and change and it was what, after two. Busy day, you'd have to admit it. They'd been driven off the road and come this close to hitting the bridge. They had their number one suspect in half a dozen bin liners at the city morgue with his dozy bitch of a girlfriend. They'd come close to catching the Molly woman as she picked up whatever package she'd been supposed to collect at the old folks' home, spent the rest of the night scouring the city for her. He'd had a brief interview with the foul-mouthed old man, got nowhere. Glared out from under his bushy eyebrows, thorny tangles to trip the unwary.

'Had a feel up her skirt, did you?' he'd sneered. 'Had a good fucking look I expect.' Defiant to the last. The old bastard was right though, what could they do to him his family hadn't already done? The DPP wouldn't touch it with a bargepole, the case would sail through the courts, see the old boy transferred to Bleakdale. Twilight years on the moors. Grinning maliciously, jabbing the arms of his chair as if they'd been alive with bugs. Christ. They'd left him to it, picked up the woman's trail. Nothing at the bus station, nothing at the train station and no known contacts in the city. Had to be Clove. Hell on bloody earth as far as he was concerned. Couple of cars keeping an eye on the main roads in, and he got Bell and his lads out checking their home addresses. Yeah, we know you've already done it, do it again. And again.

Bell had volunteered to talk to the landlord bloke, the dead girl's uncle. 'Look Roy, you know how it is, I've been told they'll have to search her room. You know, routine. I thought, as it was me, might be a bit easier for you. Up to you, of course.' Roy nodding, lifting the flap, leading the way on up under the red curtain, up to her small box room. Clothes piled on the narrow bed, picked over, discarded. Roy standing in the doorway, wife asking questions at his elbow. 'What's he doing, what's he up to?' Roy stony, stonier than the hills all around. Nothing.

Up to the home, Clove Heights. Opened up, dissected all over again. Bell had shone his flashlight over the woodpile, remembered Grainger. Great bloated carcass crawling with bugs and woodlice, bruised and scored where they'd pulled the logs from him. Shaken his head, walked on, checked the gardens, the broken-down furniture. 'They said she'd been off to Hong Kong, maybe she went early? Maybe Haberfield just went a bit nuts, took a few of her things?'

Macall blew smoke at the ceiling, annoyed the puffy-faced sergeant a little more. 'Maybe he was a little like that.'

'He was like it all right.' Louise May, the WPC, from across the room. 'Had everything, right down to her knickers.' She shuddered at the memory, stripping the warm body in the isolation room, livid purple flesh and a day's beard, the men looking over her shoulder like pervs at some damn peepshow. How had he ever imagined he was going to get away with it? Growing sense of something horribly horribly wrong as she'd fumbled with catches and pulled at unfamiliar garments. She'd known, she'd known before she'd got down to the bastard's stolen cotton pants.

'He killed her all right, I'll put money on it,' she said.

Macall watched her, wondered why he hadn't noticed her before.

'Well, what next? Permanent stakeout down here, is it?' Bell enquired, stifling a yawn. 'Check out the convoys heading for Glastonbury?'

Macall climbed to his feet, uncomfortable. 'We need a kip for the night. We'll think of something in the morning. Any suggestions?'

'You're welcome to come back with me. I've me daughter's room free.' Free all right. Free ten years since David Roberts, her maniac ex-husband, had raped and murdered her. He closed his eyes. Not now, no way. 'Then there's the settee, or the cells.'

*

They'd watched the police wander back to their cars, given them a good half an hour before Molly had nodded, Beth nosing the Fiesta along the gravel drive.

'Claire must have rung them. I told her to.'

'I told her not to,' Nicky, cross, muttered at the windscreen.

'They would have called an ambulance ... they wouldn't have left her for Christ's sake,' Molly said, strained, dog tired.

'They didn't find her,' Teomalik said quietly. 'She's where we left her.'

'Well, I'm not leaving her any longer. No way.'

'OK, OK.' Beth pulled up, they climbed out and climbed the steps, peered in the windows.

'Beth. Do you want to give me a hand?'

Beth glanced at Nicky, back to Molly. Nodded quietly.

'We'll put the kettle on,' Nicky rasped, as Molly leaned forward, unlocked the front door for them.

'Better not put too many lights on, we don't want to advertise,' Molly said.

'Right you are, Captain.' Nicky stalked along the dark passage, nosed into the kitchen. Neat, tidy. Wandered back to the reception, Teomalik bent over the desk.

'They won't have left any petty cash,' he called nastily.

Teomalik ignored him, swung himself behind the terminal, fished the tablet out of his smock and placed it alongside the keyboard. The tiny etchings were lit like electric fish, glimmering lines in the waxy grime. The youth tapped the top right-hand corner, frowned.

'They're using these ... for the stones. Can you work it?'

Nicky frowned. 'I'm a tripwriter jockey myself. New technology hasn't exactly conquered Clove yet,' he answered. Teomalik tilted his head as Nicky leaned over, flicked the switch. Teomalik's face changed colour as the terminal blipped to life.

'What do you want to do, call up your friends on the other side?'

'They won't be listening, even if I knew how to call them,' the youth answered, prodding the keyboard absentmindedly. 'But you people worship them. I've seen you,' he went on. Nicky shook his head slowly, made a face like a village idiot. 'Whoever's got Uncle's stones . . . if they try and play about with them, interfere with something they know nothing about . . .' He shrugged. Glanced at Nicky and tapped the screen. 'Skanes . . . are like lines of power over the land, like your pilings.'

'Pylons. You mean pylons.'

'Carrying your energy through the wires, yes,' he nodded. 'The skanes are creating a power grid to charge the spell. The green lines we saw. These people just don't know what they're doing,' he said, exasperated.

Nicky raised his eyebrows. 'And you'll hack in and read all about it, is that it?'

Smartass. He clenched his fists. Teomalik shrugged.

'The stones will tell me.'

Fine. Press the button, smartass.

'Type.'

Nicky leaned forward, pressed the Enter key. The screen threw up a new grid, Password?

'Password. It wants a password. If you haven't got one you can't get in.'

'Go and ask Molly. Hurry.'

Nicky straightened, drew a long, long breath. Right. Out of the front door, round the flowerbeds. Shadows moving slowly in the woodshed.

'Molly, he wants the computer password,' he called, not caring to look too closely at what they were about.

'Cannon.'

'Cannon.'

'Grainger's favourite TV show. You know. Two Ns.'

Nicky paused, stalked back down the darkened side of the house to the front door.

'C.A.N.N.O.N.,' he spelt out. Teomalik looked at the keyboard. Nicky sighed.

'Up and out of it. Let me have a go.' The big reporter took his seat, tapped the password. The screen wobbled, jumped, focused. A large rectangle divided into small squares. It was called Windows, wasn't it?

'There's a stretcher in the downstairs storeroom, grab a couple of blankets and some tape,' Molly ordered over her shoulder. Bending to lift the last of the logs from the glimmering body. She was breathing through her mouth, breathing hard trying not to smell anything. Night-time buglife scuttling for the dusty corners and knotted webs of the rotting woodshed. Molly swallowed, looked up.

'Beth?' Gentle, don't spook her, staring out over the grass, looking the other way.

'Beth?' Louder.

'I didn't notice the gnomes before.'

'What?'

'I didn't notice those gnomes... when we came down.'

Gnomes? Molly climbed to her feet, walked around the side of the shed. Dozens of stumpy shapes dotted around the rolling lawn, squatting on the broken-down furniture. Moonlight glinting on their fishing rods. Those weren't fishing... the stinky claw clutched her out of the darkness, powerful fingers clamping her mouth. Another claw seized her arm, pinched her hard. 'Be still my beauty!' Revolting obscene caller, six-packsa-day man breathing fumes over her sore neck. Molly watched other shapes detach themselves from the shadows, slink out of the untidily stacked woodpiles. *Bastard goblins back.* Eyes popping, wondering how she'd known, how the Spawn Queen had known everything except how it would end. Three creatures clamped on to Beth, her blue eyes wide over their dirty pale hands. More of them scuttling in over the lawn, along the trees, trampling the flowerbeds. Pouring out of the darkness, nightmare cocktails spilled over clean sheets.

'We have the Queen and her sister.' One of the creatures clutching an enormous spear, jabbing at Beth's face. Molly wriggled, felt the creature behind her stiffen, shake her still.

'Any more like you at home, my beauty?' A thump and an angry hiss.

'You have put hands to the lady,' the other breathed across the woodshed.

'I'll deal with you later, scumdrunk,' the one holding Molly rattled back. 'She's no queen!' Hundreds of them, packed in, packed around the woodshed, a sick nativity. Dirty shepherds gathered around the obscene cradle of logs holding Mrs Jasper.

'Wherever he's brought us, he's brought us to meat,' one of them slavered, dragging the logs from the old woman's body. Molly writhed, raked the pitiless claw clamped across her mouth. No, not that. Please God no.

'There's a light in the castle,' another called.

'Fresh trail. This way.'

'Wait!' The leader, clamping his filthy claw over her mouth, desperate to keep control of his drooling pack. She could feel him vibrate, trembling against her, something horrible sticking sharply into the small of her back and drops of hot spit running down her neck, hot breath singeing her hair.

'Hold these. We search the castle first, we eat later. Schmelker?'

A toothless skull in a beetle breastplate grinned, rolled his great purple tongue around his slack mouth.

'Jakabi, Boss Chief, we hear you,' he said dangerously. They fanned out into the night, melting into the darkness so quickly Molly wondered if she'd dozed off dreaming. If the stone was playing games with them again. Jakabi released her into the care of a fat gnome with a straggly black beard, glittering eyes.

'You watch them you leave them,' Jakabi hissed, slunk off into the darkness after his foul pack.

DEPARTURE LOUNGERS

'This means something to you?' Nicky glanced at the red-headed youth, holding a hand over his mouth as if he was going to be sick. Christ it was Molly out there doing the dirty work, as usual, he thought. Yeah. Maybe a teeny bit late for thinking about her, tea and sympathy wasn't going to get him far now.

'They've done it, opened a channel on the skane. That's what it was for, the Grimoire.'

'What . . . this?' Nicky tapped the stone tablet.

Teomalik winced, lifted it carefully from beneath the reporter's sausage fingers. Teomalik retched, coughed raggedly. Nothing left. 'They've been using the stones, whoever has them, they're doing this.'

Nicky tapped in the password again, got the same response.

Teomalik leaned back, held his hand over his dry mouth. Nicky eyed him drily.

'What's the matter?'

'The password.' He clicked his fingers, closed his eyes. Nicky sighed heavily. 'Cannon, she . . .'

'Not yours, ours,' he snapped, closed his eyes tight.

'Don't tell me,' Nicky chuckled. 'You can't remember it.'

Teomalik slapped the back of the chair in agitated frustration. 'Sounds like a mountain.'

Nicky raised his eyebrows. 'Sounds like? How many syllables?'

Teomalik, concentrating his eyebrows off, missed the heavy sarcasm.

'Loads of them. Sounds like . . . a mountain. I can see Uncle repeating it now. Sounds like . . . the mountains. They're in the north, Shibboleth and . . . and . . . it's like forgetting your mother's name,' he moaned, glaring at the ceiling, drumming his fingers on the chair.

'It's on the tip of your tongue, isn't it?'

'Well, if you'd shut your stupid mouth for a second I'd be able to remember it,' Teomalik barked, voice distorted, hoarse.

Nicky pushed the chair back over the youth's toes, making him hop back with an angry yelp, climbed to his feet and stared at him. Stared over his shoulder.

'Look, just give me a moment's peace and I'll get it,' he said, straightening up, holding his hand to his forehead. 'What is it now? More silly tricks? The old 'behind you' routine? Yes, we had that too,' Teomalik sighed wearily.

Nicky nodded.

'Talking bollocks again, wizard man?' The voice rang out in the quiet hall, making the youth jump, turn slowly.

'Molly, that was about as funny . . .'

The hall was filled with creatures, silent as dust, grinning fangy grins, gripping flinty weapons. Teomalik straightened. Nicky chuckled.

'More time fluctuations? More mirages?'

'Nicky, for once, shut up.'

The goblins dragged and prodded the four of them into the lounge. Jakabi had been all over the castle, marvelled at the fittings, the ornaments he couldn't begin to comprehend. Now he'd dragged Mrs Jasper's chair from the window, had it arranged in front of them. A dozen of his junior officers lounging in the other chairs, trying on the strange costumes they'd pulled out of sticky drawers, ragged old shawls they'd tugged from a broken cupboard, shrouded themselves. Schmelker, dipping his water pot into the stagnant tank, drinking it down.

'It's good, good water!' he called, chewing on guppy whitebait.

Jakabi watched them clambering over the furniture, dragging out drawers, rifling cupboards. He'd taken a pot, ripped the top off and swallowed half the powdery yellow contents, chammed and spat on the sticky sweet mess.

'What's this?' He held the tin up in front of the dark woman, a little unsure of himself still in front of the war band, in front of these horribly unpredictable humans. Who knows what they could come up with on their side, on their terms. The other woman, blonde as the lady but bigger, broader. He'd been a young cadet when he'd seen her billow with green fire at the battle by the bridge. He'd seen her bones, he'd helped pick her gown from the carcass. This wasn't the lady, no matter what they muttered into their claws, nodded toward her. The girl looked round nervously.

'It's custard. Custard powder.'

'It's nice. Not as nice as you though.'

'Be so good as to address your comments to me,' Teomalik said loudly.

Nicky winced, Beth eyed him nervously, still not sure whether this was happening or the stones were playing tricks on her again. Jakabi threw a leg over the arm of the chair, chuckled.

'And you are, let's see, Teomalik? The wizardboy

apprentice. Your mad uncle threw a fit back in the Sister's Slit.'

Teomalik nodded. 'You know full well who I am, the power I wield.'

Jakabi grinned, looked around the room ironically, his pasty white face split, cheesy fangs glinting.

'Really, and what power is that?' He waved his claw, one of the goblins stepped from the ranks crowded into the lounge, laid the tablet at his feet.

'Ah, Trafarnian magic bricks.'

'They are more dangerous than you know. I advise you to be very careful what you do with them.'

'Pardon me, bead jiggler, but you would seem to be in no position to order anyone.' Jakabi looked around the crowd of goblins, pleased with himself. Words shooting into his head from a dried-out old pool. Thoughts, ideas, springing and rooting in the sudden flood, carried along by bright waters running in channels around his mind. Running in channels like the dim colours running over the strange tile. If he knew its secrets. He could see it all, see everything. Jakabi the Powerlord, Jakabi the Just. The lake water must have been magic, magic all the time. Treading in it, swimming in it, bellyflopping here. He blinked, missed what the wizardboy was nattering on about.

'You are right, but my advice remains. The stones have power beyond your grubby dreams.'

Jakabi bristled. 'Enough. We're here together, where the stream flows backwards. That's enough magic for now.'

'Enough talk, we take what we want, we shag 'em, we eat 'em.' Schmelker, lurking by the window wiping his chin.

'Eat later. Eat us if you please. Let them show you their place first.'

Jakabi glared at the red-headed youth, wrapped in his wizard robes over borrowed clothes he'd never seen before. He would take time to search the whole place, have all the good things piled in front of him for first pick. He grinned. 'Show us their place? We see it for ourselves,' he answered.

'You see an old house on a hill by the stream. You haven't seen beyond.'

Nicky, racking his brains, spied the old television pushed into a corner. 'You haven't seen the magic box!' he called.

Jakabi narrowed his eyes. Nicky walked across the room, the goblins levelling their spears. Jakabi waved his hand, they let him pass, wheel the TV into the middle of the room. Nicky prayed it was working. Looked up to Molly, who nodded encouragingly.

'What do we, what does the great Jakabi's war band, need to see? We killed the Queen, we crossed over on Tilekin's breath!' Schmelker called from the corner, his sons closing about him.

'*You dung-crawling blowflies could never kill her,*' Molly rasped. Nicky winced. 'Molly!' He turned to their leader, looking at her curiously, wondering. 'Time of the month,' he hissed across at the musing goblin, running a sharp claw under his ratty-bearded chin.

Schmelker grinned, grabbed Molly's arm, tugged it toward his mouth as the girl recoiled. He glared along her arm, eyed her for a moment, caught her cold stare. Let her hand drop.

'This is what we do, this,' – turning his furious gaze on the agitated Jakabi, around the rest of the war band – 'is what we do,' he mouthed.

'Hold your water,' Jakabi growled over the growls of approval. 'Let them speak. We have all the time in the world now, all the time in their world.' He chuckled unconvincingly.

Nicky switched the set on. Christ, half-past four in the morning? All they were going to get was a testcard, for God's sake! The screen remained blank.

'Where's the remote, Moll?' Fish asked, straightening up. Oh shit. Stuffed full of bits of old gravel, wasn't going to work anyway.

Molly glared at the set. 'Try the panel at the front. You can do it manually.'

He bent down, pulled the flap down, pressed blank switches. Nothing. Nothing. Testcard. The goblins gasped, muttered. Nothing. Thank Christ for Dick Earp at NSTV.

'... killed earlier yesterday evening when they leapt from a seven-storey car park in Budgworth city centre. Police say there were no immediate suspicious circumstances but are continuing their inquiries. The mystery computer shutdown in the west continued tonight, with local companies and installations battling to contain a powerful new virus believed to have been written by a disaffected student at Budgworth University. Experts have isolated the problem to an area of north Somerset and believe the student may have hacked into systems as far afield as Dunstones Nuclear Power Station and the Space Research Station on Top Down, Hillstones. Budgworth City were beaten six–nil at home tonight in the local derby with Swindon Town. The game was marred by a pitch invasion in the second half.'

Nicky stood back, rubbed his hands over his forehead. 'Six nil? Jesus wept!'

The goblins surged forward, crowded in on the TV. Two hundred hooligans running wild over the lush green turf, bemused players and officials hurrying to the dressing room, police moving in.

'Cavalry! Look at those soddin' bastards!'

'Look at those dozy warclubs! They want lances, charging that rabble.'

'Why don't they form square, running around like headless chickens!'

Schmelker looked up from the screen, smiled horribly. 'Is this what we're up against? Daft cavalry on lumbering chargers and infantry who can't fight standing still?' He cackled.

'They're not fighting,' Nicky snapped. 'They're just playing about, juvenile high spirits,' he told the toothless old croner, remembered himself, smiled.

The goblin eyed him. 'Looks like fighting to me, a pitched battle!'

Nicky glanced back to the screen.

'The international headlines again. Fierce fighting in the Balkans as the Greek expeditionary force evacuates Thessalonika in the face of overwhelming attacks by Jihad Order forces.'

Helicopter gunships, napalm, flamethrowers. Dark bodies in camouflage gear holed and bloody. Jets screaming over rugged hills, clumps of smoke, lazy ribbons of tracer. Blocks of flats pummelled flat by rocket launchers. A woman reporter ducked down behind a burnt-out jeep.

'With UN forces cut off in the north the defence of the vital bridgehead has fallen on these volunteers from the mainland. The US has appealed directly to the Eastern Bloc to lift the jaws of death around Thessalonika, but a spokesman for Ayatollah Shimenni said his forces would not stop until they reach the sea. The sea, as you can see, is just behind me. This is Marlene Arnold, *ITN News*, Thessalonika.'

The goblins stood back, open mouthed. Jakabi fidgeted on his vinyl throne.

CHANGELING HEARTS

'Pictures! They can make dream pictures to frighten us,' Schmelker called.

'These aren't dream pictures, this is their world. This is where the stream flows backwards. I have seen it,' Teomalik piped up.

'They have wagons that run faster than arrows, great wagons running on rails . . .'

'Sometimes,' Nicky muttered.

'They wage war between the islands of the whole world, they wage war in space like our ancestors.'

'Like your ancestors, wizardboy,' Jakabi called. 'It wasn't goblins as broke the laws of our existence, brought the doom down on us all.' He stopped short, glanced round the room, astonished stares from the slower spear boys.

'*What difference did it make to you dogs anyway?*'

Nicky moaned. Molly again. Hell did she think she was doing winding them up like that? Teomalik coughed.

'*They will find you, eventually. They will come here with the weapons you see and wipe you out like ants under your boots. Believe me, I have seen how they live.*'

Jakabi waved his claw. Schmelker grunted.

'Dream pictures! We have our own power now. We came over, didn't we, without your help!'

'They have magic stones such as these, but they don't understand their power. They summoned you here by mistake.'

Teomalik closed his eyes to the screams of abuse, the threats and challenges. Nicky backed into him, the two girls falling in behind them as the angry mob surged up to them. Jakabi leapt on to his chair.

'We made our own magic! We don't need humans to summon us like a pack of dogs!' he bawled, dark eyes glinting with menace. 'We're not dogs!'

'You need your own magic too, of course,' Nicky

stammered. 'The stones bring out the magic in you,' he improvised.

Schmelker spat a wad of something horrible against a wall, wiped his toothless mouth slowly. 'Enough talk, we eat. I'm not afraid of their dream pictures!' he called, murmurs of support all around the room.

'Wait!' Teomalik called, desperate, hair hanging in his eyes. 'How strong is your magic, how far would it take you?'

Jakabi eyed him suspiciously. Humans, slippery as greased eels. Always thinking, always one jump ahead. Leaving him behind, clutching at straws, meanings, strategies. He was learning, but slowly, so slowly. They waited for him. That was something, with Schmelker shouting the odds over in the corner and his idiot sons rattling their spears.

'What do you mean, how far would it take us? It took us here,' he called.

Teomalik smiled, shook his head. 'Could it take you back? Could it take you back like it returned the Great Queen? Don't you remember how powerful she was when she came back? Don't you remember the way things were, back then?'

Outraged shouting. Jakabi racked his brains to decipher the human's meaning while the war band clamoured and barged about the four humans, uttering vile threats and prodding them like cattle in a slaughterhouse. Give me time, time to catch up with myself, he muttered under his custardy breath, watched the warlock boy stride between ranks of jabbing spearpoints, waving his arms about.

'The stones have opened a breach, a gateway between our worlds. We can come and go as we please, masters of the magic, not leaves blown by the wind!'

'Bollocks!' Schmelker yelled, glittering eyes flickering

over his followers. 'We've had enough of their tricks. We were the ones who brought them to their knees, destroyed their castles. We swept them from our lands and threw them into the sea. All they ever give us is promises, pretty talk.' He strode around the humans, picked at the girls' coats.

'I will give you one more,' Teomalik insisted. 'I promise you there is a way, a way back to Trafarionath, to a new Trafarionath. New for us all. Renewed.' He stared at Jakabi, swallowing in agitation and eyeing his slower spear boys. 'The wagon people here have been playing with the stones, they have powered the skanes, opened the breach.'

'Dreams! Promises!' Schmelker cackled.

'I will call it to you, I will open the gate!' Teomalik shouted over the angry hubbub.

'We follow no more boys,' Jakabi shouted furiously.

'*I will take you!*'

Silence. Schmelker, circling like a hyena around a lion kill, stopped dead, looked slowly from Teomalik to Molly.

'*I will take you all. I am the Great Queen now, I am she of whom you speak. Her tired flesh is in you but her spirit's here, as fresh and as powerful as ever. More so. Renewed by the breach, do you understand? I wasn't blown here by chance winds,*' she said haughtily, '*I saw you all, I saw your scurryings.*'

Nicky closed his eyes, lips moving silently on his white face.

'*Let any who would challenge me stand forth.*'

'Molly, for Christ's sake belt up!' Nicky shouted, shaking his head.

Jakabi, arms folded across his breastplate, watched quietly. Molly leaned forward, touched the red-headed youth's arm. He patted her hand, nodded.

'It is as the Great Queen has said. Far away from here. For ever. With us.'

'How? What proof?' Jakabi called from the chair, his troopers muttering nervously.

'The dream screen. I will call the dream screen.'

Molly glanced wonderingly at Nicky, shaking his head. 'What's wrong? What have I said?' she asked.

DAWN PATROLS

'Clove police, Sergeant Bell.'

'Hello. It's Molly. Molly Fish.'

'Molly? Where the hell have you been?'

'No . . . It's not Molly Fish. It's about her. Sorry. I mean, I'm not even sure I should be talking to you. I mean, it's just she rang me yesterday. She told me to ring you.'

'Hang on a minute, love. Who are you, first?'

'It's Claire. James. From the home. I work with her.'

'Right. And she phoned you, asked you to ring us. When was that?'

'Yesterday. About midday.'

Bell gesturing frantically at the exhausted DCI. Macall leaned forward, lifted the receiver on his desk to listen in.

'And Molly told you to ring us, about what?'

'Well, I rang Nicky and he said don't. Don't ring. I tried to ring them last night but they weren't back, so I thought I'd better.'

Macall raised his eyebrows. Bell, lounging on the tiny station counter, nodded slowly.

'Take it easy now, Miss James. What did Molly ask you to ring us about?'

'The home. She said . . . and this is why I thought twice about ringing you, see, because it sounds so daft.'

'Yeeeesss?'

'She said,' Claire resumed, 'we took the wrong person

to Ferndale. You know, when they had to move the old folk from the home.'

Macall sat straight, waved McNair in from the tiny office behind the station reception.

'Go on, love.'

'Molly said we'd taken old Mr Haberfield as was missing up to Ferndale, only he'd been dressed up as Mrs Jasper. I know it sounds . . .'

'And what did she say about Mrs Jasper?'

'Well . . . Nicky said not to say anything . . . to get her in trouble, you know, Molly.'

'What did she say, Miss James?'

'She said Hap had killed Mrs Jasper, taken her clothes. I know it sounds stupid but that's what she said. You still there?'

'We're still here. Where did she say he'd left her body?'

'In the woodpile. Where they'd found Mr Grainger.'

Macall was on his feet, heading for the door.

Bell sighed. 'We looked there,' he moaned, half to the receiver, half to the detective, ducking past under the counter.

'Well, that's what she said. I thought I'd better let you know, no matter what Nicky said.'

'No, no. You did the right thing, Miss James. We'll get straight up there and check it out.'

Jilly stretched luxuriously, opened an eyelid. Jesus Christ! 'Albie! Sorry . . . I was miles away.' She swung her legs from the couch, tugged her cardigan around her as Albie hopped from foot to foot. Crashed out in the principal's study, waiting for them to fix the system, get a grip on things. That was hours ago. 'What time is . . . five? Oh my God. What's happened, have I missed anything?'

Albie looked over his shoulder. He'd closed the door quietly behind himself, sneaked on in to her.

'There's some very heavy geezers downstairs. Jeffries must have called in the men from the ministry.'

'What ministry?'

Albie shrugged.

'What are they doing? Freed it yet?'

'Nope. Turned the place right over, pulled in some gear I've never even seen before, didn't let me get anywhere near it. But they were scratching their heads same as us.'

'When was this?'

'We packed it in at about half two. I hung around trying to patch in a retro-program but it wouldn't let me anywhere near. You said you were going to grab five.'

'Five?'

'You were tired, there was nothing we could do.'

'So?'

'So about three Jeffries comes down doing his nut, saying he'd had some hush-hush agency on, demanding to know what was going on.' Albie strode to the heavy oak door, opened it a notch and peered out.

'Just checking. Yeah, apparently, this program's been sending feelers out all over the place, you know, linking other networks. It was trying to run a program through to the fucking control centre at Oldstones.'

What?? 'The power station? You're kidding.'

'No way. Apparently the place is virtually impossible to crack, for obvious reasons. Their system is protected to shut down the moment anybody tries anything, you know, terrorists or stuff like that.'

'Terrorists? What, all that horoscope stuff was a hoax?'

'Is what Jeffries had the PR department tell the press. They got hold of it because their systems had crashed too. They're putting it down to some super-hacker, a mega-virus.'

'So we've got the authorities down, have we? Locked you out?'

'Of Backup yes, but you can access the program we looked at from any terminal. It's locked solid, halfway across north Somerset, they reckon.'

'Where? Have they got any information where it's tried?'

'It's tried everywhere, but it's definitely locked on to our space unit on Top Down. It crashed out Oldstones and Dunberry. They've had to switch to the coal-fired power station at Cloud Point. Localized power cuts, everything.'

'One bloody program?'

'That's what they're so scared about. It's cocked up connections to the south-west, Cornwall must be about ready to float off somewhere.'

Jilly strode through to the principal's inner office, got on his terminal. Got to be up the spout, running information through at impossible speeds.

'Not even Cantfail can do that. The printers can't cope, burned out the motors.'

'But it's running something. That means somebody is operating it.'

'To do what? What are we saying?'

Jilly looked up. 'I don't know what we're saying, but it's no bloody hacker, that's for sure. Albie, back me up here,' she pleaded, holding her head.

Albie pushed his glasses further up his nose, nodded eagerly. 'No . . . I mean . . . yes. No, it's not a hacker.'

She pushed the chair back, crossed the thickly carpeted room to the giant map of Somerset on Jeffries' wall. Ran a lacquered fingernail along the etched coastline.

'If it started here...'

'Here? What makes you think it started here?'

'It was the stones, Albie, remember?' Albie frowned. 'It started here, sends out feelers here, to Top Down, back here to Dunberry... and here to Oldstones. It doesn't make any sense. What's it trying to do, shut us down or something? Surely a more logical move would have been to cripple the Generating Board HQ mainframe. Where's that... Budgworth.'

Albie raised his glasses, peered at the map.

'Do that again.'

'What?'

'With your finger... there... to there... to there.'

'Yeah, what about it?'

'Look again.'

'I'm looking, Albie, I don't see anything.'

'You made a sort of shape. A rectangle. Run your finger more slowly, read off the places the line intersects.'

Jilly ran her finger back to Budgworth, dropped south.

'Yeah, Magnus Knoll... the old hill fort... St Margaret's Church...'

'It's a ley line, a box of ley lines.'

'A... hang on. Tumulus. Clove... Burial mound...'

'Take it a little further, see where it leads,' Albie suggested.

She ran her finger straight down the map, chuckled. 'No. That's too much. Too weird.' Her red nail hit a small notch in the map. Ancient monument. Glastonbury.

'And where did they find this guy, the old hippie?'

'Come on, Albie,' Jilly, shaken.

'They found him near Clove, right? Just here. Right

where these lines intersect. He was carrying the stones we tested. The stones did all this. They set up the grid.'

Jilly stared at the map, the colours blurring, the place names tumbling. Lines this way and lines that way. A grid.

'Why?'

DECISIONS, DECISIONS

'Dream pictures. It's dream pictures he's showing us,' Schmelker mouthed, drool running over his empty gums and dripping over the table, the keyboard.

Nicky wiped the worst from the keys, frowned at the chief. 'I can't concentrate with him blabbing in my ear,' he complained.

Jakabi waved the old veteran away. Teomalik glanced down the passage, blocked with bored goblins squatting on the floor or urinating down the walls. Jakabi followed his gaze for a moment, after his women. He could smell it on him, not fear exactly, more like punishing responsibility, concern for the others. The goblin's eyes narrowed. The way he was concerned for his war band. He'd brought them here, this place, the mad dream pictures buzzing in his ears, so many horseflies. Their wild and dangerous world, riding away with them. Looking down the passage, his scouts shoved and barged aside by the bigger spear boys, the experienced archers. Squatting and waiting, on his word. Waiting for the moment, they wouldn't wait long. Schmelker's cantankerous protests, the belly imperative. Eat first, dream pictures later. Just before they dozed off, perhaps wondering what the tall one with the raggy red mane had been bumping his gums about. Home. A new home, a better home. Gimlet-bright eyes to guide them through the woods at night. The stream turning his thoughts on their head, turning him back on himself, murky memories of fireside tales in one of the great halls beneath the cliff.

Jakabi tilted his head, flared nostrils sorting the stinks from the other room. Still quiet then, still calm. They were brooding, waiting. The initial surprise and excitement of their arrival, their captives, wearing thin. Alert, excited, but in check. For now. Overpowered. Overpowering everything else the sweet fragrance of the women. Stronger than the filthiest feet. Drenching all his war band's private biology. Jakabi sampled them slowly as he sat stiff on the desk. The girls were in the lounge under the curious gaze of two dozen spear boys, leaning on their weapons, in hand, overpowered also. A scaly, sickly audience crouched in tacky Soho sex booths, imagining. Craving. Molly and Beth out-of-work strippers at a seedy audition, sitting with knees pressed together in a couple of the chairs pulled away from the wall. Glancing at each other, trying not to catch any rolling eyes.

'I can't understand . . .' Molly raised her eyebrows at the blonde girl, nodding down at the eager faces at her feet.

'I can't understand how they can understand us, what we're saying,' she said.

Is that all? All she couldn't grasp? Fucking hell, they were sitting in a ring of four-foot-high hairless chimps, armed to the teeth with assorted sharp implements they would clearly enjoy sticking in them as much as they would their sticky body parts. Molly jammed her eyes shut, calmed herself. She was a fine one to talk. Motored on up to pick up Teomalik. Whose suggestion? His? Who you trying to kid, kid? In the bedroom, hanging on as he thrust up and at her. Whose suggestion had that been? As far as she could remember . . . they hadn't said a word. He'd said his piece, squatted on the sheets staring at his hands, on about his responsibilities to protect them all. Jesus wept, he hadn't done much protecting yet. He'd cried then brooded. What had she been supposed to do? He'd needed some comfort, wherever the hell he'd come from. Needed some comfort the same as she had. Some comfort. The tooth breaking into her, breaking through her senses, her sense. Sharp and hot, a steamy mouthful they'd passed between them. Molly chuckled, remembered his baffled embarrassment. I didn't realize... I'm sorry, if I'd known... She must have forgiven him, mustn't she? Hadn't she? Motored on up to Budgworth to pick him up, pick him out. Driven, she'd been driving, driven with her tongue running over her lips, hand clamped on the gears the way Nicky always complained about. 'You'll knock the bloody bottom out, holding it like that.' She'd heard all about it, this land of theirs. She'd heard all about its flora and fauna. Flora and fauna. She looked down at the eager, childish faces. Sunday school teachers with a class of infant archers, squatting cross-legged with their bows in their laps.

'Maybe we ought to tell them a story,' Molly whispered, bloody things could hear like bats.

'A story! Yeah, tell us a story,' one of the cadets piped up with general encouragement from his filthy colleagues.

'Make it a good one!'
'Loads of blood!'
'Loads of goblets.'
'Goblets?'
'Girl goblins.' One of the archers at the front leered, tapped her leg with an arrow. Beth swallowed, raised her eyebrows, as he tickled her thigh with the feathery flight.

'I couldn't,' she croaked. 'I can't tell them.' Molly

looked down the passage, wondered at the delay. Teomalik was supposed to be taking them away. He'd taken her away easily enough, she reflected, not bitter, resigned. He'd known all the words for her, not that he'd needed many. She'd resigned from Nicky, from all his words and his little doings. Resigned from his home. Maybe they will take me too. Take me over. What was he thinking of, what was he going to do, how would he control them? They wanted to eat them, for Christ's sake. Eat them. Yeah. Did they kill first or eat their victims the way those ancient Chinese ate monkeys, clamped head first into those special tables, serrated knives to open their hairy skulls? Molly shuddered, blinked down at the nodding heads. *Nodding heads coming at her over a dark lake.* She closed her eyes, shut the fleeting thought away.

'Well, are we going to have a story or not?' One of the archers in the front row jabbed her knee with a crooked finger, making her jump.

'A story,' she said shakily, blinking fast. 'A story. OK. Right. There was once a goblin called Rumpelstiltskin.'

'Never heard of him.'

'Shussh.' Teomalik heard the hubbub in the other room die back down, gentle whispering soothed his shattered nerves for a second. He turned back to the computer as it completed whatever program it had been running. The goblins edged back a little as the runes danced and jiggled on the dream picture box, gripped their weapons. Schmelker leaning over, running a dirty claw over the screen. Pulling his finger back as the static made him jump.

'Give me some space,' Nicky complained.

Teomalik looked up to Jakabi, squatting on the desk with his legs crossed, spear laid over his lap. 'What more do you want? This is the Grimoire, this is the gateway my ancestors made.' He pointed at the mass of data flickering on the screen. 'The magic stones have called it, opened it through the heavens. It will open for us.'

Schmelker spat on the floor. Nicky looked down, looked back at the screen. Jakabi pulled idly at the strands of wiry hair hanging from his bony chin.

'All you need to do is remember the password,' he said fiendishly.

Teomalik looked awkward. 'Well . . . it's on the . . .'

'Tip of your tongue, yes, I heard,' he sniffed.

Schmelker snorted, wiped his broad nose. 'Why are we wasting time here?' he demanded, glaring at the chief. 'Why don't we eat them and get off out of it? Out to the hills?' He looked around, appealing to the ring of fanged faces, nodding heads. 'They have good hills here.' He stamped his foot, spoilt ancient. 'Good hills for us. Woods and rocks and caves, all those cattle. We saw for ourselves. Jakabi would have us waste time looking at these dream pictures, going back to where we've come from when we've hills here for us, hills we understand. Gateways are for bead jigglers! Death to the bead jigglers!' he yelped, a flurry of angry barks and rattled weapons.

Teomalik looked around the crowded hall, rank and airless. 'Because Jakabi can see beyond his next meal,' he said stonily. 'Jakabi brought you here to get away from rocky hills and cold caves and gnawed bones. Jakabi has had a vision, has he not?'

Jakabi looked up, opened his mouth, purple tongue twitching. Watch him, snake. Trying to catch him out again. He nodded slowly, unsure whether to commit himself to this line of thinking. Wouldn't do to be bracketed with the bead jigglers if they upped and slashed them anyway. They were that close to the edge.

'Jakabi brought you here to be more than hill runners, to be more than you are.'

'We are what we are,' Schmelker growled. 'We know what we are and we know what we do. We do not squat at dream boxes making rune writing. We fight, we eat. We have come here to take.'

'Take this opportunity, go back to a new land, new hills,' Teomalik challenged.

'The gateway is waiting for us. It is wondering whether Jakabi's war band is worthy.'

Nicky swallowed, drummed his fingers slowly alongside the keyboard. Give the bastard his due, he could talk the hind legs off a donkey. He'd talked the knickers off his wife, hadn't he? Hadn't he? Eyeing him fiercely. Let these stinkers take him, let him wake up with Molly curled away on the other side of the bed, let him wake up and rub his eyes and say I've just had a really weird dream. That's all he wanted. For God's sake. He closed his eyes for a moment, thought he'd never dreamt smells before.

'It will be decided the old way,' Jakabi announced. 'We stay, we go. For stay, Schmelker.'

The old veteran drew himself up, threw out his chest and eyed his comrades, viciously proud. Proudly vicious.

'And for go, Teomalik, the wizardboy bead jiggler,' he growled.

Jakabi shook his head. 'Teomalik is of our world too. No. You will fight this one.'

Nicky looked around the room, wondering who the goblin chief had pointed out. Oh, Christ.

'Me? What have I got to do with anything? He's the one as wants to go! This is nothing to do with me at all!' It was nothing, nothing, nothing to do with him, nothing was. Molly, Teomalik, they were nothing to do with him. The bloody ugly mug with the purple flickering tongue was nodding.

'I have made my choice,' Jakabi said simply, looking from the spluttering man to the deadlier youth. 'You will fight our Schmelker. We decide everything now. Outside.'

'Well, can you put me through to him, it's important!' Jilly, strident, down the telephone to the hapless sergeant, crouched over the counter at Clove police station. Christ, he'd been up all night apologizing. Sorry for this, sorry I missed her, sorry you missed him.

'They've gone out on a search,' Bell explained, a windcheater away from throwing the receiver down and stomping off home. Let the boys from Budgworth hold the fort for a change, coming down here throwing their orders about. The way McNair had shaken his head as he'd followed the DCI out into the brisk dawn mist. Missed her? Under the woodpile? He'd searched the woodpile. Yeah, when they found the manager. Last night he'd stayed a torch beam away, running the light over the logs and broken branches.

'I have vital information for him on the Clove case,' Jilly repeated. 'I must talk to Macall. It could alter the whole thing, it could be dangerous. Do you understand?'

'It doesn't matter whether I understand or not, he's not here.'

'Well, he's got a car phone, hasn't he? A radio? I mean it, Sergeant, this could be . . . bigger. Dangerous.'

What more to say without going through the 'Are you trying to tell me . . . ?' routine. Something in the way her voice had hitched made him wince, close his eyes. How could things get any worse? 'I'll patch you through to the car. Hang on.'

Hang on. Jilly frowned, shook her head at Albie, hanging on to the big oak door in the principal's office, looking out in case those guys from the ministry came up for them.

'Doctor Freeman.' Well, there's a change. No, hang on, the sergeant. McSomething.

'Is Macall there?'

'He's here.'

'Well, let me speak to him.' She surprised herself, the venom she'd injected into her voice, cutting through everything else, the questions, the ifs, the buts, the imponderables. The impossible.

'Macall here.'

'It's Jilly Freeman at Budgworth University. Listen, those stones.'

'Still haven't cleaned your system out, then?' More pedestrian plod sarcasm.

'I'm told you haven't managed to clear yours either. That's because the stones you gave us to decipher have established a link . . . have set a pattern, some kind of grid. Somebody is communicating with it now, just like us,' she added scornfully.

A crackly pause.

'It's a virus, some program one of your bloody dope fiends has managed to infiltrate into mainframes all over the city. There's a specialist unit down from Cheltenham checking it out now.' Muffled, indistinct as if he'd covered the mouthpiece. 'Fucking stars she's seeing now. The hell they pay her for?'

'The stones have set up a link, somebody is communicating, sending messages. We can tell that much. The computer has set up some kind of framework, some kind of grid over the country. It follows the ley lines around Glastonbury. Goes through Clove, the nuclear power station. I'm trying to tell you there may be something going on which we do not fully comprehend. It might be dangerous, you might get hurt!' Determination giving way to hysteria. She could picture those dozy bloody coppers chortling away in their Granada, heading fast for God knows what. 'Clove seems to be in the middle of it. The old man who had the stones, the youngster who went missing.'

'We know about him.'

'Oh, you do, do you? Well, what about the other one? The one who escaped from your custody?'

'He forced the door with something.'

'Something. Yes. That's what I am trying to tell you. Something. Something's wrong.'

'Listen, Dr Freeman . . .'

'There's no need to be polite. Tell me to fuck off if you want. I'm just telling you, something is going on down there and we can't work out what it is. The computers can't tell us because at the moment, whatever *it* is, *it's* in control.'

The line went dead. Went dead somewhere in the middle of her outburst. Albie looked over from the door.

'No joy, eh?'

'Brain dead, the lot of them.'

'Weapons? I choose knife,' Schmelker told the crowd, drawn up in a rough circle on the gently sloping lawn. The big spear boys had taken hold of Teomalik and the girls, frogmarched them into the fresher air. Clouds tumbling up over the heights, misty outriders snaking back into the woods along the stream. Going to rain. Nicky looked at Teomalik, back to the goblin. Two feet shorter than he was but leering for the fight, a sand-blasted skinhead, a rock-jawed roughneck jabbing a bottle of meths at him.

'Wharra mak anything of it boyo?' in a hail of napalm spit. Teomalik stamping from one foot to the other. Make something of it, insist. This is your fight not mine. Not mine. Could make it his fight though, me and him. Would that satisfy them? He was about to shout it out for all of them when Molly pushed forward, tugging her bag back from one of the spear boys.

'Nicky will take the Mace,' she called.

Schmelker grinned. Great fat oaf swinging a clumsy great club? He'd gut him in a blink and watch his back.

Jakabi wanted to go back, he wouldn't have picked the big man as a worthwhile opponent. He was up to something, up to something else. He muttered to his sons to keep an eye out, stepped out over the dewy grass fingering his knife. Jakabi nodded, working his way round the inner circle, pushing some of the more eager spear boys back.

'Give them some room.' He nodded to the woman, who took her bag back and drew out a small grey tube.

'Mind yourself on that, Schmell,' one of the archers called.

'Have your eye out, that could!'

'He couldn't brain a snail with that!'

'Is he going to hit him with it or stick it up his arse?' One of Schmelker's sons, relaxing, joining the fun as Jakabi stepped alongside, paused.

'Enough. He's made his decision. No help from anybody, or they'll have me to answer to.'

Nicky looked intently at Molly, at this stranger, took the canister in his broad fist. Turned slowly.

'Be careful . . . Nicky!'

Beth, crying, trembling between two hulking spear boys.

'Watch him, Nicky.'

Teomalik, measured. Not his fight, after all. When

CHANGELING HEARTS

they'd finished with him there'd be nobody left to stand in his way. He'd get Molly by default. He let the anger flow, turned it on full steam, wound that tap round and watched the dials behind his eyes flick straight to red. The goblin ducked down low and faster than he would have imagined, ducked down and rising like a snake. He just had time to hold the nozzle straight, give him a faceful. A roar from the delighted spectators, he was going to make a fight of it after all!

MACES HIGH

The goblin staggered back on compass legs, knife tumbling from his hand as he clutched and clawed at his face. The crowd roaring him on through the choking wasps' nest the big man had thrown at him. Sporeball, witchblood brew, sucking his breath away as he staggered sideways. Cursing himself ragged, stupid to expect a human to stand there and take it, stupid to think they weren't every bit as crafty as you. Needling him, needling him through the pins and needles in his eyes. Nicky took a step nearer, brought his scuffed size ten loafer back and kicked the creature under the loin cloth. Schmelker doubled up, wind knocked out of his gummy mouth on strings of sticky spit. The crowd winced in sympathy, watched the old veteran sink to his knees.

Molly closed her eyes, holding back the feelings surging in over the sandbanks, the little boats resting at awkward angles. Relief overloaded, contaminated by damp-patch despair. They probably wouldn't honour their side of the deal anyway, they'd run rampage, a frenzy of revenge, hack them to pieces and gobble them up for breakfast. *Same as they had her. Amiarillin.* If she kept her wits, concentrated, she could isolate her, pick the darker strands of her will, her memories, shadows, raspberry ripples in the corners of her mind. Now and again she was aware of her striding out, taking the reins, taking over her tongue and her eyes. She'd stagger, shake her head, shadows melting into shadows again. Must be cracking up, must be losing my grip. She thought about Mags, for the first time since she'd heard about their shabby deaths. *The death she'd foreseen.* The fatal push she'd given her? No. Not me. Not my doing. Used, procured for the bloody witchy woman. Perhaps the boy, Puut Ra, had used Mags as Teomalik had her? Lined her up for her unwanted pregnancy, her hasty termination. Maybe that's why she'd flung herself off the seventh floor with him, when she realized what he'd done to her? She hadn't been pushed at all.

Molly concentrated on Nicky, triumphant, a great goblin in a tatty jacket, button-down shirt pulled about his neck. Towering over them, red faced, snarling. She smiled faintly. Maybe they would be overcome with emotion when Nicky stepped forward, helped the crotchety old goblin to his feet. That's what happened in the movies, final reel, old reprobate down in the dust, a bloody hand stretched out to the noble conqueror. *El Cid*. Nicky's favourite film. Molly looked up as Nicky grabbed the goblin by the ears, yanked the leathery flaps over and tugged Schmelker's face into his kneecap. A gruesome crackle and sudden splatter as the goblin's nose imploded. Nicky pushed the broken thing away, horribly savage, standing over his victim. Glared at Teomalik. Molly glanced at him, impassive, Beth, wide eyed and unable to control her trembling legs, hands clamped to her thighs.

Schmelker lay flat out on the grass, blood bubbling up from the crater of torn skin and collapsed bone. Shocked silence broken by the goblin's eldest son, stepping forward, careless and forgetful. Straight on to Jakabi's dagger. The chief gripped the spear boy's breastplate, tugged him down on to the blade. Surprise and rage etched on to the livid face, his death mask. Jakabi tore the knife aside, allowing the goblin to drop into the grass beside his father, grunting and spluttering as his innards rainbowed from the savage gash. Beth staggered against her captor, Molly stared at Nicky as he stood at bay in the middle of the ring of hostile faces. Jakabi straightened up alongside him as if he was changing sides.

'It has been decided. We go with the wizardboy.'

Murmurs and curses from all sides as Jakabi's lieutenants shadowed Schmelker's two younger sons.

'Does anybody else wish to join him?' Carelessly kicking the groaning goblin in his twisted ear. 'Then it has been decided,' he repeated. 'The wizardboy will summon the dream picture, open the gateway as he said. We will go back to our own lands. Finish him off,' nodding at the old goblin prostrate on the lawn.

Teomalik glanced at Molly, staring intently at him now, up to him. Come on, forget your fucking uncle, do something. He opened his mouth, closed it again.

'We will ride the stream backwards, ride into the night like boss Tilekin,' Jakabi continued over the hubbub. The murmuring died down but even Nicky could feel their anxious resentment, the snarled threats. Events, futures, running through their claws, running away with them. He'd done it now, hadn't he? Knocked the nasty bastard to the ground in front of his cronies. Well, at least he'd taken one of them with him. That was something.

'We came here, didn't we? Did we know where we were going, did we have a choice, once we climbed on to the great swan's back?' Jakabi strode around the ring, pushing them, challenging them. Bowed heads, nervous eyes flickering over the hills, a promise of cover and food and stone under their feet.

'I'll begin the preparations,' Teomalik said slowly. 'Back in the house.'

Jakabi stared at him, his unruly command standing in

silence for a moment before he waved his hand towards the house. Ordered them in. The ragged jangling procession shuffled up the slope toward the great grey building, dragging the bodies with them. Molly walking with Beth, Nicky behind, looking about nervously. Jakabi alongside Teomalik, dirty head level with the youth's elbow. 'You'll get us back? No tricks?' Teomalik nodded. Jakabi looked up to him, shielding his eyes against the first rays of the sun beaming over the hill. 'How? Where?'

'The Gaps. Over the hills. We must hurry or they will come for us.'

'No tricks.'

Teomalik halted, Jakabi eyeing his war band as they shuffled past, made their way up to the house.

'You don't even know the password,' Jakabi breathed. Teomalik bit his lip. 'Sounds like a mountain.' Jakabi rolled the words around his fangs, his long purple tongue.

Teomalik caught his breath. 'You overheard us. It'll come to me, don't worry.'

'The mountains in the far north, further north than Kyle, than Kelleth?'

Teomalik stared at the creature, blinked fast as his eyes popped with tears.

'The long valley between the peaks. This side, the dark one, Shibboleth. The bad place.'

'I didn't think . . . I thought you wouldn't know, the old places,' Teomalik explained.

'We have our old places too. The other side . . .'

Teomalik nodded eagerly, encouragingly. Jakabi smiled, ran his paddy thumb over his huge yellow incisor.

'In the house, no tricks.'

*

Nicky looked up as the two of them walked into the hall past the honour guard of filthy goblins. Thought for a moment of all the weddings he'd covered for the *Clarion*, the military ones where the groom turned up looking like a cross between Fletcher Christian and Lord Kitchener. All his boozy pals there with cutlasses ready to lop the heads from the bridesmaids' bouquets. Some bridesmaids. Teomalik strode over, nodded at the screen, the blue and silver rectangle, the Grimoire in all its inscrutable glory. Nicky had been pondering pressing the escape button. Well, they weren't going to, were they – escape? From this? He'd half killed their favourite champion, their star quarterback. He'd decked their bootboy, cashed in their capo. Molly and Teomalik yapping their jaws off twenty to the dozen, that wouldn't help. These fucking things were going to eat them. Guess who was going to get to be the main course? Best fillet of Hack, fried Fish. Teomalik rested his trembling hand on his shoulder. He looked as if he'd been crying, streaks in the soot and dirt on his thin face.

'Try Onomatopoeia,' he gasped.

'No thanks. Look what it's done for you,' Nicky said drily.

'Try it.'

'Ono what?'

'Onomatopoeia.'

'Where the word sounds like what it's describing. Like *piss*. Or *bonk*.'

Jakabi settled himself on the desk, dagger in his fist. 'Sounds like the mountain,' he repeated dangerously. 'No tricks, wizardboy.'

Teomalik shook his head. 'In their talk . . . it's a word that sounds like the thing it's describing,' he explained patiently.

'Like piss or bonk,' Nicky repeated.

'Bonk?' Jakabi wanted to know.

Teomalik grinned weakly, elbowed Nicky in the back.

'I would have thought splash,' Teomalik said, giving him a withering look.

'Splash, bonk, whatever,' Nicky said quickly. Maybe steer around bonk. Didn't want to give the warty little bastards any ideas they hadn't already had.

'That's the password the warlocks were using when they worked on the old stones, tried to rewrite the route functions. They tried to use their magic to impersonate the Hiehlebadian command codes, you see?'

Nicky rolled his eyes. 'Hiehlebadian?'

'It was their stone. Originally,' Teomalik told them. 'They powered up the skanes for the warlock order. When my ancestors tried to take the ship they pulled the plug. You don't mess around with the Death Priests of Hiehlebad. They realized their mistake about ten minutes after they'd taken them on.'

'Death Priests of Hiehlebad? Didn't they support Search and Destroy at Donington?' Nicky gave an exasperated sigh. 'How the fuck do you expect me to believe all this, eh?'

Jakabi raised the tip of his spear, rested it against his red neck. 'Maybe I'll stick you on this, see if you'll believe then, see if you believe when it's your blood splashed over the floor,' he hissed.

Nicky grinned weakly. 'What I meant... it sounds like a heavy metal band... you know, Death Priests.' He nodded.

'Heavy isn't the word,' Teomalik interrupted. 'Look, the warlocks adapted their stone, you see? New command words,' he grated, 'to sound like the originals, onomatopoeia. It's also a mountain, in Trafarionath. Of course, we never found out whether the warlocks had managed to adjust the stone's parameters or not.'

Nicky shrugged, tapped the password. The slowly revolving box stabilized, bright clusters of letters shining in the four corners of each compartment. The four compartments in each corner changing colour, bright blue. 'That's nice,' Nicky said. 'Looks like the top of a tub of marge.'

'That's it!' Teomalik snapped.

'What do you mean, that's it? That's what?'

'What the warlocks wanted, a gateway. A way out.'

'They pulled the sky in on all of us,' Jakabi growled. 'You and your meddling, the old fool sending the Lady and leaving her in the lurch like that. You're out of your depth as much as we are.' He stopped short, looked nervously along the hall, the puzzled scouts wondering what their daft chief was blabbering on about. Get too much like the wizardboys and he'd wind up sharing their fate, maybe.

'What are you gawping at? Watch the prisoners and mind your nose,' Jakabi barked. The scout swallowed, looked away.

'I'm trying...' Teomalik said shakily, 'to make amends. To put a few things to rights. They never wanted to open routes here.'

'Where?'

'Here. Routes from our land to yours. That wasn't the idea at all. In those days, here didn't exist. They were trying to get out, get off, not back.' He shook his head.

'You mean we were a figment of your imagination? Well, that's nice to know,' Nicky wailed, buried his face in his hands. 'Christ, they could lock us up for shit like this.'

Teomalik glared at the glowing box over Nicky's shoulder, looked from the reporter's deflating face to Jakabi's, red eyed, eager. 'The gateway? It's open?'

*

CHANGELING HEARTS

The big Granada swung heavily into the drive, grinding gravel as it pulled to a halt in front of the house. Macall leaning over the dash for a better view.

'Lit up like a Christmas tree. That bloody sergeant must have been sleepwalking,' he cursed, leapt out. The two constables in the back levered their doors open, took the steps two at a time, damn near fell through as the blonde girl opened it for them.

'Christ Almighty. Get up, you silly sods. All right, love? Work here, do you?' Macall snapped over his shoulder as the girl stepped aside to let them in. Blotchy blue eyes rimmed red, smeared make-up. The detective took a look down the passage, up the staircase. 'Any more of you here?'

The blonde nodded, hank of hair falling over her face.

'You all right?' Touching her arm, making her jump. Macall looked up as the man stepped from the reception. Him.

'What are you up to? First in at the scoop again?'

Nicky zimmered himself into the hall on shaky legs, turned the knots of his eyes on them.

'She's in the woodpile. We haven't had time to get her out. I just rang Bell back at the station.' Deadpan. Deathly pale. Black jeans and jacket pulled about, shoes scuffed. McNair waved the constables on through the house.

'I'll check the woodpile,' McNair said, turning back down the steps.

'We didn't have a chance to cover her up, make her decent,' Nicky called wearily. 'What she would have wanted.'

McNair paused, nodded. 'All right, mate.'

Macall took him by the arm, gently, propelled him toward the lounge. The blonde girl fell in behind them. 'Where's the rest of them? Your missus?'

'She's gone.'

Macall eyed him, a punctured toy, a super-bouncer that wouldn't bounce. 'Yeah, gone where?'

'You tell me.'

'With Curly-tops, I suppose.'

Nicky glared dully at him, green eyes waxy, marbles dropped in Vaseline. 'With Curly-tops. She's not coming back.'

Macall raised an eyebrow. 'Where are they headed?'

Nicky raised his eyebrows in response.

Macall sighed, watched the two constables stride back down the passage.

'They've had a bloody party, all right. Must have had a convoy in.'

Macall glanced at the big reporter. 'Bit of a rave, was it? I fucking knew it,' intently, wheeling around to look at the girl slumped behind the computer. McNair trotted back up the steps, breathing hard, nodded.

'She's there, all right. Mrs Jasper. Right at the back.'

Macall frowned. 'So what are we saying, we missed her first time round?'

'Maybe.' McNair shrugged. 'Maybe somebody went back later? I'll get Gillings down, he can give us a rough idea. Call an ambulance too.'

Macall nodded, turned back. 'Either of you two know anything about this?'

'Molly said Hap did it. She thought sometime on Saturday, during all the confusion.'

'Molly said? Why the hell isn't she here to tell us herself? Leaving her friends to call us. What the fuck's been going on? Did they take a car or something?'

'They just went.' Flatly, resigned. 'About an hour ago. You've only just missed them.'

Macall tilted his head to one side, stared at him.

'What, walked out? Hand in hand? Been wife-swapping too, have you? You just let her walk off into the sunset with this Theo bloke?' He shook his head. 'I can't believe that. You wouldn't have just let her go.'

Nicky leaned by the wall, closed his eyes, chronically tired, gutted like poor old Schmelker's eldest son. Out on the grass there, out the back. Not any more. Wherever they'd gone, they'd taken the bodies with them. Five by the time they'd finished.

'There was nothing I could do. We were finished anyway, if you want the truth. She made her mind up. She'd changed. Changed from, you know, how she used to be.'

'Grown apart?' McNair suggested, looking up from the telephone on the desk. 'So you had a party to celebrate? With the old lady lying out there?'

Nicky shook his head. 'Wasn't our party. We drove down, walked in on it. We picked Molly up in Budgworth. She'd found Hap in the home there, worked out what had happened.'

'Quite the Miss Marple, your missus,' Macall suggested. Nicky looked blank. 'So she had an inkling about this Hap character, comes here and finds the body, damn near drives us off the road getting up to Budgworth so she can expose him. You bump into her and bring her back down here. So where's Theo? How does he fit in to all of this?'

'How come she got mixed up in his lot?'

'His lot?'

'The druggies. You know, this lot,' McNair said over the receiver, nodding down the passage. Nicky shrugged.

'Hokay,' Macall breathed. 'Let's get you down to the station. You all right, love? What's her name?'

'Bethany Peters. Works at the *Clarion* with me.'

'Come along too, did she?'

'It's her car. She took me to Budgworth after Molly, brought us all back. The Cortina's still up there.'

Macall stood back, allowed the constables to escort the pair of them down the steps, into the car.

McNair finished his call, looked up. 'Most of what he says is right. We saw him going after her. He crashed. He gets the blonde to take him up to Budgworth, they pick up his missus.'

'The woman at the home said Molly had been there on her own, no sign of the other guy. They must have picked him up later. And then there's the Hap character.' He rubbed his nose. 'Sitting there with the rest of them, dressed up in the dead woman's togs. Bastard.' He rubbed his eyes, shook his head. 'Not much more we can do to the old bloke though, like he said. Even if we could convince the DPP to run with it. There's not much could be worse than sitting in a chair in a place like this.'

Macall nodded, stared over his shoulder. McNair turned to follow his gaze. The computer screen, some kind of Windows program. He squinted, couldn't make out the tiny writing.

'Christ, you're supposed to read that crap, are you? Have they freed the system yet?'

McNair nodded. 'Yeah, control says it came back on line twenty minutes ago. Press Escape, reboot and you clear all the rubbish out. So much for Dr Freeman and her bloody theories. I'll do it now.'

LOST WORLDS, LOST WORDS

Teomalik had urged Jakabi to hurry them on. The night was melting fast, heavy black pages fading at the edges, illuminating letters, words, sentences he didn't have time to read. Trees playing scarecrows against the clouds, curious sheep. Jakabi had run himself ragged, up and down the unruly column shoving his troopers back into line.

'Well, if we can't kill 'em, let's at least take 'em with us,' Ombuda, one of the loudmouths who had managed to keep his head so far, complained bitterly. The others came to a noisy halt, took a couple of wild shots at the daft sheep. Molly studied the clouds, thick and hazy at the moment but one good blow and they'd be silhouetted up here on the skyline for everybody to see. Oh, look, Mummy, some ragged children from Budgworth. What's it like to be poor? She slumped into the grass, the four guards Jakabi had assigned to her following suit gratefully, pulling and poking at their filthy footrags. One of the scouts, black hair cropped short over his large skull, nodded at her.

'Are you coming, then? Over there?' he asked, incredulous.

Molly studied him, swallowed.

'Are you going to be Queen, then?' his colleague asked, picking skin from his horny toes. A commotion out on the hill as Jakabi strode along knocking the bowmen's thin arms, spoiling their aim.

'We haven't time,' he bellowed.

'A few bloody sheep,' Ombuda protested. Teomalik paced to and fro in frustration.

'Want me to pick some bloody mint while we're at it? Get in line with the rest of them before I throw you over the fucking cliff myself!' he roared. Silence. Hiss of wind over dewy grass. A low rumble in the distance. The goblins looked over their shoulders, over the cold ridge.

'What's that?' Jakabi gripped his spear, glared at Teomalik. 'What is it?'

'Do they have dragons, then?'

'It's not a dragon, dream pictures, dream noises,' one of the archers muttered, bending to retrieve his arrows.

'It's her . . . her and her fucking swans again.'

'Let's get a move on, we haven't got all day,' Teomalik repeated over the throbbing roar, the fidgeting panic spreading up and down the tangled column. Molly on her feet shooing them on. The archers were looking up, stumbling, aiming their bows at the scudding clouds.

'It's the dream pictures . . . the flying shields!'

'Run for it!'

'It's a dream picture,' Jakabi shouted, rattling his spear above his head as the roaring closed in on them, scooped them up like a handful of dust. The war band frozen like gargoyles among the tussocks and stones. The clouds billowed and rolled over the hill, the sun breaking through the lurking mist in great white columns. A sudden howl sent them running pell-mell over the hill, throwing themselves down cursing and yelping.

The A320 Airbus came in low, wheels locking down, engines screaming on its final approach to Budgworth airport, five miles further north over the ridge. The goblins shrieked and hid themselves as the hideous bird bucketed overhead, casting a sickly shadow as they ran in circles or dropped to the buffeted grass, claws clamped to their pointed ears. Molly, running to and fro telling them it was all right, pummelled by the fearsome slipstream as the big jet hurtled over the ridge. Tired clothes torn open, big hair flowing. Jakabi, spreadeagled in a heap of sheep droppings, peered between his claws at her, arms open, head back. Screaming things he couldn't hear over the mad roar of the bird-shield-turtle picture.

'On your feet, we haven't time.' He realized it was her, not the warlock boy transfixed to the stones beside him. 'We must hurry or they'll be on us!' Striding down the heaps of trembling goblins wrenching them to their feet by their straps. Her filthy harnessed children running amok in the park, her yapping huskies straining at their leashes, mush-mush-mushing the wrong way.

'Up on your feet now!'

Jakabi watched astonished as the terrified troopers huddled back together, the Queen darting between them shaking them into line. He scrambled to his feet, groped for his spear as the tall warlock boy strode past, pointing over the misty hill.

'It's not far now . . . through that hedge . . . we must hurry!' he yelled. Cursing and mumbling, eyeing the shrouding clouds, the war band hurried on again.

Five thousand feet, a little turbulence, the bloody pilot had said. Christ, since the Bay of Biscay Andy Pheebs had been clutching the soft plastic sides of the upright deckchair they called a seat as the king prawns he'd unwisely gobbled at the goodbye party back in Albufeira took a revolting revenge on his digestive system. He'd reached for the sick bag twice only to meet his four-year-old son's calm stare.

'Are you going to do some upchucks, Daddy?'

'Bit queasy, that's all.'

'Is it the plane?'

'Yes.' Gritted teeth locked in a devilish smile.

'The way it goes up . . . and down?'

He turned across the aisle, Marion and Kaleigh by the windows. His wife smiled nervously. 'You all right?'

'Almost home.' Christ, give me the Berlin flak, give me nightfighters, but keep the fucking turbulence. They'd flown through a couple of squalls, levelled out over green fields, neat green grids studded with white houses.

'Is that our house?'

'Not yet, Neil. Another few miles yet.'

His fearless four-year-old craned his neck to peer out of the porthole, straining his harness to point out the landmarks.

'Do you think we're going to hit the hill? How can the driver see in all the cloud, Daddy?'

Andy closed his eyes. 'The pilot has radar and stuff to see where to go,' he reassured him.

'What happens if there's a power cut and the radar goes off, do we crash then?'

'No, no.' Andy waved a trembling paw at his diabolical offspring as the stewardesses scuttled to their seats, strapped themselves in. Five more bloody minutes.

'Those gnomes think we're going to crash,' Neil said, turning back from the porthole and pointing. 'They've all fallen down!'

'I know how they feel,' he muttered, leaning forward and taking one quick peek out. He sat back with a heavy sigh, wiped his hands over his eyes. Neil, who for some reason had developed an owl's ability to turn his head through 180°, stared at him, wide eyed.

'Did you see the gnomes, Daddy, hiding on the hill?'

CHANGELING HEARTS

Andy read the instructions on the headrest in front, swallowed and wondered what to say. Yes, was the word that came to mind.

Running now, panting over the dips and folds out on the open down. Bare seams of grey rock elbowing through the deep lush grass, rabbit trails in the grey dew. The swifter scouts, recovering from the shock of the giant turtle-bird-shield dream picture, running on ahead, veering off from the shuffling, muttering war band. Teomalik, putting on a sprint to catch up with Jakabi, who had hardly raised a sweat, pointed on ahead. 'Better keep them back . . . we'll be there soon.' Jakabi shouted something in his hoarse goblin talk, gave a piercing whistle. The scouts slowed, drifted back toward the main group. Molly in the middle of a crowd of chattering chimps torn between leering at her and tapping their dirty foreheads in some kind of homage, nodding. Teomalik looked up as the last runner trotted on, peering over his shoulder. Gone. The astonished goblins dug their feet in, held on to neighbours as the war band came to a stuttering stop out on the top. Teomalik striding out ahead, peering down the sudden gap. He looked around, the bare fields, bent trees giving him no clue to his whereabouts. Molly and Jakabi trotting up beside him.

'I thought it was nearer the road,' he moaned.

Molly peered down the ridge, pointed. 'There's the road. We want to follow this one along, then cut over that field and along the hedge.'

'What if we're seen?' Teomalik hissed.

Jakabi shrugged. 'We fight, we kill,' he leered.

Molly closed her eyes, shook her head. 'There's nobody about. Hurry them on.'

Jakabi waved the war band up and along the narrow chasm, the goblins taking it in turns to take a peek over the edge.

'Are we there yet?'

'How much bloody further?'

'Did you see Ombuda? One minute there, next minute,' the goblin clicked his claws.

'Best thing for him, uppity skunk.'

'He won't be missed.'

'*We* won't be missed.' A small archer at the back, looking over his shoulder at the broad trail they'd stomped through the grass. The column wound along the smaller gap, filtered through the scrubby hedge at the bottom of the field and hurried on along the dry-stone wall beside the road.

'Down!'

They threw themselves into the chalky brambles at the foot of the wall, listened to a dream-picture chariot-box rumble by along the other side. Up again, along the wall, up over the steep slope.

'Careful, we're here.' Teomalik out ahead, arms outstretched. The gap, an immense limestone mouth half a mile long and God knew how deep, smiling crookedly over the face of the down. They edged closer, looked at one another. Well, what now?

'The door? The gateway you told us about?' Jakabi snorted, rolling his spear in his claws menacingly. Teomalik breathed deeply.

'This is it.'

Molly checked her watch. 'Fifty-three minutes. We left at three thirty,' she told him, nervously winding it. She stopped, stared at it. No more, no point, no time.

'Well,' Jakabi snorted. 'What do we do?'

Teomalik raised his eyebrows, nodded to the gap. 'We go down.'

'Down? We can't climb that! What do you think we are, mountain monkeys?' Patience not so much wearing thin as dying of malnutrition.

'Schmelker was right. We should have hidden ourselves, we should have stayed!'

'They would have wiped you out,' Teomalik said stonily. 'They would have destroyed you like a handful of maggots, stuffed your bodies and shoved glass beads into your eye holes, put you on show at their circuses. When they'd finished some of them might . . . might have suggested you should have been spared. Kept in a zoo. Kept for some tests. They would have wondered all sorts of things, once they'd stamped you out.' Molly looked over the band, catching gimlet glares and residual leers. 'It's true. They would have come after you. Cleaned you out like cockroaches,' he said. A squall of shouts and threats. Teomalik turned to the gap.

'This is the gateway. This is the gateway the stones have set for us.' He nodded encouragingly, took the tablet from Jakabi. Molly peered at it. Exactly as it had been before, tiny runes in twelve boxes around a central panel, hairlines glinting dimly beneath a layer of waxy grime. Teomalik ran his fingers over it, tossed it over the edge. Astonished silence.

'There is no going back. We go down.'

'We can't fucking clamber all . . .'

'We jump.'

'What?' Jakabi tore at his arm, raised the spearpoint to the boy's fleshy chin. 'Do you think we're that stupid? You stand here and watch us, I suppose? Watch us jump and then go home for your blasted tea?' he raged, froth hanging from his fangs.

Teomalik, ashen, shook his head. 'I'll go first.'

Jakabi threw his arm down, barked with laughter.

'Chickening out already? What's to stop us staying, if you've gone?'

'Nothing.' Teomalik shrugged. 'You can go back the way we came, wait for the silver birds to fly down for you, the silver chariots to run you over like rabbits in the road. You can run over the hill like headless chickens until they trap you and catch you. You'll pray for death, you'll wish you'd never been born, what they'd have in mind for you. I have seen their world,' he insisted.

Molly eyed him, tugged her coat around her, shivering, exhausted. What had he seen of their world? A tired old news report, some tired old folk? Police who had to doctor the evidence before they'd believe their own eyes? She could talk. Couldn't believe her own eyes, couldn't believe his eyes either, and they were all she had to go on. Lying eyes and snivelling confessions. Those funny old fellers who liked to call in at the police station, own up to anything that was going.

'And your world is so much better,' she said flatly.

Teomalik looked at her quizzically. 'Are you asking me or telling me?'

'I don't know.' She flung her hand up, tugged her hair out of her drawn face. 'I'm asking you,' she said crossly. 'Jesus Christ, what do I have to do?'

Teomalik looked from the crying woman to the muttering goblins. Was it his imagination or had they closed in behind her, shivering and bleating like sheep in a snowstorm? Her anxiety breeding panic in their itchy skulls.

'You've brought me here, to this,' she accused. 'You could have dressed it up a bit, your precious Trafarionath. I mean, you could have tried to sell it to me.' He was shaking his head, he'd misunderstood, again. Molly closed her eyes. Well, it's not like we expected from the brochure, is it? Miles from the beach and the food's so greasy. She glared at him, stepping from foot to foot, her ropy rep. Reluctant Redcoat.

'What I want to know is, would I really want to go there? If I could come and go between, make up my own mind?' she went on. 'Say something,' she pleaded.

'If there was time . . . if she hadn't . . . you know . . . if I hadn't . . . if I had a choice . . .' Teomalik raised his hands, hopeless and bloody helpless.

'We've got a choice,' Jakabi snapped. 'We stay or we jump.'

The tall youth shook his shaggy head. 'We don't have a choice. All this has been foreseen, it's already decided,' he said quickly.

Jakabi wheeled round and glared at Molly, thrust the spear toward her breast.

'Then you go. You jump, then we jump, all together. He won't trick us, once you're gone,' he said intuitively. Molly looked at Teomalik, red hair hanging limply, plastered to his skull. Nicky's fishing jumper tugged and baggy over the green smock he'd arrived in, what, a few days before. Jump over the fucking cliff? What the hell was he talking about? She blew a cloud of vapour, laughed bitterly.

'Me, jump?' she asked incredulously. 'I thought there'd be a gateway . . . a door . . . something you could walk through,' she chattered nervously.

Teomalik nodded. 'You step out, you step through. It's all the same. Would it make it any easier if there was a massive big door with funny writing on it?'

'Yes, it fucking well would, now you come to mention it,' she snapped.

'Boss Jakabi . . . we've got company.' The scout with the stubble Molly had spoken with earlier, pointing a trembling spear behind him. A host of white shapes, cloudy faces, misty eyes, staring at them, surrounding them. Out of the grass, out of the cracks, the spirits of the fallen. The shades of the dead. Unstitched jumpers, pulled threads. The goblins closed in, jostling and shoving their weaker comrades to the front, weapons clattering.

Jakabi looked furiously at the boy. 'You said no tricks!' he growled.

'It's not a trick. I've seen them before. We jump, we close the breach behind us, we seal the gateway. We release them.'

Jakabi snarled, weighing the spear in his claw. 'They're your ghosts, not ours!'

'They're trapped the same as you are. They're trapped in the gateway, lost in the void between the worlds,' Teomalik insisted. 'We've given them the stones. All they need now . . . is us. We have to go before the breach can be sealed. Now throw the bodies over,' he grated.

Jakabi looked down, the eight hacked goblins the boy had insisted they drag along with them. Caked with blood, features battered by the sharp rocks, their bumpy journey over the hill. Jakabi waved his hand. The quaking spear boys rolled them to the precipice, pushed them over. They fell like baggage, colliding sloppily with pitiless stone columns and crowns.

'They're waiting for us. There isn't any time. We must go now,' he called, staring at Molly. She ground her lips together, features frozen, staring at the pit beneath her feet. The goblins edged away as Teomalik walked up to her, lifted her hand.

'Think about what I've told you. The Spawn Queen . . . when she attacked me in the stream . . . she had seen all this. She had foreseen her own death. She stabbed me with the tooth, stabbed her magic into me to give to you. She had foreseen her own rebirth,' he insisted quietly. More muttering in the ranks.

'We get back over, she's going to be after us for that,' one of them hissed in Jakabi's twitching ear. He waved the spear boy back, concentrating.

'She wouldn't have allowed them to . . . if she hadn't been confident . . . she'd come back. In you. Do you see?'

Molly stared into his wrong-coloured eyes. 'Why didn't you mention any of this before?'

'Because you wouldn't have believed me. Maybe you would have tried to alter things, work around it. Things would have been different.'

'You knew . . . all along about the tooth?'

'I told you . . . it was hers. I told you all I could,' he insisted. 'You step out, you come with me, with us. She knew, she knew you'd come to her, come back with her.'

'And I make it better. I make everything all right over there.'

Teomalik, eyes watering, pulled at his nose. 'She must have known . . . she must see some sense in it.'

He went on mumbling about fickle fucking fates but she'd closed her ears to him. The buck stops here. Time's up. Same as it had been for Jonathan and his family, for Mags and for Mrs Jasper and Hap and everyone else. Her turn now. New life awaits, over there. Molly closed her eyes, peered into the darkness inside her head, and was aware of her, standing forth, coming out of her closet. *Her* closet. Taking over the reins, the strings of her life as if she'd already jumped, bailed out of the burning bomber of this life into the flak-black slipstream of . . . The slipstream. The new Queen of the catwalk. Amiarillin. A tall gangly girl with coils of dark, grapy hair. Standing self-consciously under her gaze. Smiling shortly, embarrassed maybe. Try me on for size. Sorry about this. She opened her eyes. 'I don't want to be her. I don't want to be her zombie,' she cried.

Teomalik gripped her arm. 'You aren't, you won't. Suggestion, remember? She'll suggest things to you sometimes, she'll live through you.'

'How do you know?'

'How do I . . .'

'How do you know she'll be content with that?'

Teomalik opened and closed his mouth.

'What?'

'Because if she doesn't, I'll take you back,' he whispered. 'But she won't,' he repeated, louder for the benefit of the suspicious goblins, pressing in and away from the shadow host. 'Look, we've got to go. I'm coming with you. I'll be there . . . the other side.'

'*Like your precious uncle promised my sister?*' she crowed, cold, harsh, astonishing the fidgeting goblins who edged back from her towards the crowding shadows, trapped between a rock and a hard place. Teomalik looked blank.

'Tarkemenis loved her. She'd bewitched him. He would have done anything for her, up to and including making the spell to send her over.'

'But he didn't go with her, he didn't follow. He left her here alone, and you know what happened,' the Molly creature grated, clenching her white fists.

'He didn't, but I would, I'd follow you anywhere,' he said simply.

'Trafarionath.'

'Wherever.'

'Promise.'

'Come on, all this talk,' Jakabi growled. 'Are we going to go or not? Are we going to ride the swan brothers? Like Boss Tilekin?' Embarrassed silence.

'She can jump, give us a sign,' one of the archers suggested. 'Then we'll know to jump too.'

'If she jumps we jump,' Teomalik shouted. 'What's

the matter with you all?' He turned round, held out his hand as Molly threw her arm over her face, wrenched herself by the hair. The goblins edged away again, Teomalik stepping forward, halted in his dewy tracks by her sudden screeching.

'Get your fingers out of my head, you slimy bitch!' Skin puckered around her tightly clamped eyes, picking her out, the gangly girl in the shadows recoiling from her own flaring spirit. Molly trawled the vaults of her memories, the childhood nightmares sleeping fitfully beneath quilts of dust and patchwork webs. Pulled the sheets and shrouds away, released herself, all of what was left of herself. Rats. Horrid slick-furred slimy-tailed biters, hurrying across the floor towards the cowering girl. Out of it, out of it you fucking let's pretending witch. The brown bodies surged up the girl's legs, swarmed over her gauzy frock. She screamed, raked her nails down the blackboard of her sanity, began to spin as the rats clawed her chest, scrabbled and scurried for her blurred features. Eat the witch bitch out of my head, throw her out of the window! The girl spun, top heavy, with rats clinging by tooth and claw to her shredding clothing. Flying off like furry shrapnel, faster and faster. Brown lumps of fur twitching and dissolving on Molly's threadbare carpeting, mattress ticking pillows lining the walls, padding her reeling brain. The whirling dervish stopped still, raised her banshee arms above her mad bitching eyes and glared back.

'Get out of your own head before I turn my rats on you, Lady,' she called brazenly. Molly's lips moving in all directions, dribbling and drooling, yapping like a dog dreaming of the chase.

The goblins stared, bug-eyed bug-eyed bugs. 'That bloody Spawn Queen's repeating on her like she repeated on me,' one of the archers gasped.

Molly backed away, crawling on the wet grass like a blind pup. Over her shoulder, over the last sandbag of herself, she saw the Witch Queen in all her glory, standing triumphant like a bloody she-wolf gladiator, spreading the great slimy nets of her cloak from her long brown arms. Draping them over the cowering woman as if she was wrapping a baby in swaddling clothes. Swamping, sealing. They saw her leap to her feet, full of fire, totter along the edge like a drunk driver on a white line. Drunk with her own powers, flexing and flowing. Teomalik raised his hand, touched her frozen fingers. She smiled, stepped out. For a split second, the tiniest fraction of time, Teomalik felt her snap tight shut on him, trapped by her snare stare. Who was she? Who was she now? She was gone. A bump, a short yelp. He clamped his tongue between his teeth, looked iron eyed at them.

'We go, together. Spread out. Spread out!' he bellowed. He took Jakabi's claw, tugged the spear from his hand and threw it down into the pit.

'We go, together. Say it!'

'We . . . go . . . together.' Weakly, uncertain.

'We go now!' He jumped, pulling Jakabi with him, pulling the suspicious spear boys and the reluctant archers and the scornful scouts and the hangers-on. Over and out. The misty shapes withered as the breeze brushed the hill, swept them away with the last of the night.

EPILOGUE

A WALK IN THE PARK

'Take care now, not too close to the stream!' The big woman hauled the broken-down buggy over the muddy ruts, going against the grain of the badly ploughed track. It was a bugger at the best of times, and about as manoeuvrable as the *Tirpitz*, loaded down with three bulging bags of shopping. Extra shopping, she reminded herself. They'd already motored out to the new Tesco's at Rookton, bought seventy quid's worth on Saturday. The boy had chomped through most of it already, and she'd had to shoo him away from the doughnuts before they'd cleared the checkout. Dave would go mad if he found out. He hadn't been too keen on taking care of the little starver in the first place.

'Not too near the stream!' Steph repeated, struggling to keep the buggy wheels out of the ruts. Kids bringing motorbikes down here, shouldn't be allowed. She paused to catch her breath, watched the boy hop skip and jump over the ploughed path and disappear into the bulrushes like a sawn-off Sioux, his little bow and arrows clutched in his remarkably powerful fist. He'd punched Dave on the nose already, not too keen on having his toys tidied away. He was a steady sort of chap, Dave, but he didn't take kindly to being mugged by toddlers.

'Walter! Come away from the water, I won't tell you again!' But she would. She knew she would. The little tearaway was becoming more disobedient by the day.

He'd recovered all right, after all he'd been through. Too young to remember much about it, the crash and all. Losing his parents and then his elder brother a few weeks later, well, it was no wonder he was a bit hyperactive. She watched the toddler fit a rubber-tipped arrow to the plastic bow, stalk through the rushes toward the edge of the ornamental lake. A couple of mallards regarded him, beady eyed under their sergeant-stripe wings. He'd have someone's eye out with that bow, if he wasn't careful.

'Walter! Will you come away! Don't you dare shoot those ducks. Nice ducks. Quack quack quack.'

The boy peered over the stiff green reeds at her, a curiously resentful expression on his world-weary little face. She sometimes wondered if he was all there.

He was there all right.